Billie Starr's Book of Sorries

Also by Deborah E. Kennedy

Tornado Weather

Billie Starr's Book of Sorries

DEBORAH E. KENNEDY

FLATIRON
BOOKS
NEW YORK

BILLIE STARR'S BOOK OF SORRIES. Copyright © 2022 by Deborah E. Kennedy. All rights reserved. Printed in the United States of America. For information, address Flatiron Books, 120 Broadway, New York, NY 10271.

www.flatironbooks.com

Designed by Donna Sinisgalli Noetzel

Library of Congress Cataloging-in-Publication Data

Names: Kennedy, Deborah E., author.
Title: Billie Starr's book of sorries / Deborah E. Kennedy.
Description: First Edition. | New York : Flatiron Books, 2022.
Identifiers: LCCN 2022010774 | ISBN 9781250138439 (hardcover) |
    ISBN 9781250138446 (ebook)
Subjects: LCGFT: Novels.
Classification: LCC PS3611.E5578 B55 2022 | DDC 813/.6—dc23
LC record available at https://lccn.loc.gov/2022010774

Our books may be purchased in bulk for promotional, educational, or business use. Please contact your local bookseller or the Macmillan Corporate and Premium Sales Department at 1-800-221-7945, extension 5442, or by email at MacmillanSpecialMarkets@macmillan.com.

First Edition: 2022

10 9 8 7 6 5 4 3 2 1

For Eric, favorite human,

and

Kelleen, child whisperer

If you're not turned on to politics . . .

politics will turn on you.

—RALPH NADER

Billie Starr's Book of Sorries

Ashes

Jenny remembered his arms best. Hugging her, holding her, waving, working. Forearms, lean and tan, covered in reddish-brown hair that was often speckled with dust or paint or ash. Tattoo of his mother's name on his left biceps. Doris. A scorpion on his right. Wrists strong. Fingers nimble. A triangle of moles over one elbow. Scabby crocodile skin just below. Jenny liked to play with it, mush it around in the shape of a mouth, have it say things. *I love you. Who farted? Don't leave me.*

His face, unforgettable. White scar between his blue eyes. Nose, a little bumpy from a bar fight. Teeth, bad. Voice, not low but not high either. Heart, big. Sometimes too big for the world he was born in. That was her father all over. Sweet-tempered and short-changed. Small beer.

"A lot of ugly in this world, beautiful," he told her. "Got to make our own pretty."

Pete talked like that. Like a hick Hallmark card. A fan of country music, the White Sox, Marlboro Reds, and Cher, he was also superstitious. Never stepped on a crack, never walked under a ladder, threw out mirrors when he broke them, and gave Jenny an impossibly soft purple rabbit's foot for her fifth birthday.

"Luck, sweet pea. Good and bad. Sometimes it's all we've got."

For most of his life, he built cabinets and countertops and

installed them in houses that his boss, Bob Butz, a local Realtor, sold to people who didn't care that men like Pete existed. Then, when Jenny was sixteen, when she needed him most, he died. She held his hand as it happened, felt it grow stiff and cold. She'd wanted to drive him to the hospital, but he refused. Didn't like how hospitals smelled. Too sad, those places, he said. Too many blue walls and white coats and code reds.

When Jenny called her mother to break the news, Carla was annoyed more than anything, irritated that her ex-husband would choose that day of all days to give up the ghost. She had tickets to a Kenny Rogers concert.

"And I'm fresh out of black dresses."

Pete had moved to Crooked Lake by then, to a little motel at the dusty end of a dead-end gravel road. The last place he'd been truly happy, he said. Jenny had been happy there, too, when, during a long-ago spring break, Pete brought her with him on a job. While her father and a small crew of men worked on a house across the water, Jenny sunned herself on the public beach and ate lunches of peanut butter and jelly in the motel room in front of game shows and soap operas and terrifying documentaries about serial killers. In the evening, she and Pete walked to a nearby tavern for fried fish dinners and Pete told her all about the fancy family who owned the house he was working on, about the fresh-squeezed orange juice they drank and actual butter they ate and the tennis rackets and skis and motorboats they owned and the pictures on their walls of places they'd traveled to—New York City, the Grand Tetons, Yellowstone. People like that saw the world up close and in person. People like Jenny and Pete saw it in magazines and on TV. It was fine, though. They weren't mad about it because, before they went back to the motel for the night, they had time to venture out onto a nearby dock to look at the stars. Arm around Jenny's shoulder, Pete pointed out constellations, told her stories about ancient men who used to steer by them, his voice full of awe.

"This is my happy place, Jenny. Right here, right now, with you. As good as it gets." Jenny, sleepy and full, agreed. A perfect week of nothing much.

But then that week was followed by months and months of Pete getting sicker and sicker. Coughing. Always coughing. Divorce in there somewhere, Jenny dividing her time between her mother's house and the motel. Pete only stopped coughing when he stopped breathing. Carla's best friend, Vi Gregor, called his death a blessing. He's at peace, she said. His suffering is finally over.

Peace? Jenny wanted to die along with him, follow him into the fire, come out the other side light as air, feeling nothing.

On a gray day in July, shivering, she scattered Pete's ashes at the end of their star-watching dock, teenagers from the city skiing by, hooting at her, slaloming right through the line of white and gray. Just like that, Pete went from being son of Doris, father of Jenny, knight in torn tee shirts, to debris. It was too fast, that transformation. And too unsung. Jenny should have brought fireworks, planted a cross or something. Instead, she went home and slept for twenty hours straight, dreaming of motorboats and mermaids, swords and stones and fish food.

She never admitted it to anyone, but she took to praying to Pete like you would a saint, begged him to protect her the way he used to. She felt stupid doing it, idiotic, but she did it anyway, and when she became a mother, she asked him to look after Billie Starr, too, to keep her safe from dangers Jenny felt unqualified or unable to counter. Bullies. Lightning strikes.

Maybe it worked or maybe it was just luck, the good kind. Either way, Jenny had come this far—twelve years—without him and it was 1991. A famous basketball player, thirty-two, had just announced that he had AIDS. A famous rock star, forty-five, had just died from it. A postal worker shot up his office, and a former KKK grand wizard just barely lost a race for governor of Louisiana.

Jenny, twenty-eight, turned off the news. She was alive somehow and so was Billie Starr, and when she remembered to, Jenny kept the velvety purple rabbit's foot with her, held it close. Sometimes she forgot all about it. But not about him. Pete. Bony-kneed. Red-necked. Starstruck. He'd loved her. The only one who did.

Book One

She woke to snow on the ground, a dripping sink, and her neighbor's cats at her door, begging for food. The dripping sink and begging cats—Jenny was used to that. Her house was old, her plumbing was shot, and her neighbor, Marcus Rye, often forgot to feed Gertrude and Yo-Yo, and so it had fallen to her to give them two cans of tuna each day—one in the morning and one at night. The snow, though, that was new. The first of the year, it turned her scrubby lawn into something pretty for once, and, standing on the back stoop, cats winding around her ankles, Jenny looked at it— the sparkle, the purity of it—and thought that maybe, just maybe, what she was about to do wasn't so terrible after all.

She gave the cats their breakfast and poured herself a cup of old coffee. She didn't bother heating it up. The microwave would wake Billie Starr and Jenny wasn't ready for that. Not yet. She still needed to shower, shave her legs, "get dolled up," as her mother put it. And she needed time to figure out what she would say when she saw him. The first words. They seemed important. Monumental, even. Life and death.

The man's picture was in an envelope on the counter next to the toaster. Jenny gave the cats a head pat and went back in, pulled the picture out, studied it. The men in black suits told her to be on the lookout for a weak chin and large, liquid eyes. Also a

halting gait. The photograph obviously didn't show his gait, but the weak chin was there, and his eyes reminded Jenny of a puppy's. He had a full mouth and shiny skin and thinning brown hair. His brows were bushy and unkempt and his sideburns were out of style, but he wasn't ugly. More gentle-looking, and his sweet smile gave Jenny pause.

Still, the men in black suits told her that if she didn't take the job someone else would, and maybe that lady wouldn't be as cute as Jenny or as kind. It was her choice, the men said. They weren't there to pressure her. They were simply presenting her with an opportunity, the likes of which rarely came along for girls like her.

Girls like her. Jenny knew what that meant.

She put the photo down, drifted into the living room to the large picture window that looked out on the front yard. The snow gave the sky its light, made the early morning world glow baby blue. Four sets of paw tracks wound around the big locust tree. A rabbit had been by, and a deer. Gertrude and Yo-Yo picked their way across the drive back to Marcus's, the beige single-wide dark this time of day and missing some siding.

Jenny lived in an old brick schoolhouse at the top of a sharp S curve on a small stretch of road that, a hundred years before, had its own railroad station and post office. That was ancient history, and Acorn Street was part of Benson now. Five miles outside town, bordered by farmland and patches of woods, it was a lonely spot on the map, a nothing sort of place that everyone pretty much forgot was there. Then, the previous August, a drunk twentysomething missed the curve and drove right into Dorothy Renfrow's house, killing her and her entire collection of African violets. The Fort Wayne news carried the story. A few Indianapolis outlets, too. The twentysomething went to jail for a month. His parents were important somehow. Or anyway rich. The house, a haven for raccoons and blackbirds, had yet to be repaired or torn down. It looked like

a punched-in face. And Dorothy, about as a friendly as a thistle, wasn't missed by anyone.

After the accident, the city installed a blinking yellow sign to alert drivers to the coming curves. It throbbed all day and all night, a sour signal that pulsed through Jenny's dreams and made the houses on Acorn Street look even worse than they already did. Marcus's trailer was an eyesore on its own. There was the missing siding, but also several cracked panes, a mountain of soggy mail on the front step, and a charred west wall from the night he'd left the stove on and set fire to a bunch of phone books. And the blinking made it seem like the cops were forever stationed in Dorothy Renfrow's front yard, radioing for the coroner.

Jenny's house wasn't much either but she loved it anyway, cherished its creaky wooden floors and odd nooks and crannies. Even the window above the kitchen sink that let in wind and snow and rain was just more proof of its character, its uniqueness. Most of all, she loved that it was hers. She'd used her tiny inheritance from Pete as a down payment and filled it with Goodwill furniture, cute antiques, candles. How long, though, before the bank took it all away? A collection agent named Kevin called often now, called early, and the flashing sign reminded Jenny that she was three months behind on her mortgage payments. *Mortgage mortgage mortgage,* its blinking seemed to say. *Loser loser loser.*

The sign pulsed at the same rate as the mantel clock Jenny's mother had given her for her last birthday, a hideous rococo thing Jenny hated but couldn't get rid of because Carla would call her ungrateful if she did. Carla considered rococo "high culture." Also anything that suggested "Asia at its finest." Her apartment was cluttered with porcelain figurines of white-wigged men and women at leisure, her walls dotted with prints of geisha girls and sumo wrestlers. Rooms at war with themselves.

The sign and the clock reminded Jenny that time was running

out, that, like Pete, like Dorothy Renfrow and her violets, she, Jenny Newberg, would die someday and so would Carla and Billie Starr and Jenny's best friend, Lyd Butz, and Marcus. Good business for Hiram Hardacre, the town funeral director, but bad news for everyone else. Gertrude and Yo-Yo, they would die, too. And the locust tree. The bunny and the deer, wherever they were. Everything. Everything and everyone would die and then what?

Jenny finished her coffee and padded down the hall to take a shower.

"Mom?"

"Yeah, pumpkin."

"I'm not a pumpkin. I'm an airplane."

"Oh, okay. Zoom!"

"I don't zoom, Mom. I roar."

"Roar!"

"You sound like a bear. Plane roars are different."

Billie Starr had dressed herself that morning. She'd dressed herself every morning since she started school three years before and refused to take Jenny's advice on anything that had to do with clothes. Underneath her bright red coat, she wore an orange sweatshirt, a turquoise skirt, and black, sparkly kneesocks. Her white gym shoes lit up when she kicked her feet, sending little red signals against the passenger seat.

"What are you?" she asked Jenny.

"What do you mean, sweetie?"

"I'm not a sweetie. I'm an airplane."

"Of course."

"I asked you what you are."

"I'm your mom."

"But what else?"

The farms flashed by, field after field of spent cornstalks, bent

and sharp in the frigid soil. White wooden foursquare houses sat off the road, surrounded by barns and pickup trucks and earthmovers. Long driveways in this part of the county. And short fuses. A few weeks ago, one of the farmers, Lorne Keck, shot at his wife for making a runny pie. No one was exactly shocked by the news. Lorne and Trish had a reputation for being "volatile," and Lorne collected antique revolvers, haunted gun shows on the weekends. Many in town were, however, surprised to find out that shooting at one's wife was an offense worthy of arrest. "Didn't it matter that he missed?"

Lorne was still in the county lockup as far as Jenny knew, and she hoped he'd be there for a long time. He was an old friend of Pete's but she never understood what her father saw in him. Once, when she was spending the weekend with Pete at the dead-end motel on Crooked Lake, Lorne dropped in on them, carrying a pizza and a twenty-four-pack of Milwaukee's Best. While Pete coughed in his bed, Lorne cued up a pay-per-view boxing match between two aging heavyweights. Then he proceeded to eat all the pizza and drink all the beer. He smoked so many cigarettes that night, one after the other, Jenny had to go outside in the freezing cold just to breathe.

"Mom?"

"Yeah, sweetie."

"I told you I'm not a sweetie. I'm not a sweetie or a pumpkin or a honey. I'm an airplane."

"I'll try to remember."

"And I asked what are you besides a mom and you never answered me."

"I'm sorry."

"You're a sorry?"

"Sure."

"That doesn't sound very interesting."

"I guess it's not really."

"Well, I'm going to Paris because I'm a plane. Mr. Richardson said we can go anywhere we want to in our imaginations."

Mr. Richardson was Billie Starr's teacher. A nice-looking man in his midthirties with sandy hair and a baseball player's body, he'd asked Jenny out once at the beginning of the school year. His wife had died of ovarian cancer the previous spring. Jenny had taken a week to think about it. In the end, she turned him down, said she didn't think it would be appropriate, since he was her daughter's teacher. Sometimes at night, though, lying alone in her bed, Jenny regretted her decision, wondered what it might be like to go on a date with a decent man.

"Mr. Richardson is right," Jenny said. "You can go anywhere you want. In your mind."

"See you when I get back."

"See you."

Billie Starr disappeared into her own world then, tracing pictures in the frost on the window with her index finger, singing as she did so—"Freray jacka, freray jacka, dormay-voo, doomay-voo"—and making airplane-taking-off-and-landing sounds. She did this almost every time Jenny drove her to school. The make-believe destination wasn't always Paris, though. Sometimes it was Disney World. Other times the Grand Canyon or Niagara Falls or the California redwoods. And she wasn't always a plane, either. For a long time, she was the Batmobile. Before that, a bullet train and before that, a stagecoach.

Jenny couldn't remember playing such games when she was Billie Starr's age. She was just herself, Jenny Newberg, going to school, Jenny Newberg at school, forgetting to listen, flubbing up on tests, and Jenny Newberg leaving school, feeling the weight of all her failures lift off her shoulders until the next day when she would have to go back and do it all over again. Finally, when she was sixteen and a half, she was Jenny Newberg *not* going to school, Jenny Newberg dropping out. Jenny Newberg on her own, hunting for jobs and a place to live, Jenny Newberg discovering, as Carla had warned her, that money did not grow on trees.

She passed more farms—the Johnson place, the Winkler place, the Shields place—and a trailer park where Randall Leffert, Billie Starr's father, had lived for a while after he lost his job at the feed store. Jenny heard from Lyd that Randall had moved out of the trailer park a few weeks ago, that he was seeing someone, a hairstylist from Crooked Lake who vowed to fight off any woman who showed the slightest interest in him.

"Literally," Lyd said. "Chick used to be a wrestler."

After the trailer park came a cluster of grain silos, a park, and finally the school on the left, teeming with traffic.

"School is my favorite thing," Billie Starr said.

"I know, baby."

"I'm not a baby! I'm an airplane!"

"Okay, okay. How's your landing gear?"

Billie Starr kicked her shoes, red arcs in the half-light. "There and fully functional."

"Good. We're on our descent."

The elementary school wasn't the same one Jenny went to. That school—which Pete's father helped build—had been torn down years ago. Modern, brick, single-story and sprawling, the new school sat at the edge of town on land that used to belong to the Lefferts. Carla liked to go on about how the Lefferts owned Benson, Indiana, called them their "corporate overlords," but the truth was the Lefferts were dying off. They were packing it in and in many cases, packing up. The still-alive ones were taking their money and moving in droves to gated communities in Florida and Texas and North Carolina, all of them, it seemed, except a handful of police officers—and Randall. Randall swore he'd never leave Benson, even though his parents had decamped for a place called Orange Blossom Gardens the year before. He couldn't bear to part with his daughter, he said, but he made no real attempt to be a part of her life, just showed up on Jenny's porch late at night, drunk, high, or both, crying into his shirt collar and hollering at Jenny about

wanting to see his daughter, begging her to give him back his balls. She refused to let him anywhere near Billie Starr on such nights. As for his balls, those were his problem.

"Mom?"

"Yeah."

"You're going in the out way."

"Shit."

"You shouldn't say 'shit.' It's a bad word."

Jenny was in a game of chicken with a line of minivans. An angry dad waved at her from behind a windshield dotted with state park stickers. Then he started honking.

"You need to turn around," Billie Starr said.

"I'm trying."

"You're messing the whole thing up."

The school parking lot was a minefield. Every morning, Jenny was shocked she got out of there alive. It was mostly an issue of space. The lot had been big enough five years ago, but when the Lefferts started selling off their farms to developers, subdivisions began popping overnight—Birch Meadows, Willow Lake Estates, Juniper Ridge. No one could keep up with the growth, and everything was overcrowded now—the grocery store, Pike's Pizza, Dr. Harme's office. Dr. Frank's office, too, and the Brown Derby, Benson's one cloth napkin restaurant. The school parking lot was just an extreme example of both the overcrowding and the mismanagement thereof. Someone—Gladys Mock, Jenny assumed, the school's principal, who was on the verge of retirement and had been Jenny's terrifying sixth-grade math teacher—was always switching the car lanes with the bus lanes and the in with the out in an effort to supposedly make things more efficient. Jenny couldn't keep it straight.

"Mom, this is taking forever," Billie Starr complained.

Jenny carefully backed up onto the roadway, hoping to shoot forward into the designated "in" lane before the minivans blocked her way, but she was too slow. They streamed by her in an endless

line of blue and white and maroon. Very patriotic, those vans, Jenny thought. Like a big, rumbling American flag. Desperate, she parked in a small patch of gravel behind a fire hydrant and a utility shed.

"Time to fly," Jenny said.

Billie Starr sighed heavily and grabbed her unicorn backpack. "Fine."

Five more minivans sped by. Five more frustrated, pinched faces peered out at Jenny as if she were personally responsible for the crowd of cars and shifting lanes. She pulled her coat tighter around her thin dress. The coat covered what she needed it to—the cleavage, the arrow necklace pointing to it, her bare arms. But what about her hair—high, curled, sprayed to unnatural stiffness—the too-heavy blush, the eyeliner? Jenny had overdone it. She'd over-done it and now, because she had to run Billie Starr into school instead of just dropping her off at the curb, everyone would see her looking like this, a woman in her late twenties who should know better.

The snow, so sparkling back at home, was melting here into sooty slush in the drains, green and brown patches around the trees. Jenny and Billie Starr hustled clumsily up the winding sidewalk past the buses and toward the front doors of the school. On the way in, they ran right into a pack of moms, all perfectly put together and clutching thermoses of tea and sleek, stylish purses. For some reason, they gave off an odor of cinnamon—probably the tea—and created a low sort of hum with their talk of their husbands and houses and special diets. They reminded Jenny of a hive of bees, but Lyd called them the Mummies. A few were old schoolmates of Jenny and Lyd. Aging cheerleaders, high achievers who'd only recently started watching their weight. Most were transplants from Fort Wayne who lived in the new subdivisions (which the women and their chubby, beige husbands moved to because housing was cheaper here than in the city) and spoke up at PTA meetings about

the need for more computers in the library and healthier food options in the cafeteria and the inappropriateness of showing fifth graders videos about their changing bodies. Also about evolution and the moral and economic advantages of certain Marxist principles. That last one had been a mistake, apparently. Wrong tape in the player.

Jenny ducked her head, tugged Billie Starr behind her. "Hurry, hurry," she whispered. "Step on it, airplane." But it was no use. She'd been spotted.

"Jenny!"

It was Ashley Batchelder, former cheerleader, current PTA president, mother to Terri, eight, and recently divorced from Ken Batchelder, city councilman and the owner of the asphalt company on Route 20. Ashley was on the school board. Ashley was very active in the community. Ashley didn't have to work. According to Lyd, head teller at Benson Bank and Trust, Ken paid Ashley an insane amount of alimony. So she volunteered. She headed up the annual Boy Scout popcorn fundraiser and the Girl Scout cookie sales drive. Sometimes, like now, around Christmas, she hosted parties at her house where she sold makeup and kitchen gadgets and quilted bags. Jenny had gone to a few of the parties, not because she wanted any of the products, but because, when Ashley issued the invitations, she made going sound like giving back. In the end, though, everything was too expensive, and Jenny always went home empty-handed. Embarrassed, too, ashamed she couldn't afford a fifty-five-dollar cheese grater.

"Where are you headed in such a hurry?" Ashley asked.

She and a few of the other Mummies moved in on Jenny, a cloud of beautifully coiffed hair, all of it styled in exactly the same way and modeled after an actress in a television show Jenny tried to watch but couldn't. It was too stupid. All the characters complained constantly about not having enough money, but Jenny never saw

any evidence of their poverty. No collection agents named Kevin ever hounded them, and their apartments were as perfect as their teeth. Maybe that's why the Mummies liked the show so much. It reminded them of themselves.

"We're late is all," Jenny said.

Ashley smiled. "Aren't you always late?"

Jenny tried to smile back. She could feel the foundation on her cheeks cracking.

"You're looking . . ." Ashley raised one of her eyebrows, plucked thin and boomerang shaped. "Interesting."

Jenny quickly surveyed the women around her, their attractively tailored coats, their elegant pants, their boots so clean and in fashion, and felt cheap and trashy. Back in her bathroom with her candles and cracked mirror, Jenny thought she'd looked pretty, but now that she was surrounded by all the prettiness that money could buy, she knew she was wrong. Her purse wasn't like their purses. It was scuffed and out of style and packed with free-sample perfume and dry lipsticks. Her outfit, her hair, her makeup and eyebrows and earrings, were all in bad taste. She was bad taste. Even her pantyhose were the wrong color. Too dark. Jenny wanted to rip them off and go back to bed.

"I have a funeral to go to," she said to Ashley.

"Oh, I'm so sorry."

"Me, too, but that's life, right? Death."

"I guess so," Ashley said. "For some people."

Billie Starr was tapping her foot and tugging on Jenny's coat. "Mom . . ."

"Well, I should—"

Ashley put a thin hand on Jenny's shoulder. "It's really good we've run into each other. The gals and I were just talking about the second-grade field trip to Chicago. It's going to be so much fun. We're taking the kids to the museums and to the Magnificent Mile

for some shopping. Christmas is coming up, you know." She peeked around Jenny at Billie Starr, back to making airplane sounds. "You do want to go, don't you, Billie Starr?"

Billie Starr stopped roaring and nodded shyly.

"You need to sign her permission slip," Ashley said to Jenny. "And pay the fee, of course. It's nothing. Seventy-five is all. A small price to pay for memories, don't you think?"

Jenny couldn't remember hearing about any field trip, and the last time she checked her bank accounts, she had maybe a hundred dollars to her name. But no matter. After this morning, she'd be flush. She'd be set. She could afford to send Billie Starr to a million Magnificent Miles.

"A very small price," Jenny said.

"Before you go," Ashley said, twinkling. Where did that twinkle come from? Her bright white teeth? An emptiness behind her eyes? "Did you get the invite to my party?"

The invitation was at the bottom of Jenny's kitchen trash. Not quilted bags or gadgets this time. Knives. Something called Cut-Corp that, according to Ashley's perfect handwriting, could slice through car doors like butter. "I did. Yes. Thank you."

"I'd love to see you there. We all would, wouldn't we, ladies?"

The Mummies hummed their assent, nodding their heads in unison. Jenny felt dizzy, a little hypnotized standing there. "I'll definitely try."

Talk then turned to the nativity scene in front of the courthouse. A tall brunette whose name Jenny could never remember was complaining about Mary and Joseph. Their faces were so worn you could hardly tell which was which, and baby Jesus was missing a nose. It was verging on sacrilege to put out such an ugly display, the dark-haired Mummy said. Disrespectful. A sin. Should they maybe start up a collection to buy the town a new one?

Billie Starr tugged on Jenny's sleeve again. "Mom, announcements . . ."

"I should go," Jenny said.

"Of course." Ashley took a sip from her travel mug. "Don't forget the field trip! I wouldn't want Billie Starr to miss out."

The Mummies moved back, and Jenny and Billie Starr hurried inside and down a long hall toward Mr. Richardson's room. On the way, they passed five other classrooms, all of them full of kids throwing things at one another and picking their noses and coloring on their desks. Jenny wondered how the teachers could stand it, day in and day out. The chaos. Not to mention the smell of pencil shavings and glue and crayons and wet wool. Windex, too. And old vomit.

"God, Mom. You're so slow."

"Sorry, sorry."

"You're Sorry, remember? Not me."

"I remember."

"You're basically just saying your name over and over again. Every time you apologize. It's weird."

"Sorry."

"Mom!"

Jenny put her head down, sped up, slammed right into the hard body of Principal Gladys Mock who, judging by her safety orange vest, had been helping the crossing guards direct traffic outside. She turned slowly in her sensible shoes and looked down her long nose at Jenny just as she used to when Jenny was thirteen and couldn't remember how to calculate the area of a rhombus. Or what a rhombus was.

"Running in the halls is strictly prohibited."

"I was just trying to get Billie Starr to her classroom on time—"

"Perhaps if you weren't already tardy . . ."

"You see, we were pretending to be airplanes—"

"Actually," Billie Starr said. "I'm the airplane." She pointed at Jenny. "She's a sorry."

Gladys Mock obviously did not care who was what. "The fact remains that you, Miss Newberg, are an adult and, as such, you should know better than to set a bad example for our students."

Staring at Gladys Mock's extremely clean fingernails, Jenny was a girl again, ordered up to the chalkboard to solve an equation. Something x times something y equals something else. The answer always eluded her. z? z squared? It was arbitrary. It was alphabet soup.

"And while I'm glad you're suddenly very concerned with promptness," Gladys Mock was saying, "Ashley Batchelder tells me you have yet to fill out Billie Starr's permission slip and pay her fee for the second-grade field trip."

"Yes, I'm—"

"You missed the registration deadline, but it just so happens that there was a last-minute cancellation, and, out of the goodness of her heart, Ashley Batchelder is willing to give your daughter the extra seat."

"That's wonderful. I'm so—"

"There are limits, Miss Newberg. Remember that. There are rules in this world. Just because you don't respect those rules doesn't mean they don't apply to you."

Billie Starr, who'd been circling slowly around a discarded eraser and a pair of earmuffs still wet with snow, made another small roaring sound.

Gladys Mock watched her for a moment, shook her head. "Now get on. You don't want to be any later than you already are."

Mr. Richardson's room was at the very end of the hall across from a broom closet. Baby-blue lockers lined the walls to the left of the door. On the other side, a bulletin board, covered in sparkly snowflakes, announced the students of the month. Billie Starr's name was right in the middle.

Jenny felt a burst of pride, seeing it there. But she was irritated with her daughter, too, for making her a target of the Mummies, of Ashley Batchelder of all people. And of Gladys Mock. "Why didn't you tell me about the field trip?"

"I tried like six thousand times." Billie Starr kicked her shoes against the wall, the soles flashing like tiny ambulances. "You just weren't listening."

"Do you really want to go?"

"Everyone else is going."

"It's a lot of money."

"You always say that."

"I do? Like when?"

"Like when I told you I wanted a computer for Christmas. You said computers cost a lot of money."

"They do cost a lot of money. I was just telling you the truth."

"You weren't telling the truth back there. You lied to Terri's mom."

"I did not."

"Then someone really died?"

"People are dying all the time . . ."

"So, you're not going to a funeral then."

"No."

"Why'd you tell her you were?"

Jenny stared at a locker for a moment. Number 123. Lucky kid. Was the combination just as easy to remember? Inside the classroom, Mr. Richardson was writing spelling words on the board—*pine, gift, lights, song, ribbon, stocking.* How comforting, Jenny thought. Christmastime as one big cup of hot chocolate.

"Actually," she said, "I'm going to a job interview and I just didn't want anyone to know, because if I don't get the job and I've told a bunch of people about it, I'll feel bad."

"Really?"

"Really," Jenny said. "And anyway, it doesn't matter."

"The interview?"

"Me lying to Terri's mom. It's not a big deal."

"You told me all lies matter. You told me all lies count."

"I lied."

Billie Starr rolled her eyes and hoisted her backpack higher up on her shoulder. She was so skinny. Too skinny. Like Carla that way. She had Randall's thick nose and high forehead. His pale skin, too, and his tendency to turn pink when he was nervous or guilty of some-

thing. Her mouth, full-lipped and wide, was Pete's. All Billie Starr had inherited from Jenny was her hair. Red. Curly. Often unmanageable. Jenny kissed that hair, told her she'd see her in the afternoon.

"Be good."

"I'm always good."

"I know." Jenny pointed to the billboard. "Nice job, student of the month."

Billie Starr blushed and roared and zoomed through the doorway, arms out at her sides like wings. Mr. Richardson spotted her, smiled, gave Jenny a wave. Jenny waved back. Then she started to walk quickly down the hall, Billie Starr's beloved announcements in full swing. Something about choir practice, the fifth-grade spelling bee, the third-grade plant show . . .

"Miss Newberg?" It was Mr. Richardson. He was trotting after her, a pink piece of paper in one hand. "I was hoping to get you to sign Billie Starr's permission slip. For the field trip to Chicago? And to collect her fee. Is this an okay time?"

"Now's great," Jenny said. Why was everyone so obsessed with this field trip? You'd think it was a pilgrimage to a holy place the way they were all going on about it. "I can't believe I forgot to pay. Let me just write that check out to you now."

"Perfect." Mr. Richardson gave her the paper, stepped back. Ever since she'd rejected him, he seemed to take great care to keep his distance.

The permission slip consisted of two paragraphs of information about the date and time of the trip, topped with crooked clip art of a generic city skyline. Scheduled for the coming Saturday, the trip would be "an educational and fun introduction to one of the Midwest's cultural treasures!" Kids should bring a warm coat, comfortable shoes, and a packed lunch. Jenny pressed the paper against a blank space on the wall next to a glass-encased fire extinguisher, signed it, gave it back. Then she filled out a check as quickly as she could and handed it over, too.

"I should go," Mr. Richardson said. "The kids will resort to cannibalism if I don't."

Jenny laughed. "That could get messy."

"Very."

Mr. Richardson looked like he might want to say something more, but then his attention was caught by the sight of a small, pale boy with a pointy nose standing under an exit sign. The boy had stringy black hair and a rash on his neck and was whispering to something in his palm. Mr. Richardson walked over to the boy, spoke softly to him about needing to get to class. The boy started like a frightened animal and dashed off down the hall. The thing he was talking to fell from his hand. A cockroach. Mr. Richardson followed the boy, smiling at Jenny over his shoulder. She checked her watch. Late again. Always late. That's how Carla often described her—"My daughter, late for the party."

The announcements were over now and the woman who read them every day had launched into the Pledge of Allegiance. Jenny put her hand over her heart out of habit. Behind her, a chorus of high voices chanted in singsong rhythm, one nation, under God, indivisible, with liberty and justice for all.

$\mathcal{L}$yd said no way.

"Don't do it. You can't do something like that. Not you. Someone else might get away with it, someone more sophisticated and secretive and scheming, but you? Uh-uh. It'll backfire." She took a long gulp of orange juice and finished her French toast. Lyd used to diet a lot, to agonize over her weight. She didn't anymore, said that whole obsession was a big, fat waste of time. She had five pants suits she wore to the bank during the week—black on Mondays, navy on Tuesdays, red on Wednesdays, brown on Thursdays, and green on Fridays. The suits looked good on her. So did the matching power pumps she paired with them. She had

a soft face and a hard stare. She started nibbling from Jenny's plate. "You know I'm right. I'm always right."

Jenny let Lyd talk. It was what Lyd did every Monday morning when they met at the pancake house for coffee: talk, lecture, try to get Jenny to "see sense." Jenny understood. Lyd, overall overachiever, saw it as her duty to tell Jenny, chronically underemployed underachiever, how to live her life. Lyd had been doing it since they were girls. Get some sleep, Lyd said. Study more. Also, quit dating idiots. Read a book, read a newspaper, toughen up, wise up, lawyer up. The last was in response to Randall's failure to pay child support, but Jenny couldn't afford a lawyer.

Unlike Jenny, Lyd had graduated from high school, top of the class. She was smart and practical and knew things Jenny didn't about annual percentage rates and easements and tax write-offs. She had an apartment on Poplar Street, a full set of encyclopedias, basically new, and a subscription to *Time*. Also actual ambitions. She planned to wait out her boss, Larry Dodge, who wasn't in good health, and be running Benson Bank and Trust before she turned thirty-five.

"Please tell me you'll rethink this thing," Lyd said. "Please tell me you'll change your mind."

The pancake house was full. Fresh coffee smell. Toast, too, and spilled syrup. Clang of flatware getting dumped into a sink and washed. Clink of cups. Comforting.

"I'll think about it," Jenny said.

"Really think about it?"

"I'm thinking about thinking about it."

"Oh well, I feel so much better."

Jenny did her best to follow Lyd's advice. Her house on Acorn Street—that was Lyd's idea. Lyd had heard the house was for sale from her uncle, Bob Butz, who'd also been Pete's boss. (Benson, Pete often said, was a small world. So small you just might meet your own self on the street, coming *and* going.) Bob helped Jenny

negotiate her mortgage. Then he hired her as a receptionist in his real estate office. It was a good job—easy, anyway, and came with health insurance for her and Billie Starr. For three years, Jenny paid her bills and was content, answering phones and typing up and sending letters, until one day Bob cornered her in the break room and shoved his hands up her skirt. Jenny didn't know what to do, so what she did was scream and kick him in the crotch. An instinct, that's all that was. A reflex. Bob fired her on the spot. Then he made her promise not to tell anyone what happened, especially Lyd. Jenny agreed, only because the whole thing was humiliating and sweaty and something she would prefer to forget. When she thought of Bob's hands on her, she felt nauseated and ashamed. Untouchable, too. Tainted. Bob fired her four months ago. No one else, not even the pancake house or Pike's Pizza or the Brown Derby, would hire her. The kindly managers all gave her the same excuse—they were fully staffed, they said. Not in need of help at this time. We'll keep your application on file. Then they hustled off to answer the phone or do a load of dishes.

"I'm serious," Lyd said. "Are you listening to me?"

"I'm listening."

Their waiter, a Winkler boy—that forehead—refilled their coffees. Lyd waited for him to leave to say, "I don't think you realize what you're getting into. You never think ahead, Jenny Newberg. You just do what feels good or seems right in the moment. I mean, the whole Randall saga is proof of that. You don't stop and consider what's next."

Behind Lyd, a family of six squeezed into a booth. The kids began play-fighting with their straws, sword style. Every once in a while, a straw would whack Lyd on the head. She kept talking. "This is a lot more complicated than it looks on the surface. I mean, did you get anything in writing from those guys? A contract? Anything?"

"It's fine, Lyd. Really. I've got everything under control."

Lyd rolled her eyes skyward. "Oh, Jesus. I know what that means. Translation: everything's a mess. We're in opposite world now, folks."

"Don't worry about me, okay?"

"Easier said than done."

"I don't worry about you."

"I wonder why."

"Can we change the subject?"

"To what? The weather?" Lyd grabbed a saltshaker, tapped it like a microphone. "Well, ladies and gents, it sure is nippy out there. Don't forget your hat and gloves when you leave the house this morning. Also, news flash, Jennifer Natalie Newberg is about to blow up her life. Just thought you, our loyal viewers, would like to know."

"Why are you freaking out about this? It's a job. I'll do it and it'll be done. I'll finally have some money. No big deal."

"No big deal? This is the biggest of big deals. This is the kind of thing you regret for the rest of your life."

"Like having my daughter?"

Lyd pushed her plate away. "Not fair."

"Pretty fair."

When Jenny first found out she was pregnant with Billie Starr, Lyd had lobbied her to have an abortion, arguing that bringing a baby into her situation would only make things worse, especially given that Randall Leffert was the father. Jenny refused. It was the one time she'd defied Lyd, and Lyd, who fell in love with Billie Starr the moment she set eyes on her, had to admit, at least in this instance, that Jenny had finally done the right thing.

"Billie Starr is not going to thank you for this," Lyd said. "Mark my words."

"She's my kid. I think I know what she needs."

"In the name of all that's holy, Jenny, you're so naive. If you want to do what's best for Billie Starr, call those men and tell them it's off.

I'll give you the quarter. Hell, I'll give you a whole roll of quarters. Call the men, call their wives, call their mothers, call their kids, call their dogs. Call all of them and tell them you were wrong to accept this gig and you want out. Do *that* for Billie Starr. If all you need is money, come to the bank, apply for a loan. I can help you out."

The Winkler boy was back. He wanted to know if they needed anything else.

"Just the bill," Lyd said. "And a brain for my best friend."

Jenny smiled at the boy. He smiled sloppily back and tripped on his way to the kitchen. Jenny's smiles had that effect on men. It was almost too easy. "How's work?" she asked Lyd.

"You think you can distract me as easily as you distracted forehead over there?"

"Come on," Jenny said. "We haven't talked about you at all."

"You know that you look like a call girl."

"Do I?"

"The eye shadow's a bit much."

"Seriously, I'm dying. Tell me all about the most recent scandals at Benson Bank and Trust. Don't leave anything out."

As head teller, Lyd knew the town's secrets. It was all there in how they handled their money. She knew who was genuinely broke and who was pretending to be broke for tax purposes. She knew who was skimming company funds off the top and padding their own pockets and drowning in debt, and, even though she was supposed to keep such things to herself—"under penalty of law"—she often spilled the beans to Jenny, who swore she wouldn't tell a soul.

"What if this man they want you to sleep with is some sort of predator type?" Lyd asked. "He could be a monster. A rapist. A murderer. A serial rapist slash murderer."

Jenny remembered the man's puppy dog eyes, his goofy haircut. "I don't think so."

"You could get killed. You could be one of those stories on the five o'clock news: body of single mother fished from the river."

"What river?"

"A lake then."

The father of the family in the next booth met Jenny's eye over his daughter's head, attention probably caught by the words *body* and *river*.

"Could you lower your voice a bit?" Jenny asked.

"Could you do me a favor and make the right choice just this once?"

Jenny switched tactics. "I had a run-in with the Mummies this morning. Ashley was ragging on me about not signing Billie Starr up for some field trip. About not paying my way. And then she brought up the knife party she's having on Sunday. Did you get your invitation?"

"Yeah," Lyd said. Nothing fired her up like Ashley Batchelder, whom she referred to as Head Mummy in Charge. "She brought mine to the bank with her, along with her monthly PTA deposit. Do you know what she said to me? She said, 'Lydia Butz, as I live and breathe! I didn't know your hair could get any shorter!' It was all I could do not to return the compliment. 'Ashley Batchelder, I didn't know you could be any bitchier.' She's the worst."

"*The* worst," Jenny agreed.

"So that's how my week started. With Ashley *Bitch*elder. Right after her, a politician's wife came in and withdrew a shit ton of money. It set off alarm bells for me, but Larry was all casual, said she was a regular customer. Regular, my ass. I'd never seen her before. I swear, Larry'll run the bank into the ground one of these days. And, then, on Friday, Marcus showed up in a kimono, ranting about a government-sponsored conspiracy involving the moon landing, General Motors, and genetically modified mosquitos. He's really losing it, isn't he?"

"How'd he get into town?" Jenny asked. "He's not supposed to drive anymore."

"He walked."

"In this weather?"

"Yeah. Larry took him to Dr. Harme's. We were worried about frostbite. Marcus was fine mostly. A little chilled. Dr. Harme gave him some Tylenol and a set of scrubs to wear. Then Larry drove him home, made him promise he would go straight to bed and not cause any more trouble."

"Anytime Marcus says he won't cause trouble, he always does. I should check on him later."

"You should check on him now," Lyd said. "Blow off those Black Suits whoever they are and go make sure your sweet and crazy neighbor isn't frozen to death."

Jenny pulled a ten-dollar bill from her ugly purse and tossed it Lyd's way. "I have to go."

"Jenny—" Lyd reached for Jenny's hand.

"I'll call you."

"You better."

"I will."

Maybe she would. Maybe she wouldn't. Either way, she'd make sure that Billie Starr came out a winner in the whole deal. Jenny would see to that. What was the worst that could happen, anyway?

The plan wasn't complicated, not really. The Black Suits had hashed it all out for her in a grimy booth in the back of Benson's Gas America, aroma of hot dog water and disinfectant heavy, competing. Step one: drive to Fort Wayne to a pay phone in the parking lot of a downtown Shell station. The men had given her a map of the town and a phone number to call. The number was written on a scrap of graph paper. If Jenny was still committed to going through with the job, she was to call that number and, when the tallest of the Black Suits answered, the one with the deep voice—bright, silver hair, too, and strong chin and air of authority—she was to deliver this one simple line: "The oranges are ripe."

"Easy peasy?" said the man with the higher voice. He was short and fat with rolls of flesh around his collar and was always sniffling. Maybe he just had a cold. A circlet of black hair topped his head like a doughnut and his salt-and-pepper mustache was spotty.

"Lemon squeezy," she replied.

The fat man had laughed at that, clapped her on the back, said she was a smart cookie. "Lemons, oranges," he said. "Someone knows her citrus fruits."

If she changed her mind, got cold feet, the men told her to skip the drive and call from her house. In that case, the one with the deep voice instructed her to tell them, "The oranges are rotten." That's how they would know the deal was off. Regardless of what she decided, she was to set fire to the paper the number was written on, turn it to ash, and grind it under her shoe. That was step two.

It was all so ridiculous, so hard-boiled and strange, but here she was, making the drive. She had the map of Fort Wayne on her passenger's seat and had written out detailed directions to the Shell station on an old electric bill. The phone number was in her coat pocket. She had matches there, too. And Pete's purple rabbit's foot for luck.

After making the pay phone call, she was to drive around the corner to a McDonald's where a woman—also in a black suit— would be waiting for her in the ladies' bathroom. Step three. That woman would equip Jenny with a device that would pick up every word the man said. The man with a weak chin and bushy eyebrows and halting gait. The man with the gentle smile. Jenny was supposed to get him to say incriminating things, things like how much he wanted her and how sexy she was and how his wife would be furious if she knew what he just did with Jenny in a hotel that rented rooms by the hour.

The men told Jenny exactly which hotel to go to. They'd scouted it out, apparently, found it satisfactory for the purpose and marked

it on the map, too. The Riverview Inn. It had a red roof and a pool out front, they said. Oh, and a cannon. Antique. Out of commission. You can't miss it.

"Is it on a river?"

"No," said Tall Black Suit. It was across the street from a lamp store and an accountant's office.

The hotel was step four. She was getting ahead of herself. Jenny still didn't know the name of the man she was supposed to coax to the hotel. The Black Suits—whose names were also a mystery—said she didn't need to know. They simply called him "the Candidate." The Candidate was a politician running for some sort of office. According to the Black Suits: (a) he was a bad man; and (b) by sleeping with him and exposing him as a bad man, Jenny would be doing a service to her country; and (c) he adhered to a morning routine that rarely varied. C, the Black Suits said, was the most important part. The other stuff, well. That was for the voters to decide. Jenny was just giving them a little nudge in the right direction.

According to the Black Suits, the Candidate showed up at the same Scott's grocery store in downtown Fort Wayne at 10:30 A.M. every day, bought the same cup of coffee and doughnut from the same bearded baker, then went to the same checkout lane—no. 3—and bought the same newspaper: the *Journal-Gazette*.

"Pinko-commie rag," growled Fat Black Suit.

"Just stick to the plan," said Tall.

"Fine, fine." Sniff, sniff.

On his way to the checkout lane, Fat Black Suit said, the Candidate picked out an orange. Sometimes two. Then he ate the fruit a little later, usually before the doughnut and typically in his car, discarding the peels out the window. No matter, both men said. Jenny should approach him in the produce section. He tended to linger there, over the oranges, looking for the best one.

Ironic because that's where the Black Suits found her, in the

produce section of a grocery store, only that store was in Benson and Jenny was buying apples. They said they knew she was the one for the job the minute they saw her.

"You have just the right air of understated elegance," said Tall.

"And the Candidate has a thing for redheads," said Fat.

She'd made it to the city. The streets were gray and wet and wide. Nearly deserted. The snow had melted here, too, into a soft slush like cake icing along the roadside. A rat rolled around in it near a storm drain. Then it slipped between the bars and was gone.

Jenny missed the Shell station on the first try, only found it the second time around because the car in front of her was pulling in, too. The station was small—four pumps, a glorified convenience store, a couple of newspaper boxes. The phone booth was in the back corner of the lot behind a large propane tank. Jenny parked next to the tank, got out, glanced around. No one seemed to be watching her. A middle-aged woman in a huge coat was pumping gas. Another sat in her yellow hatchback, reading a book. Why would you read a book here of all places? The sky was white and far away. A blank slate.

Jenny needed gas—she had just enough to get back to Benson—but she thought she'd fill up after the job was done and she was flush and relaxed. She pushed her way into the phone booth, pulled off her gloves, dropped a quarter in the slot, and dialed the number. The phone rang twice. Then a man's voice answered. It was Tall Black Suit, the silver-haired one with the imposing chin. She could tell by the gravelly way he cleared his throat.

"It's you," the man said.

"It's me."

The middle-aged woman in the huge coat had finished filling up her tank. She got in her car—a boxy sedan—and drove off. The woman in the hatchback was still reading. A blind man with a Seeing Eye dog walked by on the sidewalk, cane bumping the concrete in a gentle, drumlike rhythm.

"The oranges are ripe," Jenny said.

Tall Black Suit sighed. Jenny could hear water running and a television tuned to some sort of game show. Clapping. Celebration. And then a womp womp sound when someone made a mistake, lost it all.

"Our suppliers will be thrilled," Tall said. "I mean it. They'll just be tickled pink."

The gentle hiss of produce sprinklers reminded Jenny that she had to pee. There'd been no time back in the McDonald's restroom. The woman who met her there was all-business, brusque, in a hurry. With her haughty air and man hands, she was a lot like Gladys Mock. She told Jenny to go straight to the oranges. Don't dawdle, the woman said. Then she looked at Jenny sharply as if to say, I know your kind. Yours is the kind that dawdles.

The grocery store was shinier, cleaner, newer than the store in Benson. It had an organic food section and a fresh flower department. A bank branch, too, and pretty displays everywhere. Even the cash registers made a different sort of beep—softer, easier on the ears.

A man with a bucket and a mop tipped his hat to her. It was a butcher's hat, spattered in blood.

"And how are you, little lady?"

Before Jenny could answer, a tiny, beady-eyed woman in a hairnet told the man to go back to the meat counter, to get a new hat, make himself presentable.

The man spat on the floor. "I'll presentable you," he said. Then, when Hairnet threatened to have him fired, he mopped up the spittle and walked away.

At the end of a line of registers was a magazine rack. Jenny ducked behind it, shrugged off her coat, left it on the floor. The woman back at McDonald's had scolded her for her thin dress,

asked her what she was thinking, wearing something so cheap and flimsy when there was a wire to hide. Jenny hadn't known the wire would be bulky and awkward. She'd just wanted to look cute. Typical bimbo, the woman said. Then, sighing, she lent Jenny her black silk vest, cinching it at the back as tight as it would go with a safety pin.

The effect was surprising, sexy even. Jenny felt like a Las Vegas cocktail waitress. Or a cigarette girl. Still, it wasn't comfortable, and sweat dripped into her underwear, the pin pinching the soft skin around her spine.

The oranges rose up in a pyramid shape in the middle of the produce department, an enormous pile of pale, waxy fruit surrounded by green bunting that Jenny assumed was supposed to look like grass. But that didn't make sense. Oranges grew on trees. Jenny's mouth was dry, her palms wet. She'd bitten her tongue back at McDonald's. Every once in a while, she tasted blood. And the cold coffee she'd drunk too fast back at home.

There was no one near the display, no man with bushy eyebrows or a weak chin or a halting gait. There was just Jenny in her come-hither outfit, clutching her keys.

The Black Suits had schooled her on what to do if the Candidate didn't show up right away. She should stall, they said, bide her time, look natural. The woman at McDonald's got more specific.

"Pick up the fruit, examine it like a housewife would. Sniff it. Put it back. Repeat."

She plucked an orange from the top of the pyramid, turned it over in her hand, returned it to its spot. If the Candidate really took his time getting there, she was to roam around from stall to stall, putting items in her cart as she saw fit. But Jenny didn't have a cart. She'd forgotten to grab one. She was too nervous. And suddenly he was limping toward her. She knew it was him immediately. There were the eyebrows, the sunken chin. He had a newspaper under his left arm. In his right hand, he balanced a coffee and a dough-

nut. The bakery was at the back of the store. He was probably se-
lecting his doughnut while she pretended to be a housewife. He
talked to everyone he passed—the butcher in his new hat, the hair-
netted woman, a little girl screaming for a balloon. The Candidate
pulled a balloon from a bouquet above a rack of Christmas candy
and handed it to the girl, told Hairnet to put it on his tab. Then he
saw Jenny. He stopped. His smile disappeared, replaced with a look
of curiosity. Maybe a little lust. Jenny dropped her keys, crouched
down. The Candidate rushed over, got to the keys before she could,
scooped them up. Then he placed his paper and coffee and doughnut on the floor, rose, took her hand, dropped the keys into her
open palm, and gently, one-by-one, folded her fingers over them.

Jenny couldn't remember what she'd planned to say to the man
when she saw him. He had sleep in his eyes and a cold sore on his
lower lip.

"What's your name?" he asked.

"I need to pee," she said. "I need to pee so bad I think I'm going
to die."

The man held the orange up to her right breast, shook his head,
said, "No, no. It's all wrong. It's a peach. Your breasts are peaches.
I'd like to make a pie."

Jenny thought of Trish Keck and her runny pies, of Lorne Keck
and his .38. Men were always comparing Jenny's breasts to peaches.
She was used to it, tired of it. Bored. Her breasts had brought her a
lot of misery over the years. First, there were the awkward, smelly
high school boys pawing her in the backs of cars and movie the-
aters, in her parents' basement, in their grandparents' basements, in
cemeteries. Then there was Randall. High school sweetheart, prom
date, first time. He liked to sleep with his head between her breasts,
drooling on her nipples, his stubble giving her red, painful rashes
that itched on their way out. The most recent was Bob Butz who,

just before he fired her, admitted that his idea of heaven would be to sit in a chair across from her naked body and stare at her chest. For the rest of his life.

"You're so beautiful," the Candidate said. "You're the most beautiful woman I've ever seen."

He seemed to have forgotten that he wanted to know her name. The Black Suits told her to remain as anonymous as possible. Jenny had worried briefly that anonymity would make the Candidate suspicious—"Won't he think I'm a hooker?" she asked. Otherwise why would a twenty-eight-year-old woman seduce a fifty-something man in a grocery store? The Black Suits said it would all work out fine. Never, added the fat one, underestimate a horny man's powers of self-delusion. And if he seems hesitant, just bat your lashes and stare longingly at him. Touch his arm. Make your voice nice and breathy. Flatter him. Pour it on thick. Give him some rigmarole about how much you admire his work as a public servant and how you find him oddly magnetic, irresistible even, probably because of the daddy issues you're trying to work through in therapy.

"Therapy?" Jenny said.

"Trust me," Fat Black Suit said. "He'll eat it up. Like a twelve-ounce filet."

Fat Black Suit was right. The Candidate swallowed it all whole, even though Jenny stumbled on "magnetic" and "daddy issues." After some hesitation at the store and in the parking lot outside her car—the man, perhaps used to being watched, followed, admired, kept looking around, scanning the spaces for someone he knew maybe, or a member of the media (Jenny could only guess)—he agreed to come with her to the Riverview, which Jenny said belonged to a friend of a friend. *I've followed your career from afar.* Batting her lashes. *I'm a big fan.* Staring longingly. *What you do, so inspiring. You have my vote.* Lie after lie after lie, all delivered in a breathy voice she hadn't used since high school when, in a period of

temporary insanity, she was obsessed with winning Randall away from Ashley Batchelder née Shields. Apparently, that voice was just as powerful now as it had been then.

"Do you have any idea how gorgeous you are?" the man asked.

Her beauty was like her breasts. Men liked to talk about it, and they liked her heart-shaped face, too, her cornflower-blue eyes, her thick, curly hair, her womanly hips, her small waist. Carla, though, told her to be careful. She'd get fat if she didn't watch it.

"I mean, you're perfect." The Candidate twirled a lock of Jenny's hair between his fingers. He studied the hair like it was a wonder of the world. "And I'm . . . well." He laughed. "I never do things like this." Then he sat up in bed, sheet creeping down his thin, mostly hairless torso. "No, that's not right." He wagged his finger at nothing, at no one, maybe at the television, which was at least ten years out-of-date and off anyway. "I've *never* done anything like this. It's like I lost my mind back there in that store and the truth is, I feel fine without it. Who needs a brain? What good are brains anyway?"

The wire was on the floor in the bathroom under her dress. Jenny wondered if it was still picking up the man's words. No matter. She did what the Black Suits had asked her to do. While she was still clothed, she got the Candidate to say a lot of lusty things and to admit that she was his dream girl, his wife be damned, and then she'd excused herself, said something dumb about slipping into something more comfortable, came back out, naked, and, holding her breath, closing her eyes, she climbed on top of him. She'd done her job and she'd done it well, despite herself. Despite everything really. All that remained was to collect the money.

The man, though, wasn't ready to let her go. Technically, he hadn't finished—his pager buzzed a few times and he'd lost what he called his "concentration." He wanted to give it another try.

"Next time, next time," Jenny whispered. She kissed his greasy forehead and tiptoed back to the bathroom to get dressed. In the

dark, it was difficult to find the light switch. Her hand kept hitting empty space. The man must have heard her nails scraping the wallpaper. He told her the switch was higher up, just above the gold-plated antique revolver candleholder.

The Riverview wasn't like the motel Pete died in or any motel she'd ever been to, the rooms in those places blandly interchangeable, each one just like the other, except for the bronze number on the door. The Riverview was hunting lodge meets corporate boardroom meets divorced stepdad's bachelor pad. It was ugly and musty and the carpet, both here in room 186 and in the lobby, was strewn with cigarette and cigar ash.

Jenny flipped the light on and hurriedly stuffed the wire into her underwear. Then she pulled on her dress and tried to hide the bulge with the brusque woman's black vest. It was easier when she had help, but it would do for now. It would get her where she had to go, which was away. As quickly as possible. She spit on a square of toilet paper and wiped the mascara from under her eyes, pinched her cheeks, smoothed her hair.

"Can I call you?" the man asked from the other room.

Jenny froze. The wire was digging into her hip now. "Sure."

"How?"

"What do you mean?"

"What's your number?"

"I'll give it to you."

"When?"

Jenny stepped into her shoes. "Soon."

"What are you doing in there?"

Her neck hurt from where the man bit it. She fingered the sore spot, wondered if what she'd just done with him showed on her face. "Putting myself back together."

"Come to bed."

"I can't."

"Why?"

"I have to pick up my daughter from school."

The minute she said it she regretted it. She hadn't meant to tell the Candidate anything real about herself, but she'd already let it slip that she was from Benson, town of 3,891. Benson? The man said, surprised and delighted. Why would anyone be delighted by Benson? Jenny hadn't found out. They were in the middle of the whole thing and lost the thread and he was kissing her so neither of them could talk anyway.

He seemed to be fiddling with the TV. She heard the dial click from station to station, releasing flashes of voices, a bit of song. Then silence. "Idiot box," he mumbled. And then, more loudly, "You don't look old enough to have a daughter."

"I started early," Jenny said.

"That's the way to go. You have the energy, right?"

"Right."

What she'd just done—wrong. So wrong. Was there now any difference between her and a prostitute? Jenny couldn't see one. She flipped the bathroom light off, stood for a moment in the dark, glad that Pete was dead. She wouldn't have been able to face him. Then again, when she did something she wasn't proud of—yelled at Billie Starr for tracking mud into the house, let Randall fuck her on Memorial Day because she was too tired to say no, ate an entire bag of Doritos in one sitting in front of *Oprah*—Jenny wondered if her father was watching her somehow, if guardian angelship was like a two-way mirror and he had a direct feed into her world through the magic of heaven/the afterlife/wherever he was now, now that he wasn't here. She sincerely hoped not. For both their sakes.

Jenny's thoughts on religion were vague, uninformed by any actual instruction. What she understood of Christianity was courtesy of television shows and movies and the few attempts she'd made to read the Bible. None of it was clear on what people in heaven (or

hell) knew of people on earth. And what she'd read of the Bible was not comforting. God's actions seemed all rather arbitrary and cruel, and people—women mostly—were always being punished for something they didn't do.

Jenny hugged herself briefly, went back out to face the Candidate. He'd gotten dressed, too, and was fastening his belt. He'd missed a loop on the side, but she didn't tell him. She felt suddenly shy. Should she give him a fake phone number? Just make one up?

"I'd like to see you again," the Candidate said.

"But . . ."

"But what?"

"You're married."

The man shoved his left hand into his pants pocket. "I guess I am. Sort of."

"Sort of?"

"I mean, I'm completely married as far as that goes. Have the certificate to prove it. And the photo album and mortgage and place settings. My wife just doesn't like me very much anymore."

"I'm sorry."

"I wouldn't call it a tragedy. If I'm being honest—and why not? This seems like the perfect time to be honest—I never should have married her. She shouldn't have married me. We were young and stupid and now we're stuck. I mean, who would take me now? I'm like a beater truck, all worn-out and rusty. I'm worse than that. I'm a beater minivan."

The Candidate wasn't attractive, not in a conventional sense anyway. He was a little hunched and had a dandruff problem. But there was something charming about him. He'd been gentle with Jenny and his trim body was clean. Smell of soap and spice. Going to bed with him had been easy, tolerable, not stomach turning like she'd thought it would be. She was glad, though, that he hadn't finished. Neither of them had considered the matter of condoms until things were pretty far along, and Jenny couldn't remember

where she was in her cycle. About halfway through maybe? That was the danger zone. Standing there in the ugly hotel room, Jenny had a moment of retroactive panic, thinking about what could have happened, about the abortion clinic Lyd had wanted to bring her to when she first got pregnant with Billie Starr. Jenny was pretty sure she saw it on her drive to the hotel. It was just down the street from the Riverview. An old mansion with a subtle sign over the front door, it looked harmless enough. Sandstone steps. Young women going in and out, hiding under hooded coats.

Jenny had left her own coat—and Pete's lucky rabbit's foot—back on the grocery store floor, and she was starting to wonder if she'd ever be warm again. When the Black Suits paid her, she'd buy a new coat, a better one, maybe one like the Mummies wore, smart and gathered at the waist, no coffee stains on the cuffs. The Candidate had tried several times to get her to wear his, but she had refused. The gesture reminded her of high school–era Randall, always trying to get her to wear his letterman jacket, only in this case the coat wasn't an homage to jockdom. Far from it. Gold corduroy with brown patches on the elbows, it made the Candidate look smart, professorial. He was wearing it now and rifling through a hard-sided briefcase, scattering papers. Jenny wondered if he might be someone important, someone she should have heard of. Unlike what the Black Suits claimed, he didn't seem like a bad man at all. Not a rapist, not a serial killer. Take that, Lyd. He seemed kind, maybe a little confused, bewildered not just by Jenny's interest in him but by life in general.

"My wife wanted kids," he said. "That's what it came down to, I think. Why she married me. She wanted to be a mother, rather desperately, if I'm remembering correctly. But we're past that age."

"Past what age?"

"The age of wanting things desperately."

"Oh."

"And of baby-making. We never had kids. We have dogs instead."

"Dogs are nice."

"Not my wife's."

"What's wrong with them?"

"They bite. And they shit in my shoes."

Jenny smiled. The Candidate smiled back, a little ruefully, and started to come toward her, arms outstretched. If the Black Suits hadn't told Jenny about his halting gait, she probably wouldn't have noticed it. The limp was subtle. She wondered how he got it. War injury? Childhood illness? Maybe one of his legs was just longer than the other. A stuffed deer head was on the wall behind him. He gave the impression of having antlers, a full, ten-point rack as he approached.

"If you could just stay a little longer . . ."

There was a knock at the door then, two quick raps and a woman's voice announcing "Housekeeping!" Jenny could tell the Candidate was getting ready to send the maid away, but this was her opportunity for escape, and she took it. She kissed the man's cheek, told him she'd be seeing him, and then darted out the door into the lobby. The maid, a round woman in a Kiss tee shirt, cart brimming with cleaning supplies, watched her run by.

"I'll find you," the Candidate said.

Jenny waved but did not turn around. She pushed through the lobby's double doors and went straight to her car. She'd parked it next to the pool, where a dead bird lay frozen in the deep end on top of a tarp. Trapped in ice, it was a sad sight, the frigid, tiny body, the claws all but gone, eyes pecked out, but Jenny couldn't help it—she felt incredibly light. It was as if her stupid shoes could catch flight and she was a bird—undead, unfrozen—or a plane on her way to Paris. She would have money. Finally. She could get Billie Starr that computer. She could pay her mortgage. She could make plans.

Two trucks spun out in front of her on the icy roads, but she simply drove right through, blessed, untouchable, and the snow came

down like a curtain, like wave after wave of sparkling, perfect applause.

The Black Suits weren't where they said they were going to be, which was a café a few miles from the Riverview in a shopping center helmed by a Sears store and a movie theater. Step five. Another spot on the Fort Wayne map, circled in red. Jenny supposed the men were on a different errand or maybe in the bathroom. Either way, the three of them—four? Would the woman from McDonald's make another appearance? Jenny hoped not—hadn't settled on a specific time to meet because, as Tall Black Suit said, "Jobs like this, you have to let them run their natural course."

Fat Black Suit agreed. "Don't rush it," he said. "Get there when you get there."

The café was small and mostly empty. A young man sat by himself by the window. He was writing in a notebook. Frantically. As if his life depended on it. Maybe it did. And a woman and her daughter took up the restaurant's one booth. They were having lunch—soup and salad and bread—and laughing about something. The daughter was Jenny's age, the mother Carla's. They were chubby and ruddy-faced and happy-looking.

Jenny wondered idly what that would be like: to be happy and comfortable in one's mother's company. In just a short visit, Carla usually managed to squeeze in at least three insults and two passive-aggressive insinuations that Jenny was living her life entirely incorrectly. Inevitably, Carla would bring up Doris, Pete's beautiful, red-haired mother he'd worshipped as a boy and often said gave Jenny her looks and her sweet nature. Carla clearly considered the comparison a liability. Doris threw herself from her bedroom window the day she turned forty. Depressed, Doris was, about getting old, losing her looks. "Died facedown in the dirt," Carla was all too happy to report. "At least your house is single story."

A waitress came to take her order. Jenny had fifteen dollars in cash. The men had promised to pay for her lunch. Everything on the menu, besides coffee and a cup of soup, was at least ten bucks.

"Coffee, please."

"Cream?"

The waitress was young and cute, just out of high school, if Jenny had to guess. Piercings glinted out in unexpected places— under the girl's lip, at the tip of her tongue—and her hair was piled into two separate buns on the top of her head. She had on striped purple-and-black tights, a short jean skirt, and a tight tee with a dragon on it, flames blazing across her breasts. Not peaches in this case. Lemons. Why was Jenny thinking like this? *Someone knows her citrus fruits.*

"Yes, thank you," she said. "And a cup of soup."

"Broccoli and cheese or the bisque?"

Jenny didn't know what bisque was. It sounded fancy. French maybe. "The bisque."

"Good choice." The waitress started to walk away.

Jenny called her back. "Have two men in black suits been here by chance?"

"Men in black suits?"

"I know it sounds strange . . ."

"Haven't seen anyone like that. It's been pretty dead. The snow, I think. Keeps people at home. Bunch of pussies. Bunch of pansies." The waitress clicked her pierced tongue against her teeth. "Be right back with the coffee."

Jenny crossed her legs, settled in to wait. The men, she assumed, would be here soon. In the meantime, she would amuse herself the way fancy women who ate bisque on a regular basis amused themselves. She smiled softly, watched the ruddy-faced mother and daughter laugh some more, compare Christmas lists. The mother wanted a pair of gold earrings, the daughter a DustBuster. The scribbling young man was writing intently, but once in a while he

took dainty sips from a large mug and raised his eyes to the ceiling, as if seeking inspiration. He had dark hair, a five o'clock shadow at noon, and was alarmingly thin. The skin under his eyes was blue. He didn't seem to be eating anything. Jenny wanted to buy him some bisque. Maybe she would, when the Black Suits gave her the money. Then again, the payment might be in check form, in which case she'd have to go to the bank, cash it, listen to a Lyd lecture, come back . . . Oh, the very real struggles of the very rich . . .

The waitress brought the coffee and a small, silver pot of cream. Jenny couldn't remember the last time she'd had real cream in her coffee. She poured it in slowly, savoring the way it ribboned the darkness, made little underwater worlds there. Didn't people use tea leaves to predict the future? What about cream swirls? One branched out like a tree—all the avenues she could take. Another spun in on itself. Full circle. Jenny brought the cup to her lips, preparing herself for the delight, for joy of decadence in the middle of the day. It had been so long since she'd treated herself to anything.

At that moment, an old woman burst into the café and Jenny lowered her cup in surprise. The woman entered in a wave of snow and cold. Her feet were wrapped in garbage bags. She wore a quilt for a coat and a Chicago Bulls beanie and mismatched gloves. She filled up the shop with her bulky body and the stink of urine and gasoline. Cheap red wine, too, and fried food. It was her face that most surprised Jenny. Her skin was ravaged by age and weather, a constellation of basketlike lines and broken blood vessels, but the woman had obviously been beautiful once. Her beauty wasn't like Jenny's, though, or how men were always describing Jenny's beauty to her. Soft, the men said. Easy on the eyes. This woman was striking, her profile chiseled like a monument. While the happy mother and daughter stared at their mostly empty plates and the young writer man hid behind his notebook, Jenny watched the old woman produce a piece of paper from under her quilt coat and wave it

around. The paper showed what looked like a child's drawing of the earth with a big red *X* over it.

"I'm here to warn you about the end of the world," the woman announced.

The waitress, who'd been sorting silverware, turned and faced the woman, clearly bored. "You warned us about it yesterday."

The old woman planted her feet more firmly. Tiny trickles of muddy water ran off the trash bags, wormed their way out in all directions. "It's the end of the world."

"Then why are we all still here?"

"The world is ending."

"If you're not going to buy anything, you need to go."

"Buy something? You want me to buy something when the world is ending? Where are you all going to be, with all your boughten things, when the eternal blackness comes?"

The waitress was unmoved by the woman's pleas and her obvious predicament: insanity and homelessness. One of them probably the result of the other. The chicken *and* the egg. What Carla would call the "double whammy."

"I'll call the cops like I did yesterday," the waitress said.

"The cops, the cops," the old woman pooh-poohed. "Who cares. They're nothing. You're nothing. It's the end of the world."

"I'm nothing, huh?"

"We're all nothing in the face of the coming apocalypse. You'll see." The old woman pointed to the waitress first, then to everyone in the shop in turn. "You'll all see soon enough. And then you'll wished you'd listened to me."

The waitress toyed with the ring in her nose. "Well, until the world actually ends, we're going to keep serving food and drinks to paying customers, which, let me guess, you aren't one."

The woman shuffled her messy feet. The plastic made a sucking and swishing sound against the floor. Suck, swish. Suck, swish. Meanwhile, the heretofore happy mother and daughter busied

themselves with coats and dollar bills and change. Their faces were pinched, their whispers annoyed. *Why we even bother coming downtown anymore. Beyond me. We should have just had a nice cup of tea at home. Seriously. Honestly. These people.* They were put off. They were leaving.

"You can run but you can't hide," the old woman told them. Then she focused her attention on the young man with the notebook. He'd stopped writing for the time being, but the woman must have noticed his scribbling, because she made great, looping letters in the air with one of her charred fingers and said, "Write it all down, my boy. Write it all down, but your words are going to burn up anyway and no one will read them and nothing that you do today, here, now, matters one little bit."

The waitress crossed her arms over the flames on her chest. "What do you want us to do?" she asked. "Seems to me, if the world is ending, and nothing we do matters, then that applies to what you're doing right now, too."

The old woman lost her confident posture. She was a landslide standing there. "I'm just trying to warn you."

It dawned on Jenny as she watched the scene before her unfold, as her coffee and soup got cold, that the Black Suits weren't coming. They were never coming. They were never going to pay her. And she was a fool. It was just as Lyd had predicted. She hadn't insisted on a contract or written agreement of any kind. She'd burned up the paper with the phone number on it. She had no way of contacting the men, no way of making them hold up their end of the bargain. And wasn't that their plan all along? They must have known she was naive and trusting when they picked her for the job. They'd flattered her, told her she was the prettiest girl they'd ever seen. Like magazine/movie actress pretty. "This place"—meaning Benson, although they expanded it to Indiana, the entire Midwest, America in general—"doesn't deserve you," they said. "You're bound for bigger things. Better things. The world's your oyster."

Jenny believed them. She ate it up, like peach pie. Like bisque. Never underestimate a broke single mom's powers of self-delusion. A headache exploded behind her eyes. She wanted to cry but was too stunned at her own stupidity to start.

Girls like her.

End of the world.

She didn't wait for the bill, didn't have to. She'd already done the math. She fished the fifteen dollars from her wallet and slid it under the cream pot, thanked the waitress. Then she told the old woman she was welcome to her coffee and soup if she was hungry.

"What makes you think I'm hungry?" the woman snarled. "What makes you think I want your charity?"

"She was trying to be nice," the waitress said. "Can't you even appreciate when someone's just trying to be nice?"

Jenny grabbed her out-of-fashion purse full of worthless checks and old lipsticks and capsule-size tubes of free sample perfume—no money there and no answers, either, just blank paper and the futile munitions of vanity—and left. The world was still there. Cars people dogs snow. Streetlights traffic lights sidewalks storefronts. A sofa, too, for some reason sitting in the middle of an intersection with a sign stuck to the center cushion: FIFTY BUCKS OR BEST OFFER. VEGAS OR BUST.

Carla was on the front stoop when Jenny got home. She had on her favorite purple coat and white snow boots and looked very self-satisfied sitting there, smoking. Gertrude and Yo-Yo leaned against her, purring loudly. Cats loved Carla and Carla loved cats. She even said she thought she might have been one in a past life. The apartment complex where she lived didn't allow cats. Otherwise, Carla often said. Otherwise, I'd be the biggest fucking cat lady you've ever seen.

Jenny was surprised to see Carla this time of day. Typically, she'd be packing cookies in a factory near the interstate, a job she'd had

for twenty-five years. She'd gotten Jenny work there several years ago. Much to Carla's embarrassment, Jenny only lasted a week, a disastrous week that involved a hundred pounds of windmill cookies having to be thrown out because Jenny pressed the wrong button at the wrong time. To Jenny, it was a poisonous place, full of gossip and sabotage and backbiting. Carla enjoyed that atmosphere, thrived on it even, but the mere thought of it, combined with the memory of trying to stack cookies in tiny cardboard trays flying by on a conveyor belt for eight tedious hours on end, made Jenny sick to her stomach. So did the smell of her mother's clothes at the end of a shift.

Carla didn't smell like cookies at the moment. She smelled of cigarettes and snow. "My younger self wouldn't be caught dead in that outfit."

"Hi, Mom."

"Where's your coat?"

"At the cleaner's."

"Bradley's or Marsh's?"

"Bradley's."

"I don't approve of Bradley's. They ruined two of my favorite blouses."

"I know."

"Marsh's is the place."

"They were closed."

"Marsh's never closes."

Jenny's key was sticking in the lock. She needed to oil it, the lock. Or get a new key. Or a new lock. How much did new locks cost?

Carla blew a smoke ring over Jenny's shoulder. "So, who died?"

"What?"

"Saw Ruth Shields at the pancake house. Ruth told me that Ashley told her that you had a funeral to go to today, which, I assume, is why you're all dolled up, although what kind of funeral you'd wear that to is beyond me."

"Someone should rename this town Rumor Mill. Or Gossipville."

"Someone should rename you Miss Sterious."

Finally, the key turned. Jenny invited her mother in for coffee.

"Got something stronger?" Carla asked. "I'm in the mood for a celebration."

"I'll check."

The house was cold and dark. Jenny started flipping on lights. Had she turned the heat down? She couldn't remember. Maybe the furnace was on the fritz. How much did new furnaces cost?

Clearly convinced that Jenny wasn't paying attention, Carla snuck back to the front door, let in Gertrude and Yo-Yo. Jenny had asked Carla repeatedly not to do that—they had fleas and worms and their fur often came off in clumps—but Carla wasn't one to follow orders. The cats entered the room cautiously, eyes darting. Then they leaped on the couch and started cleaning themselves. Mirror images.

At least Carla had left her cigarette butt outside. Jenny wondered if it was still burning. Probably not. Carla always put her cigarettes out very emphatically, like she was killing something. A sugar ant. Jenny's self-esteem.

"Was it one of your dad's people?" Carla asked, patting Gertrude's head. "Those Newbergs never show me any respect. Just shut me out. All I did was dare to love your daddy more than anything and then that love destroyed me."

"It wasn't anyone you know."

"Loved your father more than anything. And it wasn't an easy job, I'll tell you that much. Pete made it hard to love him. Still, I did the best I could. I perseverated, and they shunned me, like the Amish. That's what it was like. A good, old-fashioned Amish shunning."

Jenny went to the kitchen, got out the coffee and a filter, filled the pot with water. The faucet was still leaking. *Drip drip drip,* in rhythm with the sign in front of her house, with Jenny's pounding head, with the red light on her answering machine—messages from Lyd, probably, a lecture about truth and consequences, and from

Kevin the collection agent. Jenny had yet to meet Kevin face-to-face. So far, they'd talked only on the phone. Kevin's voice cracked often. He said "in any case" every other sentence. He always started their conversations by pretending to be interested in Jenny's life. And then he got down to business. "In any case, we'll be talking about this soon." "In any case, the bank empathizes with your difficulty." "In any case, this is the kind of debt that doesn't go away."

Carla followed Jenny into the kitchen, peeling off her gloves and patting her hair, which had seen one too many curling irons, far too many boxes of grocery store coloring kits. For years now, Carla had been dyeing it a sort of white-blond. It was dry and stiff and stuck out in little puffs around her ears. It reminded Jenny of tumbleweed. Or a million tiny spiderwebs.

"It couldn't have been someone I don't know," Carla said. "No one sneezes or dies or gets married or pregnant without me knowing about it."

"As a matter of fact, Mom, this was someone you don't know."

"What'd they look like? You know I never forget a face."

Carla claimed she had a photographic memory, swore she knew all the people and streets and neighborhoods and bridges and lakes of Whitley County, Indiana, by heart, but Jenny had never seen any evidence of it. What Carla seemed to remember most clearly were insults, both real and imagined. She was good at airing grievances and holding grudges. Her true superpowers.

"It doesn't matter what they looked like," Jenny said. "They're dead."

"They? So it was multiple people?"

"No. I mean, forget it."

"And this person died of what exactly?" Carla asked.

"Can we not talk about it?" Jenny said. "It's making me sad."

"Okay. Fine. Geez. So sensitive today. And purple eye shadow is not a good look for you."

Jenny could still feel the Candidate's breath on her neck. Warm,

hurried, a butterfly caught in her hair. She rummaged through a cupboard, looking for a bottle of wine or the whiskey Lyd left behind by accident last summer. No luck.

"You'll have to settle for coffee," she told Carla. "What are we celebrating anyway?"

The last time her mother came over to celebrate, it was because she'd won $3,000 in the lottery, money she used to buy a bunch of expensive makeup at L. S. Ayres in Fort Wayne, a couple tickets to Disney World, and a ball gown she never wore. She took Vi Gregor with her to Florida, didn't even ask Billie Starr to go, and then a hurricane ruined the trip. Carla used the occasion to write a long, angry letter to the Orlando tourism board.

She sat down at the kitchen table, sniffed the peppermint-scented candle Jenny was using as a centerpiece. Her nose was upturned and bright red and flaking. She looked old. And exultant. "I'm getting married."

"You're getting married?"

"Don't sound so surprised."

"It's just . . ."

"It's just what?"

"I didn't realize you were involved with anyone."

"Well, I am."

"Who's the lucky guy?"

"Bob."

"Bob who?"

"Bob Butz."

Jenny dropped the filter on the floor. Then she picked it back up, inspected it for dust and cat hair, plugged in the coffeemaker. "You're marrying Bob Butz."

"Indeed." Carla sat back, studied her left hand where a new, gaudy diamond solitaire hung from her bony ring finger. She closed her hand to hold the ring in place. "He's getting it resized."

The ring had to be fake. It was Bob Butz all over—playing the

grand gentleman, when in truth he was always counting pennies, cutting corners. Back when Jenny still worked for him, she helped Bob throw parties he claimed were incredibly generous and lavish but were actually bring-your-own-everything. And she listened silently as he bragged to clients and friends from Fort Wayne, people he called "movers and shakers," about his modern, state-of-the-art facility, showing off the new furniture and fancy wallpaper and pretty sinks in the bathroom, all the while leaving out the fact that the roof leaked and the copier was always breaking down.

"Do you know what Bob told me the other day?" Carla asked. "He told me that his idea of heaven would be to run his hands through my hair for the rest of his life."

Jenny had succeeded in turning on the coffeemaker and now, for some reason, she was in front of the refrigerator. She'd opened the door, had planned to get something out but could no longer remember what that was.

"I know Bob's not your favorite, and he wasn't Pete's either," Carla said, "but you and your father—you ask too much of people. Bob's only human, okay? And so am I."

Milk, Jenny thought. Milk for the coffee.

Carla patted her hair again. Very into her hair all of a sudden. "I'll be the first to admit that Bob's not as handsome as your father was, and his sense of style leaves a bit to be desired, but he's more than his perm and his clothes. For one, he's sweet on me like you wouldn't believe, and he'll take care of me in my old age, which is more than I can say for someone I gave birth to."

"Mom—"

"You'd throw me in a home before I could say 'wheelchair aerobics.'"

Jenny sniffed the milk. It was past its expiration date but smelled fine. She put it on the table next to the sugar bowl, along with two mugs and a spoon. "Congratulations."

"Say it like you mean it."

"I just did."

"Didn't sound sincere to me."

Jenny's headache was in her neck now, too. And her stomach. "Do you have a date set?"

"We're thinking June."

"June is nice."

"June *is* nice."

Carla stirred milk and sugar in her coffee, took a drink, and immediately started coughing. Coffee went everywhere. Jenny got up to fetch a paper towel. Carla waved both hands around for a while, eyes watering. She'd had a smoker's cough since Jenny was a teenager. It had gotten worse recently. Unlike Pete's, Carla's fits generally left Jenny unmoved. She knew her mother was about to blame the whole thing on her.

"You make your coffee too strong," Carla said.

"Sorry."

"One scoop of coffee for every cup of water. How many times do I have to tell you?"

"You should see Dr. Harme about that cough."

"Humph." Carla flicked a crumb from the table. "I'm done with Dr. Harme. Going to Dr. Frank now."

"Why? What happened?"

"Dr. Harme was inappropriate. He was above his station." Carla pulled her cigarettes from her purse, tapped on the pack, put them back with a disgruntled look. "Anyway, Bob's got a cousin with a barn out on Turtle Town Lake. The cousin said we can use his place for the wedding and the reception as long as it's before July because that's when he needs it for his cows. Or his horses. Anyway, for something. Bob says it's a very elegant barn. Very pretty. And we're in agreement—no churches. We're not churchy. I'm going to wear my lottery money gown."

Jenny sat back down at the table across from her mother. Her hands were shaking again. The day seemed so long, like it would never end.

Carla squinted at her. A flash of actual concern flickered in her eyes. "Are you okay?"

"I'm fine."

"You look terrible."

"Thanks."

"You know what I mean. You're hiding something from me. What's going on?"

"Nothing."

"You're not sleeping enough. I can tell by those lines around your eyes. And your arms are getting fat again. Your neck, too. Doris had fat arms and a fat neck. You have to watch that."

"I will, Mom."

"Seriously, what's going on?" Carla asked again. "You can't keep things from me, dear daughter."

"Nothing's going on. I swear. But I do need to get Billie Starr from school soon."

"Sure, sure, shoo me away on my big day."

"Don't you have to get to work anyway?"

"The boss gave me the afternoon off. I told him my news and he said, 'Go forth and be happy.'" Carla spooned more sugar into her coffee. "He knows I'm short-timing it. I might quit tomorrow. Who knows? And then I'm never going to pack another cookie ever again. Bob and me, we're moving in. We're going to get a house in one of the richie rich subdivisions and live like the other half does."

"Good for you, Mom," Jenny said.

"It is, isn't it? It is good for me." Carla's triumphant mien melted slightly when she looked down at her coffee. "I really wanted to laugh it up a little."

"I'm sorry," Jenny said.

"Sorry, sorry. You're always saying you're sorry. Have you noticed that? My younger self never apologized for anything."

"Sorry."

"And now you're apologizing for apologizing. What sort of example is that for Billie Starr?"

"I don't know."

"Like you have to apologize for living, for daring to draw breath, that's what."

They drank their coffee in silence for a while. Jenny couldn't taste it. It was warm and that was all she wanted for the moment. And to have the chance to change her clothes and sink into the floor somehow and disappear.

"So, this person who died," Carla said. "Was she gay?"

"What? Why?"

"Your outfit. I can see someone wearing that getup to a gay funeral."

"It wasn't a gay funeral."

"That's good."

Was it? Why was that good? Gay people died, too. Gay people had to have funerals. Carla was probably thinking that her younger self wouldn't be caught dead at one.

"You know I think Lyd is gay," Carla said. "It's her lips. Gay women have thin lips."

"Lyd's lips aren't thin."

"And she's sweet on you. Always has been, since you were kids, since the day you met."

"That's not true. Lyd and I are just friends."

"You sure that's how she sees it?"

"I'm sure."

Carla toyed with her ring. "Doris had a gay friend, you know. It was her gay friend that found her, all dead in the dirt."

Jenny got up, went to the living room to check the time. The ugly mantel clock told her it was almost three. *Tick tock, tick tock, tick tock.* Billie Starr would expect her in five minutes. It took at least ten to get to the school. "I really need to go, Mom."

"Fine. Fine." Carla sighed from the kitchen. Her chair squeaked

on the linoleum. She made a loud show of dropping her coffee mug in the sink. "But do me a favor. Ask Billie Starr what color she wants to wear to the wedding. I'd like her to be a flower girl."

That would be a tricky conversation. Billie Starr hated what she called "scratchy dresses," said they should be outlawed, along with pointy-toed shoes and too-tight headbands.

Carla joined Jenny at the mantel, where framed photographs of Billie Starr sat at odd angles, an imperfect record of childhood milestones—first Christmas, second Halloween, third birthday. Carla leaned in, studied Jenny's favorite of all the photos—the one of Billie Starr in front of her winning science fair experiment (a demonstration of how rivers, when left alone, cleaned themselves, board behind her reading HUMANS RUIN EVERYTHING).

Carla ran a skinny finger over the ticking rococo clock—"You need to dust more"—and made her way to the door, stopped on the threshold, reluctantly put her gloves back on. Probably hated to hide that ring. "Don't be mad at me, but I've asked Vi to be my maid of honor."

Recently divorced from her fourth husband, Vi was working on securing a fifth, a Wakarusa bail bondsman. She was, Carla often complained, spending a lot of time out of town.

"I'm not mad," Jenny said.

"I guess I mean maiden, don't I?" Carla asked. "*Maiden* of honor. That's what you call them when they've been married before, and Vi, well. You can't say she's the driving snow."

"I think it's 'matron' of honor and 'driven' snow."

"Whatever."

Carla had another short coughing fit. When it was over, she waved in the direction of Jenny's two hanging baskets, the flowers dead and snow-dusted, the plastic hooks starting to bow and crack. "You really should throw those out," she said. "They're hell on my allergies."

Jenny walked over to one of the baskets, yanked it down, and threw it into the yard. Then she did the same with the second. Both

made sad thumping sounds as they toppled on the ground, soil spilling out. A squirrel ran over, sniffed at a few brown leaves, then shot off in the direction of Dorothy Renfrow's house, where a pair of cardinals were making themselves at home on a shelf above the kitchen stove. Jenny was surprised no one had looted that stove. Or the shelf.

"Happy now?" she asked Carla. Her head was the size of a planet. Pounding. Pounding. What was she going to do? What options did she have? How much did options cost?

Her mother blinked, lit a cigarette. "You sure you're okay?"

"I'm fine."

"You're acting very strange."

"I'm just tired."

"Hmm." Carla's smoky breath made amorphous clouds in the air. "One more thing while I'm here. Bob would like us all to go to dinner as a family. He got us reservations for tomorrow night at the Brown Derby. Seven. Sharp."

"Why?" Jenny said.

"He wants us to bond before the wedding. Bob cherishes family. And he was hoping to talk to you about maybe coming back to work for him. I told him not to count his chickens, that you're as stubborn and defeatful as your father, but he has hope. That's Bob for you. Hopeful. Not defeatful." Carla stood on Jenny's front stoop and watched the snow fall with a contented smile. "I can't believe I'm getting married again. It's crazy how life works, isn't it? Me about to get hitched for the second time and you . . . well. You're still young, as they say. Youngish, anyway."

With that, she walked regally to her car, Gertrude and Yo-Yo pawing her coat, trailing her like a furry, purring train. Jenny imagined for a moment her mother in her lottery money ball gown, sweeping into a barn and melting in Bob Butz's arms. Then she thought of going back to work for Bob, her new stepfather. Taking notes. Dodging pudgy hands. Hopeful, not defeatful. She was going to be sick. There was nothing she could do about it. She hadn't eaten since breakfast and the

headache made everything worse. Her mother's news, too. Jenny got to the bathroom just in time. She fell to her knees, held her own hair back, let it happen. She let herself cry, too, finally, head hanging over the toilet bowl, wire falling from her underwear.

What would Pete say if he could see her now? Could he see her now?

In the kitchen, her faucet dripped. The furnace did not come on. Jenny was freezing. Someone shot around the Acorn Street curve, crunch and roar of gravel, shriek of tires. She pulled herself up, blew her nose, brushed her teeth. She didn't have the luxury of feeling sorry for herself. She wasn't a bisque woman. She wasn't a cream-in-her-coffee woman. She was an end-of-the-world woman, and she was late. Again.

*D*inner was peanut butter and jelly and cut carrots. It was what Jenny had around, what she didn't have to shop for, and something that didn't require actual cooking.

"We had this same dinner last night," Billie Starr said.

"I know."

"It's not even healthy. The jelly isn't anyway."

"That's what the carrots are for."

Billie Starr zipped her coat up. She had on a scarf and hat. Jenny did, too. The thermostat read fifty-nine degrees. It had fallen five in the last half hour. How low would it go before morning?

"I'm cold, Mom. Can you turn the heat on?"

"It's not working."

"Why?"

"I'm not sure."

"Can you fix it?"

"I'll call someone soon."

"How soon?"

"Soon soon."

"You always say that."

"Do I?"

Billie Starr didn't answer, just studied her sandwich like it was a science project, a riparian system. From all angles. Skeptical. "Why were you so late today?" she asked.

"I told you. Job interview."

"Really?"

"Yes."

"Did you get it?"

Jenny grabbed a matchbook, lit the peppermint candle. The scent was sweet, melted sugar. "The job?"

"Yeah, Mom. Duh."

"I don't know yet. You have to let such things run their natural course."

Billie Starr munched on a carrot, her small pale face made even smaller by suspicion. "Terri's mom was there on time. You know, the one you told you were going to a funeral. She waited with me."

When Jenny finally got to the school that afternoon, Ashley Batchelder was on the sidewalk of the car pickup lane, leaning over Billie Starr like a protective tree, whispering something in her ear that made Billie Starr snort with laughter. When Ashley saw Jenny, she straightened up, smiled, hands still on Billie Starr's shoulders. Possessive. Smug. She's glad I'm late, Jenny thought. Every time I'm late or look "interesting" or can't afford her stupid kitchen gadgets, she loves it. My fuckups are her fuel.

"She was quite happy to tell me that she had somewhere else to be," Jenny said. Fort Wayne, picking up supplies for her knife party. Ashley said again how much she hoped to see Jenny there. It was going to be so much fun. All the gals, all together.

"She's nice," Billie Starr said.

She'd stab you through the eye if it would help her sell a lidded bowl. "I should just let you ride the bus," Jenny said. "That's what I should do."

"The bus comes at five in the morning, Mom."

"Six thirty."

"Whatever." Billie Starr leaned toward the glowing candle at the center of the table, took a long whiff, hair dangerously close to the flame. "When are we getting our Christmas tree? Putting up the tree's my favorite part."

Jenny moved the candle, blew it out. She'd forgotten all about a tree. She usually bought a live one from the Boy Scouts. They sold them from the Benson Market parking lot every year, and Jenny could often count on one of the dads—Cash Hardacre or Luke Enyeart, flirty with her, strict with their sons—giving her a "pretty single mom discount."

"So, when are we going to get it?" Billie Starr asked.

"Soon."

"Like, as soon as we get the furnace fixed? Or not as soon? Or sooner?"

"People from Oklahoma are called Sooners," Jenny said.

"And people from Indiana are called Hoosiers, but you didn't answer my question."

"We'll get it next week sometime, okay? After your field trip."

"What if all the good trees are gone by then?"

"We'll get a sad tree and make it happy."

"That only happens on TV."

Jenny couldn't eat anything. Her headache had mostly subsided. Her gut, though, was one big knot. No room for food. And she kept seeing things in her peripheral vision that weren't there—men in black suits, snow falling from the ceiling, her mother's engagement ring, catching light.

"Why is Grandma getting married?" Billie Starr asked.

It was as if the kid could read her mind. "I don't know," Jenny said.

"Is she going to move out of her apartment?"

"Probably."

"Do you think she'll give me some of her pictures?"

"The geisha ones?"

"No, the sumo wrestler ones."

"You'll have to ask her." Jenny made herself eat a carrot. It tasted like basement—mold and mud. She set it aside.

"Everyone at school is saying Mr. Richardson's going to marry Terri's mom."

"Mr. Richardson's dating Ashley Batchelder?" Of course, he would pick the former cheerleader. Men. They always did.

"Do you love Dad?"

"Where did that question come from?"

"My brain. So, do you?"

How to answer that? When Jenny was a teenager, Randall would often run all the way from his parents' farm at the corner of the county to Pete and Carla's house, covering a little more than four miles each way and showing up at Jenny's window, pink-faced and beaming. He'd throw rocks at the panes and beg to be let in her room or, at the very least, get a few kisses and feels before he turned around and ran back, and Jenny had loved him with the optimistic, self-erasing kind of love that's only possible when one is a virgin who watches too many romantic movies about beautiful heroines leaving the men in their orbit breathless with need. By the night of Billie Starr's conception, at a drunken Super Bowl party thrown by one of Randall's friends, Jenny was none of those things. She was a disillusioned twenty-year-old looking for a job and letting her ex screw her in the host's parents' cluttered bedroom. Smell of cinnamon potpourri wafting over from the dresser. Teddy bear curtains. Coats from the other partygoers at her feet.

"I did once," Jenny said. "A long time ago."

"But not more than once? And not now?"

Jenny was saved by three loud knocks on the front door. Billie Starr, seemingly done with love, ran to answer it. Jenny followed her. According to the mantel clock, it was closing in on eight. Too early for Randall. Maybe it was Lyd come to tell her she told her so. Or, more likely, Kevin the collection agent. Collection agents stopped

calling after a while, didn't they, just started showing up at your house? Carla and Pete dealt with a few back in the day. That was Jenny's childhood—falling asleep to the sound of her parents fighting in the middle of the night, lots and lots of yelling about some woman at work and some man down the street, and then waking up to busted lamps and windows and vases, to Carla and Pete, exhausted, bruised, and dirty, snoring on the couch in nothing but their socks while annoyed people knocked impatiently on the door, insisting they be paid or else. Carla often sent Jenny out to deal with them. To stop them in their tracks, Carla said. What kind of heartless bastard's going to harass a kid? Jenny got them to go away by promising them they'd be paid tomorrow. That was the ticket, according to Carla—promise them money, give them a timeline. If they didn't leave, burst into tears. Jenny was prepared to do all three tonight if necessary.

Billie Starr had parted the curtains. The blinking yellow sign flashed on her face, gave her a ghostly look. Jenny shivered again. They were so vulnerable out here. Two girls in a run-down old schoolhouse with nothing but trees, a couple of cats, and an old man who was rapidly losing his mind for company. As witnesses.

"Who is it?" Jenny asked Billie Starr.

Billie Starr shrugged. Her little hands were turning blue.

Jenny paused. She could turn off all the lights, drag Billie Starr into the bathroom to hide. Surely Kevin wouldn't dare to break into her house?

The person knocked again. Jenny told Billie Starr to close the curtains, come away from the window.

"Why?"

"Just do it."

Billie Starr reluctantly did as she was told. "You're acting crazy."

"Anybody home?" It was a man's voice, muffled by wood and wind.

"No!" Billie Starr yelled. "No one's here."

The man outside laughed. "Good to know. Would whoever just said that consider talking to me for a moment? I promise, I don't bite."

He didn't sound like Kevin the collection agent. Jenny sighed, opened the door like a kid ripping off a Band-Aid, and there, on her front stoop, was the Candidate. He held a clipboard bursting with papers. Snow fell on him, flecked his eyebrows, melted there. It wet his papers, too. The top one was mush. When he saw Jenny, he broke out into a huge grin.

"Ha!" the man said. "Can you believe my luck? I hoped I'd see you again."

Jenny stepped back, bumped into Billie Starr, who'd traded her spot at the window for one right behind her mother, sandwich half in one hand.

"I was out canvassing Benson," the man explained. "Didn't I tell you I'd be in your neck of the woods tonight?"

"I don't think so."

She would have remembered that. Or would she? At that moment, she was having a difficult time recalling anything the man had said to her, both at the grocery store and the hotel. She remembered mostly butterflies and oranges, her ruined pantyhose, the hotel cleaning lady wielding Windex like a gun. Was that right? No. The maid hadn't pointed anything at her. She'd stood like a statue, let Jenny run by her without a word. The guns were all inside the room.

"Can I come in?" the man asked. "Pretty chilly out here."

It wasn't much warmer in her house, but Jenny didn't know how she could refuse. She moved aside. Billie Starr moved with her, a scowling, apprehensive shadow.

The man stomped his boots as he came in, shook off the snow, then apologized for making a mess of the rug. "My manners are terrible. I was born in a barn. Literally. And not very far from here, either, in 'Busco."

"Churubusco?" Jenny hadn't been there in years. It was another small world, Benson rotated ninety degrees. Same pasty-faced people, same two-block, brick-buildinged downtown, different zip code.

"Do you know why Churubusco's called Turtle Town?" the Can-

didate asked. He was looking at Jenny, but his words were clearly for Billie Starr. He paused, put on a very serious face. Hamming it up, in his element. "One day this farmer's out walking his property and he sees a giant turtle in his pond. I mean giant. We're talking head the size of a hubcap, shell as big as my car out there." He raised his arms in an O-shape over his head. Billie Starr was taking an interest. She'd raised her eyes to him, and her suspicious squint was gone.

"I'm telling you," the man went on, "this turtle was huge. Gargantuan. The farmer, he's like, 'I can't keep this to myself. I have a giant turtle in my pond. That's something worth sharing. I have to tell my friends.' So he does. He tells his friends who tell their friends who tell their friends and before you know it, the farmer's giant turtle has made the national news. Churubusco's on the map. It has its own Loch Ness Monster, only it's a turtle and"—the man lowered his voice—"it's very, very shy."

"What do you mean, 'shy'?" Billie Starr asked, finally coming forward.

The Candidate turned the full wattage of his politician's smile on her. "And who are you?"

"Billie Starr. Who are you?"

"I'm George." He reached his hand out for a shake. Billie Starr transferred her sandwich to her left hand and gravely obliged him.

George, Jenny thought. She'd never known a George. It suited him.

Billie Starr did not agree. She was scowling again. "George?"

"Kind of old mannish, isn't it?"

"Yeah."

"It was my father's name. I'm a junior."

"A junior?" Billie Starr asked.

"Just means I'm not as important."

"So what happened to the turtle?"

"What do you think happened?"

Billie Starr shrugged. "They killed it?"

"Nope. Believe it or not, no one wanted to hunt it. They just wanted to see it, and they kept seeing it. A fin here, a flash of shell there. They named it Oscar for the farmer who first spotted it. But it never came out when it was convenient, when the cameras were rolling, so people started to doubt, to get bored, to think the farmer made the whole thing up. But I know it's real. And do you know how I know?"

"How?"

"I saw it. I've seen it a hundred times. I grew up on that farm."

Billie Starr's eyes widened. "Cool."

"Yeah. Some people say Oscar's dead, but I don't believe it, not for a minute. I think he's swimming around in the deep end, biding his time."

Billie Starr took a bite of her sandwich. "My grandma's getting married in a barn on Turtle Town Lake."

"You don't say? Well, what a co-inky-dink."

"Did you come here to tell us about turtles and barns?"

"Not exactly." George ventured a little farther into the living room. He presented his clipboard to Billie Starr. "Would you like to sign my petition?"

"What's it for?"

"I'm trying to keep people from dying from dust."

"Dust? How do you die from that?"

"You inhale it," George said.

"That's weird," Billie Starr declared.

"It is," George said. "It's very weird. Hence the petition."

Jenny retied the belt on her robe and wondered what she must look like in her striped scarf, boots, and one of Randall's old Colts hats. "I'd offer to take your coat, but you'll probably want to keep it on. I think my furnace is broken."

George took his coat off anyway, tossed it onto a nearby chair. The chair was covered in cat hair. "Well, then it's your lucky day. I happen to be an expert in old furnaces."

"Yay!" Billie Starr said, clapping.

"You don't have to," Jenny said. "I'm sure you're really busy."

"Nope. Done for the day. So, where's the faulty unit?"

"In the laundry room."

"Another coincidence!" George said. "So's mine."

Jenny led him there like a woman in a dream. Was this really happening? George followed her, whistling. Jenny pointed toward the furnace—olive green and ancient, huddled in the corner with the water heater—and said again, "You don't have to do this. Really. We'll be fine."

"You won't be fine. You'll be on the morning news—two girl-shaped icicles found in the old Acorn Street schoolhouse, pretty, but dead. That is not going to be on my conscience." George pulled off a large metal panel, peeked and poked around, whistling more loudly now. Jenny recognized the tune, one of Pete's favorites: "Two Silhouettes on the Shade." He put the panel on the floor, tapped his foot. "Just as I suspected."

"What?"

"Your pilot light's out."

"Is that bad?"

"Probably not," George said. "You got a match? And a flashlight?"

Jenny did, in her junk drawer. She went to the kitchen to fetch them. Billie Starr was at the table, studying George's petition, her red head bent in concentration, finger moving across the paper as she read.

It wasn't the pilot light. Well, it was, but it was more than that. "Bet you a hundred bucks it's your thermocouple," George said, having tried three times to get the pilot going.

"That sounds expensive."

"I can fix it, but I'm going to need some tools. A socket wrench, probably. And an adjustable. Have those, too?"

Jenny shook her head. She usually borrowed tools from Marcus. "My neighbor might. I need to go over there anyway, but I don't want to keep you."

"Don't be silly. What else am I doing?"

Being married, Jenny thought. And running for some kind of office. "Can you wait with my daughter? I'll just be a minute."

George readily agreed. He blew on his hands, smacked them together, made a satisfied humphing sound. Then he joined Billie Starr at the kitchen table. The two of them huddled over his petition as if it were a map of an unknown land. Jenny hurried out the front door, mumbling to herself "socket wrench, adjustable, socket wrench, adjustable," so she wouldn't forget.

The wind hit her first, an open hand to the face. Then the cold. It crept in the crevices between her clothes and skin, mean, sharp, as invasive as Bob Butz. Her nostril hairs tingled and froze. She ran across her yard to Marcus's, snow crunching under her feet. The moon came out from behind a bank of clouds, shone bright and white across the uneven, gray expanse of Marcus's trailer and the various additions he'd built over the years—a bathroom tacked on and sinking into the ground, a screened-in porch with no screens, a garage so full of junk there was never any room for his truck—and the blinking sign did its usual, sickening work. Jenny climbed a set of rickety stairs and banged on the front door. She used to be shyer about violating Marcus's privacy, but that was before he'd set fire to his kitchen, before he'd gone partially deaf. Now she knew that if she didn't make a racket, he'd never realize she was there.

Most of the time and as far as Jenny knew, Marcus lived like any old man. He ate, he slept, he yelled at his cats. And he made Billie Starr a series of increasingly odd presents—a doll with hair from one of his old mops, a beer can planter. Most recently, he'd brought over a wooden birdhouse with no hole for the bird to go in. Billie Starr didn't care that the gifts were strange or smelly or hard/impossible to use. She cherished them anyway—even hung the birdhouse on a birch branch outside her window—and she and Marcus were firm and fast friends. Once in a while, though, he'd have what Dr. Harme

called "one of his episodes." The previous week, he'd sent the entire Benson Market into a panic when he waltzed in, brandishing a
loaded crossbow. A month before that, he'd headed up a protest of
one in front of Pike's Pizza over the fact that Troy Pike had started
putting cheese on the bread sticks. A step too far, Marcus said. Why
break what was already fixed? Also, he was lactose intolerant.

What really freaked the locals out, more than the picketing, more
than the inconveniently wielded weaponry, was his tendency to dress
up like a woman once in a while. When Jenny first moved to Acorn
Street, she often glimpsed Marcus dancing in women's underwear in
his kitchen, usually to a polka. Sometimes honky-tonk. He liked to
call himself a shameless hedonist. "What's life without pleasure?" he
said. "Empty. Less than zero." That was his attitude, what he called
his "modus operando." Cleaning was clearly not something he found
pleasurable, and stepping foot into his house was like entering a disaster zone. Jenny never knew what she'd find there. Trash, usually,
in lumpy, slimy piles. Cat shit, too, and hair balls. Since Marcus often
forgot to close his doors in summer, mosquito larvae had been known
to make a home for themselves in the bathtub. He was responsible for
at least three police reports per month and several emergency midnight Bible study meetings at which a few ministers had suggested
Marcus be committed to a mental hospital in Fort Wayne for the
good of the town's youth and moral standing.

Jenny could hear music playing. The TV, too, was throbbing at
maximum volume. It lit up Marcus's curtains from the inside, rattled the windows. It was like watching a poorly designed spaceship
readying for launch. She put her ear up to the door, listened for
Marcus's heavy footfalls, the scratch of his slippers against dirty linoleum, or his voice telling her to hold her horses already. He probably hadn't heard her knock, too much noise, so she tried again,
waited, huddled inside her clothes in an effort to make herself a
smaller target for the wind.

When he still didn't answer, Jenny went ahead and tried the knob. It turned easily.

"Marcus?" she called. His living room smelled of cat and Old Spice cologne. The only light came from the television and a red lava lamp next to the couch, a dark, brownish tweed number with a ripped back panel and wooden slats holding the arms up. Marcus had taken a steak knife to that couch one night, said he had no choice, his furniture was trying to kill him. One of his bad days.

The TV was tuned to a local news report on a toy drive for kids in need. Jenny hovered near the entryway. "Marcus? Are you there?" No response. "Hello, Marcus?"

Still nothing, so Jenny picked her way to the kitchen, stumbling on a bowling ball bag and an overturned box of kitty litter. With the exception of the bag and the kitty litter, the house was relatively clear. Not clean, but easy to navigate, and, unlike her house, warm. Jenny stood under a heat vent for a moment, relishing the rush of hot air. Then she peeked around the corner and gasped. Marcus, dressed in a French maid's outfit, skinny hairy legs on full display, was at the stove, tending to a pot of spaghetti sauce. Trish Keck, wearing a heavy poncho and men's jeans, swayed next to him, waving a wooden spoon and singing along to a song blasting from the radio. The tune was melancholy but Marcus and Trish were clearly in a celebratory mood. A pie (homemade? runny?) rested on the kitchen table next to a few lit candles and two place settings.

Trish had long, yellowish gray hair, nothing but split ends. Her face was long as well, a little jowly, and her body reminded Jenny of a funnel—big up top, skinny down below. Marcus was no beauty, either. He had a head shaped like a football, narrow shoulders, a potbelly, and varicose veins and age spots and flaky skin, but their happiness transformed them for a moment into something worth looking at. Marcus grabbed the spoon from Trish's hand, dropped it in the sauce pot, spun her around the room with the grace of a gen-

tleman trained for such things. Then, pausing under a low-hanging light, they kissed. Jenny felt like a spy, an interloper. She fled, let herself out the same way she came.

Clouds were back to blocking the moon. She fumbled her way through Marcus's garage shelves, trying to find a wrench, socket, another wrench, adjustable, but didn't know what those were. Her fingers grazed frigid nails and hammers and screwdrivers of varying sizes. Then she hit on something large, wrench-like. Jenny grabbed it. Then she found what felt like another wrench, only slightly bigger and more complicated. Was that an adjustable? She grabbed it, too. Both tools were large and heavy. She could probably kill someone with them if she had the notion.

That's when it occurred to her that, almost without thinking, she'd left her one and only daughter with a complete stranger. What the hell was she doing? Being a horrible mother. Being an idiot. Theme of the day—Jenny Newberg doing moronic things. Not thinking ahead, not considering the consequences of her actions. *Dumb mom,* the blinking sign said as she stumbled toward her house. Agreeing with Lyd entirely. *Slut mom. Whore mom.*

Jenny tripped again, this time over one of the spare tires Marcus kept in towers scattered around the yard, cursing herself and her life and her luck. Gertrude and Yo-Yo approached her from the shadows, mewing. As she ran, all the nightmare scenarios Jenny had ever entertained about all the ways Billie Starr could be lost to her ran through her mind, played like a movie behind her eyes, now watering from the cold. Billie Starr bloody and crying on the ground, her clothes ripped off by some faceless, horrible maniac; Billie Starr blank-eyed and cold to the touch, neck bruised and crushed by another faceless, evil psychopath; Billie Starr a black hole in the house, gone. Just gone.

Jenny stopped short on her own sidewalk. A deer was blocking the door. A doe. Not young but not old, either. She stared at Jenny,

ears twitching as the snow fell on her. With the exception of those ears—almost comically large and erect—her body was completely still. Underneath her right front hoof was an empty tuna can. The blinking street sign strobed the deer, turned her dun coat a dull gray. But she was beautiful all the same. Stunning and wild. Most of the deer Jenny had seen over the years were dead, killed by semi-trucks or inept hunters. Spring in Benson was a parade of carcasses. Jenny hated the sight, but Marcus often dragged the remains home for stew. There was a pot of it in Jenny's freezer right now. She could never bring herself to eat it. She held her breath, met the doe's gaze. Was the doe a mother? She was alone right now, but maybe she had fawns waiting for her somewhere. The doe blinked. Jenny blinked. It's almost as if they understood each other. About what, though? How heartless the world was? How carelessly it could kill you/shrug you off/swallow you up? The doe's white tail snapped in the wind. Then, quickly, gracefully, she leaped away, dashed across the road to Dorothy Renfrow's yard and vanished behind a line of pines.

Jenny exhaled, came back herself. *Dumb mom,* the sign said again. *Slut mom, whore mom. Loser. End of the world.*

If the world ended tomorrow, Jenny wouldn't have to think about rent or bills or field trips or her own mistakes ever again. Everyone would be wiped out—everyone. All at once. Nothing to lose. Nothing to mourn. If the world ended tomorrow, she would be free.

Inside her house, though, a mundane domestic scene—Billie Starr in the kitchen with one of her textbooks from school, George reading companionably over her shoulder. No blood, no blank eyes. Everything right and in its proper place.

"See?" Billie Starr was telling George. She pointed to a page in her book. "See what I mean?"

Jenny heard the usual dripping of the sink and ticking of the mantel clock, the metronomic beats that measured out her days,

but behind those sounds was a soft hum, a hum combined with a whistling. The hum was the furnace, the whistling the sound of hot air pouring through the vents. Had George fixed it without the tools? How had he done it?

"The screws were pretty loose," he explained. "Just used my fingers to get the problem piece out and cleaned it with a sponge from the sink. You should be fine now."

Jenny set Marcus's wrenches down by the door. "Thank you."

"Don't mention it."

Billie Starr shut her book and thoughtfully crunched on a carrot. "I was telling George about the Indian slaughter that happened right where Dad grew up, where all those new houses are now. Terri lives there. Dexter, too, and Hannah and Laurel and Kyle and Kylie. A bunch of white people. George said he'll fix it."

"The slaughter or the subdivision?" Jenny asked.

"Both," Billie Starr said. "But the slaughter mostly."

George smiled sadly. "I said I *should* fix it, but genocide's not a furnace. I can't go back in time and bring those men and women back to life. That damage is done, I'm afraid."

"Then what's the point?" Billie Starr asked.

"Of what?" George asked.

"Your petition. Talking about stuff. Doing anything about anything."

"Good question."

"Mom says that to me all the time and then never gives me a real answer. Marcus—that's our neighbor—is the only one who really ever answers me. He says I shouldn't be so full of white guilt all the time, that I have to live my own life the best way I know how, but I don't think it's guilt exactly. I think it's knowing things."

"Quite the precocious little girl you have here." George grabbed his coat and clipboard. He thanked Billie Starr for the history lesson. Then he handed Jenny his business card. "Call me tomorrow. That is, if you're not too busy. I have a proposal for you."

Jenny glanced down at the card. ELECT GEORGE SHEPHERD, it said. INDIANA'S NEXT AND BEST GOVERNOR. Gold letters on a background of navy blue. With a thudding heart, she thought of the wire that was lying in plain sight in the bathroom trash can. Was it still transmitting sounds to the Black Suits? Had they heard her vomit? Weep? She had no idea how wires worked, if the thing was still on or not. The woman back at McDonald's told her not to worry about such things. "Just be pretty and . . . you know."

Billie Starr trotted over, curious. Always curious. She scraped at the card with her fingernail. "That's the state flag."

"A proposal?" Jenny asked George.

"The best kind." He leaned toward her, mouth cupped as if to tell her a secret. Billie Starr leaned in, too. "A job," he whispered. "Working for my campaign."

Jenny shook her head and backed away from him.

"Just some secretarial work, not worthy of you, I'm sure, but do me a favor. Mull it over."

Billie Starr was nodding enthusiastically. "Mull it over, Mom."

"We'll see," Jenny said.

"That means 'no,'" Billie Starr told George.

"I sincerely hope not." He bowed to them both. "Evening, ladies. Take good care of each other." Clipboard over his head, papers scattering in the wind, he left. He didn't stop to gather loose sheets, just ran to his car and drove away, one headlight out.

Billie Starr turned to Jenny, hands on her hips. "Was that the job you were talking about? Working for George?"

What was one more lie? "That was it."

"You should take it."

"I should?"

"George would be a good boss."

"Bedtime for you, little girl."

"I'm not little. I'm precocious."

Mr. Richardson had used the very same word in a recent parent-

teacher conference. His ironic tone suggested that he found Billie Starr both delightful and exhausting.

Jenny gently nudged her daughter down the hall to the bathroom where her early morning attempts to be sexy were still evident— crumbs of blush in the sink, spent cotton balls covered in nail polish on the floor and in the trash can, a pair of fake eyelashes on the counter, lashes-up, dead centipedes. Billie Starr didn't notice. That, or she didn't care. She dutifully brushed her teeth, humming the same song George had back in Jenny's laundry room. She even seemed to know the words. "Two shilloettes on the shade," she said. Mouth full of foamy paste, she asked Jenny what a "shilloette" was.

"Silhouette," Jenny said. "It's your shape, basically. Seen through something like a curtain."

"Or a shade."

"Yes. You're getting toothpaste on the mirror again."

"Oops." Billie Starr spit into the sink, rinsed, wiped the mirror with a towel, white streaks everywhere. She pointed to the wire in the trash can. "What's that?"

"Nothing."

"It doesn't look like nothing."

"It's just something I broke."

"Like the furnace?"

"Sort of, but really the furnace broke itself."

"I'm cold still."

"You won't be when you get under all your blankets."

"Fine." Billie Starr stuck her tongue out at Jenny. "I'm going." Then she zoomed to her bedroom, arms out, a plane again. On her way where? Paris? "Nah," she said. "The Taj Mahal."

Billie Starr had a poster of the Taj Mahal on the wall opposite her bed, and next to it was a mural she and Marcus had painted of the schoolhouse. Of Marcus's trailer, too, and Gertrude and Yo-Yo. Hugging the house and trailer was a golden cornfield spanned by a double rainbow. The mural was clumsy, childish, but cheerful.

Jenny supposed it was what Billie Starr wished their little plot of land looked like. No scrubby yard in this version, no towers of tires—just green lawns and tiger lilies and lilac bushes. Bees, too, fat and buzzing, and birds and butterflies.

Billie Starr's room was a lot like her wardrobe. She was in control here. Nothing matched. Somehow, though, it was the most comfortable space in the house. Her headboard was covered in glow-in-the-dark stars, and a model of the solar system hung, mobile-style, from the ceiling over her dresser. The solar system was another gift from Marcus. Surprisingly, all the planets were in the right place.

Billie Starr climbed into bed, pulled her covers up to her pointy chin. Jenny had grabbed an extra quilt from the hall closet. She shook it out on top of Billie Starr's Princess Leia blanket and Winnie-the-Pooh sleeping bag. Billie Starr was still in her winter hat, but her hands weren't blue anymore. The furnace was going full force.

"Where are your gloves?" Jenny asked.

"What gloves?"

"The yellow ones."

"Lost them."

"When?"

"Like a month ago."

"Why didn't you tell me?"

"I did. You probably just forgot. Like with the field trip."

"We'll go out and get you a new pair tomorrow."

Wasn't there a church on Filbert Street that gave them out for free? If you were poor enough. Toys, too, according to the news report she'd heard at Marcus's. Jenny hoped it wouldn't come to that, but if faced with the choice between becoming a charity case and having nothing to give Billie Starr for Christmas, she'd gladly pick the former, town gossips be damned. And this being Benson, there would be talk, some of it kindly meant, the rest of it spiked with

self-righteousness. How sad, one of the Mummies might say. Not being able to afford a single gift for your child. Can you imagine?

Jenny kissed Billie Starr's smooth forehead. "'Night, honey."

"I'm not a honey. I'm the Concorde."

"Sweet dreams, Concorde. I love you."

"I love you, too, Mom."

Jenny flipped the light off and gently pulled the door closed until it clicked. That click was usually the sound of her having done her duty for the day, the sound of small triumphs, of getting Billie Starr to school and picking her up and feeding her and tucking her in, all somehow without killing her or, Jenny hoped, damaging her irreparably. It was Jenny's cue to relax, have a cup of tea, watch something on TV, and then go to bed herself. But she had to do something first. She hurried to the bathroom. Wet tiles soaked her socks. Water from Billie Starr's toothbrush probably. Minty smell. Jenny briefly checked her reflection. It was a habit. A crutch. Mirrors reassured her that, no matter what crisis befell her, she was still beautiful and that beauty had to count for something. But would her skin pay the electric bill? Her breasts for gas in the morning? And, if she really thought about it, wasn't it her beauty that got her here in the first place?

She grabbed the wire from the trash can. It was a spider in her hand, the kind that bit you and left rot behind. Jenny didn't look at it, held it as far away from her body as she could. In the hallway, shadows of her arm and the spider wire climbed the wall. Outside, the wind was still roaring. She followed the deer tracks to the first of the dead flower baskets and buried the wire under a mound of snow and loose dirt. "Are you listening, Black Suits?" she said to the spot. "Can you hear me?" She stomped once on the wire, twice, three times to kill it for good. "You're the evil ones. I know it now. You're the bad ones. Not George Shepherd. You."

The stomping wasn't working, though. The wire snaked itself

out underneath her foot like a live thing, like something that might take root, suck nutrients from the soil, bloom in spring.

"You," Jenny said once more. Another stomp. For good measure. Then she ran back inside.

*P*ounding woke her from the middle of a dream about the end of the world. Pound, pound, pound, rap, rap, rap. Thud. Thud. Thud. Something about threes. Why threes, though? The dream was the sticky kind. It remained with Jenny as she shot out of bed and stumbled down the hallway, clouding her consciousness, blurring the lines between what was real, the waking world, and that other place full of tornadoes in winter and blizzards in summer. She still wasn't sure whether a huge sinkhole had indeed opened up under her house, threatening to swallow her and Billie Starr and Gertrude and Yo-Yo and Marcus Rye whole—Carla, too, and Pete and Randall and Trish Keck and Mr. Richardson (everyone, it seemed, gathered together for a party of some kind, a celebration that involved a cookout and a menagerie of piñatas, bird, deer, cat, tuxedoes, cats in tuxedoes)—or if that was just her brain playing tricks on her. Otherwise, she would have known better than to answer the door, would have been able to think first before letting Randall in. As it was, he blended in perfectly with the rapidly disappearing images from her dream, shedding candy like a piñata, head swollen and spongy as a balloon. He wasn't speaking the language of celebration. Or of disaster, for that matter. He was telling her she was no better than he was. She was trash, in fact, a slut, the kind of woman who got pregnant at the drop of a hat and then refused to let the father of her baby have any contact with it.

But your baby isn't an it, Jenny's fuzzy mind thought. Your baby's a she. A human. That's why I've put a sinkhole between us.

"You think you're better than me," Randall said. "What are you? A Newberg. A Newberg? Might as well be an iceberg for all the warmth I get from you."

Jenny was gradually coming to, realizing her mistake. How many times had she pretended to be asleep/not home/dead maybe? Just so he would go away. Moonlight filtered through the gap in her living room curtains. Sign light came in, too. *Why now why now why now.*

He knows, Jenny thought. He knows what I did with George and is here to take Billie Starr away from me. *Horrible mom. Whore mom. Girls like you.*

Randall crossed his arms over his chest, squinted threateningly at Jenny. That squint meant she was dealing with Randall the Crusader. Jenny never knew which Randall she was going to get. Sometimes he was Weeping Mess Man. Weeping Mess Man wanted Jenny to forgive him for being a piece of shit to her and Billie Starr, begged her to fix him somehow, prop him up, give him hope, tell him he wasn't so terrible before sending him on his way. Other times he was Utterly Logical Man Who Understood That He and Jenny Should Never Have Had a Child in the First Place but Since They Did, They Needed to Figure This Out, Make a Plan, Maybe Bring in Outside Help. Utterly Logical Man usually passed out midsentence. And then there was actual Randall, sober Randall. Once in a while, she ran into sober Randall on the street and he was shy, cagey, in a hurry to be away from her.

Randall the Crusader looked like he hadn't slept in days. His shirt wasn't buttoned right. A bubble of hairy belly poked through. There was a wet spot of urine on the crotch of his jeans. His thinning hair lay flat against his skull in some places, stuck out like feathers in others. Dime-size, scaly sores dotted his cheeks and chin. He wasn't wearing a coat. Where had he left his? Maybe he'd completely forgotten to put one on.

"I know my rights." Randall stabbed the air with his right index finger. Then he studied the motion, seemed dissatisfied, switched to his left. "You have to let me see her. If you don't let me see her, I'll have no choice but to take her away from you and have my cousins in the police department throw your hot ass in jail." Another stab,

followed by a stumble and the jarring of her curio cabinet, full of clay figurines Billie Starr had made in art class. They made a low tinkling sound as Randall steadied himself. Then they went silent.

The house was warmed through now. Even the leaky spot over the kitchen sink was comfortable. The wind had obviously died down. No howling in the eaves, no creak of trees outside. Out of habit, Jenny filled the teakettle, set it on the back burner. The Crusader rarely finished his fuming in under an hour.

Randall had picked up a sheet of paper from the kitchen table and squinted at it. "What the hell is this?"

It was George's petition. He'd left it behind with Billie Starr, who'd covered the list of signatures in airplanes and fluffy clouds and Eiffel Towers.

"Nothing important," Jenny said.

"Well," Randall said, "in that case." He held the paper up like a bullfighter's cape. Then he ripped it in half. The two pieces skidded to the floor and disappeared under the refrigerator. Randall was triumphant for a moment, then confused. "I just want to see my daughter."

So, it wasn't about the Black Suits, about Jenny sleeping with George at all. She was both relieved and annoyed. "You *can* see her," she said. "I'm not keeping her from you. But she's in bed now, Randall. She needs her sleep. She has school tomorrow."

"I know that. You think I don't know that? It's Tuesday, for fuck's sake."

"Actually, it's Monday."

"Actually, you're a bitch."

"Maybe I am, but you only come here after she's gone to bed and you're drunk. I'm doing what I think is best for everyone."

Randall started pacing, lumbering between her couch and the kitchen, punctuating his pacing with a lot of growling and sucking in of nostrils and balling of fists. It was just one phase of the Crusader's multilayered attack on Jenny's nerves. The attacks all tended

to play out the same way, beginning with the pounding and the belittling, transitioning into pacing and ranting, and ending with him crying on her couch over his bad luck in choosing to reproduce with a stone-cold frigid she-beast who wouldn't know kindness if it raped her in the face.

Right on schedule Randall, at the front window now, curtains opened wide, launched into a rant about how Jenny had sawed off his balls, how she'd systematically dismantled his manhood in an effort to, stab, stab, stab: "You know."

"I'm sorry, Randall," Jenny said, "but I really don't."

"Yes, you do. You're just acting like you don't to put me off my guard, to tear me down."

Randall stumbled across the carpet, braced himself against the wall between the kitchen and the living room, ear up to the plaster, drumming against it, tapping softly, softly, as if trying to sense something hidden inside. "Empty," he said. "Like your soul." He pivoted away from the wall, tried to arrest Jenny with his eyes but was obviously having trouble focusing. "Hollow. Like your heart."

The teakettle whistled. Jenny went to it, poured hot water into the mug, watched the steam rise up in soft, comforting clouds. Randall was back in the kitchen, pulling on his earlobe. Jenny saw then that some of it was gone. The skin there was mottled and singed.

"Remember that day when you and me, we went to the mall?" Randall asked. "How we got our ears pierced on the same day? No more studs for me, which is fine. Remember when I was a stud? Your stud?" He came at her, arms out. A net. "Sleep with me, Jenny Newberg. Sleep with me and tell me you believe in me even if nobody else does. Tell me my ugly ear isn't important."

Jenny grabbed her tea, dodged him, moved into the living room. It was a dance they'd done a thousand times. "I think you should go."

"Oh, do you? Do you think I should go?" Randall followed her, yanked hard on the door of the curio cabinet, and pulled a clay bird from the top shelf. He held it aloft, started talking to it, a drunk

Mary Poppins. "Look at Miss Holier Than Thou over there. Thinks she knows what's best for everyone. For me, for our daughter. But she doesn't know anything about anything." He dropped the bird on the floor. It broke in three pieces.

"Please, Randall. I'm so tired. Can we do this some other time?"

He gave the bird's broken belly a soft kick. It rolled into the corner of the room where the wrenches were, the socket and adjustable Jenny had borrowed from Marcus to help with the furnace. A smile stretched across Randall's chapped face. It was a sick smile. It made his top lip bleed. He started to move toward the tools, fingers growing clawlike. Jenny set her mug down and pushed him out of her way.

The wrenches were like weights in her hands. She held them over her head, wielded them as best she could. "I'm not going to let you hurt me or Billie Starr. Do you hear? I won't let you."

"Not worth it." Randall did a drunken two-step to her couch, collapsed there in jerky increments—headfirst, hitting the armrest, followed by ass, on the edge, and feet, right on the pretty throw pillow Jenny had bought at one of Ashley Batchelder's stupid parties. The one thing she could afford, its shirred white surface showed two cardinals in a lacy green tree, musical notes shooting out the beak of one of the birds, a gust of words from the other: YOU MAKE MY HEART SING. "Nothing, nothing cunt. That's what you are. A cunt of nothing." A sob or chill or wave of nausea shook Randall's body, and a solitary tear dropped down his left cheek into his open mouth. Then he was snoring.

Jenny stood over him, mantel clock ticking, sign outside blinking blinking blinking. The details of her sinkhole piñata dream were fading, but one image remained clear. It was Randall holding a wrapped gift, presenting it to Jenny shyly, blushing like he used to, hair still full, back straight, all his youthful handsomeness intact. The gift was a new purse for Jenny and inside the purse was a computer for Billie Starr and inside the computer was a program

that would save the world. Billie Starr just had to unlock it some-how.

Everyone at the party had breathed a sigh of relief, even Carla, who was clinging to the side of the sinkhole, feet dangling over empty space. The world was going to be okay. The world was go-ing to be fine, and they had Billie Starr and Dream Randall to thank for it.

Real Randall, Randall the Crusader, farted. The fart roused him slightly. He turned over on the couch, mumbled something about Jenny Newberg not knowing kindness if it fucked her in the heart.

She was going to get him a blanket but decided he would be fine in his clothes. She left the tea where it was—she was too tired to drink it—and, on her way to bed, picked up the fragments of the broken bird and put them in the trash. She took the wrenches with her.

*I*n the morning, Billie Starr ate her banana and stared at her fa-ther, who'd tumbled to the floor in the middle of the night and was filling the small living room with the stink of cigarettes and whis-key and bad beer.

"Why does he do that?" she asked, eyes narrowed in disgust.

Jenny was trying to choke down some cereal. It tasted like the cardboard it came in. "Sleep? We all need to sleep."

"Drink so much."

"He's probably sad about something," Jenny said. "A lot of people drink to forget that they're sad about something."

"Do you? Drink to forget you're sad?"

Jenny could count how often she'd gotten drunk on one hand—four times with Randall in high school and once with Lyd after she got the job in Bob Butz's real estate office. She didn't like the taste of alcohol, didn't trust the grandiose ideas it gave her—I could be a model or an actress, her buzzed brain thought, if I could only get

out of this town—or the extra-ugly reality it hit her with in the morning when, shoveling Tylenol into her mouth, she had to come to terms with the fact that she wasn't destined for bigger things after all, that she was, in truth, nothing more than a pretty fish in a small pond, a nobody, who, by the time she was forty, would probably go in search of someone's second story.

"Not really," she said.

"Is that why you won't marry Dad?" Billie Starr asked. "Because he's drunk all the time?"

Jenny got up, took her cereal to the sink. "I bet you can't wait for Saturday. The field trip. That's going to be a lot of fun."

"Maybe that's why he's sad, because you won't marry him."

"We've gone through all of this before."

Billie Starr took a gulp of water, swished it around in her mouth, swallowed it thoughtfully. "Beer doesn't even taste good."

"How do you know that?"

"Lyd gave me a sip once. It was gross."

"I'm glad you're not a fan."

"But seriously, Mom," Billie Starr said. "Why do people drink?"

"They have to, I think. It's a bad habit, like biting your nails."

Billie Starr studied her nails. "But biting your nails doesn't make you fall asleep when you shouldn't or do or say stupid things."

"True."

Randall snored loudly and turned over. His jeans had crept down his ass as he slept, revealing bright red bikini briefs, decorated in puppies and kittens and skulls.

"Why is he even here?" Billie Starr asked.

"He wanted to see you, but you were in bed, so I told him he'd have to wait."

"And now that I'm up, he's asleep."

"That does seem to be the situation." Jenny checked the mantel clock. Quarter to eight. "Time for school, young lady. Gather up your stuff."

Billie Starr rolled up her banana peel, chucked it at the sink. It landed on the counter next to George Shepherd's card. "I'm not a young lady," she said grandly. "I'm a petition."

"A petition?"

"George said last night that petitions can change the world for the better. I'm a petition."

Jenny grabbed her car keys from a bowl on top of the curio cabinet. Billie Starr put on her coat. They both paused in the living room for a moment, watching Randall twitch in his sleep. A spider crawled up his neck into his hair.

"Are you just going to leave him there?" Billie Starr asked.

"He can see himself out."

"What if he robs us? Or pees on the floor like he did that one time?"

"Shhh. Let's go."

"Or pukes on the couch." Billie Starr peered into the cabinet, opened the door. "Hey, where's Tweetie Birdie?"

"Tweetie Birdie?"

"The robin I made in kindergarten."

"Maybe she flew away."

"Clay robins don't fly."

"We'll find her later."

"Dad broke her, didn't he? Because he was drunk and sad. He dropped her."

Jenny hurried her daughter outside where the day was dawning blue and white. Snow just barely covered the grass. It was the fine, flour-like kind of snow you couldn't do anything with. No snowballs, no snowmen, just feathery cold in your fingers. Gertrude and Yo-Yo, content, recently fed, sniffed around the wire. The sign across the street blinked rhythmically. Two blackbirds swooped in and out of Dorothy Renfrow's eaves, shrieking, fighting over some scrap.

Billie Starr watched them for a while, thinking of what? Her broken robin? Then she buckled herself in the backseat, face still

thoughtful. "Hey, Mom, didn't you tell me once that Grandpa Pete made countertops?"

Jenny turned the key in the ignition. The gas gauge needle hovered on empty, but the car started anyway. This car, this old Honda Jenny had bought when she still worked for Bob Butz—it had yet to fail her. She tapped the steering wheel affectionately. "Yes, Grandpa installed countertops."

"And he died of a lung thing," Billie Starr said. "Grandpa did."

"Cancer probably, yeah. Why?"

Billie Starr sighed. "Just sayin'."

"Just sayin' what, exactly?"

But Billie Starr had retreated into her own world. She was gazing out the window at the Keck farm, where Trish, clad in a puffer coat and cowboy hat, was scraping frost from the windows of Lorne's yellow International Harvester pickup.

"Don't smoke cigarettes," Jenny told her daughter.

"Or drink beer?"

"Yes."

Or meet men. Or fall in love with them. Or get pregnant. Don't get any older. If you get older, I won't be able to protect you.

On the roadside in front of the Keck house was a dead deer, face still, eyes open, belly distended, ready to burst. Was it the same deer? The one from the night before, hoof in a tuna can, tail flicking snow away? It didn't matter which deer it was. Deer in the headlights. Deer in a ditch. Deer beautiful and perfect and now no more.

Randall didn't rob them or pee on the floor. When Jenny returned from taking Billie Starr to school, the living room was empty, quiet. He'd left a note behind on the couch. His scrawl was the same as it'd been in high school when he sometimes left love letters in her locker. This was not a love letter.

I meant what I said last night. You can't keep my daughter from me. I'm getting a lawyer. I suggest you do the same.

So, here was Utterly Logical Man, making an appearance on paper, delivering an ultimatum. Jenny crumpled up the note, threw it outside with the overturned flower baskets and the wire. Marcus Rye was on his front step, calling for Gertrude and Yo-Yo. In his kimono and slippers, legs bare, hair flyaway, he was no longer transformed by happiness. He was a scarecrow, gaunt and lost-looking.

Jenny kicked an empty tuna can off her stoop. It shone in the snow like a tiny hubcap. Marcus heard the clatter, waved. "Doing okay over there?" she asked. He didn't hear her, so she asked again, yelling this time.

"Hanging in," he yelled. "You?"

"Same."

Marcus pointed to the blinking sign across the street. He always did this. Every time the two of them hollered at each other from their separate stoops, he brought up the sign. It was one of his obsessions. "That thing is the bane of my existence." When he used words like "bane of my existence" it meant he was having one of his good days. "I called the city about it, you know. And the county."

"Did you? That's smart." Jenny's heart beat in rhythm with the sign's blinking. *Lawyer, lawyer, lawyer.*

"You know what they said?"

Jenny did know but pretended not to. "What did they say?"

"That I should be thanking them. That we should be thanking them. For saving our lives. Can you believe it? Bunch of morons. Bunch of idiotic, busybody bureaucrats."

A few cars wound through the curves in front of them—a truck driven by Lyd's boss, Larry Dodge ("Spying on me!" Marcus said), and an El Camino, Troy Pike at the wheel. Marcus shaded his eyes. "Cheese on the breadsticks. What's next? Chaos. The abyss." He turned to Jenny. "How's our girl?"

"She's good. At school."

"As she should be."

"She's going to Chicago this weekend."

"Morocco?"

"Chicago!"

"Ah." Marcus nodded. "Big shoulders. Good pizza."

The wind whipped up, pushed feather-light snow across the yard in white waves. Clouds as big as cruise ships raced each other overhead. One blocked out the sun, threw Jenny and her little world into shadow. The yellow sign throbbed on. *Empty empty empty*— both her bank account and her gas tank. She'd gotten Billie Starr to school on time for a change that morning and maneuvered her way through the parking lot like a pro, smiling at the Mummies as she drove away, but the whole time she was worried her car would sputter to a stop, right there in the drop-off lane, right in front of Ashley Batchelder, who, shivering gamely in her exercise clothes and taking small sips from her shiny travel mug, was having a particularly good hair day. Somehow Jenny made it home. On fumes probably.

"Have any gas I could borrow, Marcus?"

"Bass?" He made a wavelike motion with his hands. "Ran out of fish months ago."

"Not bass," Jenny said. "Gas!"

"Oh gas! Yeah. Got a couple of cans in the garage."

"Can I borrow some?"

"Sure, but you should have some extra lying around, too, little lady. What are you going to do when the government comes through with the tanks?"

The threat of martial law was another one of Marcus's obsessions. It was why he hoarded things and kept a crossbow and a machete in his closet, already stuffed with skirt suits and bustiers and feather boas. "Just in case the powers-that-be try to subdue me into abject compliance," he often said.

"Hey," he said, "I saw someone sneaking around your house last night. Lurking. Peeping in windows."

"Randall you mean? He came by around midnight."

"Don't think so. Taller than Randall. Dark coat. Orange hat. I grabbed my ax and scared him off."

"Thanks."

"Don't mention it."

At that moment, Gertrude and Yo-Yo came bounding out of Jenny's bushes. They ran toward Marcus, ears flat against their heads, yowling. Marcus scooped them both up and, waving at Jenny once more, went back into his house.

Dark coat, orange hat, blinked the sign. *Dark coat orange hat. Peeping peeping peeping.* A Black Suit? George? Jenny circled her house, looking for footprints, for evidence of a lurker, but found nothing. The soft snow would have erased it all anyway.

Just inside the door were Marcus's wrenches. Jenny had put them there so she wouldn't forget to return them. Perhaps it was for the best that she'd forgotten. They'd be handy weapons in case a Black Suit or Randall the Crusader surprised her in the middle of the night. Or Randall All Lawyered Up. Of course, Randall could afford a lawyer. He had Leffert money. His parents would pay for it.

The living room was still full of his presence. It smelled like a bar. The couch cushions were dented from where he'd slept most of the night, and a cigarette lay bent in half in the middle of the carpet, unlit, leaking tobacco. Jenny plucked it from the carpet, tossed it in the trash can under the kitchen sink. It landed on George's business card. She'd thrown the card away that morning, wanting to bury it the same way she buried the wire and her memories of what she'd done in that ugly motel, glassy dead animal eyes staring down. Her skin was cold now. She was a statue standing there, emotionless, made of marble. No, she whispered to herself. You can't possibly. Don't be ridiculous. Don't be an idiot. Think ahead. Think of the consequences. But another voice—her shoulder angel? Or the devil

himself?—told her she didn't have a choice. She was out of money. She was out of time. She was out of gas. She needed a lawyer. She retrieved the card, hurriedly dialed the number embossed on the back before she could change her mind. George answered. She knew his voice by now, just as she'd known the voices of the Black Suits. No citrus fruit this time, though. No code.

"I'll take it," she told him. "I'll take the job."

There was a short delay. Phones rang in the background. Jenny heard typing and laughter and someone yelling out random numbers and counties. Fifteen Kosciusko, thirty-four Blackford, one hundred and one Tippecanoe. Then George said, "Is this who I think it is?"

"Who do you think it is?"

"The pretty, redheaded single mom from Benson with the wonky furnace and smart daughter who wants me to save the Shawnee?"

"Yes."

"What's your name, pretty single mom from Benson?"

"Jenny Newberg."

"Jenny Newberg. A lot of optimism there."

"I guess."

"When can you start?"

"When do you want me?"

"Right now." He laughed. "Right now. Always. Forever."

Jenny was at the kitchen sink. She put her fingers under the faucet, felt the freezing water drip down. I'll fix it, she thought, turning her hand over, studying her wet palm, her lifeline, her love line, her fate line. All of them short except for the fate line. Carla, who'd studied palmistry one summer, said that meant Jenny was destined to die young (Doris) and love once (Randall). But what did Carla know?

I work for the future governor of Indiana. How would that sound to Lyd and Carla and Randall? To Bob Butz and Mr. Richardson

and Ashley Batchelder and the rest of the Mummies? *Just the other day, my boss, the governor, was saying* . . .

"Tell me where to show up," she said.

George gave her an address, asked if she could be there in an hour.

"Yes."

In the back of her mind were the Black Suits, the ammunition she had given them and the question of how and when they would deploy it. But wasn't there a tiny sliver of a chance that the wire hadn't worked, that the men got nothing from the whole encounter? Maybe that was why they had failed to show up at the café, failed to pay her. For the first time since she'd accepted the men's offer, since she'd slept with George for money that never materialized in a motel arrayed with guns and cigar ash, it occurred to Jenny that she might be in the clear, that everything was going to work out fine.

Book Two

George Shepherd had chosen an old storefront on Main Street in Churubusco for his campaign headquarters because he was, he said, a hometown boy at heart. He wanted Jenny to answer the phones.

Had she done reception work before?

Yes.

Could she file?

Yes to that, too.

And send out letters and lick stamps and be friendly to people who were screaming at her about things that weren't her fault?

Yes yes yes.

"You're hired," George said.

He'd brought doughnuts and coffee. They ate at a small, rickety table set up near the front window. The view was of turn-of-the-century redbrick buildings and cars parked at an angle. Snow moved like opaque curtains up the street, chasing the wind. White light filtered through the dirty glass, dulled by old tape and the remnants of blue and pink lamb and bunny decals. According to George, the store used to sell secondhand baby clothes. Cribs, too, and changing tables and diaper pails. Before that, it was a hole-in-the-wall tavern, the kind where drunks would pass out in their barstools and have to be dragged home by their boots.

"The bartender rounded them up at the end of the night and

drove them home," George said. "I used to drink Pabst right here, right where we're sitting. There was a booth in the corner with wooden benches. That's where I courted my wife. I etched our initials into the side. *G.S. + B.K. = T.L.* Guessing that bench is long gone now. Sawdust. Like the sentiment."

Jenny waited for his translation. Her lips were coated in glaze. She licked them contentedly, watching two men in their seventies hobble into a barbershop across the street. Right behind them was a young mother, pushing an infant in a stroller, a look of pure bliss on her upturned face. She had no idea, Jenny thought. No idea what was in store for her. Babies grew up, became kids. Bottles and diaper changes and naps gave way to desires voiced often and loudly. Suddenly, your little one wanted answers to life's big questions. And computers for Christmas.

George pretended to scratch letters into the table's Formica surface. "George Shepherd plus Brenda Keck equals true love."

"That's sweet."

"If you say so." He leaned back, studied her. "You look like a Titian sitting there."

Jenny had dressed carefully that morning, more carefully than she had when seduction was the aim. She'd combed through her closet for her best Bob Butz Realty work clothes, spent several minutes trying on different outfits, hoping to find the perfect combination of attractive and modest, professional yet pretty. She'd settled on a form-fitting blue blouse under her least-worn black pantsuit and sensible faux leather pumps, no knee-highs. The no knee-highs decision was a mistake. She'd stepped in a frozen puddle on her way to the car, and, since she'd left her coat back in the Fort Wayne grocery store, she had to work hard to keep her teeth from chattering.

"What's a Titian?" she asked.

"He was a painter. Beautiful red-haired women were his specialty."

Jenny still did not know how she felt about this man. Was she

attracted to him? Or simply grateful because he'd just explained that she'd be paid twice a month and that the first check would come in a week? Was there a difference?

"Wait," she said. Things dawning slowly. "Brenda Keck? Any relation to Lorne?"

"They're cousins," George said. "Brenda is from Benson, believe it or not. Keeps an apartment there and retreats to it when she's bored with me. It's a small world we live in."

"Very small," Jenny agreed.

"I'm Lorne's lawyer. Didn't want to take his case—one can't help pitying poor, long-suffering Trish—but family's family, eh?"

Jenny thought of Randall's note—*I'm getting a lawyer. I suggest you do the same.* The paper was probably getting snowed on now, melting to nothing. She glanced around at her new workplace. The carpet was dirty, the walls pocked with nail holes and small dents. A light over her head buzzed and blinked. Besides the small table, the room was furnished with five metal desks, four computers, a printer, three phones, a radio, a wall of file cabinets, and a fax machine. Nothing was plugged in. Boxes of business cards lay about in disarray, along with piles of posters and yard signs. A tower of printer paper leaned up against a refrigerator covered in magnets that matched the business card George had given her the night before. The whole office was roughly the size of Jenny's house and about as clean.

She was dismayed when George had first flipped on the lights, but then he explained to her that he'd been running the campaign out of his living room until now—that's where he was when she called—and that he'd be bringing his staff to the office tomorrow to help her get things set up.

"You'll love my team, a great group of guys." George stood up, started to plug things in—the computers, the fax machine, the refrigerator, the phones. "I haven't made my official announcement

yet, so a lot of people don't even know I'm running. That all changes on Saturday."

"What happens Saturday?"

"I'm giving a speech right there." He pointed to the sidewalk, where two blackbirds were fighting over a soggy piece of bread. "That's when I'll announce my candidacy. Can you be here?"

Saturday. Saturday. Jenny knew she had something to do on Saturday, but what was it? The word *Morocco* came to mind. The second-grade field trip. Duh, Mom. Duh. "I can be here."

"Wonderful." George leaned toward her, put a hand on her knee. No wedding ring today. "Tell me more about yourself, Jenny Newberg."

"There's not much to tell."

"I don't believe that for a minute. Look at you. You have that kind of face."

"What kind of face?"

"The mysterious kind, the kind that hides a million secrets. Fess up. You're fascinating."

"I'm not. Honestly."

"Tell me the boring stuff then."

Jenny wasn't used to having to treat relative strangers to her autobiography. Every time she'd applied for a job it was in Benson where her prospective bosses were already well acquainted with the basic facts of her life and had ready-made opinions about how she'd lived it so far and where she'd end up. Pete's girl. High school dropout. Single mom. Pretty but impractical, bound to lose her bloom in her thirties and turn into one of *those* women—working long hours in a thankless place, bitter-mouthed with disappointment. A Carla-in-training. But George knew nothing of her history, and his warm regard unlocked something inside of her. She told him more than she intended to, began to ramble, touching on Billie Starr's birth and Pete's death and her friendships with Lyd and Marcus, the bank,

Gertrude and Yo-Yo, her little house on Acorn Street and what it meant to her. While she talked, he smiled the same smile from the photograph the Black Suits had given her—soft, rapt. For a few intoxicating minutes, Jenny felt like the only person on the planet. It was a good feeling, but a fleeting one. While she struggled to explain what had gone wrong at her previous job—Bob Butz handsy in the break room—George interjected.

"You know," he said, drawing his fingers together under his chin in a steeple shape. "I think you and I are a lot alike."

"We are?"

"Let me count the ways." He started ticking off their many similarities, beginning with the fact that they were both from small towns, towns most people had never even heard of, which meant they had to work hard to be acknowledged, to stand out, get their proper due. It was exhausting, that work, but worth it, yes? Because they were also very ambitious. Driven. To succeed, definitely, but also to make the world they lived in a better place for others.

"We care deeply about people, even if that caring sometimes comes at great personal expense to ourselves. Wouldn't you agree?"

Jenny wanted to recognize herself in the portrait George was painting but thought he was giving her a little too much credit. She was just about to say so when he took her hand.

"I want to talk about that morning at the Riverview," he said. "What it meant to me, what I hope it meant to you."

Jenny pulled her hand away, stood up. "That's okay. We don't have to—"

"I know I told you I was past the age of wanting things desperately. I spoke too soon." George rose, limped toward her. No ten-point rack behind him this time, just a water-stained wall. "We'd have to be careful obviously. The campaign, the press, we'd have to be incredibly discreet, but . . ."

He was suddenly so close Jenny could smell the sugar on his

breath. She froze. Was he going to try to kiss her? Here, in full view of a bunch of old men getting their gray beards trimmed? Should she let him? The last time she fought off an advance from her boss, everything ended in disaster. At least for her. But George wasn't Bob. He was charming and sweet. Kind. Also old enough to be her father. And married.

He stepped back a bit. "I'm coming on too strong, aren't I? I do that sometimes, get out over my skis. I'm sorry. But I thought, since we already started something—"

"Yes, of course. It's just that . . ." Jenny sat back down, fiddled with the zipper on her purse.

"I understand," George said, flashing that smile again. "This is a lot to take in. New job. Besotted boss. But think about it, okay? Tell me you'll think about it."

"I'll think about it."

"Good. That's all I ask." He downed his coffee, apologized for being so incredibly rude on her first day, but he had a few errands to run. "Coffers to replenish, babies to kiss, etcetera." Would she mind holding down the fort until he got back? "I'm just glad I don't have to school you on the issues. The fact that you're all up to snuff on my platform is going to make everything that much easier."

His platform. Dust, something about people dying from it. But what else did he stand for? Jenny had no idea.

George paused in the doorway, threw on his coat. "Do you believe in fate, Jenny Newberg?"

Fate. As in everything happened for a reason? Ashley Batchelder had tried to sell Jenny a pillow that said that once, needlepoint unicorn smiling up at the words, spelled out in a rainbow. "I don't know."

"Well, I didn't believe in it. Then I met a beautiful girl in a grocery store." George winked at her and left, humming.

Unsure of what to do in his absence, Jenny sat for a while at the

rickety table, finishing her coffee, twirling her Titian hair. Maybe she should straighten things up, clean, organize, but she saw no evidence of a broom or vacuum or paper towels even, and she wouldn't know where to start. She could practice her phone voice, which had grown rusty since Bob Butz fired her—*Hello, you've reached the campaign office of George Shepherd, Indiana's next and best governor. How can I help you?*—or play around on the computer, the copier, the fax machine, try to figure out if they worked the same way Bob's did. She didn't do any of those things. She continued to sit in the uncomfortable chair George had pulled out for her, watching the blackbirds spar in the snow. Then the birds dispersed, shot up squawking, and a woman appeared in the doorway, tall, broad-shouldered, square-hipped, holding two smallish yippy dogs by matching blue leashes. The dogs strained at their collars, filled the air with squeaky barks and musky breath. Their mistress wore a bulky yellow coat and an unflattering stocking cap over her gray, feathered hair. She dropped the leashes, and the dogs, tails wagging wildly, darted from desk to desk to refrigerator, sniffing and making strange snarfing noises. Black and white and low to the ground, they had fat, sausage-like bodies, floppy ears, and thick, bristly fur. One ran over to Jenny, nipped at her foot. The woman calmly told the dog to heel. Instead, it leaped off toward the yard signs, lifted his leg, and peed on George's face.

Jenny put on her best receptionist's smile. "Can I help you?"

"I'm not sure." The woman gave Jenny a once-over. "Can you?"

"If it's Mr. Shepherd you want, he just left to run some errands. I could take a message."

The woman drifted farther into the office, picking up posters and setting them back down, checking cords, eyeing the stained carpet. The dog that had tried to bite Jenny was running in circles around the copier, snarling at some invisible foe, while its brother or sister ate his or her way through a box of business cards. The woman gazed indulgently at the dogs, apparently amused by their

hijinks, and continued roaming through the office, fingering supplies. She reminded Jenny of a bear in a campsite hunting for food. While she lumbered about the room, Jenny had gradually and unconsciously made her way toward the front door. Fight or flight? She knew herself. Flight.

"Actually," the woman said, stopping at the one desk without a computer, leaning on it, "I wanted to talk to you."

"To me?"

"I'm Brenda Shepherd, George's wife."

Jenny tried to hide her shock with busywork. She gathered up napkins and coffee stirrers, plucked crumbs from the floor. Paper clips threaded the carpet. Staples, too, and a few diaper pins. She hadn't thought much about this woman whose husband she had seduced, but in the fleeting moments when she had imagined her, she pictured someone small, birdlike, made tragic and waiflike by a lack of love. The real Brenda Shepherd was large and mannish and seemed like the kind of person who would be utterly unbothered by something as ethereal and impractical as romance.

Jenny rose, pulled herself together, and gave the older woman another smile. "It's so nice to meet you, Mrs. Shepherd."

"And you, too, Miss . . ."

"Newberg. You can call me Jenny, though."

"Nice to meet you, Jenny."

They were at an awkward distance from each other—too far apart to shake hands—so Jenny offered a clumsy wave, wondering how it was that Brenda Shepherd knew of her at all. Everything had happened so fast that Jenny assumed George hadn't had time to discuss his plans to hire her with anyone, not even his wife, with whom, to hear him talk about it, he shared very little beyond a surname and a house and these two undisciplined dogs. And how had that conversation gone?

Honey, I'm thinking of hiring this delightful young woman I met yesterday in the produce section.

Oh, how nice, dear.

What are her qualifications?

Well . . .

"George says you're very passionate about Democratic causes."

"I am," Jenny said. "Very passionate."

"I guess it makes sense that he'd hire you." Brenda sat down at one of the desks, crossed her legs in the shape of a four, ankle on knee. Her socks were thick red wool, pilled and slouching around her shoes. "That's how the world works, isn't it? Pretty young things, passionate about human rights, over aging wives who can't seem to get worked up about anything anymore."

"Wait," Jenny said. "Do you mean you were supposed to have this job?"

Brenda didn't seem to hear. The dogs had started fighting over a pen in the corner by the file cabinets. Their heads made hollow drumming sounds against the metal. Brenda whistled at the dogs to stop, but they kept fighting, growling, baring teeth. She raised her voice to be heard over the din. "Look at them, so playful, so full of life."

One of the dogs had succeeded in yanking a clump of fur out of the other one's tail and was trying to swallow it, gagging and drooling. Brenda laughed and retrieved the fought-over pen from the floor. It was destroyed, full of holes and as amorphous as egg white. She tossed it back on the floor with the fur and chewed-up business cards.

"Boys will be boys." Brenda licked her finger, wiped at a sticky spot on the desk. "Do you have children, Jenny Newberg?"

"A daughter. Billie Starr."

"Billie Starr. That's pretty. How old is she?"

"Eight."

"A good age."

"If you say so. Sometimes I think I preferred the years when she couldn't talk."

The dogs had finally settled down. One was lying on the floor, chewing on a poster. The other was licking the refrigerator door.

"I don't know if George told you," Brenda said, "but he courted me right here, in this very room, back when it was a bar, a peanut-shells-on-the-floor kind of place."

"He did tell me."

"When it came time to propose, he took me out on Turtle Town Lake in his dad's fishing boat, gave me a circle of fishing wire for a ring. Silly. Smelly. But it was the last time I remember being happy. Sometimes, I take Roger and Wilfred there, think about what my life might have been like if . . . I hope I'm not boring you."

"Not at all," Jenny said.

Brenda clapped at the dogs. Her hands were slightly swollen, her nails bitten to the quick. "Roger, Wilfred, come here!" The dogs ignored her, continued exactly as they were. "I spoil them, but who wouldn't?"

Jenny just kept smiling. Her face was starting to hurt from it.

"You get to be my age," Brenda said, "and you start living your life backward, spending a lot of your time in your own head because it's better than . . . what's out here." She gestured at the messy room, clapped at the dogs again. This time, they listened. They stopped what they were doing—licking their crotches—and came to their mistress, tails wagging wildly. She gave each a few pats on the head. "You darling little idiots. Let's let Miss Newberg get back to work."

The dogs pulled her to the front of the office, bumping into each other, tangling their leads. "Oh," Brenda said, turning. "Do me a tiny favor? Don't mention it to George that I came by. He doesn't like me to bring the dogs into his offices, says they make a mess and a racket." She gave Jenny a final, appraising look and let the dogs yank her out the door, which clanged shut behind them like a broken bell.

Outside, snow began to fall, big fat flakes, wet feathers rocking down to earth. The moment the snow hit the concrete it melted, turned the road and sidewalks into slick, dark mirrors that doubled the parked cars and squat brick buildings, made a mirage of the

city block, gave it the appearance of hovering dreamlike in midair. Suddenly, all the phones in the office rang at once. Jenny ran to the phone nearest to her, picked up the receiver. The smooth black plastic was cold but reassuring in her fingers. She was back in familiar territory, answering phones for a man.

"George Shepherd's office, Jenny Newberg speaking. How can I help you?"

The quiet on the other end was as heavy and cloying as steam. Jenny could hear someone breathing. Smoking, too, it seemed. There was a sharp intake of breath, followed by a noisy exhale.

"Hello," she said, more loudly this time. "Can I help you?"

More drawn breath, more exhalation, and then a man laughed in her ear. Jenny recognized it somehow, that laugh.

"Hello? Is anyone there?"

"Be careful," the man said. "You're a lightweight in a heavyweight's game."

Jenny got a chill. The hairs on the back of her neck stood up. "Excuse me?"

The man laughed again. Then he hung up. The moment the line went dead, there was a short electrical hiss and all the lights in the office went out, one after the other. Jenny sat in the dark to wait.

She and Billie Starr were late for Bob Butz's family bonding dinner, but it didn't matter. The Brown Derby waiting area was packed and hot with bodies and the slight young hostess told Bob it would be ten minutes, maybe twenty, before they could be seated. Bob, who'd made the reservations, was seriously displeased.

Carla whispered to Vi that the hostess was a Leffert, some relation to Randall undoubtedly. Just look at those ears.

"Everyone in this town is a Leffert or related to one," Vi whispered back.

Including Billie Starr, Jenny thought. Stuck in a corner with Vi

and Carla and a very scratchy fake plant, she just wanted the whole evening to be over.

Vi had been invited to join them—probably because she was to be matron of honor—and accompanying her was Ed, her Wakarusa bail bondsman. He was a swarthy man with a small head and huge, painful-looking belly, which he kept rubbing with his right hand in smaller and smaller circles. Next to Ed was Lyd and next to her was Billie Starr. Billie Starr showed Lyd her new gloves, a pink sparkly pair she'd picked up at the church on Filbert Street. That trip was what made Jenny late. The old lady in charge of running the clothing bank insisted on showing them down into the church basement herself and then, when they got to the room where the winter clothes were stored, the door was locked and she couldn't remember where she'd put the key. A half hour elapsed before she found it under a coffee mug. Then Billie Starr took her sweet time picking out her gloves, trying on pair after pair after pair, before finally settling on the pink ones because, she said, they were "distinctive." Lyd acted like they were the most amazing things she'd ever seen. The two of them were completely ignoring Jenny. That wasn't all that out of the ordinary. Jenny often felt like a third wheel in their company. Sometimes she suspected that Lyd, with all her ambitions and strong opinions, understood Billie Starr better than she did.

"I am most seriously displeased," Bob told the hostess again, self-importantly patting his perm.

"I'm sorry, sir." The hostess was busy with menus and napkins and silverware. Her cheeks were flushed and there were beads of sweat on her upper lip. "We had to accommodate a large party just now and that's why we're a little behind."

"Did this large party have reservations?" Bob asked.

The girl blinked at him and dropped a spoon.

"I'll take that as a no."

"We'll get you in as soon as we can."

"Not good enough," Bob said. "Not good enough. In fact, un-acceptable." He turned and surveyed the room, a beige, inoffensive purgatory, yeasty odor of bread and old deodorant hovering. "Is customer service dead?" he asked. "Is this really the best we can hope for in this day and age?"

No one answered him. Kids hid behind their parents' legs. Parents pursed their mouths. An old couple occupying the area's only bench mumbled something about manners and meat loaf.

Carla and Vi clearly didn't mind the delay. They were too busy with wedding planning to care about something as minor as some-one stealing their dinner reservation. While Jenny counted ceiling tiles, they discussed catering options ("I want elegant," Carla said, "Chinese, maybe, or just really small food of some kind; small food is always elegant"), the flowers—orchids (expensive, inconvenient) and roses (too boring?) versus carnations (tacky?) and irises (but aren't those for funerals?)—and the song for Carla and Bob's first dance.

"He suggested 'Stand by Your Man,' can you believe it?"

"You're kidding."

"Although I do stand by him, of course."

"Sure you do, but that's not danceable."

"That's what I said, Vi. I said, 'That's not danceable.' Too fast for a slow dance, too slow for a fast dance. Right?"

"Right."

Carla and Vi also debated the matter of DJ versus live band—Carla was in favor of a band but Vi said they could be unpredictable and on drugs—as well as white cake versus chocolate ("White," Vi said, "seems more bridal somehow") and whether or not Carla should take Bob's last name.

Carla seemed to be on the fence about the name change. As eager as she was to get rid of "Newberg," "Butz" wasn't so great either. "But 'Mr. Stand by Your Man' is traditional, so . . ."

"I guess you don't really have a choice."

"It'll be nice to put those Newbergs behind me. You know how I feel about those people."

"Ooh boy, do I."

"They've shunned me, my own husband's family," Carla said. "They've straight up shunned me just for loving Pete the best I could."

"The best you could."

"And he wasn't easy to love."

"A difficult man if ever there was one."

Carla looked like she wanted to say something more, presumably about Pete's being difficult, but at that moment she had one of her coughing fits and could only wheeze and sputter. When she could speak again, she bumped Jenny backward with a bony hip. "Stop crowding me, girl. You're taking all my air."

"Sorry," Jenny said. Twenty-one ceiling tiles. Twenty-two, twenty-three, twenty-four . . .

"Hear that?" Carla asked Vi, thumbing Jenny over her shoulder. "'Sorry.' That's all my daughter says these days. Sorry sorry sorry. She might as well be that old board game."

Vi laughed. "Do not pass go, do not collect two hundred dollars."

"Wrong game but right idea." Carla shook her head and scooted close to Vi again, her husky voice low and conspiratorial. "Enough about me. What's Ed's story? Could we be headed for a double wedding?"

Vi pulled on the collar of her dress, talked into it. "I just can't tell," she said. "He's so mysterious."

Ed was still rubbing his belly. With the other hand, he scratched at a neck pimple, made a low humming sound, then checked his fingernail for pus.

"One can only wait and hope," Vi said.

"Us women," Carla said. "We have it hard."

"The hardest."

Jenny was counting her thirty-fifth ceiling tile when the pretty hostess called out "Butz, party of seven! Butz, party of seven!" as if Bob weren't standing right in front of her. The kids in the waiting area giggled. Even their parents smiled. Carla raised her eyebrow at Vi like see? See what I'm up against? The table the hostess showed them to was at the back of the restaurant, by the bathrooms, and Bob's displeasure only increased.

"The worst spot in the whole place," he said.

The hostess looked pained and, like Jenny, eager to escape. "It was our first available, sir."

Carla sat down, motioning for Bob to join her. "This is a party, honey bear. Let's just be happy."

Bob smiled tightly and sat down next to Carla. "You're right, sweet tart. We're here to celebrate. To celebrate family." He rearranged his face into an expression of contentment, of bounty to bestow, puffing his rather small chest. "Everyone, please, order whatever you want. Tonight, I'm sparing no expense. Let's eat, drink, and be merry."

There was no good place to sit. Billie Starr was sandwiched between Lyd and Ed the bail bondsman. Then came Vi and Carla. Jenny, hanging back, ended up in the spot nearest the men's room, with Bob Butz to her right and an empty chair to her left.

"Thanks so much for coming tonight," Bob said to her, shaking a napkin out over his khaki lap. "It means a lot to me and your mother."

"Billie Starr and I wouldn't miss it," she lied.

"I've always wanted to be a grandpa and a dad and here I am, getting doubly blessed in one fell swoop." Bob winked at Jenny. "I suppose you've had your suspicions all along, eh? I told your mom, I told her, 'That daughter of yours knows what's up. She's onto us.' Didn't I, Carla? Didn't I tell you?"

Carla wasn't listening. She'd lit a cigarette and was studying the menu with a pirate's squint.

"Well, anyway," Bob said, "I'm sure you knew about our love affair before anyone, you being so perceptive and all."

"I had no idea," Jenny said. "I didn't know you were dating."

Bob opened his own menu, ran a beefy finger down the list of appetizers. "I see. Well, that's fine then." His finger stopped at loaded potato skins. "That's just fine."

Jenny had assumed that he would avoid talking to her out of embarrassment. The last time the two of them had seen each other was when he was firing and threatening her. Instead, over the course of the hour-long meal, he appeared determined to engage her as much as possible. He began by chronicling Carla's many assets—her hair, her eyes, her legs that "went on for days"—and then moved on to more substantive qualities like her work ethic and toughness, what he called her "mettle."

"Just look at her," Bob said, but his perm was blocking Carla from view. "They don't make women like her anymore."

Jenny had ordered the fish and was now regretting it. The white fillet swam in a pool of butter and parsley, flavorless and limp. She did her best to eat what was on her plate, but it was heavy lifting and eventually she gave up and focused on the bottles of champagne Bob had bought for the table, pouring herself glass after glass until Bob asked if she was okay.

"I'm fine," she said. "Can we get another?"

"Another bottle?" Bob asked.

"Yeah."

"Well . . ." Bob hesitated, glancing at the other glasses, gauging, Jenny assumed, whether another bottle would be necessary, weighing expense against reward. "This *is* a celebration."

"Exactly," Jenny said. "It's like you said—occasions like this don't come around every day."

Bob raised his own glass, cheers-ed her. Then he slapped her back and called for the waiter. "One more bottle of bubbly, if you please, sir. My soon-to-be daughter's a little thirsty tonight, and you

know, I think I'll soon have more than just my marriage to celebrate. Something big."

The waiter, trying to take the order of the neighboring table,
gave Bob a brief up-nod and continued scribbling on his notepad.

Jenny helped herself to another glass of champagne. "Something
big?" she asked Bob.

"Nothing I want to bore you about. Business, is all. Backroom
kind of stuff. But, while we're talking shop, I was wondering if
you might consider coming back to work for me. On a trial basis,
of course, just in case we find that mixing business with pleasure
becomes too tricky."

"Oh, well, thanks so much," Jenny said, "but I just got a new
job, actually."

"Is that so?"

"Yep."

"Doing what exactly?"

"Same stuff I did for you."

"Congratulations."

"Thanks."

The champagne was so sweet it made Jenny's teeth hurt. It tasted
like carbonated grape juice but was going down easier, now that she
was on her fourth or fifth glass. *Why do people drink, Mom?* Because,
Airplane, because Ms. Precocious Petition, they had a long day/shit
week. Because their furnace broke and their mom was marrying a
sexual harassing phony. Because their beloved dad was dead. Because their best friend had every right to say "I told you so." Because
the deadbeat father of their child showed up drunk at their house in
the middle of the night, called them a nothing cunt, and would soon
be suing them for custody. Because people like Ashley Batchelder
existed. Because tuna fish wasn't free and neither was gas or good
coffee or bisque or computers. Because they'd been given a job they
weren't qualified for and weren't sure they could do and, if a certain
sex tape were released to the public, they would be solely respon-

sible for bringing a good man and his entire campaign crashing to the ground. Because life hadn't turned out the way they thought it would, or maybe it had turned out exactly the way they were brought up to expect, and that was worse.

Across from Jenny, Lyd and Billie Starr were playing with pats of butter, which, at the Brown Derby, were shaped like roosters. It was one of the restaurant's claims to fame. Lyd's rooster was hiding behind her water glass. Billie Starr's was crowing from atop her rye roll. Vi, clearly annoyed by their game, picked her teeth with her fork while Ed sawed at his steak, a large, much-marbled T-bone. Once in a while, he volunteered a fun fact about bail bonds—something about the practice dating back to ancient times, another something about having to moonlight as a bounty hunter—and then Vi, stroking his shoulder, informed the table that Ed was a portrait in courage, truly one of the unsung heroes. Other than that, there wasn't much conversation. Carla, who'd hardly eaten anything, was smoking happily, blowing rings out over the table.

Jenny followed the rings' progress as they lost their shape, wobbled into nothing and joined the soft lavender rainbow that spanned the room. The waiter brought a third bottle of champagne, uncorked it with a flourish, and placed it in front of her. She gave him a grateful smile. He grinned back at her, and, not paying attention to what his hands were doing, knocked Bob's water glass into his lap.

Bob jumped up, cursing, slapping at the waiter as he futilely tried to mop up the ice from his crotch. "You're making it worse!"

"I do apologize," the waiter said.

Bob yanked at his perm. "What's happened to this place?

"Sir?"

"The Brown Derby used to be classy. It was the place to go, the place to bring your family for a nice dinner. Where'd the quality go? Where'd the class go?"

"New ownership," Vi said.

"Out-of-towners," Carla agreed. "Double whammy."

The waiter apologized several more times, but Bob continued to fume. It was only when the manager offered the table a free round of desserts that Bob finally calmed down.

Jenny sat through the entire scene at a distant, amused remove, sipping champagne, studying the waiter's strong, pleasing profile. So her smiles still worked. Of course they did. They'd worked on George, hadn't they? And on countless men and boys before them. Maybe her smiles and her peach pie breasts would transport her out of Benson, land her in a better, more exciting place where she and Billie Starr could start over, have a different sort of life. Just one more drink . . .

"Jenny! Jenny Newberg!"

George Shepherd was waving and limping toward her, the halting gait more pronounced than ever in the carpeted blandness of the Brown Derby dining room, his hair and skin dull in fake candlelight. He approached the table warmly, smiling and shaking hands. Billie Starr offered George an enthusiastic high five, introducing him to Lyd and proudly showing him her pat of butter, starting to melt in her fingers. He wiped butter off on his pants and told Lyd it was very nice to meet her. "Any friend of Jenny's," he said. Lyd shot Jenny a questioning look. Like, is this *the* guy? Jenny got very busy with her tasteless fish. Next to her, Bob Butz had stiffened, back, apparently, to being seriously displeased. He ignored George's offer of a handshake and stared straight ahead. His face, unhealthily red, matched his medium rare sirloin.

George parked himself in the empty chair next to Jenny and took a sip from her champagne glass. "So, are we celebrating your new job, Jenny Newberg?"

"New job?" Carla asked.

"I just hired this young woman to be the receptionist at my

campaign headquarters." George pulled a handful of business cards from his breast pocket and passed them around. "I'm running for governor."

Lyd studied the card, one side, then the other, eyebrows raised. Billie Starr started clapping. "Woohoo, Mom! You got it. You got the job."

George patted Jenny's hand. "She got the job."

"We're not celebrating that, though," said Billie Starr. "We're celebrating family, because my grandma is marrying Bob."

"Congratulations!" George said to Bob, who still wouldn't acknowledge him. George leaned forward, tried to get Carla's attention. "And to you, too, Mrs. Newberg."

Carla stamped out her cigarette in her coffee cup and lit another. "Soon to be Mrs. Butz, thank you very much."

George cheerfully took in the room, oblivious—or maybe just indifferent—to Bob's apparent fury. "Place is crowded tonight, eh? I was shocked we were able to get a table with no reservations. The hostess told us we slipped in right under the wire. I'll admit, I might have thrown my name around a bit."

"You took our reservation," Bob growled.

"What's that?" George asked.

"The Derby is not what it was."

"Sorry to barge in on your party." George snuck another sip of Jenny's champagne and squeezed her shoulder. "Was just on my way to see a man about a horse."

He headed for the men's room and the free desserts arrived—brownies drizzled with raspberry sauce, a scoop of vanilla ice cream on the side. Jenny guzzled more champagne. One more glass couldn't hurt. And another. And then just a teeny bit for the road. Like Kool-Aid, this stuff, she thought. Like fizzy water. While everyone but Jenny and Carla dug into their desserts—Carla was, she announced, trying to lose weight for the wedding—the waiter

brought the check. Bob grudgingly left him a five-dollar tip. No one asked Jenny about George or the job. The table became a feeling, the room a cloud she could float away on. George must have walked by again on the way to his own table, but Jenny missed him. As the dinner slid toward its inevitable end—gravy-stained napkins, greasy plates, atmosphere of letdown, of disappointment—she closed her eyes. Conversation washed over her, none of it important.

So full. Why'd I eat so much?

Not even that good.

That's what I thought. Not worth the calories.

My meat loaf was burned. Stingy with the salad dressing even.

I told you, new owners.

From Ohio, they say.

Oh, Ohio.

And the chef's from Florida, so.

The brownie was yummy, though.

Billie Starr, put down that butter rooster, you're making a mess. I hope you'll act like a lady at my wedding and not a hooligan.

Hooligan. Billie Starr repeating *hooligan*. I like how that sounds, Grandma. Hooligan.

You can like how it sounds but don't be what it is.

Jenny opened her eyes on a yellow blur. People stood up. Chairs were pushed in. Hugs happened. A wet kiss landed on her cheek. Billie Starr put on her new gloves and waved at her. Jenny waved back, or she thought she did. Were those her hands? How was her hair? Why was her nose so cold? Who was that behind her, fussing? Where, someone was asking her, is your coat? "Don't you know it's freezing out? Don't you know it's snowing?"

*L*ight came through the gap in her blackout curtains white and harsh. Jenny squinted at the beam, the dust spiraling inside it, her eyes a desert, her head sloshy and sore. Billie Starr was in the door-

way, fully dressed, backpack over one shoulder, new gloves on and everything.

"Get up, Mom. Get up. We're late. Again."

Jenny raised herself up on her elbow and quickly fell back against the pillows. Wave of nausea. Mouth sticky. Sour grape taste on her tongue and filmy teeth. "How late?"

"It's already eight. I've tried to wake you up like five hundred times."

"Sorry."

"Lyd said you'd be like this today."

"Lyd? When did Lyd say that?"

"She said you'd say that, too."

Jenny took a deep breath. Spinning, the world. At first, anyway. Her dresser and side table and closet door rotated on a dial, refused to stay still. Then the room stopped its whirling and began to jerk up and down instead. Piston motion, like an earthquake. Billie Starr sighed, studied her reflection in Jenny's vanity, her sharp face pale and irritated. Jenny concentrated on her daughter's slim frame, tried, through sheer effort of will, to get her to stop moving. It didn't work.

"Lyd drove us home," Billie Starr said. "You were too drunk. You could hardly walk."

"Oh God."

"She drove us in our car so you'd have it here and Bob Butz and Grandma followed us so he could take Lyd back to her car at the restaurant." Billie Starr stopped for breath. "It was all very complicated. Lyd told me you wouldn't remember anything, that I'd have to fill you in. That's what I'm doing."

Jenny rolled over, enjoyed the dark coolness of her sheets. She just needed a little more time. Twenty minutes, a half hour, to steady herself. Then a shower and coffee. Maybe some dry toast.

Billie Starr plunked down on the side of Jenny's bed. The mattress swelled, then sank. "You kept telling Lyd that they didn't pay

you. They didn't pay you, you said. You did it all for nothing. Who's they? And what did you do for nothing, Mom?"

Into the pillow: "I'll tell you when you're older." These pillows are my true love. I will never leave them.

"I hate that answer."

"What else did I say?"

"A lot of stuff about how you needed to take the job with George even though it's crazy because Dad is suing you for something."

"I did? I told Lyd that?"

"Uh-huh, and she said she told you years ago to get a lawyer, but you said you didn't have enough money for a lawyer. Are lawyers really expensive?"

Jenny raised herself up on her elbow, tried to meet her daughter's intense gaze. More waves. She dropped down again. "Yes."

"Is that true? That we don't have enough money to hire a lawyer? And what is suing anyway?"

"Don't worry about it. I have everything under control."

"It doesn't look like you have everything under control."

"Looks can be deceiving."

"Mr. Richardson told us that the other day. He was reading us a story and the book he was reading had an ugly, beat-up cover and he said, never judge a book by its cover, that pretty things can sometimes be ugly inside and vice versus. When he said that, he looked right at me. Mom, am I ugly?"

Jenny was up now. She'd managed to foist herself out of bed and was fumbling through her dresser drawer for a bra and underwear. Her nightgown stuck to her and gave off an odd smell. She ducked into her closet and stepped out of it. Clothes. A monumental challenge. She stumbled on a pair of heels, jarred her shoulder against the doorjamb. The bra clasp refused to cooperate. The pair of underwear she'd grabbed was period-stained and had two holes near the waistband. Better than nothing. She'd told George she'd be at the office by nine.

"No, honey. You are not ugly."

"How do you know?"

"I just know."

"How do *I* know you're not just saying that because you're my mom?"

"I wouldn't lie to you."

"But you lie to other people."

"You're not other people."

"Well, no. I'm me." Billie Starr, back at Jenny's vanity, held a pair of earrings up to her unpierced lobes, shook her head, picked another pair. "Why did you get drunk at Bob Butz's family bonding dinner?"

Skirt or pants? That was the real question. Shirt or sweater? "I don't know."

"I think Lyd was mad at you."

Jenny tossed the bra aside. Commando, today. With a jacket.

"She said you really should have called her back, and then she helped us both into bed."

"That was nice of her."

"Lyd's always nice. She's my friend."

"She is."

"Grandma was pretty mad at you, too."

"Because I was drunk?"

"Yeah."

"Like she has room to talk."

"Why would someone need room to talk? Talking doesn't take up much space."

"If it did, you'd need to walk around with a football field attached to your face."

Jenny pulled a pair of pants and a blouse from their hangers without seeing them. Did they match? Who cared? She just needed to cover herself. From the room, silence. No chatter. Still buttoning her shirt, Jenny stepped out, bare foot coming down hard on a hairpin.

"Fuck fuck fuckety fuck fuck."

Still nothing from Billie Starr, who never missed a chance to judge Jenny for her foul mouth. She was at the window, looking out on Acorn Street. Tapping her fingers against the glass in rhythm with the blinking yellow sign outside, she bit her lip and scrunched up her eyes, obviously trying hard not to cry. Crying wasn't something Billie Starr did very often. She'd always been a stoic child, and Jenny was sorry she'd said what she said, wanted to take it back, but she was too hungover to do even that. She couldn't hold on to a feeling for long. It was soon replaced by dizziness and vertigo and a roar in her ears that was like the sound of Pete's saw back on the rare day when he worked from home—wheel spinning so fast it looked almost stationary, dust flying, Pete in goggles grinning in the gloom. Jenny put her hand over her heart. It was galloping strangely. How to even get started this morning? She'd simply have to do it.

"Give me five minutes," she told Billie Starr.

Billie Starr was stubbornly maintaining her silence. She crossed her arms over her chest and stalked out of the room, light-up shoes sparking red against the wood.

Jenny stood in front of her vanity mirror, wrestled some silver hoops into her ears, thought about a belt. Black or red? Her shirt was pink. Red, definitely. While she accessorized, she mumbled to herself, grousing about her luck, her choices, her life, telling the mirror that if she hadn't had Billie Starr, if she'd followed Lyd's advice and aborted her, she would not be in the position she was in, broke, struggling, all but desperate. If she were childless, she could do what she wanted, which was not drive a kid to school for the five gazillionth time. And not just any kid. Her kid—Billie Starr Newberg, the know-it-all nitpicker who never met a question she wouldn't ask, who, when Jenny made a mistake, outright refused to let it go. Child as bad cop, as anchor, as ballast, as pain in the ass. And yes, she was ugly, but maybe she'd grow out of it,

and even if she didn't, that was probably for the best because it was the ugly covers, people like Lyd, who succeeded in life, while pretty covers like Jenny got drunk on cheap champagne at the Brown Derby in the middle of the week and couldn't find their stupid hairbrushes.

Jenny gave her reflection a quick once-over—not great, but not horrible, either—and turned around, everything in the room on a sickening, lurching delay. There was her bed, a mess of sweaty blankets, her nightstand—dusty—the painting of a potted plant she'd picked up at a garage sale, also dusty, her window, cobwebs in one corner, her closet, the hairpin, the belt she'd decided against. There was the doorway to the hall. She should walk through it. That's what she should do, but Billie Starr was standing on the threshold again, actual tears coursing down her cheeks.

"How long have you been standing there?"

Billie Starr's skin was a mix of fish belly white and painful pink blotches.

"What did you hear?"

Her daughter chewed on her lips, snot ballooning out of one nostril.

"I didn't mean it, okay? I'm just in a bad mood."

Again, nothing. No movement. No words. No sound of any kind, really. Only tears and a scowling face.

"I was just talking to myself. I'm sorry. Really, honey—"

Billie Starr didn't let her finish. She stalked off a second time and was swallowed up in the dark of the hall. Jenny followed slowly behind, stopping once to lean against the wall, to breathe. Under her right hand, a new ding in the plaster. Where had that come from? Jenny ran her fingers over the spot, stuck her thumb in. A perfect fit.

Billie Starr had flung open the front door and left it to let in the cold and the cats. There were Gertrude and Yo-Yo again, kitty clockwork, mewing pathetically, their coats stiff with ice.

"Fine. Fine. Come in. I can't fight you today." Jenny hurried to the kitchen, opened two cans of tuna, gagged, and filled a serving bowl with water, set all of it down in front of the refrigerator where a mess wouldn't matter much. The cats came running.

She kept a litter box around for them in the pantry. She pulled it out, kicked it into the middle of the room. "Do your business in there. And stay off the furniture, okay?"

In the driveway, Billie Starr clung to Marcus, who was filling Jenny's gas tank from a red metal can. He'd thrown a lined flannel coat over his flimsy kimono and opted for a pair of rubber boots instead of his usual slippers. No socks, though, and no pants, and his bare skin was chapped and purple. Gas dribbled out onto his right hand.

"Shit, overshot it." He wiped the gas off on his robe and tenderly patted Billie Starr on the shoulder. "Now, what's all this about, little missy?"

Billie Starr shook her head, wiped her face against Marcus's side, accusing eyes on Jenny.

"Maybe I have something that would help." Marcus produced a fifty-dollar bill from his pocket and handed it to Billie Starr. "For your trip to Morocco."

"Chicago," she said.

"Get yourself something nice, okay?"

"Okay."

Jenny thanked Marcus for the gas. "The cash, though," she said. "That's too much."

"It's the least I can do for my favorite girl." Marcus gave Billie Starr another pat. "Learn lots of stuff. Come home even smarter."

"At school or in Chicago?" Billie Starr asked.

"Both," Marcus said. "And take it easy on your mom, okay? It's not easy raising someone as special as you."

"Mr. Richardson says that if something is easy, it's not worth doing."

"Who's Mr. Richardson?"

"My teacher."

"Sounds like a wise man."

"He is," Billie Starr said. "He's really nice. He wanted to date Mom but Mom turned him down so he's dating Terri's mom instead."

Jenny gritted her teeth. "Billie Starr—"

"Ah, romance." Marcus said. "Complicated. Don't I know it?" He grabbed his gas can, spun slowly around, a lost look in his soft eyes. "I feel like I'm forgetting something."

"Gertrude and Yo-Yo?" Jenny ventured. "They're inside."

"Just so they're safe and warm. I'll get out of your hair then."

It had snowed more overnight, enough to cover the wire and most of the dirt from the broken flower baskets. This snow was the heavy kind, wet and soft, packable. Last year around this same time, the three of them had had an impromptu snowball fight right here on the lawn, laughing and pelting each other with wet clods, a mismatched but happy little family. Not today, though. Billie Starr was already in the backseat of the car, strapped in and staring at her newfound wealth, and Marcus was shuffling off toward his house, kimono lifting in the wind. The cats whined at the picture window. Jenny sighed and let them stay where they were. Across the street, the yellow sign was doing its relentless blinking. Today's message: *champagne champagne champagne. Regrets regrets regrets.*

The ride into school was a quiet one. So was the drop-off. Jenny ran Billie Starr to Mr. Richardson's room like she had too many times before, the two of them rushing headlong like usual, the hallways empty, clean, echoing, only instead of playing the sorry and airplane game, they were very much Mom and Daughter, the former asking over and over to be forgiven, the latter refusing to say anything. When they got to Mr. Richardson's door—closed, goddammit— Billie Starr ducked Jenny's hug and moved away, wide mouth set

in an angry line. Jenny felt suddenly sticky with hangover sweat. She would have to talk to Mr. Richardson, explain why they were late again. She knocked on the wooden door, stepped meekly back.

Mr. Richardson peeked his sandy head out. He had chalk on his cheek.

"We're late again," Jenny said. "I'm so sorry."

"Actually, your timing's impeccable." Mr. Richardson smiled at Billie Starr and opened the door to let her in. "I was just starting to read 'A Christmas Carol' to the class."

Billie Starr hustled into the room, pulling off her hat and gloves, shaking out her bright hair. Not ugly. Beautiful. Jenny waved at her daughter's back and told it she'd see her after school. Fake cheer, an act put on for Mr. Richardson's benefit, overcompensating. Very Mummy this morning except for the fact that she probably smelled like old champagne.

Mr. Richardson joined her in the hall, shutting the door quietly behind him and shoving his hands in his pockets. "Do you have a second to talk, Miss Newberg?"

"Sure."

Mr. Richardson moved away from the door, still taking care, it seemed, to not get too close to her. "Is everything okay?"

"With me? I'm fine." She'd forgotten to brush her teeth or put on deodorant and was second-guessing the red belt. "Doing great really."

"That's good to hear. And how's Billie Starr?"

"What do you mean? She's fine, too."

"If I'm being honest, I'm a little worried about her. There's the lateness, of course—"

"That's all my fault," Jenny said. "Believe me, if my daughter could drive, she'd be here on time every day. She'd be here an hour early. She—"

"Principal Mock and I had a short conference with Billie Starr yesterday."

"Why would you do that?"

"We just wanted to make sure that everything was okay at home."

"Everything *is* okay at home."

Mr. Richardson pulled a pen from his breast pocket and started clicking it open and closed. The pen was from Lyd's bank. Jenny had five of those pens in her junk drawer. Everyone in town had that pen.

Jenny steeled herself. "What did she say?"

"Gladys?"

"No. My daughter."

More pen clicking, some rocking back on his shoes. "She said that you're getting a lot of phone calls about missed bills. I gather she's scared that maybe you've run out of money."

"I see."

"And I guess she's been having a lot of stomachaches lately. Headaches, too."

"She never said anything to me about stomachaches or headaches."

"She probably doesn't want to upset you. Billie Starr's a very empathetic little girl."

"And precocious."

"Indeed."

"It's interesting that you would bring all this up with me today, because I just got a new job."

"Oh!" Was there a hint of disbelief in his tone, or did Jenny just imagine it? "Well, congratulations."

"I'm working for George Shepherd. Maybe you've heard of him. He's running for governor."

"That's really wonderful, Miss Newberg. I'm so happy for you."

"Yeah, and I'm wanted back at the office so, if you'll excuse me . . ."

"Of course. I hope I didn't offend you. I just wanted to make sure—"

"I'm not offended."

"Good. If there's anything you or Billie Starr ever need . . ."

"We don't need anything from you."

Mr. Richardson bowed his head and withdrew, opening the door and releasing for a split second the roar of eight-year-olds left on their own. Then the door shut behind him and all was quiet.

Jenny balled her fists. She could tell Mr. Richardson a little something about stomachaches and headaches. There was a sea of red behind her eyes, a tornado swirling in her gut. She supposed Ashley Batchelder's daughter never had to worry about collection agents or drunk dads or broken furnaces and blue hands. And would Principal Gladys Mock have dared quiz a Mummy's child about her homelife without asking permission first? Not a chance. That sort of indignity was reserved for moms like Jenny. The ones with shaky finances. The kind who couldn't afford a lawyer. Jenny had to walk by Gladys Mock's office on her way out. Another wooden door but this one with a brass nameplate at eye level. Jenny let the saliva rise, waited for it to collect in her mouth, aimed. Fired. The spit hit the *G* and snaked down the door. Jenny watched it for a moment, satisfied, sure that if Pete were watching her at that moment from heaven, he would be proud of her. She hocked a second loogie at the *M*. On her way out, she ran into the boy with the pet cockroach. He was huddled near the doors, talking to his palm again. And itching madly behind his ears. Did he ever go to class? Did anyone care where he was?

"Have a good day," Jenny told him. Then she hustled to the parking lot, the cold a relief. It cleared her head. She was over it, the hangover. She was fine. She had everything under control.

"Health care for every family, a no-brainer," Max said. Max was George's chief of staff. A tall man from south Chicago, he cursed a lot and yelled even more and threw things—coffee cups, pens,

staplers. Also, after having told a Republican operative to die a slow and agonizing death, a phone. He was handsome and intimidating and intense. A little scary. Jenny tried not to look at him. "An end to income inequality," he added. "Very doable. Raise taxes, of course, but make it sound like you're not raising taxes. An end to abusive workplace practices—this policy area focused on but not limited to activities that actually endanger workers' lives, i.e., toxic chemicals, unsafe equipment, long hours, general lack of safety protocol, inhumane treatment of assembly line workers, immigrants, immigrant assembly line workers, mothers, minorities, the elderly, the poor, the addicted, the otherwise marginalized. More money for AIDS research. Gun control. Oh hell yeah."

The federal assault weapon ban was obviously a big help here, Max said, but there were still plenty of Uzis that had been grandfathered in. Get those Uzis and AK-47s out of the hands of whackjobs. Get said whackjobs the psychological help they needed instead of throwing them in jail, where they were sure to grow more whackjobby. Criminal justice reform. Did Jenny realize that the majority of Black men in the United States were incarcerated? It was generational racism in action. Speaking of action, affirmative action, very much pro, but this issue took some finessing to convince skeptical, Protestant, work-ethic white Hoosiers. ("Talk about your racism, fuck's sake."). Show said racist white Hoosiers the faces of the movement, the success stories, cute black kids from Gary who'd gone on to make good. Tug at the heartstrings.

"Hey," Ted said from across the office. "I'm one of those kids."

"Wanna be in a commercial?"

"Um, let me think about that for a minute." Ted glanced down at his watch. "No."

"Too bad. You'd look nice on camera."

"While you exploited me to score political points with conservative douchebags?"

"I guess you could put it that way—"

"Again, no."

Max turned back to Jenny. And then, he said, when all that was accomplished, environmental protections to halt and even reverse something called "global warming" and the depletion of "the ozone layer." Regulations to dramatically decrease something else called "greenhouse gases." Greenhouse gases caused global warming and the depletion of said ozone layer, and, if leaders like George didn't do something soon to address both problems, they'd all be living in a desert. No water, no food, no nothing. Nada. Just a hellscape full of zombie people drinking their own piss.

Jenny was writing it all down. Or trying to. She'd mastered her own form of shorthand while working for Bob Butz—he often dictated to her at the end of the day, using the occasions to pace around her and play with her hair as he "brainstormed," and Jenny had always been good at spelling—but Max spoke so quickly and peppered his sentences with so much off-the-cuff commentary that Jenny couldn't keep up. He apologized a few times for throwing a lot at her on her first couple days with the campaign, but George had made it clear that Jenny "knew her stuff" so . . .

"Did you get all that?" Max asked.

Jenny scribbled more notes. A picture of a zombie. A doodle of a urinal. She stopped writing and clasped her notebook to her chest. "Got it."

She was supposed to use what Max was telling her now to draft "an eff-you letter" to the Indiana Chamber of Commerce. Jenny didn't know what the Chamber of Commerce was, but it sounded official and important and like the kind of organization you didn't want to send an eff-you letter to.

Max, though, was adamant, a little giddy. He flopped down at the desk he'd claimed earlier that morning—the biggest one with the newest computer and speakerphone—and wrote the letter for her. He was picky and insisted on composing the bulk of the letters

himself, so all she had to do was type up his handwritten words—scrawled carelessly on coffee-stained yellow legal pads—correct her own mistakes, and send the letters out. "Let's sign it, 'While we're here, fuck yourselves from here to next Tuesday. Your friend, George Shepherd.'"

The rest of George's team—Ted (chief strategist, mild-mannered, very into bow ties and cats and plants) and Hideo (crisis coordinator/technology guru, Hawaiian, high-energy, long-distance runner)—laughed and added their two cents:

Ted: "P.S. May your greed land you in the Seventh Circle of hell."

Hideo: "P.P.S. Your mom says that she admires my policy regarding corn subsidies. And my cock."

George was running as a progressive alternative to the incumbent governor, a good-looking, soft-spoken Democrat with deep pockets and even deeper family connections—his father had been a longtime senator who was almost universally beloved—but to hear Max and Ted and Hideo talk, it was as if there were no incumbent, no Democrat, to beat. The Republicans in the race were the focus because they were such, in Max's words, "craven, ruthless, greedy twat holes." Their platform, Max said, was a study in cruelty. Tax cuts for big business while the poor, working class, and even middle class struggled to pay for basic life necessities like food, shelter, and health care. Environmental destruction in the name of economic prosperity. Blatant hate and discrimination in the name of religion. And so many kickbacks for cronies it'd make Jenny's head spin.

Jenny's head was already spinning. With the campaign team officially moved in and now hard at work, the hours she spent in George's campaign office went by like one long, exhausting dream. She was so busy taking down letters and making calls and filing reports and memos and policy papers—so much filing—that she was forced to do something she hated: ask for help with Billie Starr. Carla would do in a pinch and Marcus in a moment of true desperation,

but Lyd was Jenny's go-to babysitter and by far Billie Starr's favorite. Too bad Lyd considered Jenny an irredeemable idiot at the moment. Jenny knew she had no choice. Shortly after lunch on her first full day working for George, she held her breath and dialed the bank.

Larry Dodge answered, his voice bright at first, interested. Then, when Jenny asked for Lyd, he sighed. "I'm the manager of this bank, and no one ever calls for me. Do you know how dispiriting that is?"

"Sorry, Larry."

"Can't you just pretend that you wanted to talk to me about something important?"

"Like what?"

"Like interest rates."

"So," Jenny said, "what are the interest rates these days?"

"Horrible," Larry said. "I don't want to talk about it."

"But you asked—"

"Do you realize we're in a recession?"

The eff-you letter Jenny typed to the Chamber of Commerce mentioned the recession, but she hadn't really paid attention to that part. "I think I heard something . . ."

"It's a disaster. We're all going to be out on the street by New Year's." Larry sighed again. "Anyway, I'll transfer you."

"Thanks."

To Jenny's immense relief, Lyd agreed to pick up Billie Starr from school, feed her, and help her with her homework. "The math stuff anyway."

"Gertrude and Yo-Yo will need to be let out, too," Jenny said. "You sure you don't mind?"

"Nah. It's a slow day here," Lyd said. "Larry can't be mad if I leave early. There's nothing to do. I almost wish someone would come in and rob us just to keep me awake."

"I'd do it if I could."

"How you feeling today?"

"Me?" Jenny looked down at a letter on her desk. It was from a

labor union organizer at the GM plant in Fort Wayne. Something about a photo op, George taking a tour of the assembly line floor. "I'm fine. Totally fine."

"Not just a teensy bit hungover?"

"Nope. Good. All good."

"Wow. You should be studied," Lyd said. "You were pretty out of your gourd. Speaking of, you know that taking that job was absolutely insane, right? Absolutely fricking certifiable. And I'm not sure about that George guy. The way he just drank from your glass last night, he acted like he owns you or something. It was kind of gross."

Ted was watching Jenny from his desk near the bathroom. She smiled at him. "I have to go."

"Okay, okay," Lyd said. "We'll talk about it later."

"We don't have to."

"We do, though."

"Bye, Lyd."

"Bye, hotshot."

Jenny hung up the phone, started to draft a reply to the man at the GM plant. The campaign office had lost its lackadaisical look, was organized and bustling and mostly clean, thanks in large part to Ted, who was more than happy to help Jenny vacuum and dust and replace the burned-out fluorescent tubes in the overhead lights, the ones that all went out at the same time the day before when the prank caller hung up.

"What else is a chief strategist for?" Ted joked, lemon Pledge in hand. "Seriously, guys, what's my job description again?"

"At least you have things to strategize," Hideo said. "I've been on the job now and George hasn't given me a single crisis to coordinate. Not one."

They chatted for a while about a recent sex scandal involving a Democratic candidate for president. Then they agreed that George was the least likely man on the planet to be accused of having an extramarital affair.

"Do you think George and Brenda do it?" Ted asked.

"Ugh," Hideo said. "I hope not. She'd want to get the dogs in on the act."

"Gives new meaning to the phrase 'doggy style.'"

"Barf, dude."

"And George would insist on delivering a speech on trickle-down economics."

Hideo slunk over to Ted, whipping off his tie. "Oh Roger," he moaned. "Oh Wilfred."

Ted played along. "Ronald Reagan's heartless disregard for the financial well-being of everyday Americans has proven to be the single most harmful economic policy enacted in the history of our republic."

"Supply side gets me so hot." Hideo squirmed, spanked Ted on the ass. "A little to the *left,* Brenda. Not the right. You should know me better than that. Who do you think I am? Henry *Kiss*inger?"

"No, you're Clarence Thomas and you're dying to give me a Coke."

"Come on, girl. That pubic hair isn't gonna drink itself."

They pretended to make out for a while, then broke apart, laughing, smell of imitation lemon hanging in the air.

It was obvious to Jenny that Ted and Hideo adored George and believed in his campaign, but they also made fun of him constantly. They made fun of everything, saving the bulk of their mockery for the men and women who described themselves as "strict family values voters" and dropped by to inquire earnestly into George's stances on things like prayer in schools (against because, according to a contemptuous Hideo, the separation of church and state was obviously a thing enshrined in the First Amendment) and so-called welfare queens, a concept the family values voters seemed very worried about but that Ted dismissed as a pure racist fiction invented by the right to smear hardworking single mothers, most of whom happened to be Black. *Hypocrites,* Max agreed, when the voters,

having been given a bag of free campaign materials, were safely out of earshot. *Fake fucking Christians.*

George wasn't in the office for Ted and Hideo's Kissinger performance. He was in Fort Wayne, giving an interview to a local TV station.

"Flirting with Stephanie Shine," Hideo said.

"Who's Stephanie Shine?" Ted asked.

"Hot blonde from Action News."

"Oh her."

"Yeah her. I wouldn't mind coordinating her scandal."

Like George, Max missed the talk of Brenda and doggy style and hot blondes. He came in at the end and told everyone to get back to work.

"We're not paying you to gossip like girls," he said.

"You're hardly paying us at all," Ted said.

Hideo agreed. "I could make more money as the Churubusco prostitute."

"Hey," Max said, "don't knock her 'til you try her."

Jenny bit her tongue and kept her head down. Meanwhile, the telephones rang constantly, and the fax machine was forever whining atop a table crammed with printer paper, bumper stickers, and buttons. At first, when she answered the phone, Jenny worried about the Black Suits, that they might call the office again and breathe heavily in her ear or, worse, let the cat out of the bag about her and George and their rendezvous at the Riverview, but the sheer volume of callers made it impossible to focus on anything for long. Even though George hadn't officially announced his candidacy, people had obviously gotten the word, and they had a seemingly endless set of demands, most of which were far beyond Jenny's power or pay grade. They wanted promises that George would do this and not that, support this cause, repudiate that one, put speed bumps up on their street, do something about the pollution levels in their local lake, throw someone in jail for stealing their kids' swing set,

free someone else for a crime they didn't commit, declare a state holiday in honor of their dog, declare a state of emergency because their cat had been poisoned. On and on and on, seemingly without end, but Jenny didn't really mind it. The flurry of activity kept her busy, made the time go by fast, gave her the exhilarating sensation of being a part of something bigger than herself. In addition to the eff-you letter to the Chamber of Commerce, she typed up one to a newspaper in Indianapolis about George's refusal to take any money from the oil and gas sector and another to a pharmaceutical giant about his plans to pressure the insurance industry to reduce the prices of popular prescription drugs. She also composed several emails—all to newspapers, most of them in the southern half of the state, the region most likely to go for the Republican challenger—and couldn't help clapping happily when Hideo showed her how to send them over what the team called "the World Wide Web." It was all so exhilarating and new and strange. Either this web thing hadn't existed when she worked for Bob Butz or he wasn't connected to it. Probably the latter, considering Bob's stinginess.

The men never seemed bothered by Jenny's requests for help or clarification. They all gloried in explaining to her the maddening complexities of the copier and just why the Republicans' approach to public health would prove particularly disastrous. The more they talked, the more disconnected Jenny became from the reality she'd always taken for granted. It was as if the woman she'd been before, the one who struggled to afford tuna and considered politics as far removed from her life and untouchable as a distant planet, was replaced by an entirely new woman who cared very much about things like demographics and water quality—or anyway, thought she *should* care—and so when, later that night, she arrived home to find a Pike's Pizza box and half-consumed two liter of Pepsi on the counter and Lyd on the couch watching a nature show, her own house didn't seem real to her.

"Well, look who it is," Lyd said. "Miss Newberg goes to Wash-

ington." She'd traded in her red Wednesday pants suit and power pumps for a jean shirt, corduroy pants, and hiking boots. There was a plate of pizza crusts beside her.

"How was she?" Jenny asked.

"A perfect angel," Lyd said. "She's asleep."

"I owe you." Jenny kicked off her shoes, sat down next to Lyd, nibbled one of the crusts. "Not just for tonight, but for the Brown Derby fiasco, too. I can't believe I got so drunk."

"It was bizarre, wasn't it? Meeting your new boss there, the man you—"

"It was."

Lyd looked for the moment like she planned to linger, so Jenny made a show of yawning, stretching, rubbing her eyes. "I'm so tired," she said. "The last couple days have been a roller coaster."

"Maybe we should trade jobs. Mine's a graveyard."

"Larry seems pretty low."

"It's the recession. I think I saw him sneak some booze into his coffee this morning." Lyd turned the TV off. "Oh. I almost forgot. A man named Kevin Lipshott called."

"Did he say what he wanted?"

"I let the machine get it. He said he needs to talk to you ASAP. Only he didn't spell it out. He pronounced it—A-sap. I hate people who do that. Who's Kevin Lipshott?"

Jenny leaned her head back, closed her eyes. "No one important. Do you think you could do this tomorrow night, too?"

"Speaking of messages, you realize that I've left you, what, three in the last two days? Do you ever listen to your machine?"

"Oh yeah. Sorry about that. I've just been so busy."

"Sure." Lyd brushed crumbs off her shirt, went to the front door. Her voice quavered with sudden anger. "I get it. Time flies when you're sleeping with your boss."

Jenny sat up. "Ouch."

"Please tell me that you're getting a good salary at the very least."

"I'm getting paid on Monday."

"Oh my God, Jenny. You don't even know what they're paying you, do you? You just took the job the same way you agreed to do those Black Suits' bidding, no questions asked."

"It's a real job, Lyd. I thought you'd be happy for me."

"What happens when those Black Suit guys you told me about release the tape they made of you and George?" Lyd asked. "What then? If word gets out, you'll be done in this town. You'll be done, period."

"You're overreacting."

"Am I?"

"Maybe they haven't released that tape because it didn't work. Bad connection or something."

"Jenny."

"Lyd."

"You haven't returned my calls because you know I'm right about this and you don't want to hear it."

"I told you, I've been swamped—"

"And when you finally do call, it's because you want something. It's because you need a babysitter."

"You seemed perfectly willing to watch Billie Starr, acted like I was doing you a favor, getting you out of work."

"That's not the point."

"What *is* the point? If you don't have time—"

"I have time. It's you who doesn't seem to have any time."

Jenny went to the kitchen, poured herself a glass of Pepsi. She drank it too fast. The bubbles were in her nose. "Well, how about we just cut to the chase and you lecture me some more on my poor life choices. I assume that's why you called."

"Actually, no. That's not the reason." Lyd grabbed her coat from the hall hook. "This is how it always plays out, our friendship—me telling you something and you just ignoring it, you just refusing to listen to what I say."

"Seriously?" Jenny dropped her glass in the sink. It cracked up the side, sent shards of glass into the drain. "That's our friendship? That's how you see it?"

"What other way is there? It happens over and over and over."

"The only thing that happens over and over and over is you telling me how to live my life and then, when I don't follow your advice, you get the chance to say 'I told you so.' And you love it. That's what our friendship is. You always being better. And now that I finally have a good job and a chance at something, you can't stand it. You want there to be something wrong with it. You want me to be Jenny Newberg the slacker, the underachiever. If I'm not, then what are you?"

"There *is* something wrong with it. You're working for a man you slept with for some sort of underhanded scheme. This can't end well. Don't you understand? Why aren't you hearing me?"

"I'm hearing you loud and clear as usual."

"Ha ha, Lyd the loud talker. Funny. Really good joke." Lyd was having trouble with her coat. Her hands shook and one of the arms was the wrong way out. "I can't do this tomorrow night," she said. "I have plans. What a shock, right? I know what everyone in Benson thinks about me, what you and Carla have assumed for years. Poor ugly Lyd Butz, right? Hanging around pretty Jenny Newberg like a bad smell."

"I have never said anything remotely like that to you or anyone else."

"Maybe not, but you've thought it, haven't you?"

Sweet on you. How many times had Jenny heard Carla say that, her scratchy smoker's voice equal parts boastful and disgusted. *Since you were kids.* And how many times had Jenny pretended not to believe her?

"It must boggle your mind to realize that I have a life outside of you, but I do and it's great." Lyd gave up on her coat, angrily folded it over her arm. "And believe it or not, pretty only gets you so far in

this world. It doesn't make you worthwhile or interesting or better than anyone else. Pretty doesn't make you special."

"Wow, thanks for that information."

"You're welcome."

"I don't know why we're even fighting right now."

Lyd ran her hand through her hair, bit her lip, shook her head. It was as if she were trying to talk herself out of something. The faucet dripped five times in the interim. "Good luck finding another babysitter," she said. "Good luck with everything." Then she slammed the door so hard behind her that Billie Starr's clay figurines rattled in their cabinet.

Jenny turned the TV on, flopped back down on the couch, nibbled some on the pizza crust, but she wasn't hungry. The mantel clock ticked on relentlessly. *Good luck good luck good luck. Hotshot hotshot hotshot.* The nature show Lyd had been watching was about monarch butterflies and something called "overwintering," and Jenny tried to concentrate on it for a while, to learn something, educate herself, but that was no good, either. She was confused and exhausted and sad and passed out in her clothes, her last conscious thought of Black Suits and black cats, all of them crossing her path again and again and again, weaving, darting, dripping ink until the path wasn't a path anymore, was a shadow with big shoulders and two waving tails, cast by nothing.

*J*enny spent another day at the campaign office filing, typing, copying, answering the phones, and listening to the team argue about how best to hammer the incumbent governor—a "milquetoast nonentity" in Max's words—and the Republican candidates in the press. Also about how to polish George's rather folksy image into something more sophisticated and urbane. As to the latter issue, Ted suggested that a good haircut might do the trick. Hideo thought it came

down to George's relentless kindness. A little more edge couldn't hurt. Max's opinion was that they were all looking at it the wrong way. George's very appeal was a direct result of his aw-shucks reputation. People loved him because he was salt of the earth.

"You mean white," Ted said.

"He can't really change that fact," Max said.

"No," Hideo said, "but he doesn't have to act so white all the time."

"Has he ever listened to a single rap song?" Ted asked. "Or even Janet Jackson?"

Max shrugged. "He likes Oprah."

"Can you all stop talking about me like I'm not here?" George asked. He looked folksier than ever, coming out of the bathroom and adjusting his belt.

"Oprah doesn't count," Ted said.

"Oprah doesn't count?" Max asked. "Tell that to like six gagillion women."

Hideo was staring dreamily into space. "I bet she smells really good, Oprah. Like a tropical island mixed with melted butter and money."

"That's racist," Ted said.

"Is it?"

"Yes."

"I thought I was being nice."

"Jesus."

The office TV was tuned to a speech one of the Republican candidates was giving at an Elkhart RV manufacturing facility about environmental regulations killing small business. Blocky white vehicles stretched to the horizon. George and Max walked over to the TV, watched the candidate work a crowd of pink-faced people holding foam cups of steaming coffee. Wind ruffled the speaker's stiff, gray comb-over.

"What about you, Jenny?" Ted asked. He was watering a cactus he'd brought from home. "How can we remake George's image into something more palatable to the jet-setting Hoosier crowd?"

Jenny didn't feel qualified to weigh in on the question and didn't have to. Ted and Hideo talked over her—and each other—constantly.

"The jet-setting Hoosier crowd?" Hideo scoffed. "The kind that drives buggies, you mean?"

Ted was born in Gary but grew up in Shipshewana, the only Black kid in the entire town. The Amish jokes were all aimed at him. "I quit. I quit with you people."

"Hey," Hideo said. "*You people?* Who's the racist now?"

"What George really needs is a cooler car—"

"That's nuts, not to mention incredibly capitalist—"

"It's more consumerist, but okay, Karl Marx—"

"Brenda's the problem. He needs to dump her for Stephanie Shine."

"Dude, the sexism. I was reading Hannah Arendt the other day—"

"Don't throw Hannah Arendt at me, and besides, I'm not sexist. Most of my friends are women."

"Oh boy. Most of my friends are women. Care to comment, Jenny Newberg?"

Typing typing typing. "No."

Jenny's relative reticence didn't seem to bother them. They were warming to her anyway. That morning, Ted had asked what she thought of a particularly colorful tie, and Hideo told her about a mule ride on his native Molokai that ended in a leper colony, "the prettiest leper colony you've ever seen." Then Ted showed her pictures of his cats, two Siamese, one black with gold eyes like Gertrude and Yo-Yo, and a few of his plants, mostly cactuses. He called them succulents. Jenny listened to them talk but was mostly focused on her work. She had to be. She was barely treading water as it was,

and by dinnertime on Thursday, was so deep into a letter-writing campaign to some of George's top donor prospects that she forgot everything else—the screaming fax machine, her own lack of qualifications, the Black Suits, the fact that she had a daughter and a best friend who were still very angry with her, the fact that said angry daughter was now in the dubious care of Carla, who'd only agreed to watch her that night if she could smoke in the house. Then the phone rang.

Max answered it before Jenny could. She watched his typically intense demeanor melt into one of disbelief. He stared at the receiver for a moment and then hung it up. "The fuck?" he mumbled. Then he hustled to the fax machine and waited, hands on his hips, shaking his head as the paper spooled out.

Ted froze, watering can in hand. "What is it?"

"George!" Max shouted.

George had followed him to the machine. "I'm right here."

Max handed him the fax.

George read the contents silently to himself, passed the paper back to Max. "Ridiculous. Absolutely ridiculous."

"Of course, it is. Rank, amateurish nonsense, but we have to deal with it."

Hideo came rushing over. "A crisis?"

"Don't sound so excited." Max folded up the fax, put it in his pocket. "We need to have a serious conversation about hiring a security detail."

George dismissed the idea out of hand. "Nope. We talked about this. Not interested. It's too expensive and I don't like the optics."

"That was then, this is now. You can't win if you're dead." Max raised his hands, as if to announce the winner of some sort of prize. "Welcome to the show, folks!"

"What show?" Ted asked.

"Yeah," Hideo said. "What did that fax say?"

Max and George ignored them both, sequestered themselves

in the back corner of the office behind the file cabinets and printer paper. Meanwhile, the Republican candidate on the television was wrapping up his speech, growing more and more animated as he challenged his audience to fight back against "the loopy left" hell-bent on destroying everything Americans held dear—their freedom, their love of country, their sacred relationship with God and family. He ended with a prayer in which he implored that God and His beloved son, the savior Jesus Christ, invest His holy warriors with the courage and bravery necessary to counter the pinko commie wave that was coming, the socialist onslaught that threatened to swallow them all up in a sea of politically correct culture, liberal ineptitude, and the blood of a million aborted babies. "We will march," the man roared, "we will fight—to the death if necessary—and we will prevail!" The crowd sent up an amen, spilling coffee and cheering wildly and throwing stocking caps in the air. Hideo flipped the TV off and returned to his desk, sighing.

"I'm the crisis coordinator for this campaign," he complained. "How am I supposed to coordinate if no one tells me anything?"

Ted nodded. "It's like they forget we're even here half the time."

"Think the fax was an assassination threat of some kind?"

"For what?" Ted asked. "Daring to sport bad sideburns? I mean, George is as inoffensive as they come."

"Not if you're a right-wing crazy. You heard that guy just now, railing against the pinko commie wave. George is that wave. We're that wave."

Jenny felt feverish. Hot, cold, then back to hot. Was that a Black Suit on the phone just then? Had he said something about her, the rendezvous at the Riverview with George? The phone rang again. This time, Jenny answered it, heart in her throat. "George Shepherd's office, how can I help you?"

"You don't have to be all Newberg high horsey with me."

"Mom?"

"Glad you can still recognize your own mother's voice."

"Is Billie Starr okay?"

"She might not be for long."

Jenny gritted her teeth. "What do you mean?"

"What I mean is Randall and his girlfriend are on the front stoop right this very minute, demanding they be allowed in to see her."

"Oh no," Jenny said.

"Oh yes."

And Randall, whom Carla described as drunk *and* disorderly (double whammy) was threatening to get the police involved. "You know what that means," Carla said. "The cops in this town are all Lefferts. They'll take Randall's side before you can say thick blue line."

"Stall him. I'll be there as soon as I can. Don't let him in. If you let him in, he'll never leave."

"He's not leaving now."

Jenny's alarm must have shown on her face, because, after she hung up, George, peeking his head over the file cabinets, asked her if that was more "Deep Throat crap." She shook her head, started to shut down her computer. Leaving like this, on just her third day— was that a fire-able offense? George came over, sat on her desk, asked her if she was okay, scuffed loafer swinging. Was something wrong at home? Was there anything he could do? His kindness. It just made her feel worse. She didn't deserve it.

"If you tell me what's up, maybe I can help." George smiled and patted her hand. "I'm well connected, you know. I'm kind of a big deal."

She explained the situation as quickly as she could, too tired, too worried to whitewash. George nodded as she spoke, apologized, said it was all his fault for keeping Jenny at the office so late. Would it help to bring Billie Starr to work with her from now on? Jenny assumed he was joking but he assured her he was completely serious.

Hideo, right then helping himself to a soda and sandwich from the refrigerator, could use Billie Starr's expertise, George said. And the whole team would benefit from her youthful enthusiasm, especially Ted who, with his cats and cactuses and crush on Bea Arthur, was old before his time.

"I heard you," Ted said.

"Good, I wanted you to," George said. Then he put in a quick call to the Benson County sheriff, a friend of his, not a Leffert, and asked him to send a deputy to Jenny's house to scare Randall straight. "That should take care of it."

Much to Jenny's shock, it did. Later, in Jenny's living room, Carla, confessing to having panic-chugged two beers in the span of thirty minutes, reenacted the entire confrontation. She made Jenny be Randall so she could be the cop, whom she described as a "stone-cold dreamboat." Carla/Dreamboat Cop jumped out from behind a chair and told Jenny to "stick 'em up." Jenny as Drunk Randall was instructed to slide to the floor and crumple into a ball, shrieking "don't shoot don't shoot don't shoot!" Then Carla grabbed Jenny's robe from the hall hook and sloppily tied it around her waist, waving her arms and hollering about her rights, her rights, her civil rights.

"I'm Randall's girlfriend now," Carla explained. "Eileen. You wouldn't believe your eyes if you saw her, dear daughter. Old, dumpy, and sour. Randall Leffert is scraping the bottom of the barrel. Anyway, this Eileen person kept insisting that Dreamboat Cop radio his supervisor, but Dreamboat Cop stood his hot ground. He gave her the what-for on civil rights, I'll tell you that much. Then Randall and his ugly other half just drove away. They had to. Dreamboat Cop was threatening to arrest them if they didn't." Carla was impressed by Jenny's new boss in spite of herself. "It's always good to know people who know people. I dare the Lefferts to crow over us after this. And the Newbergs, too. In their face. In their snobby, self-righteous face."

As exciting as the evening had obviously been for her, Carla was still relieved when Jenny told her she wouldn't need her to watch Billie Starr the next night. Babysitting had really cut into her wedding planning, she said. It was like a full-time job—choosing the florist and the caterer and colors—but she was determined. No generic "I take thee for my awful wedded blah blah blah" for her.

"My wedding to your father was about as blah as it got," Carla said. "This one is going to be different. I want it to knock Benson's collective socks off. Speaking of socks, I told Billie Starr she'd have to wear tights under her flower girl dress and she pulled a face a mile long. She could use a crash course in good manners, dear daughter. That's not my job. That's yours."

Jenny gently nudged Gertrude and Yo-Yo out onto the porch and walked Carla to her car. Carla paused, hand on the driver's-side door. "I've been thinking a lot about stamps lately," she said.

Snow began to fall, soft flakes that dissolved like sugar in water the minute they hit the ground. According to Billie Starr, an idea that Jenny had grown up with—that every snowflake was unique—was a myth. A lot of flakes were duplicates, just like the others. It made Jenny sad somehow, knowing that. *Pretty doesn't make you special.*

"Stamps?" Jenny asked.

"The ones that will go on my invitations. Do you think I should spring for the 'Love' ones? I mean, they're just going to end up in the trash. On the other hand, they send a message, don't they?"

"What kind of message?"

"That Bob and I are classing things up a bit, that our wedding is going to be nice, a real do, not your cheapskate American Legion shotgun affair that everyone else settles for around here."

"Go with the 'Love' ones then."

"They're twice as expensive as the flags."

"I thought all stamps cost the same."

"Show's what you know."

"So, it's the flags, I guess?"

Carla sighed. "Thank God I have Vi to talk to about these things. *She* gets it. And she isn't afraid to have actual opinions, unlike some human weathervanes I know."

Having said her say, Carla climbed in her car and roared away, front windows each open a crack, cigarette smoke and the first few lines of a twangy country song snaking out. Jenny couldn't quite place the tune, couldn't tell if it was a male or female voice lamenting a lost love and a cursed life, but it sounded familiar, reminded her of being Billie Starr's age, of what it was like to be a small girl caught in Carla's angry orbit, being punished for doing something Carla's younger self never would—crying in public, peeing her pants, having the affrontery to speak when not spoken to. Across the street, the yellow sign blinked on and on. *Love stamp love stamp love stamp. Crisis crisis crisis.*

Over breakfast the next day, Jenny told Billie Starr about George's invite to join her at the office after school. Billie Starr said haughtily that she'd think about it.

"You can't think about it. You have to come with me."

"Why?"

"I don't have a babysitter lined up for you."

"I'm not a baby."

"I'm aware of that."

"I can sit myself."

"You're too young."

"I want Lyd again then."

"What's wrong with Grandma?" As if she didn't know.

"She smokes all the time and drinks stinky beer and watches bad TV."

"How about this? How about you be a good girl and come with me to George's office like I'm asking you to do?"

"Like you're *telling* me to, you mean."

"Fine, I'm telling you, but that's one of the fun parts about being an adult. You get to tell kids to do things while you, the kid, get to live a charmed life of no responsibility."

Billie Starr wouldn't eat the cereal Jenny poured her. She pushed it away, flipped through her library book, which seemed to be about different dog breeds. "This boy at school, he looks like a greyhound. Fast and pointy. His name is Judd Pickens. He's been suspended."

"For what?"

"Spitting on the principal's name or something stupid like that."

Jenny grabbed Billie's bowl and took it to the sink, rinsed it out. She thought of the boy with the pet cockroach and stringy black hair. Fast and pointy. "Spitting on the principal's name?"

"On a brass thing outside her office. I don't know. It's dumb."

"Pickens. I'm not familiar with any Pickens."

"He's from Mississippi. His grandpa made countertops like Grandpa Pete and he got sick. A lung thing, too. Judd and his family moved here to take care of him. He died last week."

Gertrude and Yo-Yo were staring at Jenny from a spot below the window. Blinking eyes very judgmental. "That's too bad."

"I know Judd didn't do the spitting but he's really poor and sometimes he smells and so people are always accusing him of bad things. They suspended him because they'd already given him like four detentions and bathroom duty. They ran out of other ways to punish him. When I'm president of the world, I won't allow that to happen. I'll make sure there's real justice for everyone, even ugly people. Ugly covers." Billie Starr shut her book and slid it into her backpack. "It must be so difficult for you, Mom, trying to figure out what to do with me, who should watch me and where to take me, especially when you didn't even want me in the first place."

"Billie Sta—"

"Dad wants me, though. He came over last night to see me. He has a girlfriend named Irene."

"Eileen."

"I bet she wants me, too." Billie Starr slung her backpack over one shoulder. "Did I tell you? Judd Pickens and I are writing a book together. We're calling it *The Book of Sorries* because you and his mom are always apologizing for things but nothing ever gets better. It's going to be a bestseller."

"You'll make a lot of money then."

"We're not doing it for the money. We're doing it for the good of the world."

Jenny fed the cats, drove Billie Starr to school, and dropped her off without incident. Then she sat in the parking lot for several minutes, trying to get up the courage to walk right into Gladys Mock's office and confess to being the nameplate spitter. "It was me," she rehearsed in her car. "I spit on your nameplate. Me, Jenny Newberg, poor, hungover single mother, not Judd Pickens, poor, smelly scapegoat boy. It's not our fault we're poor. It's the fault of the system. I know all about the system now. George and Max and Ted and Hideo are teaching me and it's bad. It's corrupt. Capitalism kills." But in the end, she didn't do it. She knew she'd have an enormous stack of faxes waiting for her back at office, not to mention a slew of phone calls to return. There was no time, and she didn't have the courage anyway, so she left. She left Judd Pickens to his own devices, arriving at the campaign office just as Ted was coming out. He held the door open for her, asked if she might want to join him for a cup of coffee.

"There's a really good shop a block from here."

Jenny thought of her empty wallet, her soon-to-be overdrawn checking account. Everyone in the office seemed to drink coffee constantly, to need it to function. She'd already had more cups in her first week with the campaign than she normally had in a month. "No thanks. I should really get to work."

"Come on," Ted said. "Don't make me go by myself."

"Well—"

"I'll buy. And I have juicy gossip."

"About what?"

"That fax that came in yesterday. The one that made Max and George shit their pants."

A long black car drove slowly by them then, window rolling down, then up. Was that a head of steely gray hair Jenny saw? Or was she being paranoid? Just because you wore a black suit didn't mean you drove a black car.

"If you come," Ted said, "I can expense it."

Jenny relented. She was curious about the contents of the fax. Curious and full of dread. She still felt like two different people— the woman who filed papers on George's infectious disease strategy (under *D* not *I,* because the disease folder was a catchall) and the furious spitting woman with no coat who'd prostituted herself at a cheap motel and was desperately waiting for her first paycheck to clear and the other shoe—black—to drop.

The café was in an old house behind the post office. It was small and warm and quiet. Paintings of covered bridges and cute signs about caffeine and muffin tops lined the butter-yellow walls. A man in a bowler hat greeted Jenny and Ted enthusiastically from behind a baker's case full of pastries, bagels, and doughnuts. The place was empty otherwise. They found a table by a bay window and an elaborate model train display of an old-fashioned Christmas village. The track and strands of lights wound up a wooden mountain to a mini–North Pole, colored bulbs blinking along the way like tiny checkpoints.

The glow gave Ted a halo. "Christmas," he said. "Shit. I haven't bought a single present. Have you?"

"No."

"I understand you have a daughter to play Santa for."

"I do. And she's mad at me."

"What for?"

Jenny squirmed. That ugly comment. Why did she have to say that? She was no better than Carla. "A lot of things."

"Don't let it back up on you too much. When I was a kid, I used to get mad at my mom all the time, but you know what? She's one of my best friends now. She got me this." Ted proudly straightened his tie—a satin, diamond-shaped bow decorated with blue donkeys. "She thinks working for George is a dead end, but she's voting for the other guy, so . . ."

"The Republican?"

"Dear God no. The incumbent. She's worked with him some. They're friends of a sort. Mom's a lawyer, big into women's rights. My family's all pretty political. Being Black in Indiana will do that to you."

The man in the bowler hat brought their coffee. Jenny took a sip without thinking, burned her tongue.

Ted blew on his. "And Asian, for that matter. Hideo and me, we met at IU. We were in student government together. Max came to campus one summer, recruited us to help Jacobs Junior with one of his reelection campaigns. I don't have to tell you what a legend Jacobs is."

"Sure, yeah," Jenny said. "Jacobs."

"Anyway, it was Max who convinced us to hitch our wagon to George's star. He said it might be dim now but watch out. And now here we are." Ted ripped the tops off three sugar packets and emptied them into his coffee all at once. "You know, George never said where he found you."

"Oh, he didn't find me exactly."

"What do you mean?"

"More I found him."

"Where?"

"In a grocery store."

"You're joking."

What had the Black Suits told her to say? "He's a great public person. Magnetic."

"George, magnetic?"

"I used to follow his career from far away."

"It might have been better for you if you'd kept your distance." Ted looked around the café—still empty—and lowered his voice. "So, whoever sent that fax, whoever called yesterday, is claiming to have possession of a tape of George doing something . . . let's say *untoward,* with a woman who is most certainly not Brenda."

"Untoward?"

"Uh-huh, and they're threatening to give the evidence to all the local TV stations and newspapers and basically blow up the campaign unless—get this—George pays them fifty thousand dollars."

"Fifty thousand dollars?" That would buy her entire house.

"It's obviously insane. We're operating on a shoestring as it is. Doesn't help that a big donor Max was counting on yanked his support. By the way, want to come with me and Hideo to the plasma donation site next week?"

"What's plasma?" Jenny felt like Billie Starr, peppering poor Ted with so many questions.

He shook his head. "Stick with us and you'll find out. It's almost too ironic. Here Hideo and I were just joking about George getting embroiled in some sort of sex scandal and in comes this creepy fax. Guess that's what Max meant when he said 'Welcome to the show!'"

In which I'll have the honor of playing the part of the villain, Jenny thought. Or the idiot. Or both. She tried to take another sip of her coffee but the lump in her throat wouldn't let her. If the tape came out before she got paid by the campaign, she'd be worse off than she was before the Black Suits found her. Not just desperate and out of choices, out of chances, but disgraced. Done. Period. And it sounded like Monday's paycheck was guaranteed to be underwhelming at best, probably wouldn't even cover a computer, let alone a mortgage payment. Why was Lyd right about everything?

Ted was eyeing her closely. "Wait. Don't tell me you think there's some truth to the whole thing? That George is embroiled in a seedy, clandestine affair?"

"No, of course not." Jenny shuffled her feet. Grains of sugar under her soles. Soggy paper packets, too.

"Yeah, me neither, but, just in case, he's agreed to let Max hire a security detail. I guess there've been a few answering machine messages of a vaguely threatening nature. Max thinks they're threatening anyway, so a couple cops who typically work the night shift are going to follow George around for a while."

"That's good."

Ted raised an eyebrow.

"Isn't it?"

"I'm not all that happy about the prospect of having the police around all the time."

"Why?" Jenny asked.

Ted was not laughing anymore. No joke. Dead serious. "They kill people like me."

"People like you?"

"Jenny. Are you really that naive?"

"Maybe these cops will be the good kind."

"I wish I believed that kind existed."

Jenny considered the cops she knew. Tony Leffert, Randall's cousin, had spent a lot of high school harassing Lyd because she refused to go out with him. He TPed her house on weekends, got his friends to throw food at her during lunch. He was a lieutenant now. And Fred—Randall's uncle and the Benson police chief—was more than happy to tell Jenny every time he pulled her over for a minor traffic infraction that the only reason she was getting off with a warning was because she was young and cute and "a known quantity." Ted was most definitely not a known quantity around here.

He finished his coffee, took two dollars from his wallet, and anchored the bills to the table with his empty cup. "Ready to head back?"

"Ready." She followed him outside, where a line of schoolchildren, dressed as shepherds, angels, and wise men, plodded behind an extremely tall nun hollering for order. An icy rain had begun to fall, and the kids, heads down, shivered in their robes.

"Joseph!" the nun shouted. "Get your finger out of your nose. And Mary, stand up straight."

A girl in robin's-egg blue snapped to attention, and, in doing so, dropped a doll on the sidewalk.

The nun grabbed the doll and stuffed it inside her habit. "Be more careful with the baby Jesus, or I will replace you in the program faster than you can say 'Holy Ghost!'"

"Forget a security detail," Ted whispered. "George should hire that lady."

Jenny caught the eye of the little girl, gave her what she hoped was an encouraging smile. The girl stuck her tongue out at her. Then she walked off with the rest of her class, smirking and pretending to pray.

The campaign office was full of people and noise and dripping umbrellas. Jenny didn't have time to check the fax machine or even turn on her computer. Max rushed her the moment she was in the door, asked if she wouldn't mind meeting with a few people who'd dropped in unexpectedly, hoping for an audience with George.

"He's double booked at this point. Fuck, he's triple booked." Max handed Jenny a letter from a woman with Hoosiers for Healthy Families. "She's going to want you to promise that if George is elected, he'll push for big bumps in the Medicaid and food stamp budgets. Tell her that while you, Jenny Newberg, obviously can't promise anything, George is definitely on the side of expanding health care access to everyone in the state and that he's a firm believer that a good life begins with good nutrition, that his voting record reveals a man clearly committed to the needs of the disadvantaged, especially children, blah blah blah. Improvise if you have to. Got it?"

"Got it."

"Once you get rid of this"—Max read the letter over Jenny's shoulder, motioned to a proud-looking woman in a navy blue skirt suit, sitting very straight in a chair near the front door—"Regina Hoffman person, I need you to chat with a couple of guys from the city about today's setup. The stage for the speech and whatnot. They're really into bunting, I guess. Who cares? Let them have their fucking bunting."

"Yes, sir."

Max squinted at her. "You look nervous."

"Not at all. I'm fine."

"Good, because it's all hands on deck at this point."

Jenny invited Regina Hoffman to join her at her desk, did her best to assure Regina that, while she, Jenny Newberg, couldn't promise her anything, George firmly believed that poor kids deserved good food and access to health care. "Maybe even more than other kids."

Regina crossed her legs, dark hose hissing. "Excuse me?"

"I just mean that George's voting record speaks for itself."

"We don't think it does. We want a guarantee that George will advance our cause, or he won't get our endorsement. It's that simple."

"Like I said, it's not my place to give you any guarantees, but—"

"Then why am I meeting with you? Seems to me that if Mr. Shepherd were truly committed to eliminating poverty in the state of Indiana, he would have had time to tell me so himself."

Jenny opened the top drawer of her desk, closed it. Opened the bottom one. Closed it, too. Stalling. "I think it's so great, how your organization helps people who are struggling—"

"The work is hard, but we keep trying."

"It's such a coincidence that we're talking today because I have a friend who's in a rough spot. Financially." Jenny started to gather up some swag—a button, a bumper sticker—then left them where they were. Regina Hoffman did not look like a woman who

would care about swag. "This friend of mine, she's never used government benefits before. She was embarrassed to try, I think. Ashamed, which isn't right, but people around here, they can be so judgmental, so nosy."

"People everywhere, I imagine."

"Right. Anyway, I was wondering if you could tell me how she might go about applying for, I don't know. Food stamps? Medicare? Things like that."

"Is your friend over 65?"

"Um, no. She's my age."

"Then I think you mean 'Medicaid.'"

"Right. Yes. Medicaid. I'm a bit new to these things—"

Regina Hoffman stood, smoothed her skirt. "With all due respect, Ms. Newberg, the information you seek is not part of my job description."

"No, I know, I'm sorry. I shouldn't have presumed—"

"My work involves meeting with candidates like your boss and gauging their level of support for what we do, and if that level is not, in our opinion, satisfactory, I endeavor to educate the candidate about why and how they might go about changing their stance. Sometimes it takes multiple meetings to iron out our differences. I often meet with five candidates in one day. You might not realize this, but, like Mr. Shepherd, I, too, am very busy, so if your friend's situation does not change for the better, I suggest she contact the state benefits office directly."

Jenny could feel the blush at her hairline. "Thank you. I will."

"Please also inform George that he'll be hearing from us, and he might not like what we have to say."

Ted walked by just as Regina Hoffman was showing herself out. "That go okay?"

"Definitely," Jenny lied. "It went really well. They're getting back to us."

Her time with the Churubusco city councilmen was more

successful. Both in their early seventies, white, faded, and bald, they could have been brothers or even twins. Jenny didn't catch their names, couldn't tell them apart. They were, as Max had warned her, very concerned about bunting, and she was happy to be able to inform them that they were free to decorate the podium just as they pleased. Smiling, they settled on eight yards of red, white, and blue draped bunting and three pleated fans of the same. Then they asked Jenny if she could sew some stars onto the fabric. To symbolize patriotism. We can't have the conservatives claiming a monopoly on love-of-country, they said.

She told the men she didn't sew.

Do you know anyone who does?

Not really.

You're George's receptionist, aren't you?

Yes.

My, my, times *have* changed.

Having left the councilmen outside to find their own seamstress, Jenny helped Hideo decide who they should set out chairs for—the mayor, Brenda, the bunting enthusiast city councilmen, a couple other politicians from Fort Wayne, an old former state senator who was pushing eighty, a donor from Indianapolis—and how they should arrange them: semicircle in front of the lectern. Hideo said the rest of the crowd could stand. He and Jenny also had a quick conference about tent versus no tent. The rain had stopped and the local meteorologists were predicting a cold but clear evening. No tent, then. A tent would look weak, Hideo said, and George, being a Democrat, couldn't afford to look weaker than he already did.

A little before three, Jenny ducked out to pick up Billie Starr, who was still pretending to be deeply interested in her book about dogs.

"I thought we could pick up our Christmas tree. What do you say?"

Billie Starr shrugged.

"A big one. A happy one, not a sad one."

No reaction. Head stuck in that book.

"Not sure there will be time to decorate it tonight. Maybe we can do it tomorrow, when you get back from Chicago."

Billie Starr flipped a page, read aloud to herself a paragraph about Basenjis and yodeling. Jenny knew she was not supposed to be listening, was, under no circumstances, to comment, so she did what she did best lately—drive somewhere she didn't really want to go.

The Benson Market parking lot was quiet. Clouds hung low and heavy over the store and a smattering of pickup trucks and minivans and sedans speckled with road salt. A Salvation Army bell ringer posted outside the front doors wished everyone a Merry Christmas as they rushed by him. No one donated, no one returned his greeting. The trees were on the south side of the store, sectioned off by a makeshift fence and a blue-tarped tent and a sign on which someone had painted the Boy Scout oath. The oath was all there, the parts about duty to God and others and the self, to being strong and moral and straight. The *h* in *oath* had worn off over time, though, and no one had bothered to correct it. That tickled Billie Starr, who, in the past, while Jenny looked at trees, liked to quiz the Boy Scout volunteers about what they liked to put in their oatmeal. Not this year. Billie Starr obviously wasn't in a talkative mood and there weren't any Boy Scouts in sight anyway, just a slope-shouldered woman with a Benson Market apron tied over her coat. She greeted Jenny and Billie Starr with an outsize wave as they approached. Dark hair like a curtain down half her face. Name tag on her chest—HEATHER.

"We got white pine and blue spruce," Heather said. "White pine has the soft needles and blue spruce has the poky."

"White pine," Jenny said.

"Blue spruce," Billie Starr said.

Jenny gave her daughter a quick side hug. "We can do poky."

Billie Starr squirmed away, hid behind a large stack of wreaths.

Heather gestured toward the stack with a flourish that made

her hair fly off her face for a moment. Then it settled back, heavy, hiding one eye. "We also have wreaths."

"Just a tree, thanks."

"Sure. Sorry. It's a habit. This isn't really my job. I'm usually in one-hour photo. The Boy Scout dads asked me to cover for them while they took a coffee break and I said sure. For the variety. All day, I ask people if they want doubles. Over and over and over. You want doubles? By the way, you want doubles? They're free. Not everybody knows that." Heather pulled what Jenny assumed was a blue spruce—very poky—from a pile. "This one's nice." She held it upright, spun it around. Missing most of its middle section, its trunk was crooked like a river and the top was splayed out like a fan or a sad hand hanging, waiting for a high five.

Billie Starr peeked out from her hiding spot. "That doesn't even look like a Christmas tree."

"Billie Starr."

"There's no way the angel's gonna fit up there."

Heather tossed the ugly tree and moved on to a different pile, pulled another blue spruce off the top. "Or this one maybe."

Pyramid-shaped, healthy, about six feet tall, it would fit nicely in front of the picture window where Jenny always put her trees. "What do you think?" Jenny asked Billie Starr, who was fingering a holly leaf. Having given her opinion twice, she could not be prevailed upon to give it again.

"We'll take it," Jenny said.

"You sure?" Heather asked. "It's fifty bucks."

No pretty mom discount today. Billie Starr was waiting, watching. *She has stomachaches. Headaches. She thinks you've run out of money.* Jenny swallowed hard, wrote out what was almost guaranteed to be a bad check to Troop 3198, and handed it to Heather, who, after three tries, managed to yank the tree through a hollow drum filled with white wire netting. All those crisscrossing,

interconnecting paths, Jenny thought. All the ways things could go right or wrong. The many holes a human could fall through.

Heather was staring intently at her, head cocked like a bird's. "Hey, I've seen you before."

"Yeah," Jenny said. "I shop here a lot."

"I mean I've developed your photo."

"You have?"

"Yeah. For this really angry-looking guy. Pocked skin. Lots of nose hair."

Jenny rubbed her nose. "You're probably mistaking me for someone else."

"I don't think so. You were outside an old schoolhouse with a little girl. *That* little girl." Heather pointed at Billie Starr. "He got doubles, the mean guy. His type always does."

Was she talking about Randall? He was angry—check—and he'd had acne as a teen, nothing major but pockets of scars remained, mostly on his temples. As for his nose hair, Jenny had never really noticed it. The idea that he might be carrying around a photograph of her was disorienting, more disturbing somehow than his midnight rantings. So was the thought of him snapping her picture without her permission. Was he pining for her in secret? And what if his wrestler girlfriend found out?

"And there's something else I know you from," Heather said, still eyeing Jenny through that wave of hair. "It'll come to me later. Lyd says that's just me. Stuff always comes to me later." She drifted over to Billie Starr at the wreath stack, told her she could have some pine branches to take home if she wanted them. They made good bouquets, Heather said. Better than flowers.

"Hey," Jenny said to her, "did you just say 'Lyd'? Lyd Butz?"

But Heather hadn't heard. She was helping Billie Starr gather pine boughs, shoving more branches into her arms than she could possibly carry. Billie Starr muttered a quiet thanks.

Jenny started struggling with the tree, dragging it by the trunk along the ground, when someone shouted her name.

"Nice Tannenbaum."

It was Buddy Winkler. Jenny had gone on a few dates with him back in high school even though that high Winkler forehead made him hard to look at. All smiles and muscles now. A sweet, easygoing man, he tended bar at Gill's. Jenny and Billie Starr ran into him in the library sometimes, checking out documentaries on dinosaurs and books on home improvement projects. His house on Elm always seemed to have sawhorses in front of it. Stacks of wood, too, and shingles.

Billie Starr scowled, clung tightly to her pine boughs. "That tree's dumb."

"You said you wanted poky," Jenny said.

"Not that one."

"Either way," Buddy said, "it's kinda big for such little ladies. How about I load it in for you?"

"You wouldn't mind?" Jenny asked.

"For you, Jenny Newberg? Anything." Buddy hefted the tree up on one shoulder and followed her to the car. Then he jimmied it in the trunk and tied it down with a bungee cord he found under Jenny's balding spare tire. Half the tree hung out over the bumper, but it stayed in place when Buddy tried tugging on it. "Good enough for government work."

"Mom does government work," said Billie Starr, climbing into the backseat.

"Does she now?"

"She's a pretty cover who works for the future governor of Indiana. I'm an ugly cover who ruins her life."

"Sorry," Jenny whispered to Buddy. "She's in a phase."

"I am not in a phase."

"The future governor, huh?" Buddy wiped some sap on his jeans. "Sounds big-time."

"I'm just the receptionist."

"There's no *just* about that. You should be proud." Buddy pulled once more on the Christmas tree. Satisfied, he tousled Billie Starr's hair. "Nice seeing you, little lady." He winked at Jenny. "And you, too."

Billie Starr gave Buddy her most queenly wave as he headed into the store. He stopped at the door, shoved a cluster of dollar bills into the Salvation Army bucket's small slot. The bell ringer beamed at him.

"See," Billie Starr said. "Buddy likes me."

The road out of town was a busy one. Two lane, broken shoulder. For a split second, Jenny entertained the idea of veering into oncoming traffic, bringing on the end of the world all by herself. A Ford F-150 passed. Cherry red. Then a gray minivan. A green Toyota, too. The temptation was sharp, cold, a sliver of ice in her brain. And then, just as quickly as it came, it melted, and she kept driving, past old houses and cracked sidewalks at first, then strip malls and fast-food places. Fields. Farms. Mint-green ranches with wrought iron porch rails. Light blue single-wides with fading picket fences and leaning aluminum carports. Vi Gregor's Cape Cod with its fake well out front. Jenny had seen it all a million times. Landscape as dead horse. Deja view.

"Buddy likes everybody," she said.

Billie Starr made it clear from moment one that she could not care less about the campaign office and everybody in it. It might have helped if George were there to greet her, but he'd slipped out an hour before. No one, not even Max, seemed to know where he'd gone.

"Ducking the detail already," Max mumbled angrily. "Why do I even bother?"

Jenny tried to get her daughter interested by showing Billie Starr her computer—"Look, email!" and giving her a swag bag of

button, bumper sticker, and pen—but Billie Starr didn't cheer up and come out of her shell until Brenda appeared with the dogs in tow. The team barely concealed their despair at seeing Roger and Wilfred bound around the office, snapping at chair legs, barking at nothing. Billie Starr, on the other hand, whom Hideo had put to work licking stamps, jumped up when she saw the dogs and rushed at them, as eager as they were to get acquainted.

"Corgis!" She grabbed her book from her backpack and showed it to Brenda, who patiently and kindly read the page Billie Starr was pointing to. Then she volunteered to help Billie Starr with the stamps.

Jenny watched them work together for a while. They seemed to take to each other instantly, laughing over the antics of Roger and Wilfred, showing each other their gluey tongues. Jenny had been third-wheeled over again. She wished her daughter would smile at her like that, but there was too much to do before tomorrow, too many boxes to check, to indulge in any self-pity for long. Or even to worry about the Black Suits, although they were always at the back of her mind. *Easy peasy. Lemon squeezy. You're a lightweight in a heavyweight's game.*

She was typing up Max's reply to an email from a state Democratic party operative all but demanding George drop out of the race when the phone rang. The operative's language was cloyingly polite, lots of "in the spirit of solidarity" and "for the good of the common cause" and "we're stronger together" kind of messaging. Bullshit plain and simple, according to Max, who'd composed a screed making it clear that George would absolutely not be standing down. Quite the opposite. He would not be bowing to the pressure of the mediocre and the meek. In fact, he had every intention of going public with the party's insulting letter, which was guaranteed to energize voters eager for real change—young people, women, minorities fed up with decades' worth of liberal lip service—and give them a very solid reason to switch allegiances. The cursor flashed

in the middle of a sentence about George's desire to shake up the race, blow the cobwebs from what had become a stagnant, stodgy party. Jenny had one more paragraph to go. She'd hoped Ted or Hideo might answer the phone, but they were obviously busy, Ted conferring with Max about something and Hideo on a call of his own. She picked up the receiver on the third ring.

"Hello," she said. "George Shepherd's office."

"This Jenny?"

"This is she. Who am I speaking to?"

"You're speaking to Eileen."

"Oh."

"I go with Randall."

Jenny pictured Eileen, wrinkled, dowdy, swigging cheap beer in an ugly kitchen, wrestling match on the TV. But that image was courtesy of Carla. Probably unfair. Almost certainly wrong.

"You got a second?" Eileen asked.

"Well, I am at work—"

"I know. Buddy told us."

"Buddy told you?"

"Randall and me had dinner at Gill's. Buddy said you got some gig with the governor."

"My boss is running anyway. He hasn't won yet. Did you want to know more about his campaign?"

"Is he Republican?"

"No."

"I vote straight Republican."

"I see. Then I guess—"

"Not calling about politics."

"Then what are you calling about?"

Eileen cleared her throat. "I'm calling to advocate for Randall's rights as a father—"

"His rights?"

"Which you are clearly violating by (a) not letting him see Billie

Starr and (b) siccing the cops on us when we so much as stopped by your house to say a harmless hello."

Billie Starr was a few feet away, trying to get one of Brenda's dogs to sit. He kept nipping at her fingers instead. Jenny cupped the receiver, lowered her voice. "I'm just trying to protect my daughter."

"So, leaving her with that banshee of a mother of yours is protecting Billie Starr? You and me, we must have different definitions of protection."

"Look, Randall already left me a note about getting a lawyer, so I assumed we'd be going through official channels—"

"Courts are slow. He wants access to Billie Starr now and I don't see why he shouldn't have it. Especially since you're too busy all of a sudden to watch her yourself."

"I'm working. It's not like—"

"Where is she, by the way?"

The dog that wouldn't sit was chasing Billie Starr around Hideo's desk, yipping and growling. Billie Starr didn't seem to mind. She kept laughing, egging him on.

"I don't see how that's any of your business," Jenny said.

"See? That right there is what I'm talking about. Billie Starr is half Randall, isn't she? That makes her his business." Eileen paused. Her breath was heavy, made the phone crackle. "When did you guys get a dog?"

"I should get back to my work, Eileen."

"You do that. But think about what I've said. And remember, a girl needs her father."

There was a harsh click and Billie Starr was at Jenny's elbow, suddenly interested. "Who was that, Mom?"

"A concerned voter."

"I thought I heard you call her 'Eileen.' Isn't that dad's girl-friend's name?"

"There are a lot of Eileens in this world, unfortunately."

Billie Starr gave Jenny a level look. "And a lot of liars." Then she joined Brenda in the break room, the two of them setting out water for the dogs, who, in their haste to claim the biggest bowl, knocked over both.

"Hideki!" Brenda yelled at Hideo, pointing at the wet floor. "Crisis!"

Hideo rolled his eyes, did not get up. "The name's Hideo, actually."

"Well, good for you," Brenda said, "but someone still has to clean that up."

It was Jenny who ended up mopping up the mess. After that, she finished the email to the condescending operative and worked without a break for hours, answering phone calls (all from strangers now), filing, typing. The office gradually emptied out—Brenda left first and then Ted, Max, and Hideo—and at around midnight Jenny woke Billie Starr, asleep on the ground with her dog book, and the two of them went home through a whirl of snow and wind and blue-black dark.

Billie Starr, mumbling about Eileens the world over, about neglectful moms and poisonous, foul-tasting stamp glue, stuffed the blue spruce boughs from Heather into a pitcher, brushed her teeth, and put herself to bed, while Jenny, nodding on her feet, put out clothes for the next day—her best work dress (an emerald-green shirtwaist that fell just above the knee), a pair of chunky-heeled black boots—and set her alarm for five thirty. There was no way she was going to be late dropping Billie Starr off for that godforsaken field trip. Ashley Batchelder would not be able to lord this one over her.

No Mummy-effing way.

The alarm blared. That buzzer, so harsh. The floor, so cold. Her clothes, cold too. The coffee hot, though, nice and hot, followed by a piece of toast, then feeding time for Gertrude and Yo-Yo, mewing at

the door. Freezing. Snow blowing in. Have to wake the girl. Billie Starr got up grumbling but brightened some when Jenny reminded her what day it was. Then right back to gloomy.

"Guess you'll be glad when I'm finally out of your hair."

"You know that's not true."

"You said so yourself, Mom."

"I'm sor—"

"Yeah. I know. You're sorry. You're always sorry."

Another dark drive, half asleep, under a star-studded sky, over potholed country roads, headlights picking up snowmen and overturned trash cans and drifts, soft silver hills shifting in the wind like sand dunes. School a black blot against a flat, bruised horizon. Big, rumbling bus in the parking lot. A charter with fancy seats and an upper deck. Ashley Batchelder laughing on the sidewalk with Mr. Richardson and Gladys Mock. The chaperones, Jenny supposed. Either way, a cabal. Wasn't that how Max described the Republican gubernatorial field? A cabal of crooks and hypocrites. Jenny handed Billie Starr her packed lunch—see? I didn't forget. I'm good for something. Billie Starr snatched the bag and got out, ran toward a group of winter-coated kids. Jenny shouted, "I love you, sweetheart/airplane/petition/future president." Billie Starr didn't return the sentiment, didn't look back. Her skinny body was soon absorbed into the crowd until she was nothing but a stocking cap bobbing in a sea of them.

Jenny thought about going back home and trying to get another half hour of sleep but knew it wouldn't do any good, so she drove to Churubusco instead, had her pick of Main Street parking spaces. That's when she realized the poky Christmas tree was still hanging out of her trunk. She'd forgotten all about it. Pine trees were used to cold weather, right? Hardy. Jenny gave one of its blue-green limbs a shake and made her way to the campaign office, opening the front door with the key George had given her the day before. Silent, shadowy, the large room was a four-walled photo negative

and Jenny was inside of it, groggy, feeling unreal again, disconnected. A sour smell of cold rot came from the refrigerator. Max's
old lunch, probably. Of everyone in the office, he by far ate the stink-
iest food. Jenny flipped on the lights and went to check the fax machine, where a pile of papers half an inch deep waited for her. She
started flipping through the stack. Requests for interviews. RSVPs
for the day's speech. Promises of donations. Strongly worded letters
of disapproval regarding some policy stance or another. Nothing out
of the ordinary. Then she stopped on a page covered in large, slanted
writing, the letters looking like they'd been written in something
other than ink, something viscous and dripping.

The oranges are ripe but you are rotten.
Watch yourselfs.
We'll come for what you love most.

Jenny dropped the faxes on the floor and backed away from
them, knocking over a bunch of yard signs in the process. They fell
like dominoes, fanned out, George's smiling face scattering across
the floor. The racket shattered the early morning silence and woke
Jenny up for good.

George was standing at the door in a flurry of snow, coffee and
doughnuts in one hand, newspapers in the other. "You look like
you've seen a ghost. Or my poll numbers."

Jenny tried to laugh and gathered up the faxes, started to right
the signs, too. George told her they could wait.

"Come eat with me."

She showed him the fax. He didn't look surprised. "Politics is a
dirty business."

"That first fax, the one about another woman, a tape—"

"Have some coffee."

"I feel like—"

"The cruller?"

"Sure."

George smiled and handed her a cruller and a napkin. They ate at the same rickety table they'd sat down to on her first day. The sun was just rising, flashing bright on the dirty windows, turning the crumby carpet a pale yellow.

"Don't worry about that fax," George said. "It's not in your job description."

"But I . . . but we . . ." There was nothing safe to say.

George flicked a sugar packet with his fingernail. "What's really bothering you? Did Billie Starr's dad come back?"

"No." Jenny held her coffee tightly, wished it would warm her. "That deputy your friend sent to my house was quite effective. My mom was impressed, and she's not impressed by much."

"I've had lots of dealings with the police over the years. Sometimes it pays to be a lawyer." George leaned forward. Another bad shaving job—bumps and missed hairs. "Speaking of your mom, that man she's marrying—"

"Bob Butz."

"Unfortunate name, that."

"Yes."

"Is working for me causing trouble at home?"

"Trouble? I don't think so."

"I assume Bob told you that we're not the best of friends."

"I don't really talk to him much, and he's never mentioned you at all."

"Ah, well. That's probably for the best."

"Why?"

"I've represented a number of people who've sued him over the years. And we've won pretty much every case. Bob's bitter about it. Not my biggest fan."

"Sued him for what exactly?"

George turned the doughnut box into a keyboard, typed on it.

"Flagrant and repeated violation of public safety standards, failure to disclose, breach of contract, you name it."

"When you say . . ."

"Flagrant and repeated violation of public safety standards . . ."

"What's that mean?"

"He's a slumlord, basically. He sells houses that aren't fit to be inhabited for exorbitant prices and laughs all the way to the bank. And it's not just homeowners who've gotten screwed. A lot of men who've worked for him have fallen ill. He's a proud purveyor of fake granite countertops. The dust from sawing the countertops, it gets in the lungs. Kills you if you're around it long enough, especially if your employer doesn't bother to give you the right masks or care enough to make sure your workspace is clean."

"Kills you," Jenny said. "Kills you how?"

"Respiratory failure. These tiny little slivers of particulate matter get lodged in the lungs and wreak all sorts of havoc. It's bad enough with real granite, but the artificial stuff is extra lethal."

"My dad installed countertops for Bob Butz."

"Really? Do you think he'd talk to me?"

"He can't. He's dead."

"Oh. I'm so sorry."

"We thought he had lung cancer. He was a smoker."

"It's possible it was cancer. It's also possible that your dad getting sick wasn't a coincidence. It might have been part of a pattern."

What had Billie Starr said about Judd Pickens's grandfather? He made countertops like Pete. He died, too. Of a lung thing. Jenny didn't know how to process what George was telling her, didn't know how to react. She stood up, sat back down, gulped more coffee. "I was Bob's receptionist for a while. In his real estate office. But then he fired me."

"Why on earth would he fire you?"

Because he wanted to sleep with me. You want to sleep with

me, too. Impossible. This whole situation, my whole life at the moment—impossible. "It's a long story."

"Well," George said, "whatever the reason, he was an idiot to let you go. The whole team loves you. I hope you're happy here."

She wasn't happy. More exhilarated, overwhelmed, terrified, bored. All at the same time.

"I have something for you," George said.

"For me?"

George went to the wall of filing cabinets, pulled a large white box swathed in silky red ribbon from one of the drawers, laid it in her lap.

"I don't understand," Jenny said.

"Just open it."

Her fingers shook as she peeled away the ribbon. Inside the box, wrapped up in delicate pink tissue paper, was a knee-length wool coat, dove gray, belted, lined with silk in a rose paisley pattern. She pulled it from its box, stunned.

"I noticed that you've been coming to work without a coat all week," George said. "I couldn't stand to have you shivering on camera today. And, besides, you deserve something nice for putting up with Max."

"It's beautiful."

"Let's see if it fits."

She slipped it on, buttoned it, cinched the belt tight. Exactly her size. The coat was prettier than all the Mummies' put together. Inside of it, Jenny felt momentarily transformed. Elegant. Like a woman who deserved the best of everything.

"Perfect," George said. He circled her, as if inspecting the cut of the coat, brushed something off her shoulder, came in close behind her, his lips just inches from her neck. "I knew it would be."

Max burst in the door then, ranting about an op-ed that had run in a Fort Wayne newspaper. George pivoted quickly away, busying

himself righting the yard signs, and Jenny went to her desk, stared at the computer screen, black, then blinking green.

Max was too angry to register any tension in the air. "Fuck's sake can you believe this shit? What passes for journalism these days?" he said. "The editor is going to hear from me. He's going to get an earful. Dick. That's his name. How appropriate. And I would not be surprised if this Dick person weren't on the Republicans' payroll. Now that's a story I'd like to read, if someone had the balls to write it. A thorough investigation of conservative bias in the state's largest dailies. Liberal media, my ass." He stopped suddenly, his eyes on the big white box, the red ribbon, on George, humming ("Two Silhouettes" again), and Jenny, pretending to type something while her computer was obviously still booting up.

"Forgive me for being presumptuous," Max said to George, "but it almost looks as if you purchased that coat for Jenny."

"Maybe I did."

"Did you charge it to the campaign?"

"Does it matter?"

"You can't do this shit, George. With all the weird calls and emails and faxes we've been getting, we can't afford any appearance of impropriety."

"There's nothing improper about being a gentleman and helping out a valued member of the team."

"You should clear every major purchase with me first."

"Major purchase?" George asked. "It's a coat."

Jenny started to take it off, to give it back.

"Nope, not a chance," George said. "Don't listen to Max. You look lovely."

"How she looks is immaterial—"

"Relax, Max."

"Relax, Max? You think that's clever because it rhymes? I'm the one trying to recruit some actual donors so we can keep the lights

on. I'm the one trying to save your ass from a bunch of unhinged blackmailers. If I relax, you lose. Or worse."

"This talk is officially over," George declared. Then he left to greet Ted, who stumbled into the office, his arms full of poinsettias, to, he said, spread the Christmas cheer.

He put one on Jenny's desk. "Sweets for the sweet," he said.

"Just make sure Brenda's dogs eat at least two of those," George said. "If they live to see me win this election, I will blame every single one of you."

Max went to check the fax machine, grumbling about impractical, sentimental bastards who didn't know what was good for them and irresponsible cocksuckers treating the campaign expense account like a Las Vegas ATM. "I could be in Little Rock right now, stumping for Bill Clinton," he said. "I could be anywhere but here."

Jenny shoved her hands into her new stylishly stitched pockets. Silk lining there, too. Whiff of balsam and peppermint from the collar, probably courtesy of the store where George bought it. She took the coat off and laid it gently over the back of her chair, thought about Billie Starr in downtown Chicago, a tiny white thing staring up at buildings that blocked out the sun, about Pete choking to death in that dusty dead-end motel room, Bob Butz letting it happen, the Black Suits burning everything to the ground. She imagined them hacking into Hideo's ingenious AV system and interrupting George's inspiring family-focused speech with what he'd said to her at the Riverview, all that sex talk at loud volume, the lusty words flowing over the crowd, smacking Brenda in the face and echoing up the street and into the yards and houses and ears of the would-be Christian voters who, horrified, stunned, disgusted, would turn to stone. And when they did, it would all be her fault.

George caught her eye from across the room, winked as he'd done on her first day, talking about small towns and fate and Titian. The wink made Jenny's lower belly ache in a way it hadn't in years. Sudden butterflies. From a man she would never even look twice at

on the street. She mouthed a shy "thank you," mortified to realize she was blushing. George mouthed a "you're welcome" back to her. It was too much, so she worked, and when that also became too much, she shut herself in the bathroom for a few minutes at a time, splashed water on her face, stared at her reflection in the mirror. That woman is me, she thought. That is who I am. Or who I appear to be. Jenny Newberg. The whole pie.

After lunch, she was tasked with typing up George's speech. George and Max kept adding and subtracting ideas, rearranging whole paragraphs. They fought so much and so loudly over tone, over something Max called "subtext" and George called "subliminal messaging," that Jenny wanted to toss her computer keyboard in the trash.

"Remember, Max," George said, "this is my campaign."

"Remember, George," Max said, "that Walter Mondale's one of my dad's best friends. I don't have to be here."

"We're name-dropping now?"

"Whatever it takes to get you to listen."

"Hey, get off my back. I caved on the cop thing, didn't I?"

"We need to conference with Hideo about what to do if those whackos release something," Max said. "Even if it's all a sham, we need to be prepared, to have a statement ready—"

George scratched his nose with his middle finger. "I've got your statement right here."

"I'm not kidding."

"Neither am I."

Jenny, as usual, said nothing, typing, deleting, typing some more. As the day wore on and the sky darkened outside, a crowd began to gather. Max ran to the front windows to count bodies. Ten, then twenty, then thirty. He stopped at thirty-five.

"This is really happening," he said. "This is really fucking happening. People actually came."

"Well, that's a relief," George said.

Sipping on a glass of water in the break room and flipping

through his speech, he looked completely calm. He was the only one. The office was gripped with a kind of nervous energy so palpable Jenny could almost smell it—sweat and excitement. Anticipation. Heady cologne on hot skin.

Max, hunched over his computer, yelled at George that they really needed to revise the part in the speech about increasing the minimum wage. "What we got in there now, it doesn't go far enough. It's too pussy for prime time. Same with the section on superfund sites." Ted agreed and changed his tie—from smiley faces to stars and back again—while Hideo, having completed a few quick sound checks, dragged Jenny outside, begging her to take a seat in the front row between the eighty-year-old senator and Brenda, clad in heavy, beige tweed. Jenny had hoped to find a spot somewhere near the back, to blend in, disappear, but Hideo insisted. It wouldn't look good, he said, to have a veritable sausage fest on display when George was trying hard to court the female vote.

"Politics," Brenda said as Jenny settled in beside her. Her gray, feathery hair was sprayed into a stiff helmet and she looked bored and miserable, pantyhose bagging around her ankles. She smelled like wet dog. "Nice coat."

"Thanks," Jenny said.

Brenda craned her neck and tried to cross her legs, but her skirt was too tight. "Today's Billie Starr's big adventure, isn't it? Kind of chilly for a trip to Chicago."

"I thought so, too, but no one asked me."

"No one ever asks me anything," Brenda said.

The cold obviously hadn't kept people at home. They packed the sidewalk, spilled out onto the street, everyone bundled up, filling the air with short, silver bursts of breath. Jenny spied a few familiar faces among the throng: Trish Keck in her cowboy hat, a few Shieldses, Lyd's fellow tellers at the bank—Cindy Richardson (no relation, as far as Jenny knew, to Billie Starr's teacher), and Sam Larson, a young kid just out of high school that Lyd liked but suspected

of stealing coin wrappers. Several of the news outlets were there, too, corralled into a small, fenced-in area festooned with bunting. A row of bulky black cameras crowded each other like a swarm of giant bugs. Behind them stood grizzled men in puffy vests and twill pants, joking with one another and slyly angling for better spots. The well-dressed, attractive reporters who went with the cameras stood opposite, studying their faces in compact mirrors, powdering the shiny spots, and a little behind them were two police officers—probably George's new security detail. Not Lefferts, though. Jenny hadn't seen either of them before. One was quite handsome. Tall. Blond under his hat.

George, smiling broadly, made his way to the microphone slowly, stopping once in a while to shake a hand, pose for a picture, high-five a kid, hold a baby. Watching him work the crowd, Jenny couldn't help but feel a small measure of awe. Would the cameras be turned on her at any point, the woman with whom George Shepherd Jr., very important man, was in love? Or something like it anyway.

"This is his favorite part," Brenda said in a loud whisper.

"All the people?"

"All the attention, from the women especially." Brenda reached under her chair for her purse. The bag was scuffed black pleather. It slumped on the ground like a dead thing. Brenda pulled some Kleenex from inside and blew her nose noisily.

George was at the lectern, grinning at the crowd, adjusting the microphone. He straightened a bunch of papers—papers that held the words Jenny had typed and typed again—tapped the mic, thanked everyone for coming, and announced that what he was about to give wasn't a speech so much as a manifesto, a statement of values. What he valued, he said, was every Hoosier's right to life, liberty, and the pursuit of happiness, regardless of where they were born, what god they worshipped, what language they spoke, how they grew up, whether or not they were a man or a woman,

gay or straight, Black or white. Equality above all. Compassion and empathy and the sort of clear-eyed respect and kindness that led to better outcomes for everyone, including the incarcerated, many of whom, he said, should never have been jailed in the first place.

"What do you know about it?" a woman shouted from somewhere in the middle of the crowd. It was Trish Keck, sandwiched between Sam Larson and a woman holding a sign about George shepherding his flock to a brighter future. She was shaking with fury. "Some people should be locked up. Some people should be locked up for life."

George paused in his speech, squinted out at the crowd. In the unexpected silence, with the security guards' eyes on her, Trish seemed to lose her nerve. "What do you know about it," she said again, but quieter this time. "Nothing. Not a goddamn . . ." Then she pulled her cowboy hat down low over her face and slunk away.

"My cousin shot at her, you know," Brenda said. "Over a pie."

Jenny tried to discern from Brenda's tone and the set of her face whether she disapproved of Lorne's actions, but there was no indication either way. She was as neutral as her tweed.

George, likewise unbothered by Trish's outburst, started right back in again, his delivery effortlessly smooth and funny and charming. He didn't even have to look at the paper in front of him, he was that natural a speaker. Jenny tried her best to listen, to follow along, but couldn't focus. She lost the thread of the speech somewhere in the section about hardworking families and subsidized day care and didn't pick it up again until the part about pollution and lakes and runoff from industrial farms and George and Max's plan to tackle it all, to fix it, to bring back the days of pristine water and more fish than Hoosiers could eat in a year.

While George waxed lyrical about his childhood, about trawling for rainbow trout on Turtle Town Lake, Jenny gazed around her, stared for a while at a winter-bare tree, its outline indistinct against a matte gray sky going indigo at the edges. Then something crossed

her field of vision that shocked her to attention—a man in a ripped kimono armed with a bow and arrow. Marcus Rye. He planted himself right under the tree and adjusted his kimono. It rippled in the wind, showed flashes of bare torso and hip.

"Oh no," Jenny said.

Brenda seemed to spot Marcus, too. Unlike Jenny, though, she wasn't alarmed, only amused. "George can really bring 'em out of the woodwork, can't he?"

Marcus had begun waving the bow around and screwing his mouth up as if to speak, as if to launch into his own heckling rant. Before she really had a chance to think about it, Jenny jumped to her feet and rushed toward him through the mass of bodies, bouncing off elbows, tripping over steel-toed boots. When she reached him, Marcus seemed as surprised to see her as she was to see him. She grabbed him by the arm and started to drag him away. Hideo and Ted, stationed in the back to gauge the crowd's reaction to the more controversial parts of George's speech, gaped at her, and Lyd's coworkers clapped approvingly. "Good riddance," they whispered. "Bad rubbish." The security guards obviously hadn't heard anything. They stared mutely forward.

Jenny's car was two blocks south, parked at the end of the street across from a sandwich shop. On the way, Jenny ran into Trish Keck standing outside a tavern, checking her watch, shuffling back and forth in front of the door, debating, it looked like, about whether to go in. When she saw Jenny and Marcus, she rushed over, peeled off her coat, put it over Marcus's shoulders.

"Silly man," she said. "You'll catch your death."

"I'm going to take him home," Jenny said.

Trish nodded curtly and grabbed Marcus's other arm. Together, the two of them led him through the slush to Jenny's car, pushed him gently into the passenger seat. He went meekly enough. All of his earlier fire seemed to have drained from him. His carpet slippers—gray, holes in the toes—were soaked through.

Trish shut the car door, turned angrily on Jenny. "Just what do you think you're up to, throwing in your lot with a man like George Shepherd?"

Jenny was taken aback. In the past, if she and Trish happened to run into each other—at Benson Market, Pike's Pizza—they exchanged friendly nods. Nothing more.

"I heard you're working for him," Trish said. "Doing his dirty work. I'm warning you, you're making a big mistake there."

"I'm just his secretary."

Trish's face sharpened with hate. "Those two, George and Brenda Shepherd, they're on Lorne's side. All the way."

There was a swell of applause and cheering from up the street. The end of George's speech, maybe, or a particularly stirring part. Trish was mumbling at the ground, something about young girls thinking they were really something, they were hot shit, but she knew the truth. Not hot shit at all. Cold fish.

"What was that?" Jenny asked.

Trish scratched at her shirt, at a patch above her left pocket where Lorne's name, stitched in red cursive, had been violently crossed out with a marker. "Nah. Not gonna get into it. Told myself I wouldn't, and I won't. Said too much as it is."

"Hey!" Marcus rolled down his window. "I'm here, you know! I'm still here."

"Don't get your panties all in a jumble!" Trish hollered at him.

"I will not be subdued into abject compliance!"

"I'll abject compliance you," Trish said.

Marcus shoved Trish's coat at her through the open window. "Fussy women."

"Sometimes women need to be fussy if the men in their lives are too stupid or too stubborn to dress for the weather."

"Weather doesn't affect me. I'm beyond weather."

"You're beyond something." Trish kissed Marcus on the forehead and headed back in the direction of the tavern. She hesitated

outside the front door, red neon BEER THIRTY sign lighting up her tired face. A line of young men pushed noisily passed her. She followed them inside.

"She's a drunk," Marcus said. "I've told her and told her she needs to cool it, but we all go to hell in our own way, don't we?"

"She's right about one thing," Jenny said. "You should wear more clothes when you go out in public. How did you even get here anyway?"

Marcus fingered the bow and arrow in his lap. Then he placed them both on the floor. "Where am I exactly?"

"Churubusco. George Shepherd's campaign rally. How'd you even get here?"

"I walked. I think."

"The whole way?"

"Hitchhiked some maybe. Where we going?"

"Home."

"Yours or mine?"

"Yours."

Marcus looked behind him. "You have a Christmas tree in your trunk."

"I know."

"Looks like you didn't get a fresh cut. You need a fresh cut on that tree or it won't drink." Marcus opened Jenny's glove compartment. After rifling through some papers and a pile of hair ties, he took a plastic fast-food fork from inside and stabbed his knee with it. "So, where are you taking me anyway?"

The roads were crunchy with salt. "Home."

"Mine or yours?"

"Yours."

"Good. My feet are wet. I need to put on some socks."

Gertrude and Yo-Yo were waiting for them on Marcus's front stoop. They'd killed a baby mouse and left it on the bottom step. Posing by it, they mewed proudly. Jenny gently nudged the tiny

carcass off the step with her boot and told Marcus to take care of himself.

"I'll take care of myself if I feel like it." Then he hmphed and stomped wetly inside, slamming the door behind him.

Gertrude and Yo-Yo, barred entry, rubbed up against Jenny's boots, their mewing growing more plaintive, higher pitched. Jenny made a quick trip to her house and opened two cans of tuna, set them on the porch. The cats swarmed, humming greedily as they ate. Across the street, a skinny spotted dog dug through a pile of trash at the edge of Dorothy Renfrow's yard, and the sign blinked on. *Cold fish cold fish cold fish.* Jenny brushed some cat hair from her coat and leaned against her front door, watched a gold Gremlin take the S curve a little too fast. The driver skidded toward the side of the road, corrected, and, just missing Jenny's mailbox, sped up her driveway and unceremoniously parked her in.

A delicate-looking man in a too-large navy blue peacoat and orange beanie climbed out of the car, doffing his cap and attempting a clumsy bow. "Miss Newberg," he said. "We meet at last."

"At last?"

The man appeared somewhat hurt. "I'm Kevin Lipshott, you know, of Summit City Mortgage."

So this was the person filling up her answering machine tape. And the man Marcus chased off with an ax.

"It's really pretty out here," he said. "I forgot just how open it is, how peaceful."

The usual crowd of crows over at Dorothy Renfrow's took that moment to dive-bomb the skinny dog nosing through the trash. A pathetic fight ensued. Lots of squawking and barking and growling. The birds won. They got their banana peel. The dog ran off through a line of pines, one of which Dorothy had nailed a sign to: TRESPASSERS WILL BE SHOT ON SIGHT. SURVIVORS WILL BE SHOT AGAIN.

Kevin took in the scene with a smile, like someone witnessing a heartwarming commercial or a listening to a kid saying the

darnedest thing. "We handled Mrs. Renfrow's mortgage. That's what brought me to Benson before. Too bad about what happened to her. A real sweet lady."

"She threw a beer bottle at my daughter for getting close to her bleeding heart bush," Jenny said.

"A character then. Something to be said for characters."

Yeah, Jenny thought. They threatened to call the cops on you if you let your grass get too long or forgot to bring your garbage cans in before nightfall.

"I was just in the neighborhood, and I thought, why not drop in on my favorite customer, see how she's holding up."

"This isn't a neighborhood," Jenny said. "No one's ever just here. You want to be paid."

"Oh, well now." Kevin reached down to scratch Yo-Yo behind the ears and got bit for his trouble. "Nice cats you got here."

"They're not mine. They're my neighbor's."

Kevin sucked on his wound, took a few steps back. He kept blinking. Did he have something in his eyes? Or was he just nervous? "There's another house I'm handling a little ways out," he said. "A farm. You probably know the owners, the Kecks. They fell on hard times several months back and I think they were hoping to sell and take off for greener pastures—Florida, maybe Texas—but the land's been mortgaged and mortgaged again and, last I heard, Lorne got a little trigger-happy at an inopportune time. In any case, I suppose everyone responds to stress in different ways—"

Jenny strode past Kevin to her car. Glancing down through the badly tinted windows of his Gremlin, she saw that he had a crowbar on his passenger seat, partially obscured in a nest of burger wrappers and used straws.

"I just got a job, so you can tell whoever sent you here that you'll have your money next week. Some of it at least."

Kevin wrung his hat between his hands like a dishrag. "I shouldn't have mentioned the Kecks. My boss is always telling me

to be more discreet. 'Kevin,' he says, 'you give the game away. You lose it before you've even begun to play.' But, it's hard times for everyone right now. The recession, yeah? A lot of people falling behind, losing their shirts. In any case, you're not alone, if that helps. If it makes you feel any better."

"Lots better, thanks."

"Good, good, glad to help. That's what we're all about, Summit City Mortgage. Helping people like your very self weather life's many ups and downs." Hat back on. Bowing again. Saluting. Folding himself back into his car and quietly concealing the crowbar under more wrappers and straws and some forms fished from the floorboards. He blinked up at her like she was too bright to look at. "Was a pleasure, Miss Newberg. I'll be in touch."

"I'm sure you will."

Exit collection agent, in an eddy of snow and rich exhaust. The cats were finished with their dinner and had begun bathing each other. Next door, a light came on, a frame of golden warmth in the growing dark. Marcus was in his kitchen, staring into the refrigerator. Jenny hoped he had something decent to eat. What would become of him? She could only do so much. Trish, too. A drunk in danger of losing her farm. Hard times. Hard times for everyone.

*W*hen Jenny got back to the campaign office, the lectern and AV system had all been cleared away and the launch party was in full swing. The office was still ugly, still cramped and bland and poorly lit, but the festivities made it possible for her to imagine the place a bar again, full of patrons yelling to be heard. Everyone seemed to be drinking. A few—Hideo, Ted, and a dark-haired woman in a short blue dress—were dancing on desks. The radio, tuned to the Fort Wayne rock station, was playing "Here Comes My Girl." Roger and Wilfred darted among guests, barking and snarfing up bits of food. No one seemed to mind their presence now. The wheels had

been greased enough, Jenny supposed. Even Max seemed to have loosened up. He was in a corner with Stephanie Shine, the reporter from Channel 4 Action News, laughing and showing her his socks, covered in peonies, the state flower.

So, the Black Suits hadn't pounced, hadn't released any incriminating tape. Not yet anyway. There would be no party if they had, no Hideo waving drunkenly at her, no Ted hollering, "Join us, Jenny Newberg. Kick off those shoes and let down your hair."

Jenny hung her coat up on the rack by the front door and smilingly declined. Brenda was there, sipping on a cup half full of yellow liquid. Lemonade, Jenny assumed. And not spiked, given Brenda's dull demeanor.

"I was sad to miss the end of the speech," Jenny said to her.

"You didn't miss much. A little talk about Planned Parenthood, a lot of applause, and now this."

George and the eighty-year-old state senator were helping themselves to food. The senator moved up and down the table, picking up chips and cookies and appetizers, examining them, and putting them back. George, his forehead flushed, kept up a steady stream of talk. According to Brenda, the senator had been one of George's professors back in law school. A formidable man, Brenda said. Not anymore. His pants were two inches too short and he tilted sideways when he walked. He looked like a broken umbrella. Reaching for a strawberry, he dropped a deviled egg on the floor. George moved quickly to pick it up. Then he popped it in his mouth, laughing and tripping over a stapler someone had left in the middle of the room. He'd found a discarded cup and cheers-ed the crowd. Max, fist in the air, shouted, "Cheers back at you, boss!" Then he doused the nearest poinsettia with beer.

Brenda raised her voice over the din. "Did my husband ever tell you how he got his limp?"

Jenny shook her head.

"He stopped on a highway to help a woman with a flat tire. Tire

was on the traffic side and a truck hit him. He was lucky, really. Just got grazed. The leg was broken in a couple places, and he had the chance to play the hero for a young woman who still adores him, sends him cards for his birthday and Christmas and Father's Day. Father's Day, I guess, because she considers him a dad of sorts, ever since he saved her, even though she didn't really need saving. George just eats it up. He's all about rescuing damsels in distress. It was the news coverage of that whole thing that originally launched his political career. He got to the state senate on it."

Roger and Wilfred bounded up to Brenda then, yipping and drooling. She gave them each a couple crackers and drifted away to talk to the old senator, who was inspecting a tortilla chip as if he'd never seen one before.

Jenny filled a plate with food. She wasn't hungry, but it was something to do, something to busy herself with so she wouldn't appear too much of a wallflower. Then she walked around the office, straightening the plants, collecting cups and plastic forks and tossing them in the trash, orbiting other people's conversations and catching little fragments here and there—"No, you're wrong. It was John who owned the snake"; "I said, 'Get your own glitter gun'"; "It all goes back to slavery. You know it, I know it, and Bayh knows it"; "Rumors. Rumors swirling but that's politics." At one point, she ducked outside to catch some air. On her way back in, she ran into the desk-dancing woman. A tattoo of a fairy peeked out from under the collar of her dress. Her eyes, boot black, were glazed.

"Got a cigarette?"

"Sorry," Jenny said. "I don't smoke."

The woman cupped her ear, leaned toward Jenny. "What was that?"

The music volume spiked suddenly. Jenny shook her head. Too loud for conversation.

The woman tried anyway. "You think it's just you?" she asked.

"Who doesn't smoke? I don't understand."

The woman's lips were on Jenny's ear. "There's a lot you don't understand." Then she strolled away in the direction of the food table.

Jenny was going to follow her, to ask her what she meant, but she got pulled onto the makeshift dance floor by Hideo, who spun her around, pulled her back in, pushed her out again, a sloppy East Coast swing. Someone had found an old disco ball and hung it in the center of the room. George played DJ, flipping through the radio stations, hitting the end of "Old Time Rock 'n' Roll" and the middle of "Baby, It's Cold Outside." Next came "The Gambler" and "Stand by Your Man." Carla was right. The song wasn't danceable. Everyone just sort of stood around while it played, swaying together, singing along, badly. When "We Didn't Start the Fire" came on, the whole team took turns twirling Jenny around—Hideo passed her to Max who passed her to Ted. Then they started all over again, cutting in, pushing her on to the next man. Max and Hideo didn't say much, concentrated hard on the dancing part, but Ted, smelling strongly of vodka, tried to tell Jenny something about his cats and his heart and a man named Tupac. Jenny couldn't really hear him and eventually he gave up, moved on to the black-eyed desk-dancer, who'd somehow found a cigarette to bum and was sucking on it with gusto, seemingly unaware it wasn't lit.

George grabbed Jenny then, held on to her for the length of two songs and into a third. For a short time, they were alone in the center of the dance floor, wheeling around like a bride and groom, the room full of people cheering them on. Dizzy, Jenny looked for Brenda in the crowd—"You should probably be doing this with your wife," she told George—but the faces blurred together into a pasty mass and George wasn't listening anyway, was whispering to her what sounded like a plan to meet up later, away from all these people and noise, away from his goddamned security detail. The butterflies came back, fluttering in full force. Jenny extricated herself.

"I can't, my daughter, I'm sorry."

"Don't be sorry, Jenny Newberg," George said, reaching for her waist. "Don't be sad. Be mine."

Jenny sidestepped him and checked her watch. It was nearly eight, which meant that Billie Starr's field trip bus was probably already in the school parking lot, kids spilling out, responsible parents there and waiting. She waved at George, grabbed her coat, and slipped away.

The sky was mostly clear. Glittery baubles hung from the lampposts and road signs. Red and green and gold. A soft cloud coasted over the moon, hammer shaped. Brick street to county road, no traffic to speak of. The Christmas tree was still hanging out the back hatch, bouncing gently in rhythm with the song on the radio. Let it snow let it snow let it snow. The first noel. Oh little town of Bethlehem. The silent stars go by, yet in thy dark streets shineth the everlasting light. School parking lot dark, though. It took Jenny a moment to realize that it was all but empty. Eerily quiet, too. No big, fancy charter bus pumping diesel fumes, no kids on the sidewalk saying sentimental goodbyes. Jenny checked her watch again. She was ten minutes late.

There were two cars in the whole place—a sports car and Ashley Batchelder's Ford Aerostar. Ten minutes. Two cars. Was that a math problem? Lyd would know. Jenny parked quickly. Ashley was settling into the minivan's driver's seat, telling her daughter, Terri, to put on her seat belt while Mr. Richardson loaded a garbage bag into the back. The bag was full of discarded juice boxes and crumpled paper towels smeared with mayonnaise and peanut butter and ketchup. Terri was complaining about the cold.

"Button your coat then," Ashley said.

"It is buttoned."

"Just be patient. We'll get the heat on in a minute."

"I am patient. I've been patient this whole day and you said that if I was patient, you'd get me a Super Nintendo. I want a Super Nintendo. And a Bridal Barbie. And a jean jacket."

Jenny was seeing things again, things that weren't there. In the gloom, beyond the bright puddles cast by the car's interior lights, were waving, grasping things. Mummy arms. Monsters. Natural disasters, too. Blizzards. Sinkholes. Things that could steal a daughter away from you.

"Where is Billie Starr?"

Ashley Batchelder turned, stepped back out of her car. Mr. Richardson blinked at Jenny like a child startled awake in the middle of a dream.

"Ten minutes," Jenny said. She didn't recognize her own voice. It seemed to come from the ground. From under her feet. "I'm ten minutes late. That's all. That's nothing."

No one said anything for a moment. Jenny thought she heard a coyote howl. Maybe it was just a hound.

Then Ashley smiled. The smile spread across her face like oil on water. "I'm sure there's a logical explanation," she said, stepping out of her car. "She probably went home with a friend."

"A friend," Mr. Richardson agreed. "Of course. That makes sense."

"What friend?" Terri asked. She'd found a full juice box and was chewing on the straw. "Billie Starr doesn't have any friends, unless you count Judd Pickens and nobody counts Judd Pickens."

"What have you done with my daughter?" Jenny asked Ashley and Mr. Richardson, who were standing close together now, shoulders almost touching. "Did you leave her in Chicago?"

"No, of course not," Ashley said. "I saw her get on the bus tonight. You saw her, too. Right, Sean?"

"I did," Mr. Richardson said. "She sat next to Bitsy Enyeart all the way home." He moved hesitantly toward Jenny, hands out like "don't shoot." Nice gloves on those hands. Ketchup, though, staining one finger. "Let's not jump to any conclusions. Let's all just stay calm and straighten this whole thing out together."

This was a nightmare. This had to be a nightmare. But in

nightmares, you didn't step into ice-encrusted puddles up to your ankles and feel the shooting cold through your boots. In nightmares, you didn't find yourself face-to-face with a very anxious-looking, very unsure Ashley Batchelder. That's when Jenny knew. It was Ashley Batchelder's face that told her. Ashley Batchelder was never anxious looking or unsure.

"Where is she?" Earthquake in her teeth. "Where is she?" *Where is she where is she where is she,* like the blinking yellow sign in front of her house, like the ugly clock on her mantel, like a broken record.

Ashley had a car phone. "I have a car phone," she said. "I'll call the police."

The earthquake was everywhere now. Jenny was shaking so hard in her new coat she thought her eyes might fall out. Was that possible? Could your eyes be shaken from your skull? Billie Starr would know. Billie Starr knew everything. "You gave my daughter to a stranger, didn't you? You just let her go."

"What?" Ashley was back in her front seat, punching numbers. The buttons lit up under her perfect nails as she pressed them. Nine-one-one. "No."

"Where is she then?"

Soothing male voice behind her, air of authority. "Miss Newberg."

"Get away from me, Mr. Richardson. All of you. Just get away from me."

"We only want to help."

"How can you help? How can any of you help me now?"

Ashley was telling someone Jenny couldn't see that she needed to report a missing person. Person, Billie Starr Newberg, eight years old. What is she wearing? I don't know. Jenny, what was she wearing? I mean, what *is* she wearing? Is. Sorry. Not was.

A coat, red. A hat, yellow. Pink gloves, sparkly. New. Green pants. Orange sweater. Blue socks. A walking rainbow.

"A walking rainbow," Ashley said. "Her mom's upset, not thinking straight. Anyway, it was chaos. I'm sure you understand. Field

trip parking lot, big bus, lots of kids. Kids everywhere in the dark. Everything's fine, I'm sure, big misunderstanding, but we wanted to call. Just in case."

Jenny's teeming brain took inventory. Billie Starr was missing. Also missing: the sky, the stars, solid ground. The earth heaved. She was on her knees without knowing how she got there. Nothing under control now. Snow spun around her, swept up by the wind, pricking her cheeks and forehead like needles. Salt poked through her hose into her skin. Ice shards, too. Her knees ached. Let them bleed, she thought. Let my flesh rip. What do I care? In the distance, that howl, rising and falling, a haunted, hollow wail which was really just the sound of Jenny's world falling apart. Fine. Let it crumble.

Let it all turn to dust.

Book Three

The cop was growing a goatee. He kept stroking its rather meager beginnings and telling Jenny it was his first day, that it was hard to believe he was working a kidnapping already. Most guys had to be on the force for a year or more before something exciting happened. Patrol Officer Chad Leffert. Jenny could only remember his name by glancing periodically at his badge. She could hardly remember her own. A younger cousin of Randall's. She'd never met him before. He seemed shy, a little overwhelmed. Good cop.

Carla, having driven to the station in her bathrobe, was not impressed, not with Officer Chad, and not with any of the men on duty that night, who included two other Lefferts—Fred and Tony—and a Dodge. Art, Jenny was pretty sure, although, like the Winklers, the Dodges all looked alike. Normal foreheads, but chubby and bland. Like bread dough.

Shouldn't someone be out, Carla asked Officer Chad, searching the roads and woods and fields? Was anyone doing that? She offered to draw the cops a map of the county if that would help. "It's all in here," she said, tapping her forehead.

"I assure you," Officer Chad said, "we're doing everything we can."

"Are you?" Carla picked up the receiver of the heavy black phone on Officer Chad's desk, thrust it at him. "Have you called the FBI? The CIA?"

"I'm not exactly clear on the protocol, it being my first day and all, but I don't think the CIA gets involved in cases like these."

"No one gives a shit that it's your first day. You need to find my granddaughter. You need to do your job."

"I'm trying." Officer Chad gently grabbed the receiver back from Carla and returned it to its cradle.

"Try harder," Carla said.

"Yes, ma'am."

"Don't call me ma'am."

"Sorry, Mrs. Newberg."

"That's no good, either."

"I don't know wha—"

"I am the future Mrs. Bob Butz to you."

"Yes, ma—the future Mrs. Bob Butz."

Officer Chad had made a fresh pot of coffee. Every once in a while, the machine gurgled in the corner, reminded Jenny that time was actually passing. The room she'd been ushered to was baby-puke green and windowless. Furnishings were sparse—a desk, a few chairs, that coffeemaker, and the cabinet it sat on, the whole thing Old World and ugly and claustrophobic. Jenny was having a hard time catching her breath. She'd just gotten back from making a mad dash to her house to pick up a recent photograph of Billie Starr for the police and to see if by any chance she was there, maybe locked out and half frozen but at least safe, watched over by a mama deer. She wasn't. The house was deserted. Dark. No rainbow girl, no doe. The blinking sign at the top of the curve said *missing missing missing*.

Officer Chad studied the photograph Jenny handed him—the one of a triumphant Billie Starr at the first-grade science fair. "Any other suspects you can think of?"

"Already gave you mine," Carla said.

She'd offered Randall, as well as Eileen ("In cahoots," Carla said, "double whammy") and Marcus Rye—"Sorry, dear daughter, but you know he's crazy and capable of anything."

"Not this," Jenny said.

"Was he home just now?"

"Yes, and he did not have Billie Starr."

"How do you know?"

"I looked, Mom."

Jenny had walked methodically through Marcus's trailer, ex-plaining that she and Billie Starr were playing a late-night game of hide-and-seek, returning the wrenches she borrowed as cover. She didn't want to alarm him. What was the point when he'd just forget what she said five minutes later anyway? She went room-to-room, flipping on lights, peeking in each, even the cat room, whose odor was so strong it was like a color—a gassy green curtain hanging. No Billie Starr, just stacks and stacks of magazines and newspapers and broken plates and spent toilet paper rolls and pizza boxes and fur balls.

Speeding back to the station, Jenny had watched the dark land fly by, saw her daughter everywhere and nowhere. Is she there in that abandoned house? Vision of dirty rooms and Black Suits point-ing guns. That garage? Gasoline on the ground. Lit match. That pop-up camper? Moldy cushions, rusty sink, female Black Suit muttering about the daughters of women who dawdle. That field that church that garden shed that storage unit that boat that Dump-ster? Where is she where is she where is she?

"Let's say Marcus is out," Carla conceded. "That still leaves Ran-dall and Eileen."

They were being interviewed in a room down the hall. Officer Chad had obviously been reluctant to list Randall as a possible sus-pect, and the chief pompously announced that he only called Randall in to alert him to Billie Starr's disappearance—"As her father, he deserves to know," he said—but Carla told Chad if they didn't thoroughly investigate Randall and his old and sour bit of stuff, she would tell the press that the Benson Police Department was a swamp of corruption and narcolepsy.

"I think you mean 'nepotism,'" Officer Chad said.

"You said it, I didn't." Carla sat back, satisfied, arms crossed. "And my daughter works for the future governor, so we'll make sure people hear about it. We have connections. We know people who know people."

"Well, I know Randall," said Officer Chad, "and I don't think he'd kidnap his own daughter."

Over the course of a couple hours, with cops coming in and out of the room, Jenny had caught scraps of Randall and Eileen's story. Their alibi was Gill's Bar. They'd been there all night. Just ask Gill, they said. He'll vouch for us.

The police were also questioning Mr. Richardson, Gladys Mock, and Ashley Batchelder. Ashley's statement was about as helpful as the snow falling outside, as the wind whirling around the building. She told Tony Leffert that she might have seen Billie Starr getting into a car or truck or van with some sort of "woman-type person." Or a man. She couldn't be sure. It was dark and there were so many kids running around and she was too focused on trying to keep order, she said, on making sure no one got run over in the chaos and that everyone was picked up, to keep track of exactly who went home with whom. Jenny could just picture the cops falling all over themselves, trying to reassure Ashley that none of this was her fault. That was how the Ashley Batchelders of the world were treated—like porcelain dolls, like they'd break if you doubted them or looked at them too hard or, heaven forbid, dared to suggest they might not actually be perfect 100 percent of the time.

Carla had turned her attention to Jenny, was giving her the side-eye. "That's not the coat you took to Marsh's."

"Bradley's."

"You should have gone to Marsh's."

"Marsh's was closed."

"Marsh's never closes." Carla fingered Jenny's sleeve. "How much money did you waste on this?"

"It was a gift."

"From who?"

"The team."

"What team?"

"George's team."

"I didn't know he played sports."

"His campaign team."

"Coat like that, they'll be wanting something in return."

"It's not a big deal," Jenny said.

"Sure, sure. What do I know about anything?"

"It looks really soft," Officer Chad said. "The coat, I mean."

Carla rolled her eyes, told him she had one more suspect: Lyd Butz. "It pains me to say this, her being Bob's niece and all, but we have to be realists here. She's this one's best friend and mad at her and that might mean something."

"Lyd did not take Billie Starr."

"I'm just telling this man what I know. Oh, and you're going to want to check out her girlfriend, too. That weirdo from one-hour photo."

"Lyd's girlfriend?" Jenny asked.

"Lesbian?" Officer Chad asked, his eyes lighting up with interest.

"Big-time," Carla said.

"Mom, please."

"Haven't you heard?" Carla asked. "Everyone in town is talking about how Lyd and little Miss Free Doubles have turned Lyd's nice apartment downtown into their own sin-filled Isle of LEGOs—"

"Lesbos?" Officer Chad ventured.

Carla wagged her thumb at him. "Look at who's an authority over here."

Officer Chad blushed.

"Write it down!" Carla said again.

Officer Chad scrawled "Lid Butts and One-Hour Photo,

Lesbos" next to Randall G, Eileen Dubblewhammy, and Marcus Rhine.

Lyd hadn't said anything to Jenny about a girlfriend. Was that why Lyd kept calling her, leaving messages? To tell her that she was in love?

"This lesbian lead," Office Chad said. "It would jibe with what Miss Batchelder thinks she saw."

Carla hmphed. "The Batchelders. Not even from Benson. From Arcola originally. Ashley threw herself away on a foreigner. That's how you know."

Officer Chad took a sip of his coffee, made a face, pushed it away. "Know what?"

"You make your coffee too weak. I can tell by the smell. You know what they say about a cop who drinks weak coffee?"

"Ashley feels horrible." Officer Chad ignored Carla, glanced timidly at Jenny. "She feels responsible. She thinks you blame her."

"We do blame her," Carla said. "We blame her very much. Write that down, too."

"No, we don't," Jenny said. Her voice still wasn't right. Choked, it came out in a painful whisper. "Not really anyway."

Officer Chad tapped his pen against the table. "What was that, *Miss* Newberg?"

"Light in the gophers," Carla mumbled.

"Do you mean loafers?"

"You said it, I didn't."

"I don't blame Ashley," Jenny said. "I blame myself."

Her skin felt tight on her face. There was a foul-tasting film on her teeth, and her feet ached in her nice boots. George handing her that huge white box, the campaign speech, the party and the drunken dancing, it all seemed to belong to a different world. The table where Jenny sat was fake wood covered in a layer of hard, clear plastic. Fake on top of fake. Hash marks going in every direction.

A decade's worth of cop scribble swam in her vision. If she squinted just right, she could imagine the words "Watch Yourselfs" taking shape, coming together, right there, above "plea deal" and just to the left of "murder one."

"Is it possible . . ." Officer Chad stroked his goatee some more. The hairs made tiny animal-like scratching sounds—rat in a cage, hamster in a wheel. "I mean, please don't take this the wrong way, Miss Newberg, but is it possible your daughter ran away?"

Jenny shook her head. "No."

"I'm just asking because Ashley and the school principal lady have both said that your daughter might be unhappy at home, so . . ."

"That's not true." Jenny stood, her veins pumping fire. "She is not unhappy at home."

"We're only trying to help."

"Then help," Carla said.

"I'm trying."

"Try harder."

"We've been here before, ma'am."

"That's the future Mrs. Butz—"

Jenny left. She couldn't stomach being in there any longer, and she had an idea. She knocked on the door of the room across the hall. Tony Leffert answered, hand on his gun. Ashley was crying silently at a table behind him.

"I need to ask her a question," Jenny said.

Tony stepped aside, a little reluctantly. "Be gentle," he said to Jenny. "She's upset."

"Oh, is she?" Jenny asked. "Is *she* upset?"

Ashley's nose was red, her hair stiff and stringy. There was a glass of juice on the desk in front of her, untouched, and a napkin with a cookie on it. Nothing Mummy about her now. She looked ready for her mug shot.

"Phone numbers," Jenny said to her.

"Phone numbers?" Ashley asked.

"A list of phone numbers of the kids who went on the trip. One of them might have seen something. Or maybe their parents did."

"I don't have a list of phone numbers."

"Who does?"

"I don't know. Gladys, maybe?"

Jenny turned to Tony. "Have you called the kids? Their parents?"

Tony scratched his right ear. "Don't think so. I'd have to ask Chief. Or Art. Art's in with Gladys."

These Leffert men, a waste of time. All of them. A waste. This room had its own coffeemaker. It gurgled, too.

"Don't bother," Jenny said. "I'll do it."

Art and Gladys weren't in their assigned interrogation room. They were in the reception area, talking to Ruth Shields, the station secretary and Ashley Batchelder's seventy-year-old grandmother, about stocking stuffers.

Gladys was telling Art that if he wanted to do his kids a favor, he'd forgo the toys and candy altogether, opt instead for an assortment of oranges, apples, bananas. "You know," she said. "Your basic self-contained fruits. No big dental bills that way, and no fights."

"Oh bananas *are* nice," Ruth said. "So good for the digestion. I says to Ashley the other day, 'Ashley,' I says, 'you make sure our Terri gets plenty of bananas. They'll keep her regular.' I hope she takes my advice, but you never know about kids these days. It's in one ear and out the other."

Art helped Gladys into her coat. "I'm pretty sure the whelps would kill us in our sleep if we didn't at least get them a Kit Kat or a Hot Wheels."

"That's your problem," Gladys said. "No discipline. You've always been a pushover, Art, even back in school—"

Jenny interrupted her. "I need the list."

Gladys turned. Light reflected off her glasses, shrouded her eyes. "You need what?"

"The list," Jenny said. "The list of names and phone numbers of all the kids who went on the field trip today."

"I can't give that to you."

"Why not?"

"Well, privacy, to begin with. It's against school policy to—"

"I don't give a damn about school policy. Was it school policy to let my daughter go home with someone other than her mother?"

Gladys Mock hesitated for a moment. She glanced at Art Dodge. "Isn't that your job? To make a bunch of phone calls? To interview witnesses?"

Art shrugged, said he was pretty low on the totem pole and was about to clock out anyway.

"The chief doesn't like overtime," Ruth Shields said. "He's already hollered at me twice to go home but I says to him, I says, 'Chief, I'm here 'til the bitter end.'"

Gladys tapped her foot. Galosh there. Thick gray rubber and unbuttoned at the top, varicose veins showing above her knee-high hose. What was she thinking about? What must it be like to live inside her brain? Jenny imagined an endless grid of square rooms, spic-and-span and silent. If any people were allowed to live or learn inside such rooms, said inhabitants would have to be very good at constants and variables and coefficients, at putting two and two together and maintaining perfect decorum at all times. A spacious school with no actual children inside, a jail, empty and echoing.

After what seemed like forever, Gladys took a piece of folded paper from her coat pocket and handed it over. "I'm not sure what good any of this will do you," she said. "Everyone will be in bed, which is where I'm headed, Art, unless you need anything else from me."

"Nah, teach," he said. "You're good to go."

"Don't forget," Gladys said. "Fruit in the stocking. It's a game changer."

Art nodded. "Yes, ma'am. You know best."

"She does," Ruth agreed. "She really does."

Gladys zipped her coat, was halfway out the door.

"Wait!" Jenny yelled.

She turned again, heavy eyebrow raised. "Yes, Miss Newberg."

"It wasn't Judd Pickens who spit on the nameplate outside your office. It was me."

"Why on earth?"

For treating me like I was lesser than, for making me feel small. Always. What Jenny really said was, "That meeting you had with Billie Starr without me. If you were worried about her, you should have called me first. You should have included me. You should have taken better care of her." Jenny swallowed hard, crumpled the paper in her fist. "I should have taken better care of her."

Gladys Mock didn't reply. She gazed at Jenny for a moment, pursed her lips, and left the station, not scary anymore, not larger than life, just an old woman in ugly boots. A grocery store receipt was stuck to her left sole. It flapped behind her as she walked.

Art Dodge, meanwhile, was whistling to himself. "A Holly Jolly Christmas." He stopped midnote, gave Jenny a quick pat on the shoulder. "Don't you worry. Kids are like keys. They're always the last place you look." Then he left, too, coat over his head, snow coming down hard from the dark sky, dirty-looking, like crumbs from a shaken rug.

Ruth Shields sharpened a pencil, blew the shavings into a trash can. She wasn't looking at Jenny, seemed to have forgotten that she was there. "The roads are going to be a mess," she mumbled. "That's what I says to Art, I says . . ."

Back in the room with Officer Chad, Carla was singing the praises of the county deputy who'd successfully run off Randall and his girlfriend. "A fox, that man. A stone-cold fox, and very effective, unlike some people I just met."

"I don't see how handsomeness has anything to do with it," Officer Chad said.

"You wouldn't." Carla glanced up at Jenny as she came in. "Goatee here tried Lyd's house just now. No luck."

Jenny grabbed the cop's pen, crossed out Lyd's name and wrote down her own, phone number beside it. "Leave Lyd alone. If you hear anything, call me."

Carla stood, a little stunned. "What? Are you leaving?"

"I'm going home."

"Right now?"

Jenny blinked at her mother.

"I'll come with you."

In the hall, Jenny bumped into the police chief. Light glared off his gun, blinded her for a moment.

"Miss Newberg," he said. "Sad to meet again under such circumstances."

"Yes, sir."

"Randall's pretty torn up," the chief said. "It's his opinion that this would not have happened under his watch."

From behind Jenny, Carla laughed at that idea, a laugh of pure scorn, but then the laugh turned into a coughing fit, a long one, and she staggered outside, right arm flailing.

"It's my fault," Jenny whispered.

"What's that?" The chief leaned in. A stubbled neck. Deep lines like dry riverbeds. Aftershave so heavy it stung Jenny's eyes. "Speak up, sweetheart."

Officer Chad had followed Jenny and Carla out into the hall. Tony was there, too, slurping from an old, foot-pedal water fountain. Jenny thought at least one of the men might offer some advice or information or instruction. No one did. No one told her they'd stop at nothing to find her daughter. They weren't trading theories or springing into action. They simply stood there, backs up against a bulletin board covered in MOST WANTED flyers, fiddling with their nightsticks, stroking their goatees/five-o'-clock shadows/bald heads.

Their small eyes narrowed when they looked at her. Sizing her up, weighing her in the balance, finding her wanting.

Tip of her tongue, the Black Suits. The Riverview, the wire in her front yard, the woman in the McDonald's, the oranges, the job with George, everything. Should she tell them? Should she let a bunch of beer-bellied Lefferts in on her dirty little secret? Nothing had transpired in that station to convince Jenny that these men would do anything with the information she gave them besides throw it in her face. Officer Chad would probably listen kindly, but it was his first week, and he had a goatee to grow, so rock. Hard place.

Jenny kept her mouth shut and headed for the exit. On her way, she saw Randall in one of the cheerless rooms, his arm draped around the fat shoulders of a blowsy woman who could only be Eileen. And there, at the end, was Mr. Richardson, a napkin in front of him, too, and a small cup of juice. He'd eaten his cookie.

In a better world, Jenny would have different people on her side. Actual allies. In a better world, Billie Starr wouldn't have gone missing. She would be boarding a plane to Paris, unicorn backpack and all.

The sign, the mantel clock, the answering machine—everything blinking and ticking and flashing like mad. The first phone message was from Kevin Lipshott claiming to have sincerely enjoyed meeting her face-to-face and saying he was looking forward to next week when they could both sit down and work things out, because that was what this was all about, doing the work to make sure Jenny and Billie Starr had a place to call home for years to come. The others were from the campaign headquarters. In the background of those messages, loud music and yelling, George begging her to come back to the party—"It's no fun without you"—then Ted slurring that

she'd forgotten her poinsettia, that he'd put one aside especially for her but that she'd left without it. Could he bring it by her house tonight maybe?

Carla listened to the messages from the living room. "My younger self never got calls like that."

"The one about foreclosure you mean?" Jenny heated up a cup of coffee. "Or the one about the poinsettia?"

"Both. And the plant guy sounds Black."

"If I remember correctly, you never got phone messages from collection agents because there were no answering machines in the seventies. They came to the house and you made me talk to them. Me. A kid. My younger self. And you killed every plant you ever owned, so . . ."

"Oh well, if you're just going to be hateful."

Jenny started calling the numbers on the list Gladys Mock had given her. It was closing in on midnight and Jen Anderson hung up on her before she could get her story out. So did Sal Baker, Lisa Coddop, and Ginny Dearn. Paul Enyeart was sympathetic but said all he saw in the parking lot was "a plague of foreign cars" and a lot of kids in need of an old-fashioned spanking. Jan Furhman wanted to help, too, but said her son, Josh, vomited all over himself back on the bus, so she was pretty distracted. Rick Gibson, though. He definitely saw something. Had Jenny seen it, too? Something suspicious in the sky over the school just as the bus was pulling in. A bright green light shaped like a cigar that defied the laws of physics and motion. He'd just been reading about a rash of alien abductions in Michigan. "Guess they've come for us now." Laura Hardacre tried to sell Jenny wrapping paper as part of "little Henry's church project" and promised to pray. At some point, Carla had volunteered to help make a few calls but then fell asleep on the couch, spent cigarette butt still hanging from her fingers.

Jenny had gotten to the Pickenses. There were no black check marks next to Judd's name. The marks were meant to show that a

student had boarded the bus both in Benson and Chicago. (Billie Starr had two.) So, Judd hadn't gone on the trip. Duh, Mom. Duh, because he was suspended at the time. But Jenny had already dialed the number and a woman had already answered and so here they were. Jenny tried to explain her reason for calling, but the woman interrupted her, misunderstood, was furious and slamming things from the get-go.

"If we wanted to be bullied and harassed, we could have stayed put, never left home," she said. "But no, we had to come here to take care of my dad, and did we get one thank-you from him before he kicked it? One? I'll answer that. No. We got a whole lot of grief. That's our lot. Grief from all sides. As for this stupid trip, shove it up your ass."

"But I'm not with the school," Jenny said. "Not really. I mean, I'm a parent. I'm calling because my daughter, Billie Starr—"

"Oh your daughter, your daughter, your precious daughter. Why is your daughter worth more than my son, huh? Whatever happened to her, Judd didn't do it. He's just trying to lift himself up by his bootstraps, which is what all y'all are always claiming kids should do, and then when they try, you knock them the hell down. What's a body to do with those kinds of moving targets? And if this is about the lice outbreak, I've been combing nits out of his hair for hours and he's clean. He's clean and I might even shave his head tomorrow so—"

"I'm not accusing your son of anything," Jenny said. "I didn't even know about the lice. Honestly, I—"

"Wait. Did you say Billie Starr?"

"Yes."

"Hang on." The woman hollered for Judd. There was some muffled conversation. Then she ordered the boy back to bed. "Wash your face while you're at it. I don't know how you get so dirty. You're a filth magnet, did you know that? That's what you attract. Filth." Some sighing. "He said that a girl named Billie Starr is the only one who's been nice to him since we moved here."

"She's missing," Jenny said.

"What do you mean 'missing'?"

"I went to pick her up at the school after the field trip and she wasn't there. I'm sorry. It sounds like Judd didn't go—"

"The school wouldn't let him go. I didn't have the money."

"I shouldn't have bothered you."

"Yeah, you shouldn't have." More hollering, more mumbling, a boy's voice in the background complaining that he was hungry, the woman telling him to take the stupid crackers to bed with him if he was so starving. Then an actual fight seemed to break out in the Pickens house. A series of loud crashes was followed by a little girl screaming about her hair being on fire and a boy telling her to just shut up for Christ's sake, he was doing her a favor by burning out the lice. Calm down, he said. I'll get the bucket of water ready. Jenny heard water running and the woman yelling that they were monsters, horrors, what had she done to deserve such demons? There was another loud bang and then the line went dead.

Jenny gave up on the phone list, drifted into Billie Starr's room, stared with unseeing eyes at the mess, the mural, the glow-in-the-dark constellations on the headboard. She crawled into the small, rumpled bed, pulled the covers up, smelled her sleeping daughter there on the fabric, her apple shampoo, her sharp girl sweat. A large, looping crack spanned the ceiling overhead, a cursive *G,* and Billie Starr's homemade solar system mobile spun slowly in an invisible breeze, the wooden balls hanging in midair like thought bubbles. Mercury: I'm so cold. Venus: Ashley Batchelder is very upset. *She thinks you blame her.* Earth: Where in the world is my daughter? Mars: I think I'm at war with the Lefferts and the Black Suits and men like Bob Butz who don't care about other people. *Girls like you.* Jupiter: Who was Jupiter again? Saturn: Rings. Trees are full of rings. The rings tell you how old the tree is. That fact courtesy of Billie Starr. Uranus: A silly joke about a telescope spotting something big coming out of ur-anus. From

Billie Starr, too. Neptune: the sea, the roar of it, the size, making you feel insignificant. All we have in Indiana is lakes. Lakes go nowhere. I'm going nowhere. Pluto: Mickey's dog. Why didn't he talk? And who cared about Greek mythology? Jenny had flunked that test twice.

The universe offered her nothing, so Jenny turned to Pete instead. "Dad? Can you hear me? I need you. I need your help."

No answer. There was never an answer, only silence. Not even a sign, or an omen. Pete, guardian angel, asleep at the wheel. Jenny looked again at the mural on the wall—her small, wonky house, Marcus's trailer, the corn, the rainbows, the butterflies, Gertrude and Yo-Yo stretching luxuriantly in the rays from a lopsided yellow sun. Pete would have loved that mural, would have delighted in it and in Billie Starr, but Pete was dead, probably of toxic dust stirred up by the villainy of none other than Bob Butz. And Jenny would almost certainly lose this wonky house. In any case.

She rolled over, bumped into something hard. Pushing the covers down, Jenny found a light green three-ring binder on which Billie Starr had written the words "The Book of Sorries" in large, loopy script. The *B* in *Book* was a butterfly, the *i* in *Sorries* dotted with a heart. Inside was what appeared to be a long list of apologies. Some, like the book's title, were in Billie Starr's handwriting. Others were in a sharp, small scribble, difficult, but not impossible, to make out. Next to the apologies—most of them simple "I'm sorries"—were dates and notes that apparently provided context.

"I'm sorry." Oct 31st. Mom forgot to get me a Holloween costoom. I had to go as a hobo. Again. She promised me that next year I could be a astroknot like I wanted. I'm not sure I believe her. Mom sux at holidays.

Jenny cringed, remembered hurriedly covering Billie Starr's face in honey and old coffee grounds, lending her an old shirt and some

scuffed shoes. Most of the people who answered their doors that night couldn't guess what she was.

"Sorry for living." Nov 3rd. So I asked Mom why insted of making dinner for me and Ruby she got high with that guy Gary and she said she was sorry for living but I don't think she ment it because one time when she got really, really high—not with Gary, with Jess that time—she made me call 911 so she wood not die in the bathtub without her cloths on.

So this was the record of apologies Billie Starr had mentioned, the one she was compiling with Judd Pickens. That must mean the small scrawl was Judd's.

"Sorry sorry sorry." Nov 12th. Mom got me the wrong size shoes today so I have to wear my old ones to school and they have holes in them that let the water in.

True, Jenny thought, but I got you new ones right after and they light up, so . . .

"I'm so sorry, honey-boy. Will you ever forgiv me?" Nov 27th. Mom hit me for telling every-1 that the cranberry sauce her friend JuJu maid tasted like snot. Ungreatful, Mom said. Rood. She hit me hard. I have two bruuses—one under my rite eye and one over it. They started off purple. Now they're green and pink. Snot collored.

"Ugh sorry, this is all my fault." Dec 1st. I cut my foot on a tuna can lid Mom left lieing around after she fed Gertrude and Yo-Yo. She said she'd take me into Dr. Harm for a tetniss shot but she never did.

No, because I called Dr. Harme's office and they told me your tetanus shot was up-to-date. Dear Christ, can a mom catch a break?

"Sorry, bud, but he was only a cokroach." Mom smashed Orville
with a frying pan this morning. Ruby and I berried him out next
to the lawnmoer that doesn't work. RIP Orville.

The entries were divided equally: one Billie Starr for one Judd
Pickens. Even in number if not in degree of offense. Did they talk
about that? The fact that Judd's complaints were on a whole new
level from Billie Starr's? Jenny flipped the page to a different sort
of list altogether, a catalog of "generick sorries from disapointing
adalts."

Sorry kid that's just life. (Gary)

Sorry is as sorry duzz. (Grandma Carla)

Sorry but that's our cumpanie policie. (Guy at the toy store.)

Sorry state of affares. (Lady on TV)

Sorry to anyone who was hoping for a happy ending. (Guy on TV)

Sorry I can't save the Indyans. Its too late. (Gorge)

Sorry about your luk. (Jess)

Sorry about your face. (Gary again)

As Jenny scanned the list, she found one in Billie Starr's writing.
"I'm sorry your having trubble at home." The entry at first did not
seem to be about Jenny. Next to the apology was a short explanation: "Principull Mock said this to me today because she's worried
about my helth and my future." Then: "Does my mom care about
my helth and my future?"

"Yes," Jenny cried in frustration. "Of course, I care. I care more than anyone." Then she sat bolt upright, pushing the binder to the floor. George's words from that morning came back to her: *Is working for me causing trouble at home? . . . I assume Bob told you that we're not the best of friends.* George had represented a number of clients in their suits against Bob—and George had won. How much money had Bob had to pay out over the years, thanks to George Shepherd's skills as a litigator? How much was too much? And what was it Bob said at the family bonding dinner? Something about how soon he'd be celebrating something beyond his engagement, something big and having to do with business? "Backroom kind of stuff." Suddenly, it all made sense. The Black Suits. The faxes and emails. The blackmail. And now, Billie Starr. The one Jenny loved most, a pawn in a petty plot for revenge.

Jenny ran out to the living room, shook Carla. "Wake up, Mom. Wake up!"

Carla groaned and turned over. Her robe and coat twisted around her, a cocoon. She sank farther down into it.

Jenny shook her again. "I need to talk to you!"

"No."

"Mom!"

"What?" Carla shoved Jenny's hands away, talked into the cushions. "Did the cops call? Did they find her?"

"No. They didn't call. They're not going to call." Jenny knelt next to the couch. "I have to tell you something, Mom. I don't want to tell you this, but it's important, and I need you to listen. It has to do with Bob. I'm almost sure of it."

Carla rose up on her elbows. "Bob? What are you talking about?"

Jenny gave Carla a brief rundown of the events of the last five days. Carla shook her head through it all, disbelieving.

"It's too crazy," she said. "You're lying."

"Why would I do that?"

"I don't know. Black Suits? A wire? You've got to be kidding me."

Jenny went outside, dug up the wire. Then she brought it and presented it to Carla. "This is what I wore that morning, to record everything George said. Didn't you wonder how I possibly could have gotten the job in George's campaign office?"

"Well, sure. You're obviously not qualified."

"I got it because he likes me. Because he . . ."

"Wanted to see more of you. Literally."

"Yeah."

Carla took the wire, looked it over. "My younger self would not have been caught dead doing any of this."

"I suppose your younger self would never have gone and let her daughter get kidnapped, either? Say it, Mom. Just say it."

Carla held her hands up. "Okay, dear daughter, all right, you prostituted yourself, you brought shame on you and your family. What does that have to do with Bob?"

Jenny stood again, paced. She felt like a wild animal. Trapped. The deer. The doe. She looked for it out the front window, but all she saw was the sign, blinking blinking relentlessly blinking, and Dorothy Renfrow's house filling with snow. "Bob hired the Black Suits. He put them onto me. He hired the Black Suits who hired me to get dirt on George. And he killed Dad."

"Well, now you're just ranting. You're just raving."

Jenny tried to explain to Carla all that George had told her about the dust, about Bob's business's "flagrant and repeated violation of public safety standards," and men in his employ contracting lung disease—"just like Dad and Judd Pickens's grandpa"—but Carla wouldn't hear any of it.

"You're upset. You're overtired. That's all this is."

"George has sued Bob in court several times and beat him. Bob obviously had to stop him somehow."

"Bob's a good man. You don't know him. You don't know what you're talking about."

"Remember how I 'quit' my job at Bob's real estate office?"

"Defeatful." Carla grabbed her purse and stood. She dropped a spent cigarette butt inside, huffily zipped it shut. "Not hopeful."

"It wasn't because I was defeatful. It was because he tried to attack me in the break room. He stuck his hand up my skirt. When I pushed him away, he fired me. He had me promise not to tell anyone and then I'm pretty sure he made it so no one else in this town would hire me, either. That's why I had to say yes to the Black Suits. You heard the messages. I'm broke. I'm broke, Mom. I'm going to lose my house. I had no other choice. Bob must have known that. He must have known I'd do what they asked."

"You're off the deep end. Straight off the deep end."

"He told me his idea of heaven would be to sit in a chair across from my naked body and stare at my breasts for the rest of his life."

Carla glared at Jenny for a moment. Then she had a short coughing fit. When it was over, she said, "You need to clean. It's a pig sty in here. And I won't listen to this. Do you hear me? I won't. I'm leaving."

Jenny grabbed her by the arm. "Where is he right now? Where is Bob?"

"I don't know."

"You don't know."

"I'm not his keeper. We're not even married yet."

"Mom . . ."

Carla whimpered. "You're hurting me."

Jenny loosened her grip.

"He might have said something about getting a few beers with Ed."

"Ed? Vi's bail bondsman?"

"They hit it off at the Brown Derby dinner. And they're dating best friends. It happens."

"I bet they were friends before that. I bet Ed hooked Bob up

with the Black Suits. As a bail bondsman, Ed would know some shady people."

"You're insane."

"Where were Bob and Ed going for these beers?"

"Gill's, I think, but what are you going to do? Accost Bob in a bar? Accuse him of, I don't know, extinction, right then and there?"

"Extortion."

"You'll look as loco as Marcus Rye. They'll call the cops on *you*."

"I don't care."

Carla patted her hair, straightened her back. She looked down her thin nose at Jenny, drew herself up in a regal pose. "You go down this road, dear daughter, you try to mudsling my fiancé's good name and cause trouble between us, I warn you, you won't get any help from me."

"Fine."

"You'll have to fight the Lefferts all on your own."

"Okay."

"I mean it."

"I know you do."

Carla hesitated for a brief moment, eyeing that ring on her left hand. It was still too big, had not yet been resized. "I'll write you out of my will. That's what I'll do. And you won't be invited to the wedding."

"Bye, Mom."

"You're going to regret being so awful to me. You'll be sorry. You think you know so much. There are things you don't know."

"Like what?"

"Wouldn't you like to know."

"Yes, Mom. That's why I asked. What things don't I know?"

"Defeatful," Carla said again, turning away. "Your whole life. Since you were born. Since you were tiny. Doris and Pete reincarnate. None of me in you. None."

Slammed door. Screech of tires. Crunch of snow and ice. Another dramatic exit for Carla Newberg/the Future Mrs. Bob Butz. It was nothing new: Carla saying horrible things, Carla walking away. With her gone, Jenny could breathe easier. No smoke now. No passive-aggressive belittling. Solo Jenny would be fine. She could do this. She was used to being all on her own anyway. She threw the wire in the curio cabinet with Billie Starr's clay figurines and headed to her bedroom to change.

Gill's Bar at 1:00 A.M. was life in slow motion. Low, reddish light shone on pockets of people in various states of drunkenness. Not too drunk at the tables. Pretty drunk at the booths. Very drunk at the bar itself. There was even a handful of dancers doing what they could on a small, elevated space between the bathrooms and the jukebox. They looked like swimmers in a pool, wading through a cloud of thick smoke, their heads just above water as they undulated to a song about ponytailed girls in cutoff jeans and pickup trucks parked under full moons. Howling men, jealous women. Guns waiting to go off.

Buddy Winkler was behind the bar, pouring shots for a woman wearing a cockeyed veil made of toilet paper flowers. He waved at Jenny. "Fancy seeing you again so soon. It's my lucky day."

"Hey, Buddy."

"Get you something?"

"Maybe in a minute."

Jenny scanned the crowd for Bob Butz's springy perm, but no luck. She did see Ed, though, at the bar, and a few stools down sat the skinny black-eyed woman with the fairy tattoo from George's campaign launch party, the one who'd danced on the desk with Ted and said something to Jenny about not being the only one.

Driving over, Jenny had been very confident, very sure in her

mission, but now that she was actually here and Bob Butz wasn't, she didn't know what to do. She hesitantly approached the bar. At the very least, she could make sure Randall and Eileen's alibi checked out. The eyes of the dark-haired woman and Ed were on her, bloodshot and intense. Was that Trish Keck at the end, bobbing over a brown beer? And three Mummies at a round table next to the jukebox were sucking down a round of Lemon Drops. The one who'd complained about the scandalous state of the town's nativity was the most obviously tipsy. She kept sloshing her drink on the Mummy next to her, griping this time, it seemed, about the new gym teacher at the middle school.

"Black, but that's not the problem," she slurred loudly. "I don't have a problem with that. You guys know that, right?" Mummy heads nodding, all but the one getting sloshed on. She looked skeptical, staring at her sleeve. *Of course,* the others said. *You'd never. She's just not working out, not quite like us . . .*

Jenny settled onto a stool in front of the cash register.

"How you been since this afternoon?" Buddy asked.

"Thought Gill was bartending tonight."

"He took off. Headache. And now I'm in charge of all these yayhoos."

The woman in the veil gave Buddy and Jenny a sloppy smile. "I'm not a yayhoo. I'm getting married."

"The veil sort of tipped me off," Buddy said.

"My fiancé's in cow sperm."

"Cow sperm?" Buddy asked.

"Not as dirty as it sounds. Cows aren't great at getting pregnant on their own. They need a little help. That's where my boyfriend comes in. He supplies the sperm and then they use that to get the heifer pregnant and voilà! Lots of baby cows. Without him, there'd be no hamburgers, no milk, no Klondike bars. Imagine, if you will, that world."

Buddy faked a shiver. "A hellscape." He pushed a drink toward Jenny, a Lemon Drop, probably what was left over from the Mummies' order. "On the house," he said. Then he nudged the bride-to-be's shots down the bar toward her group, four young, very drunk women admiring each other's choker necklaces. "Enjoy your Buttery Nipples."

"Enjoy your Buttery Nipples," the woman echoed, adjusting her veil thoughtfully. "We will, Mr. Bartender." Stumbling away in a cloud of vanilla perfume. "We *will* enjoy our Buttery Nipples."

"I aim to please," Buddy said. He gave Jenny an ironic grin. "I did not have 'cow sperm' on my drunken-Saturday-night-at-Gill's bingo card, did you?"

"Definitely not." Jenny took a sip of her drink. "Was Randall in here earlier?"

"Yeah. With his lady friend. I served him a few beer and bumps earlier. Or is it beers and bump? Like attorneys general?"

"Beers and bumps," said the dark-haired woman from the campaign party, cigarette behind her ear like a pencil.

"Is that your order?" Buddy asked.

"No, just my opinion."

Buddy handed her a bowl of pretzels. "You're welcome to it. Free country."

The woman took the bowl gratefully, huddled around it like it was a fire giving off warmth. "For now."

Jenny leaned over the bar toward Buddy, lowered her voice to a whisper. "Thought I might run into Bob Butz." Shaking again, watching Ed out of the corner of her eye. He'd turned his attention to the television, tuned to an infomercial about nearly painless catheters. "Did you hear Bob and that bald man over there talking by chance? Did they maybe say anything about me? Or a man named George Shepherd?"

"Give me a second." Buddy printed out a receipt and plopped it down in front of Trish Keck, but she wasn't done drinking.

"Keep it open," Trish said.

"What's the latest on Lorne?"

Trish slurped her beer. "Don't ask."

"I just did."

"How about don't ask again?"

"Sure, hon. Whatever you want." Buddy grabbed some limes from under the bar and started slicing them. Then he checked a clock over his shoulder. Hovering above the numbers, the words NO BRAIN, NO BRA, NO PROBLEM. He leaned toward Jenny, biceps popping under his tight shirt. "The self-appointed prince of Benson Realty was indeed a customer of mine for a while tonight," he said. "He left about fifteen minutes ago, but he and that guy"—thumbing Ed—"they were pretty quiet, kept to themselves. What you want with Bob anyway?"

"My daughter's missing."

Buddy jerked, cut his thumb with the fruit knife. "Fuck. Fuck's sake." Blood dripped on the limes, ran down his arm in a slippery streak. "Are you serious, Jenny? Why didn't you say something?"

"I thought maybe the cops would have called here. You know, to see about Randall, to make sure he was here when he said he was. You guys are his alibi."

"No one's called, far as I know. No cops anyway." Buddy wrapped his bloody thumb in a paper towel. "Shit, Jenny. I don't know what to say. Can I do something? Can I help?"

"I can't believe the cops haven't called. I mean, I can, but . . . ."

"We should start a search," Buddy said eagerly. "You need to get the word out. A community search, you know? The kind you see on TV where the whole town joins in, flashlights and bullhorns and whatnot. I have a bullhorn. It's right here." It was sitting on a shelf next to an inflated skeleton. Red on one half, white on the other, GILL's scribbled on the handle.

"No, Buddy, it's okay."

"It's not okay. When did this happen?"

"About five hours ago."

"Five hours ago? That's ancient history. You can't let any more time go by."

"I don't think—" Jenny started, but Buddy was already climbing on top of the bar, waving his bloody hand around.

"Attention, barflies!" he shouted into the bullhorn. "One of our own is missing. Billie Starr Newberg, the daughter of this lovely young woman right here. I'm going to start a search. We're going to comb the whole town. Who's with me?"

There was a short moment of confused silence, followed by a few halfhearted "I'm with yous" and a passionate "me!" The "I'm with yous" came from the bride-to-be and her friends. The "me" was from Trish Keck. The jukebox song had changed to "Grandma Got Run Over by a Reindeer."

"This is last call," Buddy said. "I'm not going to waste time slinging drinks while there's a little girl to be found. If you want a drink, now's the time, and it's gratis if you join the search party. Hear that, y'all? Free drinks for anyone who helps me find Billie Starr and return her to her mother safe and sound."

A flood of men in flannel shirts and dirty-kneed jeans crowded the bar, shouting out orders. The Mummies came, too, loudly debating the pros and the cons of a free drink and a few hours out in the cold versus a drink they'd have to pay for and going home to their husbands.

"Here." Jenny thrust her Lemon Drop at the Mummy who kept getting spilled on, the one with the wet sleeve, and started to make her way through the throng toward Ed. Be direct, she told herself. Get right to the point. Ask him if he knew Bob before the Brown Derby, if he helped Bob find the Black Suits, if he was in on the scheme to hire her and discredit George and kidnap Billie Starr. Back him into a corner.

Ed was one of the only people in the bar not clamoring for a drink. His highball glass was still half full and his eyes glued to the TV

where the commercial about catheters had been replaced by one singing the praises of a skillet you could run over with a car and still use to make the perfect pancake. Jenny was just about to sit down next to him when someone tugged on her arm, yanked her back.

"Come with me," Trish Keck slurred, motioning to a wooden booth in the back. "Over there."

The crowd at the bar was raucous. They banged their glasses together, threw back shots, vowed to find Billie Starr or die trying. In the middle were the bride-to-be and her fellow bachelorettes who'd finished their Buttery Nipples and were pushing their way to the front, demanding Snakebites this time.

Jenny reluctantly followed Trish to the booth. Tucked away behind a bookshelf full of antique car manuals, it was relatively quiet. The table was full of greasy glasses, fry baskets, stained menus, and crusty condiment bottles. Trish got busy marshaling the mess into some sort of map. "Your daughter is in danger." She rested her hand on the ketchup bottle, moved it like a chess piece toward the mustard.

Jenny couldn't see Ed anymore. He was hidden by a group of tall, twentysomething men. Farm boys. Dodges and Hardacres mostly. A few Enyearts. "Yes, I know. I—"

Trish arranged three sticky shot glasses into a line behind the tartar sauce. "I went to a psychic yesterday."

"A psychic?"

"A clairvoyant, whatever you want to call it. I wanted some guidance about this thing with Marcus, with Lorne. It's messing me up. I wanted answers."

"Oh, well—"

"Yeah, but all I got was a bunch of gobbledygook about planets rising and fire signs and water bearers blah blah blah. It didn't make a lick of sense and a big part of me wanted to ask for my money back, but the lady obviously needed the cash even more than I did. Her crystal ball was a bowling ball, a pink eight-pounder. Used it once. Over at Brick Lanes."

Buddy was still dispensing free drinks. Jenny played along. "So what did this psychic tell you?"

"She said that she saw in her mind's eye a little bird being stolen from its nest. The bird was so little it couldn't fly. Still needed its mom to feed it. You know how birds do. They puke into their kids' mouths. Or beaks. Anyway, what if your daughter is that little bird?" Trish took a swig from one of the cups on the table. "The lady said she heard things, too."

"Like . . ."

"Lake things."

"Lake things?"

"Water lapping, mostly. And loons."

"Loons?"

"They have a very distinctive call."

"It's December."

"So?"

"Don't loons go south for the winter?"

"I'm just telling you what she said." Trish pulled something from her pocket, pushed it across the table, knocking over two shot glasses and the mustard bottle. "And while I'm here, I thought you might want this, too."

It was a picture of Jenny and Billie Starr petting Gertrude and Yo-Yo on their front stoop at home. One corner of the photo had been torn off and the whole image was double-exposed. Hovering next to Jenny and Billie Starr and the cats were their golden, ghostly twins. It was autumn. Yellow leaves dotted the sidewalk and a rotting jack-o'-lantern leaned darkly over the steps, a fat slinky about to fall.

"Found it in Lorne's wallet," Trish said. "I was pretty mad for a while, thought maybe the two of you had a thing going."

"Me and Lorne?"

"I know, I know, a man as old as Lorne who likes to treat his wife like target practice and you all young and dewy. Like a melon. Or

the grass in the morning." Trish snorted loudly and fumbled around in another pocket, came up with a small white card, pushed it over to Jenny, too. "Give my psychic a call, ask her about that bird. Who knows? Maybe she can help. I told her this dream I have, of owning my own bakery someday, calling it Bulletproof Pies, and do you know what she said? She said open it on March fourteenth. That's pie day."

Trish had given Jenny her library card by mistake. When Jenny looked up, she was gone. So was Ed. Stool and highball glass both empty, TV showing a rerun of *The Dukes of Hazzard*. Jenny wanted to scream, to throw things. Ketchup and mustard and tartar sauce and backwash whiskey all over the walls. The Mummies and bachelorettes were pulling on their coats. The farm boys, too. Suiting up and shoving plugs of chaw in their cheeks.

Will Hardacre spit hard into his hand, wiped the mess on his thigh. "Where we headed, Buddy?"

"I guess I don't rightly know." Buddy scanned the crowd for Jenny. "Hey, Miss Newberg, where should we start?"

Morocco. Paris. A lake dotted with loons? It didn't matter where they went, but they seemed determined to go somewhere. "The elementary school?" she said.

"To the elementary school!" Buddy said, badly bandaged hand back in the air.

"To the elementary school!" the crowd echoed. A drunken battle cry.

Everyone shuffled out the door all at once, mumbling about hitching rides, about being too soused to drive, oh fuck it let's just walk. I got a flashlight in my car. Me, too. Not me, flares. Flares? What are we going to do with flares? Got a pitchfork? Ha, no. Got a gun, though, in the glove compartment. Thirty-eight? Glock. Nice. We have to stick together. We have to spread out. How old's the girl anyway? What's she look like? Cute? Fat? Hell if I know.

Jenny trailed the tossed-off words, the smell of wet wool, out into the night.

Sky like a watercolor painting dripping down the horizon, dark and deep overhead, fading to a soft heather at the tree line. Earth bumpy, hard, unyielding. Snow squeaky and shallow, blown into drifts by the road. Jenny had changed into jeans and a sweater and snow boots before heading out to Gill's, and her pretty new coat from George was surprisingly warm, but even so, she shivered violently as she trudged the length of a frozen cornfield, keeping to the row Buddy assigned her. The search party was behind the school on one of the Gregor farms. Barn in the distance. Cows mooing unhappily. A few roosters crowed, too. Confused, maybe, by the unexpected activity. A FOR SALE sign anchored the northeast corner. So another subdivision was coming. Misty River Canyon, maybe. Elm Brook Estates. (All the elms in town were dead, turned to mulch. Worm to blame.)

To either side of Jenny, a Hardacre boy. Beyond them, more flannel-shirted men and a few Mummies. The bachelorettes showed up, too, tripping, laughing, treating the search like a lark, like one more stop on their Buttery-Nippled bar crawl. The group moved together, a human combine, flashlight beams blending, bouncing. Jenny walked without thinking, thought without realizing her brain was functioning at all. This field. Before it was corn, was it soybeans? And before it was soybeans, was it wheat? And before it was wheat, was it clover/trees/weeds? Weeds are only weeds because someone doesn't want them. Billie Starr said that last summer when Marcus Rye tried to take a torch to both their yards to get rid of the dandelions. Billie Starr was somewhere thinking Jenny didn't want her. Bob Butz hated dandelions. Claimed they caused cancer. Bob Butz. Have to find him. Probably still living in that house on High Street, the one he fixed up. Scratch that. The one

Pete fixed up. Jenny would drive there, shout him awake, demand answers, make him tell her what he knew. And what had Carla meant by "there are things you don't know"? Probably nothing. Empty threat, but still. And so cold. Was Billie Starr warm? Whoever took her, did they let her keep her gloves on, her hat? Jenny should never have let her go on that field trip. Were Jenny and the rest of the bar crowd on a field trip, too? Literally. Didn't Ted say something that very morning about "literally" being used so often and applied so badly that they were going to need a new word for "figuratively"? That cornstalk was literally rattling like a dead thing. Dead thing . . . dead . . .

"I see something!"

One of the Enyearts was crouching on the ground, pointing a lit flare at a spot of earth at the field's southern edge. The human combine fell apart. Everyone rushed over. Not Jenny. She stayed where she was. Rooted.

Buddy was there in a second, grabbing the flare, moving it over the ground. He slapped the Enyeart boy upside the head. "Those are animal bones, dufus."

"You sure?"

"Dog, probably. Maybe raccoon. And at least a year old. What were you thinking?"

"I wasn't."

"Next time do us all a favor and think for a change. Don't just go off half-cocked. Her mom's right there."

"Okay. Sorry."

Buddy rose, came toward Jenny. He put his hands on her shoulders. Work gloves covering them oversize, brushed cotton, smelling of gas and garage. Pete used to wear gloves like that. "Don't worry. We're not all morons like Vic. We'll keep looking. We'll find her. I promise."

It was what she'd been wanting to hear from the cops, from all those Lefferts back at the station, but now that someone was saying it and that someone was Buddy Winkler, she was about to burst into

sobs. That or start laughing hysterically, so she rose up on tiptoe and kissed him on the cheek, nodding mutely. Then she fled across the field toward the school parking lot, broken cornstalks whistling in her wake. "Greensleeves," sounded like. What child is this is laid to rest. What dog/raccoon. How many bones had been ground into the ground here? Jenny's brain kept going, feeding her thoughts because it couldn't help it. That was what it meant to be alive. Thinking thinking always thinking, whether you wanted to or not.

$\mathcal{B}$ob Butz did not come to the door, did not answer her knock. Jenny tried the front and the back. Then she started banging on windows.

"Bob Butz, I know you're in there." His Jeep Cherokee was in the driveway, BOB BUTZ REALTY: YOUR NEW HOME AWAITS on the passenger's-side door over a painting of a perfect house, a picket fence, a stick family and a stick dog. "You can't hide from me. I know what you're up to. I know what you've done."

Bob's house was decked out for Christmas—icicle lights in the eaves, a Santa and eight plastic reindeer on the roof. Four lit-up snowmen formed a jolly army under the kitchen window. Jenny kicked the smallest one. It felt so good she kept kicking. She was still kicking when a police car pulled up, parked, idled just a few feet from where she stood.

An officer approached her, asked in a mild voice, "Excuse me, ma'am. Can I help you with something?"

Two of the snowmen had toppled over in the assault. Jenny righted them and turned to face the cop. It was the handsome one from George's rally. Blond. Square-jawed. He flashed his county badge. Not moonlighting anymore. On the beat.

"Thank you, no."

"Got a call about a disturbance, about someone trying to break into this house. Guessing you're the disturbance."

"I wasn't trying to break in."

"But you were doing your best to end the lives of these innocent snowmen here. Now, ma'am, I ask you. What did they do to warrant such abuse?"

"My daughter is missing."

The cop blew into his bare hands. "And the snowmen are behind her disappearance somehow?"

"This isn't funny. My daughter has been kidnapped."

"My sympathies. Is this a recent development?"

Jenny could tell he didn't believe her. He obviously thought she was drunk or crazy or both. "Six hours ago. Her name is Billie Starr Newberg. She's eight and dressed like a rainbow."

"A rainbow."

"Didn't the Benson police put out some sort of alert? Aren't they supposed to do that? Tell everyone in local law enforcement to keep a lookout?"

"I just started my shift, so—"

"And it's Officer Chad's first day and Art Dodge was just about to clock out, so I guess the moral of the story is that my daughter decided to go and get kidnapped at exactly the wrong time."

"Why don't you climb in my car for a minute, get warm, tell me why you're here."

"I'm here because you're all a bunch of coffee-swilling do-nothings who care more about a few fake snowmen than you do real people."

"Well, now—"

Bob Butz took that opportune moment to appear. He popped out his front door in pajama pants and a wife beater, making a big show of being cold, his perm poofier than ever. "What is going on here? Jenny! It's two in the morning."

Jenny strode across the lawn, snow up to her ankles, feet freezing. "I guess it wasn't enough that you killed my dad with your toxic dust. You had to go and ruin my life, to orchestrate the whole

Riverview scheme to take George down and for what? A few houses to flip? A couple thousand dollars? You're evil, Bob Butz. Completely evil. I bet you don't even love my mom. Using the same lame lines on her as you did on me. Pathetic."

The cop followed close behind. "Ma'am, you need to calm down—"

"I'm not going to calm down. Why should I calm down? This man is responsible for my daughter's kidnapping, I'm sure of it. He hired the Black Suits and told them to rope me into his dirty little plan. I'm going to wait here until he confesses."

Bob's red face grew pitying. "Jenny, have you been drinking again?"

She rushed up the porch stairs at him. A right hook to the nose, maybe. A hard jab to the soft gut. It would be so satisfying, but Bob retreated into his house like a bird in a cuckoo clock, holding the screen door closed with his left hand. Jenny banged on that, too.

Bob armed himself with an umbrella from a nearby brass stand. "Don't come any closer, Jenny," Bob said. "I'm warning you."

"Oh I'm *so* scared, Bob. What are you going to do? Shove your hand up my skirt again?"

"I hate to say it, officer," Bob said, "but this young woman seems to be suffering from some form of temporary psychosis."

"I'm not crazy. I'm right. Sometimes being right looks like crazy."

"What did you say about Pete? Pete and dust? Your dad died, what? Ten years ago? And you're blaming me for that? I can't help it if he liked Marlboro Reds a little too much."

"It wasn't his fault."

"We make choices in this life, Jenny, we make decisions and we suffer the consequences of those—"

"Like your decision not to protect your employees the way you should have? Like that? George told me all about it. My dad choked to death. You did that. You all but murdered him. And Judd Pickens's grandpa, too."

"George told you? George Shepherd, you mean? If you're listening to him then you really are a lost cause." Bob looked past Jenny to the police officer, who stood on the bottom step, the chiseled planes of his face casting weird shadows. "Are you just going to let her keep harassing me like this?"

The cop didn't answer. His waist radio crackled.

"Where is Billie Starr?" Jenny asked Bob. "Where did those thugs take her?"

"Why would I know where your daughter is? Last I checked, you were her mother. Shouldn't you know where she is?'

"Tell me. Tell me where she is and what I need to get her back or I swear to God—"

"Officer, please!" Bob waved his umbrella wildly. "Do something."

Jenny put her hands on her hips and faced the cop. "Yeah, officer, do something."

He smiled wryly. "Are you taunting me?"

"Maybe. Maybe I am taunting you. I'm allowed to taunt you, aren't I?" Jenny turned back to Bob, reached out, jiggled the handle on the screen door. "Free country. That's what I heard."

"You're not free to enter my home without permission," Bob said. "You are not free to do that. In fact, if you come one step closer, I'll have no choice but to defend myself."

"With an umbrella?"

"With whatever I can find."

Jenny yanked hard on the handle, put her whole weight behind it. It swung violently open, bringing a yelping Bob with it. So close. Within striking range. Jenny balled her fist, but the cop was on her so quickly and with so much force there was no use in fighting. He wrapped her up, pushed her off the porch and across the yard into the backseat of the patrol car, Bob on his porch yelling after them, "That's right. Keep the peace, officer! Keep the peace! That's what we pay you for!"

Jenny banged on the thick plastic partition between the seats,

kicked the dirty floorboards, growled. The backseat was a cold metal cage, windows reinforced with wire mesh. The cop ignored her, started the car, backed out of Bob's driveway. Santa and his reindeer and all the snowmen went dark. So did the icicle lights.

"Put on your seat belt," the cop said.

Jenny tried, but the buckle wouldn't fasten. "I think it's broken."

"Oh yeah. I need to report that."

"What are you charging me with anyway?"

"I'm not charging you with anything," the cop said. "I'm just going to take you for a little drive."

"A little drive?"

"It's called 'de-escalating the situation.' I separated you and that curly-haired man back there without incident, and now, if you don't mind, I'm going to enjoy the scenery. Once you're calm and you promise not to attack any more property tonight, I'll take you back to your car."

"I'm calm," Jenny said. "I'm one hundred percent calm."

"No, you're not."

"Would you be calm if that man was your future stepfather?"

"I guess that depends."

"He sexually harassed me."

"I gathered that from your hand-up-the-skirt remark."

"He's behind my daughter's disappearance. I'm almost sure of it."

They'd gotten to the end of High Street, every house on the block practically glowing with white and blue and multicolored lights, Santas and reindeer and sleighs, more snowmen, also mini-nativities with brand-new Marys and Josephs, their eyes and noses and mouths all very much intact. Ten minutes ago, Jenny hadn't noticed the pretty lights, the carefully arranged wreaths and tinsel and dioramas. The vibrant good cheer of a street full of plastic merrymakers mocked her, winked lewdly at her pain. The elves especially.

"My parents used to drive us up this street every Christmas," the cop said as they coasted past a small, tacky yard bumpy with

extension cords. Santa's workshop took up one corner, Mr. and Mrs. Claus overseeing the elves' progress from red, blinking thrones. Rudolph and a few other reindeer hung in midair over the mailbox, and glowing bells and holly and stars climbed the garage and the basketball hoop. "Mom made cocoa and cookies. We sang songs and shit. Corny as hell, but I miss it." The cop sighed and took a turn on Elm, heading out of town. "Name's Till. Sergeant Zach Till. What's yours?"

"Jenny."

"Okay, Jenny, tell me about your daughter. When was she last seen? Where? And stick to the facts."

Jenny told him about the field trip, the bus, the darkness and chaos and noise, Ashley Batchelder thinking she saw a "woman-type person" or maybe a man picking up Billie Starr but she couldn't be sure. Too much going on.

"Great witness," the sergeant said.

"You think?"

It didn't take long before they were in the country, houses few and far between. Those that were decorated for Christmas looked like tiny, self-contained cities surrounded by wilderness and snow. Every once in a while, the sergeant offered commentary on what, in his "humble opinion," went into an attractive display—"The all-white lights look high-class, but they're cold, don't you think? I'd go so far as to say unapproachable"; "You got to be really careful with the blinking ones, the twinkle ones—you want them blinking-slash-twinkling at the right time and in the right place. I mean, otherwise . . ."; "Symmetry only gets you so far, amiright?" Then he radioed the Benson station to corroborate Jenny's story. "It's not that I don't believe you. I do. But you were acting a little nuts back there."

There was a quick exchange over the radio, almost as confounding to Jenny as the conversations Max and George and the rest of the campaign team had about obscure matters of public policy. The sergeant threw out numbers, codes. He asked the man on the

other end if they'd put out a call to the sheriff, if they'd alerted the FBI. "This is abduction 101 stuff, dude," he said. "Have you actually done anything resembling anything to locate this girl? Have you, oh, I don't know, alerted the media? You have to know that media buy-in is huge. For kidnapping cases especially. Have you called the news stations? The papers? Anyone?" The Benson cop was defensive, a little clueless. He said something about it being his first day. Officer Chad then. He was still making excuses when the sergeant slammed down the radio. "Bunch of fuckos. Shit's sake. The FBI should be on this by now. They should have been on this yesterday." He did a U-turn in the middle of the road. No matter. No traffic from either direction anyway. He glanced over his shoulder at Jenny. "Feeling calmer?"

"I guess."

"Good, 'cause now I'm pissed." He floored it. The tires spun for a moment, then caught and the car shot forward, spooking a possum at the side of the road. It scuttled under a wire fence to safety. "Don't go back and pick a fight with your future stepfather, okay?"

"Okay."

"If you do, I'll have to arrest you, and I don't want to do that. I want to focus on finding your daughter. Do you understand?"

"Yes."

"Do me a favor and go home like a good citizen, try to get some sleep."

Jenny knew that trying to talk to Bob was pointless. Everything at that moment seemed utterly without point, pretty Christmas displays most of all. And there was no way she was going to be able to sleep. Her whole body hummed with emptiness. She wasn't two women anymore. She was a void, a blank spot. She was surprised the sergeant could even see her.

The ride back to town was short. It went by alarmingly fast considering the state of the roads, but the sergeant didn't remark on the couple times they fishtailed toward a field or when he almost

missed a curve. He cursed the whole way, said he'd always known the Benson city cops were incompetent, but basic incompetence was one thing, complete dereliction of duty another. "They should shut that station down. Just shut it down and start over, put us in charge of everything for a while. County? We know what we're doing. We know our asses from someone else's whole other ass." Houses flew by. Reindeer seemed to take flight. Santas, too. "But those guys? Heads in the sand. Heads in the fucking snow." He pulled up next to Jenny's car, jumped out, opened the door for her.

A parade of people was heading toward them on the sidewalk. It was the search party from Gill's Bar, Buddy Winkler right up front, bloody hand raised. They seemed to be marching up High Street toward the courthouse where the town's ramshackle nativity gave off a golden glow. The group had lost its earlier cohesion, as well as several members. From Jenny's count, Buddy was now in charge of a measly five men and one bridesmaid-to-be. All but Buddy, who was sober and obviously frustrated, shuffled forward like a bunch of preschoolers, running into one another, not watching where they were going. At one point, a Hardacre had to hold up the bridesmaid, drooping over a holly bush.

"That's quite a motley crew," Sergeant Till said, whistling. "I wonder if I should investigate?"

"They're looking for my daughter."

"You don't say."

"They're a sort of local search party."

"Doesn't exactly inspire confidence. Hey, you have a Christmas tree in your trunk."

"I know."

"You should put it in some Seven Up. Seven Up first, then water. It'll stay greener longer." The sergeant told her to take care of herself. Then he was back in his patrol car and speeding away.

Buddy, meanwhile, was leading his group in a "Little Drummer Boy" sing-along. They filed past Jenny, everyone air drumming to

his or her own beat, rum-pum-pumming out of time and out of tune.

"Think we'll find the girl lying in the manger?" a Hardacre boy asked.

"Yeah," his brother rejoined. "Wrapped in swaddling clothes?"

"Miracles!" Buddy yelled from his spot at the front of the line, shooting Jenny a kindly smile over his shoulder. "Miracles happen every day."

Acorn Street was peaceful. There was no indication that its youngest and most beloved resident was missing, no hint that Jenny's world had fallen apart. The yellow road sign was still blinking. Marcus's house was dark. So was Dorothy Renfrow's. Five crows perched on what was left of the roof, not making a sound. Asleep maybe. Did crows sleep? They had to. Billie Starr said they were really smart—never forgot a face, good at holding grudges. Like Carla that way. Gertrude and Yo-Yo were grooming each other on Jenny's front stoop next to a poinsettia wrapped in red plastic, note scrawled on a napkin taped to the side: "Merry Xmas, Jennie! Your dorky dance partner, Ted." Jenny let herself in, cracked her last two cans of tuna, and checked her messages. Nothing new. Nothing from any of the parents she'd called earlier, nothing from the police, nothing from Lyd or Kevin or Carla. The house was so quiet it was like something turned inside out. A pocket. Jenny emptied hers, put that photo from Trish on the counter. Couldn't look at Billie Starr's pale face, couldn't stay, couldn't stand the silence, so once she'd fed the cats, she grabbed the plant, and, unsure of what to do with it, carried it to her car, strapped it into the passenger seat, and drove. Just drove. No plan, no direction. Turned randomly at intersections. Tried to obey the speed limit. Forgot what speed limits were for. I am an end-of-the-world woman with no daughter who drives Christmas trees and plants around. "Silver Bells" came on

the radio. Flipped the station. "We Three Kings." Flipped it again. "Ave Maria." Better. After about a half hour of aimless steering and stopping, Jenny found herself in a place that struck her as familiar, but she couldn't say why. A dead-end street with an openness up ahead that spoke of water. A stream, maybe. Or a lake.

Then she saw it on her left, the motel where she and Pete stayed that long-ago spring break, the one he'd moved to after the divorce and where he'd taken his last breaths. The building was L-shaped and low-slung. Moldy roof. Same baby-blue siding, same white trim, new gravel in the parking lot. Back then, the place had been named for the family that ran it—the Jenson Inn? Something like that. According to the hand-painted sign over the front door, it was now the Cozy Cove Motel at Crooked Lake, UNDER NEW MANAGMANT.

Jenny parked next to a Buick and glanced at the poinsettia. The plant seemed to quiver slightly, but that was probably just the wind hitting it when she opened her door. The air outside was frigid and sharp, the cold deep and soundless. She followed the packed path of a child's sled down to the water. The public dock had been pulled in, but someone had placed a few lawn chairs on a lip of land near the lake. Jenny brushed snow from the closest one, sat down. The stars overhead were different from the ones Pete had thrilled to. Wrong season. Still, Jenny clasped her hands and wished on them anyway, pleaded with her father to watch over Billie Starr, to keep her safe, wherever she was.

"Please," Jenny begged. "Help me find her. Somehow. Help me find her."

"Okay."

Jenny whipped around, heart thudding. Randall. He was standing on the same sled track, smoking.

"You scared me," Jenny said.

"Maybe you scared *me*."

"Did you follow me? Are you having me followed?"

"What? No." Randall gestured offhandedly toward the motel. "Eileen and me, we're living here now."

"Oh."

"It's not a bad place really. They put in whirlpool tubs a few months ago. And they're under new management."

"My dad liked it. He died in room eight."

"We're in three."

It was disorienting, meeting Randall here in this spot sacred to her memories of Pete. Wrong. Everything wrong and upside down. Randall, at least, seemed sober. Eyes bloodshot but focused, no stumbling or ranting. He was subdued, contrite even.

"The cops let you go then?" Jenny asked him.

"Had an alibi. Gill."

"Buddy Winkler vouched for you, too."

"That so?"

"I went by the bar tonight, asked him if he'd seen you."

"Playing detective."

"I didn't go there to check up on you. I mean, sort of, but not really." Jenny sat on her hands to warm them. "Buddy's leading a search party. They're drunk mostly. And Trish Keck told me that a psychic told her that Billie Starr might be on a lake somewhere with a bunch of loons."

"Loons?"

"Yeah."

"But it's winter."

"Anyway, my car just sort of took me here. I'm driving a plant around. And a Christmas tree."

Randall took the chair next to her. His skin had the pasty look of melted wax. "What the fuck is happening?"

"I don't know."

"I mean, who would do this?"

"Carla thinks you did. Or Eileen. Maybe both of you."

"Are you kidding me?" Randall tossed his cigarette into the snow. The orange butt hissed and went black. "That's nuts."

"That's my mom. But I'll admit, I wondered, too."

"Why?"

"Oh, let me think," Jenny said. "That note you left in my house maybe? You're threatening to sue me for custody. Why not cut out the courts altogether and just take her?"

"That's not me, Jenny. You should know that."

A star streaked across the sky. A flash so fleeting Jenny wondered if she'd imagined it. "Why should I know that?"

"Because I'm better now."

"You're better?"

"I'm drinking less, working more." Randall pulled another cigarette from his coat pocket, lit it. "Eileen's helping a lot."

"So that wasn't you who passed out on my couch on Monday? Because I would have sworn—"

"Hey—"

"And Buddy told me he served you some beers and bumps tonight."

"I stopped at three," Randall said. "And I made sure to eat something."

"You want a trophy for that?"

"No. I want Billie Starr back."

"Back? You want her back? She was never yours."

"You mean—"

"I mean you never seriously tried to be her dad. All you've done is show up drunk at my house and demand to see her. That's not being a father. That's being a monster under the bed."

"I love her." Randall gathered some snow in his hands, rolled it into a ball, tossed it at the nearest tree. Missed. Tried a second time. Missed again. "It took me a while to realize it, is all."

"You love her, huh? You have an interesting way of showing it.

Why didn't you try calling her once in a while? Like before midnight when she's actually awake."

"You're different. You don't seem like you all of a sudden."

"Maybe that's a good thing."

Randall got up, walked toward the lake, turned, came back. He took a few puffs on his cigarette. In the light from the butt, Jenny saw that he had a tic—one side of his mouth kept hitching up.

"Eileen's pregnant."

Jenny supposed the polite thing to do would be to offer her congratulations, but the words wouldn't come out. Nine years ago, when she broke the news of her own pregnancy to Randall—they were at Pike's Pizza, splitting a supreme—his only reaction was to order a third beer with his fake ID and hide in the men's restroom for twenty minutes. When he finally came out, he asked if she wouldn't mind picking up the bill. He hadn't worked steadily in several months, was short on cash. "I'll get the next one," he'd said.

Randall got down on his knees in front of her, grabbed her hand. "Let's you and me find Billie Starr together. We can do it. I know we can. We can be a team like we were before everything fell apart. Please. I'm working on things. I promise I—" He stopped suddenly, cocked his head. Something crashed around in the woods, a wild turkey, maybe, judging by the clumsiness. Or a beaver. But that wasn't what got his attention. Eileen was at the top of the lane, yelling about it being three in the morning, what did Randall think he was doing, going outside in the dark and the cold and worrying her half to goddamned death, didn't he remember he was trying to be better? Is this being better? she asked. If this was better, I'd love to see worse. Then she spotted Jenny and came barreling down the hill.

"I should have known," she said to Randall. Huffing, out of breath. "Of course. You tell me you're going out for a smoke and this is how I find you."

"I was looking for Billie Starr," Jenny said.

Eileen turned. "You won't find her here."

"I can see that."

"You know what I think?" Eileen said. "I think your mother has her. She's just crazy enough to do it."

"It's late, babe," Randall said to Eileen. "Let's go to bed."

"That's what I wanted to do, but no, you had to have your smoke. So that's what they're calling it these days." Eileen's voice grew steely. She fixed her disconcertingly small eyes on Jenny. "There are some people in town—I won't name names—who are of the opinion that Billie Starr might not have been kidnapped at all if you'd just done as I requested and let her have a real relationship with her father."

Randall put his hands on Eileen's shoulders. "Now, sweetheart . . ."

"Don't 'sweetheart' me," Eileen snapped. "You know it's true. Otherwise, you wouldn't have said so back at the station."

Jenny's frozen face was numb. "What exactly did you tell the cops?"

Randall shrugged, eyes on his shoes. Untied, like a little boy's. "All I said was that you were spending a lot of time away from home and leaving Billie Starr to fend for herself."

"She wasn't fending for herself," Jenny said. "She was with my mother."

"Same difference," Eileen scoffed. "If you'd just trusted Randall more, we could have babysat Billie Starr while you worked or did whatever it was you were doing, late at night, with a bunch of strange men. We could have picked her up from that field trip. *We* would have been on time. *We* would have been there."

Jenny could not look at those eyes. She stood up, stared at Eileen's belly instead, imagined the baby growing inside. Spine and skull and tissue. Hair. Toes. Attitude.

"Fuck this," Eileen said. "I'm out." She trudged toward the motel, stopping at the edge of the hill and crossing her arms over her ample chest, glaring expectantly down.

Randall hesitated, seemed torn, cupped his mouth. Trying to get the tic to stop? Or just covering it up?

Eileen snapped her fingers—once, twice. "Don't make me do it a third time."

"I'm better," Randall whispered. Like he was talking to himself. Then he followed Eileen up the path, feet sinking in the snow.

The numbness was inside of Jenny now. She couldn't feel anything, didn't move, just stood there, wondering if Eileen was right. Maybe this was all her fault. Then she couldn't help it, couldn't stop herself. She thought about what it might have been like if Randall had tried to be better for her, the life they might have had, the family they might have made for Billie Starr out of young love and a long history. She pictured summer vacations and spring breaks, movie nights and Christmas mornings. Hurting each other. Fighting, crying, making up. The three of them figuring it all out together. But that would never happen. Randall had never offered to change, and Jenny didn't demand it.

Behind her, the frozen lake moaned. The sound seemed to come from its depths, from its very source. The moan was followed by a sharp splintering. A crack started at the shore below Jenny's feet and shot across the surface, spreading out like fingers or lightning bolts, like leads and clues that went nowhere and everywhere all at once, like a hundred icy veins in search of a heart.

S he lost a chunk of time, then another. She was in her living room, listening to the ugly mantel clock tick. *Eileen's pregnant Eileen's pregnant Eileen's pregnant.* Then, somehow, she was in Billie Starr's bedroom, staring at the Taj Mahal. It was a huge gravestone, wasn't it? A big, beautiful mausoleum you could get lost in. Without even realizing she'd walked anywhere or picked up the phone, she was trying to call the Benson police station to see if they knew anything, if they'd done anything to find her daughter, but no one answered.

Heads up their asses. Heads in the fucking snow. She tried Lyd, too—who cared about a stupid fight now—but got her machine. "Leave your name and number after the beep, but don't count on me calling you back. I'm picky. I don't like a lot of people and my time is precious, so . . ."

Beep.

Precious time. Where did it go when it passed? When it was over? Did Billie Starr take it with her in her backpack, tucked tight in her book about dogs? Or perhaps Pete held it in his palm, a handful of dust. Maybe time wasn't a thing at all, and Jenny was a ghost. Maybe every human on earth was actually dead without knowing it and only haunting the planet for a while, waiting for a ticket to a wider world, the World Wide Web. The Jenny that drove her daughter to school was gone. So was the Jenny that answered phones for a politician. Her heart was gone, too. And her mind wasn't working. What remained? A bunch of phantom limbs walking around, waving, kicking, screwing things up, not thinking of the consequences, losing everything they cared about—daughters, dads, houses, hours . . .

The teakettle whistled in the kitchen. When had she put that on? She hadn't. Buddy Winkler was standing at her stove, pouring hot water into Jenny's favorite mug, the one she got Pete for his next-to-last birthday. HOOSIER DADDY on the side.

"When did you get here?" she asked him.

"An hour ago. You let me in. Remember?"

"No."

Smiling tenderly over the steam. He handed her the tea. "You should lie down."

"I don't want to lie down. I want to know where time goes."

"It flies," Buddy said. "Even when you're not having fun. You'll be surprised how quickly it will be morning again, if you just try to sleep."

"I can't sleep."

The teabag bled black into the water. Steam from the cup drifted toward the living room. Jenny followed it, a trail, and there, right in front of the picture window, was her poky Christmas tree, up and in its stand. Ted's poinsettia was on the floor next to it, a little wilted but fine.

"How did that happen? Who put my tree up?"

"Jenny—"

"Stop talking to me like that."

"Like what?"

"Like I'm an invalid. Or a nutcase."

"I did it," Buddy said. "Just now. I went to your garage, found a saw, gave the thing a fresh cut, put the tree up and watered it. Twice. It was pretty thirsty after being driven all over Benson. I thought you'd remember. You were right there." He pointed to the couch. "You told me to hold off on the ornaments. You said decorating the tree is Billie Starr's favorite part of the whole Christmas season because you still have everything to look forward to. Wise girl."

"Precocious, too."

"Not sure what that means, but if it's good, I agree."

"I don't want to live without her."

Buddy's hands were on her shoulders again. "You won't have to," he said. "We'll find her. We will. And we'll find her alive. But you need to get some sleep first."

"Why?"

"You need your strength."

"What for?"

"For Billie Starr. Do it for her."

"I'd do anything for her."

"I know you would."

More time gone, hours and seconds and minutes erased in the blink of an eye because Jenny was in her bed without knowing how she got there and Buddy was pulling her covers up, telling her he'd be on the couch if she needed him.

Ghosts don't need things.

Oh really?

And ghosts don't sleep, either.

What do ghosts do?

Haunt places.

What else?

Howl. Rattle chains and move through walls and doors like vapor. Show up late or not at all. Pass the time in a place where time goes when it no longer matters or makes sense or does anyone any good.

Give up. Give in. Roll over. Black out.

*J*enny woke with a start to the phone ringing in the kitchen and someone banging on her front door. Phone first, she decided. It was the loudest. Then door. The clock on her bedside table blinked 3:56 but the light coming through her bedroom windows was pink and soft, so that meant more hours sucked out of the day. And a power outage.

The house smelled like loss, like something she forgot to do, and the hallway was a tunnel, shrinking, closing in, no light at the end. Whoever it was banging on her door didn't stop, just banged harder.

"Coming!" Jenny yelled. "Just give me a minute."

Buddy shot up from the couch, shaking his head as if to clear it. The poky tree was still there, nice and upright in its stand, and under the tree were Buddy's work boots and belt. He grabbed both and started putting himself together.

The banging on the door was louder now. It was inside Jenny's head.

"I'll get that," Buddy said. "You get the phone."

The phone loomed large in its nook, a beige, buzzing monster. Jenny didn't know what she dreaded most—hearing news of Billie Starr or *not* hearing news of Billie Starr. Picking up the receiver was harder than it should have been. A dumbbell in her hand.

"Hello?"

"Good morning, dear daughter." Carla coughed a few times, then spit. "Any word?"

"No."

Buddy had opened the door, greeted whoever was there with a little too much enthusiasm for the hour.

"What was that?" Carla asked.

"Someone's at my door but it's okay. Buddy's got it."

"Buddy? What Buddy? Buddy Winkler?"

Jenny should not have said anything. "Yeah, Mom. Buddy Winkler. He led a search party around town for Billie Starr last night and came over to check on me, to see if I was okay."

"Let me get this straight," Carla said. "You slept with a man on the very day your only daughter went missing?"

"He slept on the couch, Mom."

"Oh really. And what did this so-called search party find?"

"Nothing."

"Uh-huh, sounds like a Winkler."

Jenny went to the picture window, peeked through the curtains. Buddy was on the stoop with Stephanie Shine of Channel 4 Action News and a bearded man holding a camera. Jenny heard Buddy say something about asking for privacy at this difficult time and Stephanie, resplendent in red wool, replied that she understood, she really did, but all she wanted was a quick quote, a simple statement from the mother or member of the family.

"Are *you* a member of the family by chance?" she asked Buddy, rearranging her face into something soft, sympathetic.

"I have to go," Jenny said to Carla.

"Not so fast. Bob's here and he'd like to speak with you."

"Mom, please—"

"It's Bob now."

"Oh, great."

"I did not appreciate your little display last night," Bob said. "Not one bit."

"It wasn't a display."

"What was it then?"

"I need to know where they are."

"Who?"

"The Black Suits. Billie Starr."

"Not this again."

"Where have they taken her?"

"See? This is what I'm talking about. This is why I told your mom I think you might need some help. Probably professional help, and soon."

Stephanie Shine and her cameraman seemed to be discussing angles, lighting, where they should set up to get the best shot. Jenny saw her house, saw all of Acorn Street and its immediate environs through their eyes, everything ugly and sad and replete with all the signs of a life lived badly. Wrong decisions, poor choices, mistake after mistake after mistake. How else would you end up here? At the very rim of the civilized world, a daughter having fallen off the edge?

Mistakes, Bob Butz was telling her. So many mistakes. All hers. "I realize that you don't like me very much at the moment, but you must allow me to set the record straight." He cleared his throat and said something to Carla about wanting one, not two, teaspoons of sugar in his coffee. Two would be madness, he mumbled. Absolute madness. "All that stuff you said about black suits and mobsters, that's just nuts. I have no connection to the mob. And the nonsense about my business actually hurting men, killing Pete—again, crazy talk. George Shepherd has been poisoning your mind against me. That's just the kind of thing he would do."

"George didn't need to poison my mind against you," Jenny said. "You did that just fine on your own."

"That man is not who you think he is."

"Really? Who is he then?"

"He's no saint, let's put it that way."

"I don't require my bosses be saints," Jenny said. "A little integrity is nice, though. And a conscience."

"My conscience is clear," Bob said. "I would never hurt your daughter. I'm simply incapable of doing something like that. You know how much family means to me. Ask Lydia. She'll back me up. But George Shepherd, he has no family. He has no family values."

"Interesting. Family values, huh? Were you showing yours when you shoved your hand up my skirt and then fired me for defending myself?"

"Jenny Newberg, I'm disappointed in you."

"I guess I'll have to live with that."

"Working for George's campaign, it's gone to your head, made you . . ." Bob took a moment to find the right word. "Assertive."

"It's clarified some things. That's what it's done."

Bob's voice was muffled for a moment. Jenny heard Carla in the background saying he'd had plenty of time, it was her turn now. "Just a second," Bob said. "Your mom would like another word."

"Jenny, it's your mother again. I wanted to put a bug in your ear."

"About what?"

"About that dreamy cop who chased off Randall and Eileen. While I'll admit I'm not a fan of his choice in friends—I think Bob has made a pretty good case against that boss of yours—it's always good to have contacts in law enforcement and, unlike the Lefferts and Buddy Winkler, he seems to know what he's doing. You should call him, tell him I sent you. I'm sure he remembers me. We connected that night. I don't think it's overstating the case to say there was a spark, nothing Bob should worry about, of course, but an attraction nonetheless—"

Jenny hung up. Was that assertive? To hang up on one's mother while she was still talking? Jenny wasn't sure. She'd never been accused of being assertive before, but Carla had given her an idea and she wanted to follow through on it before she lost her nerve. She grabbed her coat and met Buddy outside on the stoop.

"Grand Central Station," he said. "I tried to get them to leave, but leeches, they do tend to hang around."

Stephanie Shine was untangling a mic cord. Her cameraman followed behind her like an obedient duckling. "So I'm a leech, am I? Allow me to applaud your originality. Never been called that before."

A police car rumbled up Jenny's driveway then, parking behind the Channel 4 Action News van. Officer Chad Leffert stepped out, ran a hand over his gun belt as if to make sure he hadn't left the station without his weapon. His face pink with cold or embarrassment or both, he said to Jenny, "We're having trouble locating the lesbian. Wondering if you could help us there."

Stephanie Shine's back was to him. Her blue eyes lit up as she turned. "Is there lesbian involvement then?" She thrust her mic out toward Chad, who was momentarily stunned by her star power.

Eventually, he spat out, "I'm not free to comment on an open investigation."

"You just did," Stephanie Shine said.

"Uh-huh," agreed her cameraman. "You just did. And we got it on tape."

"Well, I . . ." Chad stammered. "It's my second day . . ."

Jenny tapped Stephanie Shine on the shoulder. A pad there. The Mummies were big fans of shoulder pads, too. "Could I talk to you for a moment?" Jenny asked. "Privately?"

Stephanie smiled. Her face was feathery with foundation a shade too dark for her skin. "Of course."

Jenny led her behind the garage to a secluded corner of the yard

where Billie Starr used to keep her kiddie pool. There was still a circle of dead grass marking the spot. Stephanie tiptoed gingerly in Jenny's footsteps, avoiding puddles and tuna cans and empty plastic grocery bags half-buried in the ground. Gertrude and Yo-Yo sauntered over, meowed at her suede boots.

Stephanie smiled again, wrinkling her nose. "Cats," she said. "Not my favorite."

"I have a story for you," Jenny said. "It's a big scoop. At least, I think it is, and I'll give it to you on camera right now, right here, if you promise me one thing."

"Are you going to tell me what this big scoop is about?"

"It's about George Shepherd. You know. The candidate for governor."

"I do know him, yes."

"It's about George and sex."

"George and sex?"

"And blackmail."

"I'm listening."

"I'll tell you everything if you make my daughter's disappearance your number one focus, if you get her on TV as much as you possibly can. I heard that media buy-in is huge. With kidnapping cases, I mean."

"How do I know what you're about to tell me about George Shepherd is true? If I go live with a lie about someone like him, I could be in very big trouble. And so could you. Have you heard of slander?"

Jenny had a vague idea. Something about ruining another person's reputation? Max had mentioned suing a news outlet in Indy for slander after a reporter suggested George's stance on taxing the rich was akin to communism, but George pooh-poohed the idea, reminded Max that they couldn't sue people for having an opinion. Or, in Max's words, for being a wrongheaded, shortsighted piece of human shit.

"The story will make me look a lot worse than George," Jenny said, "and none of this is his fault. It's mine. I'll make that absolutely clear."

Stephanie Shine narrowed her eyes. Behind her, in the birch tree outside Billie Starr's bedroom window, Marcus's failed birdhouse swung in the breeze, throwing a skull-like shadow on the ground, keeping time. Hurry, Jenny thought. I'm running out.

"Okay, fine," Stephanie said.

"Thank you."

"Don't thank me yet. You might end up regretting this."

Jenny didn't think so. She marched back to the front stoop, hands clenched, while Stephanie beckoned to her cameraman, whispered something in his ear.

"Sure, yeah," he said, moving closer to Jenny, zooming in.

She remembered suddenly the words she'd rehearsed in her bathroom the week before, the ones she'd hoped would melt George's heart. They steeled her spine instead. *I've been waiting to meet you all my life.* She could see herself reflected in the camera lens—a mess, a story, a scandal. Not beautiful this morning. No wonder.

"Billie Starr's disappearance has nothing to do with Lyd Butz," she said, "and honestly? Anyone who thinks it does—you're the sick ones. It's your mind that's in the gutter." She paused, gave Officer Chad a meaningful look. "Lyd is innocent. She's also the best person I've ever known, and she loves Billie Starr like a daughter. In fact, she's been a far better role model to Billie Starr than me. You want to know what really happened? I'll tell you what really happened."

Jenny glanced over at Stephanie Shine, who was standing next to her cameraman, nodding encouragingly. Three crows squawked from the eaves of Dorothy Renfrow's ruined garage. The yellow sign blinked *slander slander slander.*

"Lyd wasn't involved. It was all my fault. I was broke. I am

broke. I haven't worked in months. I can't pay my bills. I can't pay my mortgage. So, when two men approached me in Benson Market and said that if I slept with a man they called the Candidate—and got it all on tape—they'd pay me five thousand dollars, I didn't ask who the candidate was or why they wanted to frame him, to make him look bad. I just did what they asked. I was desperate. I was stuck and I wanted unstuck. The candidate was George Shepherd, a very good man running for governor. I lied to him, told him he was my political hero, that I'd been in love with him for years because he said the right things about dust and lifting up the little people. He believed me because he's kind and trusting and I acted my part very well. George has been so kind to me. He gave me a job because he wanted me and Billie Starr to be okay. Not the two men in black suits. They didn't care. They never paid me. And now I think they have my daughter. They've been calling George's campaign office, sending threatening emails and faxes, blackmailing him. There was even a message about coming for what I love most. That's exactly what they did. They came for the person I love most in the world. Do you hear me, Billie Starr? Are you out there? You are the person I love most in the world." Jenny went inside her house, grabbed the wire from the curio cabinet, held it up for the camera. "Find the Black Suits and you'll find my daughter. And I don't care if all of this makes people think I'm a bad mother or a bad woman. All I care about is getting my daughter back. Please help me get my daughter back."

Jenny was having a hard time breathing, was overwhelmed by a need to flee, to put as much distance as she could between herself and what she'd just done, what she'd confessed to. Eyes on the ground, she made her way past Buddy and Stephanie Shine and the cameraman and Officer Chad to her car. She had to back into the nearby field to avoid the Action News van and Buddy's Ford Bronco, and she almost got stuck a few times, but her trusty Honda did not fail her, and soon she was free. Up and out. On the radio,

"Blue Christmas." In her rearview, a collage of open mouths and breath clouds and muddy snow.

The Fort Wayne gas station phone booth was occupied by a large someone in a stocking cap and a quilt. A horn honked on a nearby street. A man shouted about stop signs being a thing. Another man shouted back about turn signals being an even better thing. Jenny closed her eyes, rested her head on the wheel. In her mind's eye, she saw a pair of small light-up shoes tripping away from her. Always away. For the last year or two, whenever Jenny held her daughter in her lap, she knew that she was, at the same time, letting her go. Billie Starr was getting older. Snuggles weren't something she asked for anymore. And she was too smart to stay put. Too brilliant for Benson. She was always going to be gone, one way or another.

But it wasn't supposed to happen like this. She was supposed to grow up, go to college, chart her own course. Become president. Change the world. And then Jenny would have the honor of living in that better world, of being able to claim a tiny shred of credit for it. I did that, she'd say. To one of the Mummies. Or to a stranger at Pike's Pizza, who would be well acquainted with Billie Starr's impressive accomplishments, her selfless contributions to society, because everyone was. She was that famous. That beloved. *I made her*. Bragging a little, but that was her right as a mother. *Can you believe it? She's mine. At least she was, for a little while.*

Jenny tried to put what scattered facts she had about Billie Starr's disappearance into some sort of order, but the puzzle pieces just wouldn't fit, and her daughter as she was—not Billie Starr the news story but Billie Starr the girl—flooded her mind, pushed out everything else. Memories. Moments Jenny hadn't thought of in years. Most vivid for some reason, Jenny and a three-year-old Billie Starr holding hands on the way to the mailbox in midsummer,

casting a paper doll shadow on the parched ground, the girl a chatterbox already, so much to say about the sky and the birds and the tiger lilies. Then picking a bouquet and crushing the petals between her fingers, blowing the dust over the yard. "Orange wish," she called it. Jenny knew what she meant. Tiger lilies always smelled like potential, like something good about to happen. Then Billie Starr at bath time, still small, singing "could you be mine, would you be mine, won't you be my neighbor?" Splashing with her pruny feet, shampooed curls shining, apple scented. And what about those months when she was five and all she wanted to talk about was dinosaurs—T. rexes and triceratops and Utahraptors, brachiosaurs and pteranodons and stegosaurus and centrosaurus? Jenny thought the dinosaur obsession would never end, but it did. One day, Billie Starr's interest in the Jurassic and Cretaceous and Triassic periods dissolved, was gone like the dinosaurs themselves, snuffed out, giving way to sharks, which gave way to giraffes, which then became pangolins and pandas and stars. Places next—the Pyramids, the Great Wall, Alcatraz. After places, rainbows, unicorns, witches. Marcus made her a wand and she spent hours waving it around the yard, trying her best to resurrect dead bugs, to put brown leaves back on the trees. When Jenny explained that magic wasn't real, that you couldn't simply bring something back to life with a spell, Billie Starr grew preoccupied with the idea of death. She wanted to know where Grandpa Pete was and where bugs went when you crushed them. Mom, I don't want to die. I don't want you to die. Jenny flailing, trying to explain cemeteries, gravestones, why it was that people put flowers on a piece of engraved granite. "But Grandpa Pete doesn't have a grave." "No." "Why?" "He didn't want one." "So we can't visit him." "We can visit him in our mind." "I don't know how to do that." Most days, neither do I.

So many obsessions, so many library books and coloring books and broken crayons. All the while, regardless of whatever subject had taken up residence in Billie Starr's always-on-overdrive

brain, she was running, jumping, skipping. Refusing to slow down. Hence, the era of injuries. Two years ago. Aptly, it was fall. Billie Starr decided her life's ambition was to be an Olympic hurdler. She tried jumping the tires in Marcus's yard. End result—a broken elbow. After that, a litany of bruises and cuts and scrapes. Leaves piled up outside, wet as slugs, while Band-Aids piled up in the bathroom trash, medicinal odor, blood everywhere, Billie Starr pointing at a spot on the floor: "Look, Mom. Body ketchup." The last year or so, she'd grown graceful. Light as a feather. How had that happened? Where had the sweet clumsiness gone? Somehow, it had vanished, like the dinosaur fixation, like her innocent enthusiasm for rainbows and baby pandas. "Babies. Boring." But her laugh was still a burst of pure, unpretty joy, somewhere between a shriek and a cackle, and Jenny would give anything to hear it right now, anything to feel her daughter's skinny arms around her neck, anything for her to school her on the size of a typical pterosaur and how to pronounce "Cretaceous." "Not crustaceous. Duh, Mom. Duh." Anything to watch her spray the bathroom mirror with toothpaste and then wipe it with toilet paper. Making a mess, every time. Never learning how to do it differently. Never getting it right.

It was the toothpaste, the image of Billie Starr's face in a smudged mirror, that did it. Jenny finally fell apart. She'd been holding it together by thinking only of her next step, the next spot on the map of her messy, seat-of-the-pants search. Fruitless midnight phone calls. Check. A fight with Bob Butz in his front yard. Check. A confrontation with Randall and Eileen that got her nothing but cold. An on-camera confession that was sure to have all of Benson talking and the bulk of it calling her a sinning slut and worse. Check. And now the city. Wet, frigid, gray, impenetrable as the concrete block high-rise that neighbored the gas station, enormous wreath hanging halfway up. Happy Holidays. Check check check check. She had a to-do list to complete and by controlling the pathways her brain took from minute to minute she thought she could forestall

feeling. Focus on finding her rainbow girl. Stay busy. The crying, the melting down, that could come later. But she couldn't stop the sobbing now. Couldn't control it. She hadn't cried like this for Pete. That was different. He didn't need her. He was a grown man, he'd lived his life, but Billie Starr was just starting. She needed Jenny to be wherever she was. Whatever it took. If only Jenny could divide herself in pieces—send part of herself to the lakes, every single one of them, another part to the police station, a third part into the air where she would have a bird's-eye view, watch everyone and everything like a hawk—people roads towns rivers fields houses. Paths streams woods wells. She was finding it hard to breathe again.

When she finally looked up, the striking old woman from the fancy café, the one who hadn't wanted Jenny's charity or bisque, was pushing her way out of the phone booth and coming right toward her, motioning to roll down her window.

Jenny reluctantly obliged. She supposed the woman wanted to warn her again about the end of the world. You're too late, Jenny thought. It's already here.

"Phone call," the woman said. She pointed to the booth. "In there. For you."

"But—"

"No buts about it. Time's money, you know? Time's wasting. End of the world tomorrow. You better hustle."

The woman was clearly going to stand there next to the car until Jenny took the call, so she wiped her eyes and got out, walked slowly to the booth where the phone hung limp from its silver chain.

The woman grumbled at Jenny's back. "Did my part," she said. "Did my duty. Can't ask for more." She hobbled across the street and disappeared behind a camera shop.

Snow fell on the booth in soft clods. Jenny stepped inside, picked up the receiver. "Hello?"

A man's voice answered. Not high, but not low, either. "Hi, honey."

"Um—"

"I was worried I'd missed you. Like two ships crossing in the night. That's us these days."

"I'm sorry. I don't think I am who you think I am—"

"I know you, darling girl. I might be the only who does. I just wanted to say, keep going. You're on the right track."

"But, sir—"

"People underestimate you. They always have, because you're kind and have a pretty face, but you're smart, too, and brave and determined and you can do this. Don't let anyone tell you you can't."

"It's just that—"

"Luck, sweet pea. Good and bad. Sometimes it's all we've got."

Jenny had to brace herself against the walls of the booth. Pete's line. She checked the sky for rents, but everything looked disturbingly normal. A BAYH FOR GOVERNOR sticker decorated the booth's tiny wooden bench. Someone had marked out GOVERNOR and written "prison" in its place.

"Just promise me you won't give up."

Was she talking to a ghost? A guardian angel? Someone else's dad, more likely. Maybe every father of every girl eventually got around to saying these same words to his daughter. The only logical explanation: wrong number, mistaken identity.

"I promise," Jenny said.

"Good. Well, now that we've got that covered, I should go." The man coughed. "A voice is telling me I'm out of time anyway, so . . ."

There was a click, and then silence. Jenny put the phone back on the hook. Two middle-aged women pumped gas in the cold. Why was it always middle-aged women getting gas? Why was that their lot? The teenage cashier inside the convenience store stared blankly at three limp hot dogs going around and around like passed-out passengers on a Ferris wheel.

The booth smelled of ancient cigarettes and the phone book's plastic cover. Empty. The person who'd stolen the phone book used it for what? To start a fire, maybe, like Marcus had. What a sad fire

that would have been, unless, of course, the thief had managed to steel every phone book in the city. Maybe then it would have been a blaze worth talking about, a fire to rival the one that turned Pete's wasted body to ash. That one had burned at 1800 degrees. Hiram Hardacre, the town undertaker, told Jenny that. He also informed her that a cremation incinerator was called a "retort." Then he apologized for bothering her with trivia. It was just that people he worked with rarely said a word. "Because they're dead." He was lonely a lot. When he handed Jenny Pete's ashes, he had tears in his eyes. He and Pete had been boys together. "We used to build fires behind our houses and throw our sisters' dolls in." He regretted the dolls, he said. Felt guilty about them. "What if we hadn't done that?" he asked. "What if we'd just let them be?"

The McDonald's women's restroom was a bust. No Black Suits in the dining room or sticky stalls. The grocery store was likewise fruitless. Literally. The display of oranges had been replaced by a cardboard sleigh full of sugar cookie bells and stars. Carla very well might have packed those cookies. Jenny grabbed a box out of habit. They were Billie Starr's favorite. Then, in the checkout lane, she came back to herself. Back to reality. She left the cookies on the conveyor belt and ran. Bad luck to buy them, just asking for the jinx.

The Riverview Inn seemed at first glance to be more promising. The parking lot was full, and two men—one short and stout, the other tall and thin, both in black coats—hovered by the front entrance, smoking. But they weren't the two-bit gangster types Jenny was looking for. They were blond and young and, judging by their wedding rings and haircuts, wealthy. Jenny walked past them into the lobby.

The hotel was halfheartedly decorated for Christmas. A large artificial tree took up one corner, boxes of varying size, wrapped in

faded Santa Claus paper, arranged awkwardly underneath. Lights twinkled from the front desk and coffee cart and fish tank, where a band of silver minnows swam in a circle, a flicker of brightness in the artificially darkened room. Next to the tank stood a short, squat man sniffling loudly and flirting with the Windex-wielding, Kiss-loving cleaning woman Jenny had run by the week before. The cleaning woman sprayed the tank's sides, wiped the glass vigorously, made a joke to the fat man Jenny could only half hear, something about there always being more fish in the sea.

The fat man slapped her on the back, told her she was a pip. "Someone knows her marine life."

He'd traded in his suit for a frayed sweatshirt, jeans, a leather tool belt, and work boots, but there was no mistaking him. There were the neck rolls, the doughnut hair, the mustache. Fat Black Suit. He pinched the cleaning woman's plump arm and began whispering in her ear.

Jenny strode quickly across the lobby's thick, red carpet toward them. "Where is she? Where is my daughter?"

The man hadn't heard Jenny. He was still flirting with the cleaning lady, who nudged him with her Windex bottle. He looked up, his eyes widening for a moment. Confusion first, then recognition, then a practiced nonchalance.

"Hello, ma'am. Can I help you?"

"Is she here?" Jenny asked. "Do you have her trapped here? Which room?"

"Excuse me?" The man's voice was as high and nasally as she remembered. He sniffed, wiped his bulbous nose on his sleeve. "What are you talking about?"

"My daughter. Don't play dumb. Where have you taken her?"

"Hey, listen, I don't know who you are or what—"

"You know exactly who I am. 'Easy peasy lemon squeezy' ring a bell?"

The man tried to laugh Jenny off, smiling awkwardly at the

cleaning lady, who took that moment to retreat to a wallpapered alcove where a TV was tuned to a hunting show.

"Let's try this again. Where have you taken my daughter?"

"Lady, I have no idea what you're talking about."

"I think you do. Where is she? And who put you up to this? Bob Butz?"

"Bob who?"

"Who hired you?" Jenny must have raised her voice without realizing it, because the front desk staff, two women in their thirties who had been arguing over whose turn it was to restock the free toothbrushes, were looking at her, eyeing her with weary suspicion. One had her hand on the phone. Go ahead, Jenny thought. Call the police on me. What do I have to lose? "If you don't fess up right now," she said to Fat Black Suit, "I'll tell your bosses just what kind of man you are. I'll tell them all about your sleazy underbelly—"

"Come now, ma'am."

"I'm serious. And I'm sure you'll lose your job. You wouldn't want that, would you?"

Fat Black Suit chewed his mustache for a minute. Then he scuttled out of the lobby and into a hallway, stationed himself between the ice machine and the laundry room. Jenny followed him, remembered being in the same hallway with George. Her heart was pounding then, too. Different reason. Different rhythm. The man spoke out of the side of his mouth. What he said was hard to hear over the dull roar of an industrial washing machine and dryer going full blast.

"What was that?" Jenny asked.

"Julian," the man said. "He takes care of those details."

"Julian? Is he the tall skinny one?"

The man looked a little hurt. "I suppose he's a little taller than I am, a little on the slimmer side, but—"

"Where is he?"

"Not sure. Jules isn't what you'd call a gregarious type. He keeps his own counsel."

"Give me his number. I need to call him."

"Oh, I don't have that."

"You don't have his phone number?"

"Look, I told you. We're not friends. Jules doesn't have friends. He has people he does business with."

"Me bringing George here was your idea, I assume."

"Well, yeah, that part."

"Do you know anything about the person who hired you? Anything?"

"Like I said, you'd have to talk to Jules."

"But he's impossible to get ahold of, right? How convenient. What about the lady in McDonald's then? The one who fitted me with the wire? Maybe she'd know more than you do."

"You mean Martha? Nah. Martha was just along for the ride. A neighbor of Jules is all. A cat breeder. That's her thing, cats."

"How did the person who hired you find you guys? And why did he want to hurt George?"

"See, that was Jules again. He's the one with the contacts. He does the deals. We met at Camp Cupcake a few years back—"

"Camp Cupcake?"

"Minimum security out Terre Haute way." The man fiddled with his tool belt. A few wrenches there, not as large or menacing as Marcus's. A tape measure, too, and some pencils, a level, a hammer, and a box of nails. "Listen, I'm just a handyman. I fix things. Have a broken garbage disposal? Give me a call. And if you want a special kind of cat, Martha's your gal. Working with Jules is sort of a side project for both of us."

Jenny grabbed the man by his collar, shook him as hard as she could. Her vision blurred. He wasn't Fat Black Suit now. He was every man and woman and Mummy who'd ever condescended to

her, every person who'd done her wrong her whole life. A long list. Get in line.

"Tell me," she said. "Tell me where my daughter is or I swear, I'll kill you." She shook him some more. "I'll kill you."

"We weren't hired to kidnap any kid." The man's skin was crepey, thin, growing purple. "That's not in us. We're small-time, okay? We're good guys, really. We were hired to get you to sleep with that dippy politician guy and tape your pillow talk and that was it. Period. End of story."

"And do what with the pillow talk exactly?"

"Release it? Send it to the news stations? Not sure. Wasn't let in on that."

Staring at the man's frayed shirt, Jenny felt defeated. He no longer seemed sinister or intimidating, just rather dim and crooked, low-rent. She let him go.

"Look," Fat Black Suit said, "I'm sorry we didn't show up at that coffee shop like we said we would. The god's honest truth is that I was busy getting my ass chewed by Jules because the bugs I put in the room malfunctioned somehow. Martha, too—she got an earful for the wire not working, although it wasn't Martha's fault. Not if you ask me. It was the device, all day long. Jules took a chance on a newfangled wire, bought it from this guy who swore up and down, no tape needed. A live transmitter, he said. Voices come through on the radio, or they're supposed to, but all Jules got, waiting outside in the car, was static. A whole lotta nothing, the whole time you and that dopey man were . . . congressing. And since Jules made it clear we weren't getting paid for a botched job, there was no money to give you. It's sad, really. Discouraging. Fills one with regret. Just one fuckup after another—"

"I want to see the room," Jenny said.

"Huh?"

"The room where I took George. I want to see it."

"Why?"

"I assume you have some sort of master key."

"Well, yeah." He rubbed his neck. "There's nothing to see. Gina's cleaned that room a hundred times since."

"Just open it for me."

Fat Black Suit shrugged, mumbled about having a faucet to fix on the second floor, but he supposed he could spare a few minutes. "I'm telling you, though. It won't do any good."

Room 186 was three doors down. The paint around the black plastic numbers was scratched and faded. The knob stuck at first. There were other details Jenny missed when she was last here—the diamond-patterned rug, a print of George Washington crossing the Delaware over the coffeemaker, the emerald-green taffeta curtains covered in dog hair at the bottom. Jenny flung the curtains open, took in the view of the parking lot, where the two wealthy men were still talking, laughing, studying the antique cannon like they might actually be able to put it to some use. Fat Black Suit had flipped on the TV, sat at the edge of the bed, started telling Jenny something about how he was a father himself, he understood where she was coming from, he really did. Being a parent, it was like volunteering for open heart surgery, only to have the doctor put your heart inside someone else's chest.

"It's not yours anymore," he said. And then there was the disappointment, right? Just the other day, his daughter borrowed the car, swearing she'd bring it back in one piece, but when he looked it over the next morning, he counted "not one, not two, but three new dents . . ."

Jenny hurried around the room, looking under beds, opening drawers, scanning the closet and the shower and the vanity for anything that might somehow point to Bob Butz, lead back to him. Like what, though? A special shampoo for permed hair? One of his business cards? She found nothing. It was as Fat Black Suit predicted. The search went nowhere. Then she heard a familiar voice cutting through Fat Black Suit's monotone ramblings. She shushed

him, ran to the TV, turned up the volume. On the screen—dusty in one corner; you missed a spot, Gina—Stephanie Shine was interviewing Ashley Batchelder. Ashley, sitting cross-legged on her front porch swing and identified as a "leader in the Benson community," told Stephanie Shine that she and a group of concerned moms were raising money to put toward funding a citizen-led search party and anything else that might "help Billie Starr and her unfortunate family during this difficult time.

"It's every parent's worst nightmare, what's happening to Jenny and Randall," Ashley continued, her voice soft, velvety. It reminded Jenny of Ashley's senior prom dress, a pink plush strapless gown with a sweetheart neckline and mermaid bodice that Ashley's mom found at a fancy store in Indianapolis. A practically perfect dress and the envy of every girl at the dance. That is, until Jenny spilled Coke on it during the Hokey Pokey. "The moms I was telling you about, we're also starting a prayer chain for Billie Starr's safe return. I know that if this had happened to me, if, perish the thought, my own daughter were to go missing, I'd want all the prayers I could possibly get."

As if on cue, Terri appeared in the frame. Ashley pulled her close and kissed the top of her head. "Jenny must be going crazy right now. I can only imagine what she's feeling, how terrified and worried she must be."

The camera cut to Stephanie Shine. "Especially since she told me that her involvement in a blackmailing plot might have contributed to her daughter's disappearance."

Ashley whispered to Terri, who waved at the camera, something soft and dark in her palm. Terri swung the something in front of the camera for a moment, as if trying to hypnotize whoever was watching. Jenny leaned toward the screen, squinted. It was a rabbit's foot. Unmistakable. Purple fur. Rusty loop chain. Identical to the one she'd left behind in her coat pocket the day she'd met George. How the hell had Terri Batchelder ended up with it?

"Hi!" Terri said, waving the rabbit's foot again. "Bye!" She ran off, tossing the trinket in the air.

Ashley watched her daughter go, didn't speak for a moment. Then, shifting in her seat, she said, "I don't know anything about a blackmailing plot. We're a small, tight-knit community. Neighbors helping neighbors. That's Benson. Things like that just don't happen here."

Fat Black Suit stood, pointed at the television. "So that's your daughter they're talking about? I thought maybe you were making it up. I—"

Head roaring, an ocean between her ears, Jenny rushed out of the room, through the lobby and past the wealthy, black-coated men to her car. Flinging the door open. No seat belt. No time. Peeling out of the hotel parking lot, she clipped the cannon, grazed it with her bumper. The barrel tipped, dumping a bunch of cigarette butts and condom wrappers to the sidewalk. Dirty water, too, all over the men's expensive shoes.

The shorter of the two shouted something about women drivers. The taller one yelled at Jenny to slow the fuck down, watch where she was going.

On the highway back to Benson, oily ice patches and jackknifed semis leaking gas. Bags full of trash and abandoned cars. Mattresses rotting in ditches. The bloated carcasses of cats and raccoons.

Slow down? Jenny said to herself. No way. I'm just getting started.

The Mummies were having their knife party. A sign in Ashley Batchelder's yard welcomed walk-ins: ASK ME ABOUT CUTCORP! it said, red and green balloons tethered with white ribbon waving below. THE CUTTING EDGE OF KNIFE TECHNOLOGY. No trace of Stephanie Shine or her white van now, just Toyota Camrys everywhere. Jenny counted two in the driveway and three on the street, all of

them emblazoned with tasteful bumper stickers advertising a popular tumbling gym and a local megachurch that had its own soft rock band. She recognized the name of one of the Republican gubernatorial candidates, too—the holy warrior—on a two-toned four-door.

She couldn't decide—antique knocker or doorbell in the shape of a daisy—so she went for both. She was still slamming the knocker against the door when Ashley answered, clad in a black sheath dress, pearls, and kitten heels.

Jenny craned her neck, peeked around Ashley at the scene inside. Elegant tapered candles cast a golden glow on the silken heads of the Mummies, who lounged on couches and the floor and in chairs, sipping mimosas and nibbling baby carrots. Christmas music on low in the background. Nat King Cole.

"Jenny." Ashley looked unsure again. "Did you want to come in?"

"I'd love to." Jenny pushed past her. "I would love to come in."

The room, abuzz with chatter, grew suddenly quiet. Two Mummies, a blonde and a brunette, were just coming in from the kitchen, singing the praises of Ashley's new stainless-steel refrigerator. When they saw Jenny, they stopped dead in their tracks. The brunette—the one whose sleeve kept getting spilled on back at Gill's Bar the night before—dropped a piece of broccoli on the floor. Ashley scooted over to retrieve it, asked Jenny if she could get her something.

"Nothing for me, thanks. You might have heard—my daughter disappeared last night, so, you know, I can't stay." Jenny stepped over two more Mummies on her way to the coffee table where knives of every shape and size fanned out in a large W. She picked up one with a black wooden handle and serrated edge, tilted it so the blade glinted in the light. "Looks like the whole gang's here. I mean, why let a little thing like a missing girl get in the way of a good time?"

The Mummies obviously did not know where to look—at Ashley? At Jenny? The knife in her hand?

Ashley, her back to a magnificently arrayed Christmas tree, was staring at the empty space on the table where the serrated knife used to be. "We're not celebrating, Jenny," she said. "This isn't for fun. It's a fundraiser now. For Billie Starr—"

"Yeah, I heard. For a search party or something. Buddy Winkler already has that covered."

"A Winkler has something covered?" asked the blond Mummy. Incredulous, crinkling up her green eyes. "That'll be the day."

"We're also raising money for the nativity," said the Mummy who'd dropped the broccoli. "We all agreed, as mothers and Christians, one of our main missions must be to make sure that our town's holy family is presented in such a way that befits the sacred nature of the birth of Christ, that our tribute is both worthy and respectful. After all, cleanliness is next to godliness. . . ." She blushed and her voice petered out as she drifted awkwardly away to the other side of the room to refill her mimosa.

Jenny put the knife back on the table. Wrong angle, messing up the fan shape. Fine. Fine with it. "I need to talk to Terri," she said.

Ashley touched her pearls. "Terri? Why?"

"I think she has something that belongs to me, something that might help me find Billie Starr."

The Mummies exchanged glances, plucked eyebrows raised. Jenny supposed she sounded insane. Fine with that, too.

Ashley approached her cautiously, smiling. "I was just going to the kitchen for more napkins. Won't you join me?"

"Sure. Napkins. Nativities. What great priorities you all have."

The kitchen was warm, cozy. A soothing smell of freshly baked bread and simmering apple cinnamon potpourri wafted over from a large, oak hutch filled with gold-rimmed wineglasses. Everything in the room gleamed and sparkled, including Ashley's antique hair clip. A firefly.

She fiddled with it. "I saw you on TV this morning."

"I saw you, too," Jenny said.

"I think what you did was really courageous." Ashley had found the napkins she was looking for in the bottom drawer of the hutch. White linen. No stains. She started folding them. "I mean coming clean like that, being so honest. I admire you for it. And for defending Lyd."

"She's my best friend." Unspoken: you are not my friend. You will never be my friend. Fine with that as well.

Ashley had finished folding, was moving noiselessly from counter to table, table to island, straightening, picking up, filling trays with vegetables and cookies and cheese. "I get why you're doing this, looking for Billie Starr on your own, but isn't it best to let the authorities take care of these things? I mean, they're trained specifically to conduct such investigations, whereas you . . . Don't take this the wrong way, Jenny. You need your rest. You're obviously overtired, which is understandable. Anyone in your situation would be—"

"Where is she?"

"Terri?"

"Yes."

"I think she's in her room, but—"

"Thanks."

It had been more than a year since Jenny had stepped foot in Ashley's house—that was for a Christmas decor party (miles and miles of icicle lights and tables groaning with glittery snowmen)—but she remembered the general layout. Hall to the garage off the door by the stove, hall to the bedrooms and guest bathroom off the door by the refrigerator. She took the latter into a long, quiet corridor. Beige walls, plush carpeting, light spilling out from a room on the right. Sounds of a girl at play.

Terri was kneeling in front of a three-story dollhouse, a white-clad Barbie doll in one hand, purple rabbit's foot in the other.

"Hey," Jenny said to her. From the doorway. Keeping it friendly and casual. Scaring the girl wouldn't do any good.

Terri turned. Jenny had forgotten how much she favored her

father. It was the white-blond hair, the blunt, turned-up nose, the strong, boyish jaw. Her room, though, was all girl. Decals of unicorns and rainbows and fairy castles over the windows, the bed hidden by a mountain of stuffed animals, closet full of princess dresses. Terri was wearing one now. It had pink, puffed sleeves, a ribboned bodice, and a tulle skirt. Too big, it gaped at the neck. Jenny wondered if it, like Ashley's prom dress, had come from a fancy store in Indy. Terri looked very small inside it.

Ashley hurried passed Jenny into the room. "Terri, this is Billie Starr's mom. She thinks that maybe—"

"I know who she is." Terri stood up. "She can't pay for her house."

"Now, Terri, honey—"

"She did something bad with a bunch of Black men."

"Sweetheart, if you can't say anything nice—"

Terri ignored her mother, spoke to Jenny instead. "Do you want to play with me?"

Jenny took a few steps forward. "I'd like to, but I don't have much time." She realized that the dollhouse was, if not a perfect replica, at least a decent facsimile of the house they were all standing in, and, in the doll version of Terri's room, a little girl with bright hair was lying facedown on the bed in a position of utter despair. Or maybe she was just sleeping. Next to her, on the floor, was a tiny stereo and soda bottle. A dad doll was passed out on top of a mom doll in an adjacent bedroom. A fireman doll was in the front yard, pointing a hose at a plastic bush. He was missing his pants. A tiny dog was on the roof and a tiny toilet was in the kitchen sink.

Jenny pointed to Terri's right hand. "Where did you get that?"

Terri held out her left. "This? This is my Bridal Barbie. Mom got me her because I was patient in Chicago."

"No," Jenny said. "The other thing. The rabbit's foot."

"Why do you want to know?"

"I'm pretty sure my father gave that to me when I was about your age."

"I don't think so." Terri went to her bed and pushed a line of Pound Puppies off the edge. She lay down in the cleared space and curled up, rabbit's foot tight in her fist. Bridal Barbie fell, ignored, to the floor. "This is mine."

"I know it's yours," Jenny said. More bees with honey. "It belongs to you now. I just need to borrow it for a while. I'll give it back when I'm finished with it."

"What do you mean, 'finished with it'?"

"I think it's a clue that might help me solve a mystery. Do you know what clues are?"

"Like *Scooby-Doo*?"

"Exactly."

"I hate *Scooby-Doo*."

Ashley sat down on the bed next to her. "Sweetie, if we can help Billie Starr's mommy in any way, we should. Can you please tell Miss Newberg where you got that rabbit's foot?"

Terri shrugged in her sloppy dress, mumbled something unintelligible into a pile of pink lambs.

"Terri, darling, we can't hear you."

More mumbling. Jenny wanted to shake her.

"You're being rude," Ashley said. "Remember what I told you about Santa Claus? How he knows if you've been bad or good so be good for goodness' sake?"

"I remember." Terri slowly sat up, looked down at her feet. Bare. Toes tiny and pink, like shells. "I found it on the floor. By the one-hour photo booth."

"What photo booth?" Ashley asked.

"In Benson Market."

"Can I have the rabbit's foot?" Jenny asked. "Just for a little while?"

"Promise you'll give it back?"

"I promise."

Terri reluctantly handed it over. Impossibly soft. Rusty loop

chain. Stroking it, Jenny felt a spark. From down the hall came a
hum. Low voices chanting in a monotone. Jenny caught the words
"our Lord" and "hallowed be thy name" and "Billie Starr" and "safe
and sound." The Mummies were praying. Ashley nodded to Terri,
who dutifully brought her hands together and closed her eyes. Then
she launched into a prayer of her own.

"Please, God, don't let anything bad happen to Billie Starr. And
don't forget to punish whoever took her. An eye for an eye and
all that. Also, I would really like my rabbit's foot back, so if you
could make that happen, I'd appreciate it. And some Guess jeans
for Christmas. Thanks for listening. In your holy name, we pray."

Ashley picked up Terri's Barbie and straightened the doll's
dainty dress. "Amen."

The rabbit's foot was warm in Jenny's fingers. She dropped it in
her coat pocket, was struck by a vision of Billie Starr in this room,
surrounded by all the plastic and frills and pretty things money
could buy, while Terri Batchelder, innocently installed in the house
on Acorn Street, played under Marcus's wooden solar system and
hatched plans to save the streams. The two girls switched at birth,
Ashley and Jenny acting the part of mom to the wrong daughter. A
dollhouse turned upside down. A nightmare.

Jenny opened her eyes. She hadn't realized until that moment
that they were closed. Terri was looking at her expectantly. Poor
little rich girl with her ruffles and piles of toys, all dressed up and
no one to play with.

"Amen," Jenny said.

The Benson Market one-hour photo booth was at the back of the
store next to the pharmacy. Poster-size pictures of a pretty family of
four, all of them with perfect teeth and hair and clothes, hung from
the ceiling above a pegboard wall covered in cameras and rolls of
film and batteries. Heather was behind the counter, hovering over

a printer shooting out copy after copy of Billie Starr's face. It wasn't the same photo Jenny gave Officer Chad. In this one, Billie Starr was smiling and flashing a peace sign, a peacock in full feather at her feet. A zoo outing with Lyd, then. Jenny had almost forgotten they'd gone there together. Hot August day. They came back with sunburns and souvenir soda cups striped like zebras.

Jenny cleared her throat a few times, but Heather didn't hear her. She grabbed a pile of black-and-white Billie Starrs and set them aside. The words MISSING and REWARD framed Billie Starr's face. "If you see this child, please call 911," was in much smaller print at the bottom. Jenny realized with a start that her daughter's face was staring at her from nearly every square inch of the booth, including the floor and the cash register.

"Hello!" she said. "Heather?"

Heather looked up then, hair curtain parting. She blinked at Jenny, seemed not to recognize a real person, having clearly spent the last several hours with a likeness. "Oh, hi."

"What are you doing with all these?" Jenny plucked a flyer from the countertop. It was still warm. It was all she could do not to stroke Billie Starr's grainy cheek.

"You've seen the milk carton kids, right?"

"Yeah, I guess."

"Gonna tape these to milk cartons."

"Won't the paper get wet? Fall off?"

"Don't think so. I've got good tape." Heather held up a roll. "And I'm not stopping at milk cartons. I'm putting these on bread loaves and cereal boxes and mayonnaise and peanut butter and jelly jars. That way as many people will see Billie Starr's face as possible. Lyd thinks I'm onto something. The reward was her idea. She said, as long as we don't specify an amount, whatever money we can scrounge together will be good enough because everyone would be too busy celebrating the fact we've found Billie Starr to count dollar signs."

"Lyd knows then? That Billie Starr's missing?" What did Jenny

"Nah," the woman said. "Got my own." She turned to Jenny. "You're the mom, aren't you?"

"Yes."

"Must be a shit time for you. Hang in there."

A man from deli dropped by after that, taking with him a handful of flyers that he promised to put in the most prominent spots—in front of the sliced turkey, he said. And the fried chicken and potato salad. "Not with the rotisserie chickens, though. Might melt. Or catch fire."

Then a teen girl—a Dodge—asked for a bunch of flyers for aisle nine. She was stocking cereals. She was followed by Sonia Hardacre, who'd worked as a Benson Market cashier for as long as Jenny could remember. Sonia volunteered to paper the checkout line and candy racks while Janice Enyeart in dairy proudly took milk carton duty. They all shot Jenny shy, curious looks. And they all said the same thing about Stevie and the carts. Not. Gonna. Happen. Stevie was the cart king. Pushed those things like they were nothing. The kids they'd hired were just seasonal help, un-motivated, useless. The boss was fooling himself.

"Thank you for doing all this," Jenny said to Heather. "It's really sweet."

"I just hope it works," Heather said.

"Me, too." Jenny took a jagged breath. Being without Billie Starr this long was like an itch in her heart. Persistent. Deep. Torment-ing. There was no way to scratch it. And now here she was, playing detective, as Randall had snidely put it, a bit too far into a silly game of cat and mouse with a rabbit's foot. She put it on the counter any-way, asked Heather if she remembered seeing anyone with it in the last couple days.

"A little girl in my daughter's class said she found this on the floor outside your booth. I think if I can find the person who had this, I can find Billie Starr."

Heather screwed up her face. "Is that what I think it is?"

"A rabbit's foot? My dad gave it to me a long time ago."

"Those things are kind of sick, aren't they?"

"I guess. I mean—"

"It makes you wonder about people. Like, just how cruel are we? And where are all the three-pawed bunnies running around?" Heather paused. The printer made a forlorn beeping sound. She filled it with more paper, and the copies continued shooting out. "Not that rabbits can run with just three paws. Or two. Or even one."

"I think the bunnies were dead anyway—"

"And then someone decided it was a great idea to lop off their feet, dye them, and attach them to a chain for what? Good luck? It's gross and weird. Like hunting trophies and scalps, which is what I told this really skinny girl who waltzed in with one attached to her belt a few days ago. I asked her if she would wear a dead kitten hat around and do you know what she said? You'll never guess. She said, 'Maybe.'"

Jenny shoved the rabbit's foot a few inches closer to Heather. "Was it this one, this rabbit's foot, she was wearing?"

Heather backed away. "I don't want to touch it."

"Can you just try to remember? It's important."

"I didn't get a great look at it, to be honest. The girl wasn't here long. She told me she was developing a few rolls for her boss, but then she never came to pick them up. I'm not surprised. Who'd want a bunch of pictures of old white guys doing old white guy stuff?"

"Do you have the photos here then? Or any information about her?"

"Give me a second." Heather crouched down, plucked an envelope from plastic bin labeled A–M and read a name aloud. "Monica Jessup. We had a quick chat, not just about the rabbit's foot but about how I'd seen her a few times before, at Brick Lanes, in the bar. I don't think she bowls. I think she just drinks. That's where I

met Lyd, too. At the bowling alley, picking up shoes. We wear the same size."

"Does that envelope have the woman's address or phone number on it? I really need to talk to her."

"Is that legal?" Heather asked. "For me to just give you someone else's property?"

"You said yourself, they're just a bunch of pictures of old white guys, right? So what's the big—"

"And no one's paid for the pictures, either. The boss is already a little annoyed with me, using company resources and time to make all these copies, although he said himself that it's a good cause . . ."

"I'll pay for them," Jenny said. "I'll pay for the pictures and deliver them to Monica Jessup right now. If it helps, I won't even look at them. I'll just take them straight to their rightful owner."

Heather glanced gravely down at a flyer. Then she made a peace sign of her own, laid it over Billie Starr's splayed fingers. "Lyd told me your daughter's pretty special, that she's smart and nice and funny, all the good things a person can be and not much of the bad. I haven't met many people like that. Have you?"

"No." Jenny started to rummage through her purse for her checkbook.

Heather shook her head. "Don't worry about the money. I'll pay for them." She handed the pictures over. "Anyway, that's how I know she's going to be okay."

"How?" Jenny asked. "How do you know?"

"She's one of the good ones. God lets us keep a few of the good ones."

All this God talk. The same thing happened when Pete died. Suddenly, men who spent Sundays drunk in front of football were telling Jenny that God had a special plan for Pete's soul, that He lifted Pete up on eagle's wings to His heavenly kingdom because He liked to keep His beloved ones close, to fill His celestial hotel up with only the best guests.

The opposite of what Heather believed, apparently. "God knows that if He gets too greedy and takes all the good ones at once, this place"—she gestured to the parts of the store Jenny could see from where she was standing: shelves of shrimp and whitefish and lobster tails, slimy and gray in their plastic wrappings, an endcap arrangement of heavy-duty paper towels FOR YOUR BIGGEST JOBS, the baker lady trying to explain to an irate customer that the two-for-one deal on blueberry muffins ended three days before—"would be wall-to-wall misery. Nonstop stupid and horrible. And then we'd all just kill ourselves and heaven would get really crowded. Standing room only. God likes His space, so Billie Starr's just fine. She's waiting for us. Patiently. Safe. All we have to do is show up. Right place, right time, right milk carton. Show up."

Monica Jessup lived in a small pink house off a gravel road ten miles outside of Benson, near the Steuben County line. The house, set back in a clearing, was surrounded by scrub pines and dying ash. At least Jenny assumed Monica lived there, thanks both to the address scrawled on the envelope Heather had given her and the directions she got from a woman out shoveling her driveway.

"Oh sure, the Jessups," she said. "The girl lives with her father, I understand. Oddballs, both of them, and the dad can bark a bit, but they're mostly harmless."

An old man answered Jenny's knock. Ropey and stooped, he blew his nose into a ragged blue hanky. One of his eyes didn't seem to want to open all the way, and in the watery light of the afternoon, his forehead looked bruised. He wore a shirt that said I'M A AMMO-SEXUAL. "What do you want?" he asked.

"I was hoping to speak to Monica."

"Monica."

"Your daughter?"

"She might be."

Jenny thrust the one-hour photo envelope into the man's veiny hands. "I brought these for her."

The man turned the envelope over, held it up close to his good eye. "That's her handwriting all right. Chicken scratch. Her mother and I tried to get her to improve her penmanship but some battles aren't worth fighting." He flung the photos at a nearby table and shouted over his shoulder. "Mon! Get out here!"

A small voice from inside said, "Coming, Dada!"

The man waved Jenny in, shuffled over to a recliner and put his feet up, squinted between them at a television across the room. "My church is on." Leaning against the wall behind his chair was a shotgun, barrel up, and, next to him, an overturned laundry basket, on the top of which sat a bottle of beer and a Bible.

Church was a raised stage and a velvet curtain. A tan man in a white suit paced in front of the curtain, whispering loudly into a microphone something about Lazarus and fishes and loaves and walking on water. The man's eyes were tightly closed and his raised right arm made large arcs in the footlights as he called people to the stage to receive the healing balm of their savior, Jesus Christ. He was just offering a hand to a little boy in leg braces when a young woman skipped in from a dark hall. It was the table-dancing girl from the campaign launch party, the one with the fairy tattoo (hidden today, under a bright red scarf) desperately seeking a cigarette. She wasn't smoking now, but the house had that stale smell Jenny remembered from childhood—Pete and Carla having spent a winter weekend puffing on Camels and Merit Ultra Lights, windows sealed shut— and everywhere she looked there were ashtrays filled with old butts, most sporting red lipstick rims, all smashed into tiny lowercase *r*s.

"Hey, you're George's receptionist, aren't you?" Monica pulled her dark hair into a ponytail. No short dress or tall boots today. A long nightgown and puffy purple slippers instead. The slippers were made to look like cows. There were little bells over the toes. "The one with the missing kid."

"Yeah, that's actually why I'm—"

"Did George send you? I thought I had the day off."

"No, I . . ."

"She brought you some pictures." Mr. Jessup took a swig from the beer at his elbow, pointed it in the vague direction of the front door, where the photos sat atop a stack of magazines and grocery store mailers.

Monica raised her eyebrows, grabbed the envelope, flipped quickly through the photos, shaking her head. "Snore, snore, snore, snore. I warned George it would be like this."

"Like what?" Jenny asked.

"A bunch of Boy Scouts. Nothing but dudes paying their taxes and loving their wives and going to bed at nine every night having said their prayers and counted their blessings. Snore. Snore. Snore."

"What exactly do you do for the campaign?" Jenny asked.

"She digs up dirt on people!" Mr. Jessup yelled. "Some girls are gold diggers. My Mon, she's a dirt digger!"

"Dada, please."

"It's true," he said.

"I'm in opposition research," Monica explained to Jenny. "George hired me to research his opponents, maybe uncover some icky things."

"Icky things?"

"Sketchy business ties, tax evasion, affairs. Sounds sexy, right?"

"I guess," Jenny said.

"Not this race. Everyone's a model citizen. The Republicans, that incumbent. The most boring men on the planet. Wait." Monica set the photos down, put her hands on her hips. Sharp bones there, visible through the flannel. "This is weird. That lady running the photo booth didn't say anything about a delivery service."

Jenny pulled the rabbit's foot from her pocket, showed it to Monica. "I heard you might have had this on your belt when you dropped off that roll of film at Benson Market. I was hoping maybe

you could tell me where you found it." She blushed. I'm ridiculous, she thought. I'm making myself ridiculous.

But Monica didn't seem to think so. She clapped, did a little dance in her bulky slippers. The toe bells tinkled. "I wondered where that got to!" She plucked the rabbit's foot from Jenny's hand, rubbed her cheek with it.

"You recognize it then? That very one?"

"Yeah. Brenda's awful cousin—Lloyd or whatever—had it."

"Lorne?"

"He was visiting George at the campaign office last week and he left it on a desk. Honestly? I just took it. Maybe that was wrong of me and I know *some* people think they're weird, you know, ghoulish or whatever, but I like haunted things. Always have. Houses. Forests. People."

"You should see her room!" Mr. Jessup said. "Dead stuff everywhere."

"I have a few taxidermied dogs is all," Monica said. "My old pets. I just couldn't imagine burying them, never seeing them again, so I hired a guy to stuff them."

"Lorne was at the campaign office last week?" Jenny asked. "I thought he was in jail. For shooting at Trish."

"He was, but George got him out. On bail. He and George and Brenda, they were talking strategy. Hush-hush stuff, seemed to me. That's an unholy alliance right there."

"Strategy for Lorne's defense?"

"All I know is that Lorne guy kept making boxing metaphors, hopping around, punching the air, saying a lot of stuff about rope-a-dope and technical knockouts and going the distance." Monica swung the rabbit's foot from her finger. "Isn't your daughter's name Becky Starr?"

"Billie Starr."

"They were talking about her, too."

"What were they saying about her?"

"Book of Job!" Mr. Jessup yelled at the TV where the preacher was quizzing his audience about a passage in the King James. Mr. Jessup hurriedly flipped through his own copy, mumbling to himself about people being crushed like moths. "Here it is! Found it! 'Between morning and evening they are destroyed,'" he said, smiling. Very proud of himself. "'They perish forever without any regarding it.' Told ya. Book of Job."

Monica smiled apologetically. "Dada really likes his gospel hour." She stepped back into the hallway. Jenny went with her. The floor was a patchwork of particleboard and hooked rugs. A fluorescent light blinked gray-green overhead. "So Brenda and George and that Loren guy all got really quiet when they saw me, but I heard something about a Billie Starr, a field trip, and putting a shine on it all? George is desperate, I think. Needs something to stick. His poll numbers are bad, his money situation is even worse, and he's worried about those faxes and emails. You know, the ones about a woman and a tape and a payoff. He's sweating, is what I'm saying. And people do crazy stuff when they sweat."

Jenny was starting to sweat in her pretty coat. "At the launch party you told me I'm not the only one. You said there were things I didn't understand. What did you mean?"

"I was probably talking about the time you and George slept together at that hotel in Fort Wayne and how that place is one of his favorite places to take his, well . . ." Monica ran the rabbit's foot along the wall. It made a soft sound, fingers on a face. "Lady friends. You aren't the first woman he's bedded at the Riverview. And my guess? You won't be the last."

The bony girl's wry smile curdled something in Jenny, turned butterflies to tapeworms. "How do you know all this?"

"It's kind of my job. Seedy underbellies and whatnot. Oh, and Dada and I saw you on TV." Monica whistled. "You sure know how to torpedo a campaign, don't you?"

"I wasn't trying to torpedo the campaign."

"Maybe you weren't trying, but I'm pretty sure you succeeded."

From the living room, Mr. Jessup yelled at his daughter to bring him another beer. "And make it a cold one this time!"

Monica shrugged. "He says beer helps his spirit comingle with the divine."

Jenny was going to show herself out. Then she remembered her promise to Terri, asked for the rabbit's foot back. "My dad gave it to me when I was a girl, and I told another little girl that I'd make sure to return it to her."

Monica had been squeezing the rabbit's foot in her palm like a stress ball. She opened her fingers, looked sadly down at it. "Finders keepers, losers weepers." She gave it to Jenny. "I guess I could get one of my own. Or even make one. Our fields are full of bunnies. They die all the time. Natural causes, usually. Or Dad shoots them."

There were two bunnies crouched behind Jenny's front tires when she went back out to her car. Fluffy and fat, tiny black eyes darting, they leaped away from her and across the lawn into the safety of a small copse of fir trees, where, if they knew what was good for them, they would stay. But did anyone—man, woman, bunny, or boy in leg braces—ever know what was good for them? Jenny was starting to doubt it. To doubt everything, really. The goodness in people. Her own judgment. That she would ever see Billie Starr alive again.

Three more bunnies bolted out in front of her as she drove away. She swerved, missed them by inches. Then came the hollow echo of a shotgun firing. Once. Twice. Three times. The gray sky was suddenly full of birds. Lucky winged things, they swooped over the road in a wave and flew west, twittering. Still alive, they seemed to say to each other, to the bunnies, bloody and dying on the ground. We're still alive. For now.

The campaign office looked like a crime scene, a sticky, smoky post-mortem of a doomed thing, which, Jenny supposed, it was. There'd

been no effort to clean the place up after the launch party. Trash cans overflowed with plastic cups, smeared plates, beer cans, wine bottles, American flag hats, bunting. The room was quiet, too, disconcertingly so, and without the constant ringing of phones and whining of fax machines and shouting of vulgarities and poll numbers, it reminded Jenny very much of what it had been on her first day when George asked her to tell him more about herself, the day she met Brenda and the lights all went out at once. She tiptoed around a poinsettia on its side, a salsa stain on the carpet, and called out.

"George?" No answer. She knocked on the bathroom door, just in case. "George? It's Jenny." Opened the door. Empty except for half a dozen used toilet paper rolls, stacked in a pyramid shape on the floor.

The office was so quiet Jenny could hear a fly buzzing around a piece of half-eaten carrot cake. "Anybody here?" she asked again. More buzzing from the fly. Around Jenny's face now. She batted it away. Then the phone rang. Without thinking, she went to her desk, answered it as if she were still on the clock. "George Shepherd's office. Can I help you?"

"I hope so." Woman's voice. Breathy. Self-important.

Jenny fumbled for a piece of paper and a pen, settled for a soiled napkin and a tube of lipstick. Color: My Bloody Valentine. "What is it you need exactly?"

"This is Stephanie Shine of Channel 4 Action News."

"Oh." Jenny dropped the lipstick into a nearby wastebasket. "Hi, Ms. Shine."

"Jenny? Jenny Newberg?"

"Yes, ma'am."

"You're the last person I would expect to report to work today."

"I'm not really working. I was looking for George."

"Is he there? A man—might have been George but I doubt it, sounded gruffer, uncouth—left a really garbled message on my machine, said something about a big scoop and turtles and towns and

lakes and being somewhere in twenty minutes? It was as clear as mud."

Jenny glanced around again at the mess—the disco ball hanging just a few inches above the ground, a boom box with a broken antenna, a pile of glitter next to a discarded sock. "I'm the only one here."

"No George, either? I've been trying to hunt him down for a comment on what you said earlier. So far, no dice. Wondering if he'll confirm or deny."

"I told you the truth."

"That doesn't mean George will admit it. He's a politician. He'll say or do anything to win."

Jenny started to sit down but there was something on her chair. It was identical to the photo Trish Keck had handed her the night before in that booth in Gill's Bar, the one Trish said Lorne had been carrying around in his pocket, Jenny and Billie Starr and Gertrude and Yo-Yo, overexposed, yellow in autumn light. Jenny picked up the picture, turned it over. The slanting, ghostly Kodak stamp was scribbled over with a mess of words in red ink.

Jenny Newberg.
Late 20s
5'6"
Hair: red
Eyes: green
Slim build. Curvy, tho.
Should be wearing a dark blue coat & jeans.

Stephanie Shine was saying something about everyone in town wanting to give her the scoop of the century all of a sudden. "I'm not complaining, of course. It's just that I'm used to finding stories on my own. That's where the 'Action' in 'Action News' comes from. It was my idea, to change our station name to something a

little more gripping, something that reflected our commitment to breaking the news as it's happening. Jenny? Are you there?"

Jenny dropped the phone, didn't worry about hanging it up, ran out of the office, didn't bother locking the door behind her. People could help themselves to the filing cabinets and whatever was in them, the computers, the fax machine. They could loot the place for all she cared.

Her mind raced as she jumped in her car, flitted from clue to lead to dead end and back again. Heather among the Christmas trees saying something about an angry, pockmarked man having Jenny's picture developed. The photo Trish Keck gave her last night. Lorne—pockmarked, angry—always got doubles. And where had the other copy been until now? With the Black Suits, of course. The photo—and the description on the back—would have helped them identify her. Lorne must have hired the Black Suits in the hopes of cashing in on his cousin-in-law's campaign. Literally. And the emails and faxes and phone calls—those had to have come from Lorne, too, who, according to Kevin "In Any Case" Lipshott, was about to lose his farm. And who would have known that Jenny was also struggling because (a) Benson was a tiny town and (b) Kevin notoriously was loose-lipped around his clients. He'd admitted as much in the quick face-to-face in front of Jenny's house. All but told on himself.

Hard times had made Jenny an easy target.

And a Black Suit must have come to the launch party the night before, dropped that photo of Jenny on her chair. Or worse— someone in the campaign was in cahoots with Fat Black and Julian Keeps His Own Counsel.

The truth was like a dim ray of light in a dark room. Jenny followed the beam where it led, from Lorne who needed cash and loved boxing ("You're a lightweight in a heavyweight's game) to Brenda, woman scorned, and all the way to George. George who loved helping damsels in distress. "He got to the state senate on it." George who was eager to let Jenny bring Billie Starr to the

office where she and Brenda bonded over a mutual love of dogs. George who kept Jenny dancing past eight o'clock on a Saturday night when she should have been waiting in the elementary school parking lot to pick up her daughter. George who would say or do anything to win. Turtles. Towns. Putting a Shine on it. Stephanie Shine and the scoop of a century. Lorne and Brenda and George. An unholy alliance. A circular firing squad.

Turtle Town Lake was halfway between Churubusco and Benson on a county road that ran arrow straight between sprawling farms, an almost featureless landscape except for the fences and outbuildings and lines of leaning power poles. In the distance, Jenny saw what looked like a boy in a red hooded sweatshirt and jeans and gym shoes, leaning into the wind, navigating a slippery shoulder dotted with potholes and icy puddles. She was going to just pass him by—the lake, the light, were pulling her forward, making her mind one-track, on a mission—but he cut such a cold figure, she made herself slow down, pull over.

The boy, spooked, stumbled into a snowdrift. Pointy face, a dusty line of dirt on his upper lip. The kid with the cockroach. Behind him, on a soft, white expanse, a smattering of footprints made a circle, then led over a hill out of sight.

Jenny rolled down her window. "Do you need a ride somewhere?"

The boy talked to her forehead. "Tammy says I should never accept rides from strangers."

"Who's Tammy?"

"My mom."

"What direction you headed?"

"To Turtle Town Lake."

"Me, too. I'm looking for Billie Starr. She's my daughter."

"You called my house last night didn't you?"

"Probably. I called a lot of houses. Are you Judd Pickens?"

"Yeah," the boy said. Like he was admitting something shame-

ful. Like he wanted to take it back. "Billie Starr and I were going to go to the lake sometime, to look for Oscar."

"The giant turtle?"

"Yeah. I think maybe she's there now. Looking."

"Why don't you get in?" Jenny asked. "We can go together."

The boy brushed himself off, cautiously opened the passenger-side door. His pointy nose was bright pink. He glanced down at the rabbit's foot on the seat. Jenny tossed it in the glove compartment, turned the heat up.

"You're really Billie Starr's mom?"

"I am."

Judd got in, folded himself up like a dying spider. "How'd you know who I was?"

"Billie Starr's told me a lot about you," Jenny said.

"Like what?"

That you're poor and smelly, Jenny thought. She didn't smell anything beyond wet, unwashed hair. So his mother hadn't shaved his head after all. "You're not from here, are you? You're from Mississippi."

"Alabama, actually."

"Your grandpa made countertops."

"Cabinets."

"And you and Billie Starr are writing a book together."

"It's going to be a bestseller."

"So I hear."

As Jenny drove, past snow-laden fences and horses in blankets snuffling steam and billboards announcing the imminent second coming of Christ, the snow began to fall hard and fast. Next to her, Judd blew on his hands.

"I owe you an apology," Jenny said.

"For what?"

"Getting you suspended."

"How'd you get me suspended?"

"I was the one who spat on Principal Mock's nameplate."

"She hates me. I don't know why."

"She hated me, too. For no reason." Jenny turned her windshield wipers on high. It didn't help. The sky and road and farms all blended together into a bright blankness, a shaken snow globe. "You can put my apology in *The Book of Sorries* if you'd like."

"Okay."

"It's a little harsh, your book. Makes me and your mom sound like pretty bad people."

"It's just a rough draft."

Turtle Town Lake wasn't really a lake, more a retention pond tucked back behind a succession of small hills. Jenny turned onto a one-lane road, and the barn where Carla was planning to wed Bob Butz rose up on the right. Pretty and picturesque, it was hugged on both sides by pine trees, the lake visible through an open door. A Jeep that Jenny was pretty sure belonged to George was parked in front of it, and next to the Jeep was Lorne Keck's International Harvester pickup. Jenny looked for the men, saw no sign of them. Judd started to climb out of the car.

Jenny grabbed his arm, pulled him back. "Just sit tight, okay? Stay here where it's warm."

"I want to find Billie Starr."

"I know you do."

"She's my best friend."

"Let me see what it's like out there, okay? Take stock. And then, if it's safe, I'll come back for you."

"You're treating me like a baby. I'm not a baby. My sister's a baby. I'm nine years old."

"Sorry, Judd. I just don't want you to get hurt."

Pouting, scratching at a scarlet scab on his neck. "That's going in the book, too."

Jenny pulled the collar of her coat up, got out, walked quickly down a short slope and through a patch of long, stiff grass to the water, frozen and bubbly and opaque at the edge. Fragile pancake

pattern. A boat was stuck ten feet out, moored in ice, oars out like elbows. The snow was meal-like and blinding. Jenny squinted through the swirling storm, tried to shade her eyes, thought she saw something besides snow out in the middle of the frozen wilderness. Colors. Yellow, maybe. A shock of red. And then at her feet, a glove. Pink and sparkly. Jenny picked it up and walked out onto the ice, shuffling at first, trying not to sink, to slip, and then, when it was clear that the surface wasn't about to give way under her, she started running. In the back of her mind, a voice. Go. Just go. The voice said keep going, you're on the right track, you're a powerhouse. It wasn't just one voice, though. It was a patchwork of voices, echoing, fading in and out, piling up like the snow. Ghosts all around, Pete very near her, Pete up in smoke. That dead doe, too, done in by a car and Doris drifting down to earth and Marcus in his favorite kimono, dancing in the middle of a two-lane road, waving Trish's cowboy hat like a bullfighter's cape, calling Jenny sweetheart, telling her to trust her instincts, her mother's intuition. Jenny didn't have time to wonder why Marcus? She was too busy shedding selves—Jenny the sad little girl, Jenny the failure, Jenny the trying too hard to please a man/boss/best friend—and trying on others. She was the Concorde. She was a bullet train, the Batmobile, a turtle, a deer, a loon, a lake thing.

She turned around once to scan the shoreline. Judd had disobeyed her, was not sitting in the car like a good little boy and was, instead, watching her from the edge of the lake. And he wasn't alone. George and Lorne were with him, talking, gesturing, the wind whipping their hair and words into knots, into white noise. Jenny couldn't hear what they were saying, couldn't be bothered with them. She was in the center of the storm now, pummeled by cold, and over the million competing voices and the howl of the wind she heard it. Finally. The only voice she really needed, her daughter's crying out, calling for her.

The girl ran to Jenny, slipped some, fell into her arms. "Mom, you came for me. She said you wouldn't come but you did."

expect Lyd to do? Call her maybe. Signal in some way that she cared. The fact that she hadn't gave Jenny a hollowed-out feeling, as if she'd been scraped from the inside.

"Oh yeah, she knows. The cops think she knows too much. They came to my house and took her in for questioning a couple hours ago. Well, 'dragged' is more like it. They—" Heather stopped short. A reedy voice over the grocery store intercom called for a full cart roundup. "That's not happening," she said. "Stevie isn't here today. No one rounds up carts like Stevie. He also makes amazing paella. Do you like paella?"

"Paella?" Jenny asked.

"Yeah."

"I don't think I've ever had it."

"That's what Lyd and I were doing last night. Making Stevie's paella. We made paella and watched *Die Hard* and went to bed. Then this morning we woke up and saw you on TV. That's how we found out about . . . everything. Lyd called you a few times but you weren't home. She was getting ready to go out—to drive to your place, actually—when the police pulled up. I told them Lyd couldn't have kidnapped Billie Starr. She was with me the whole time, I said. I tried to get through to them, but they wouldn't listen."

"They wouldn't listen to me, either," Jenny said.

A woman in a white apron strode up to the booth, asked Heather for a couple copies of "the kidnapped girl" to tape to the doughnut case. She had the queenly attitude of someone used to giving orders. "I could put some on the cupcake boxes, too. And the cinnamon rolls and the scones."

Heather gave her a large pile of paper. "That'd be great, Dodie."

The woman leaned against the booth for a moment, studying Billie Starr's face. "Did you hear that call for a full cart roundup? Not gonna happen with Stevie out sick."

"That's what I said." Heather offered her a roll of tape.

Billie Starr's snow-coated hair was stiff against Jenny's cheek. Jenny thought the sheer joy and relief she felt at that moment might kill her as she knelt down on the ice next to her daughter, might freeze her blood in place, halt her heart, but that didn't happen. She warmed the girl's hands, one pink and sparkly, the other going blue, between her warm ones, whispered that she loved her over and over again. "You know this, right? I love you. I love you more than anyone or anything and you'll never have to spend another waking moment doubting that. Do you understand? Can you hear me? I love you I love you I love you."

"Yeah, Mom. I hear you."

Jenny pulled back, cupped Billie Starr's forehead, examined her face for signs of fever. Her cheeks were crimson but her skin was cool and dry. "Who said I wouldn't come?"

"Brenda. She said you were too busy with work to deal with me."

"Brenda Shepherd said that?"

"Yeah," Billie Starr said, snuggling up to Jenny like she used to when she was small. "She was here a minute ago. The dogs, too. Wilfred tore my glove off. He and Roger ran away into those trees over there." She gestured toward three lines of tracks—one of human feet, two of dog paws, leading off the lake and into a stand of oak trees, brown bark outlined in a thin line of white. "Brenda chased after them. I was going to follow her, but this guy walked up to me and told me to stay where I was."

That's when Jenny noticed that Julian Has No Friends, aka Tall Black Suit, was looming over the scene like an apparition in a green parka and gray sweatpants.

"What are you doing here?" Jenny asked him. "What do you want with my daughter?"

Julian didn't answer, simply stared straight ahead, where a crowd of cop cars had joined Judd, George, and Lorne on shore. Blue and red lights cut through the day's sooty blankness. Two officers were making their way out onto the ice, guns drawn. Tony

Leffert and Sergeant Zach Till. Stephanie Shine was right behind them, with her cameraman. Her red hat the cherry on top.

Sergeant Till got to them first. He cuffed Tall Black Suit, pushed him toward Tony Leffert, who was breathing hard from the effort of crossing the lake. Jenny pointed to the tracks in the snow snaking toward the woods, explained that they belonged to Brenda Shepherd and her dogs and that someone should try to catch up to her, that she was very much wrapped up in all of this. Sergeant Till volunteered to look for her. He started to jog away.

"You'll be nice to her, won't you?" Billie Starr asked him.

Sergeant Till stopped, squinted through the snow. "Should I be?"

"She made me French toast this morning," Billie Starr said. "And she let me watch as much TV as I wanted. She didn't hurt me. The dogs did. Kind of." She held up her bare palm, pointed to two scabbed lines cutting across in a clumsy X. "It wasn't their fault, though. They didn't do it on purpose."

Jenny grabbed that hand, covered it with the sparkly glove. Then she laced her fingers through her daughter's skinny ones, squeezed hard. She'd caught her. Billie Starr Newberg, small daughter, big brain, little bird. Jenny had caught her just in time.

*L*ater, at the police station, Jenny held Billie Starr close until the shivering stopped. It took a while. The girl was so cold, so confused by what had just happened to her and why, that Jenny wondered if they should be taking her to the hospital instead.

"I'm fine, Mom." Teeth chattering. "Really, I am."

"I'm getting you an appointment with Dr. Harme at least."

"Dr. Harme's no good," Ruth Shields said from her desk in the reception area. "Dr. Frank's where it's at. I says to Ashley, the last time her Terri took sick with the flu, this all comes of going to Dr. Harme. I says to her, 'It's right there in the name.'"

Billie Starr, still dazed, stood and followed Judd Pickens over to the station's Most Wanted wall, stared fixedly at her own face, over which someone (Ruth probably, judging by the spidery script), had written 'Not wanted. Missing.'"

"But you were wanted," Judd told Billie Starr. "That's how you got found. Because people wanted you."

"I guess," Billie Starr said. She peeled the picture off the bumpy stone, studied it some more. "Do you ever look at your face and think, 'I don't look like that. That's not me.'"

"Every day," Judd said.

There was a commotion at the front door. Sergeant Till was pushing Brenda Shepherd inside. Roger and Wilfred, wet-pawed and dirty-bellied, yipped around their ankles. Billie Starr did not light up when she saw the dogs this time. She rubbed at the wound on her hand while Judd stepped in front of her, arms crossed over his chest, legs in a wide stance.

"Someone please take these hounds from hell and put them as far away from me as possible," Sergeant Till said. "Take them both before I boot them into next year."

Brenda leaned over, pulled the dogs in close. "No. Absolutely not. They're staying with me."

Sergeant Till made a grab for the dogs' leashes. Brenda smacked his hand away.

"If you expect me to talk," she said, "if you want me to tell you anything, you have to let me have my boys."

Sergeant Till clenched his strong jaw. "You're here on suspicion of kidnapping a child, ma'am. You don't get to dictate the terms."

"I mean it." Brenda kissed the dogs' scruffy heads, then gave Sergeant Till a defiant look from under her stocking cap. "You won't get a word from me."

Ruth Shields sighed loudly, shuffling papers. "I've always said, dogs are more trouble than they're worth. I says to Art the other day—his kids are begging for a dog—I says, 'They're messy and

badly behaved most of the time and they smell.' I says, 'Better off to get a hamster. Or a guinea pig. Something you can keep in a cage.'"

Brenda hmphed haughtily. "My fur babies are perfect gentleman."

"Are they now?" Sargeant Till asked. "I wasn't aware that perfect gentlemen made a habit of crapping on the floorboards of patrol cars. Or of biting people." He rolled up his sleeve, showed Ruth his bloody forearm.

Ruth rifled quickly through a metal cabinet behind her, offered him a couple Band-Aids. "Chief's on our side of the fence. Doesn't allow any animals in his interrogation rooms as a matter of principle, but you're welcome to cell number four in the back. It's got a drain in the floor."

The dogs had strayed from their mistress's side, were sniffing at Jenny's shoes.

Brenda made no effort to rein them in. "If Roger or Wilfred did indeed do their business in your car, Sergeant Till—and that's a big if—I can only assume that was their way of commenting on your police work."

The wetter of the two dogs had the hem of Jenny's coat in his teeth and was whipping his head back and forth, as if the fabric was something he could kill. Jenny tried to wrestle free, but the dog just bit down harder.

"Maybe you'll think twice now before you sleep with someone else's husband," Brenda said.

Jenny finally shook the dog off. The hem was soggy with spittle and torn in five places. Her pretty coat. A casualty. "And maybe you'll think twice before you steal someone else's child."

"You want to pin this all on me?" Brenda said to Jenny. "Fine, but I suggest you ask your boyfriend George who planned this whole thing. All his doing. His and Lorne's. Yours, too. Want to find the guilty party here? Take a long look in the mirror."

Ruth Shields handed Sergeant Till a large ring of keys, told him to take a left at the ladies' and a right at the evidence room. Cell four

would be straight ahead. Empty. Can't miss it, she said. Then again, all the cells were empty. "Not for long, though, huh? After you get that one's statement, I have a feeling I might have to light up the 'No Vacancy' sign." Ruth chuckled to herself. Brenda scowled at her. Then Sergeant Till led her and the dogs away.

Jenny had given her statement to Chief Leffert when she and Billie Starr first arrived at the station, told him everything she knew and suspected. He grunted as she talked, wrote it all down, typing two-fingered. She told him about Lorne and the Black Suits and the blackmail, about what she thought might be Brenda's motives and George's, too. He didn't ask many questions and Jenny could tell he only half believed her, but, since she was the one to find her daughter alive, the chief had no choice but to listen.

George was in with him now, treating him to his side of the story, while Art Dodge questioned Lorne, and Tony Leffert interrogated Julian Tall Black Suit. Officer Chad, it seemed, was still operating under the assumption that Lyd Butz was the mastermind behind the whole scheme. No one had thought to let him know that Billie Starr was alive and well and in the lobby. Ruth Shields had just hobbled down the hall to give him the news when her phone rang. She sighed again, answered it, listened for a moment, scribbling notes onto a large desk pad covered in doodles.

"Roger," she said to the person on the other line. "Will do." Then she made her tortured way back toward the interrogation rooms. "Art! Fred! Tone! One of yous! Code ten fifty-five!"

The chief peeked his head out first, nodded at Ruth. Then he motioned to Jenny. "Miss Newberg, Mr. Shepherd would like a word."

"George wants to talk to me?"

"You're under no obligation."

Jenny told Judd and Billie Starr not to go anywhere. "I mean it. Don't you dare leave this building."

Judd didn't say anything, just bit down hard on his thumbnail. Billie Starr said, "Yeah, fine. Where could we go anyway?" Then

they both went back to looking at the wanted. Not missing. On the lam.

The chief's office was larger than the room she and Carla had shared with Officer Chad the previous night, but like that one, it was windowless and cold and furnished only with the bare necessities—a desk, a computer, a phone, a shelf full of ugly, black bound manuals. A coffeemaker. Creamer. A poster about use of force protocols. George sat slumped in front of the desk in a ladder-back chair. He looked older, sunken. A monument to defeat. His face was windburned, his hair a greasy mass.

"So," he said, looking up, "you weren't ever that into Democratic causes after all."

Jenny closed the door, leaned against it. "No."

"I should have known that someone as young and beautiful as you wouldn't have any real interest in me."

"And I should have known that you didn't mean anything you said."

"Jenny—"

"You hired me for, what's the word? Optics? George Shepherd, champion of the little people, offers a job to a poor single mother in an effort to lift her and her cute daughter out of poverty. That's a pretty good feature story right there. If it got any traction. Even better, imagine the fawning news coverage you'd get if you were somehow at the right place at the right time to save that cute daughter from certain death on a snowy lake."

"It's not nearly that simple."

"Isn't it? You wanted a boost, to redo what happened when you saved that girl who still sends you Father's Day cards, so you made your wife take my daughter for the night, pick her up from that field trip, ply her with promises of French toast and playtime with those awful dogs—"

"They are awful, aren't they? I've always said so. The worst dogs on the planet."

"Then, while you orchestrated a fake-but-still-real kidnapping—that's why that Julian guy was there, right? To act the part of the bad guy, scare Billie Starr some, and then run off before anyone could be the wiser—you have Lorne call Stephanie Shine in the aim of getting it all on camera. Hoping to play the hero yet again. You might even coast to the governor's mansion on it."

George shook his head. "You're making this out to be all my fault."

"Does that hurt your feelings?"

"The tacky grocery store seduction plot, that was Lorne's idea. And Brenda bankrolled it. To get back at me for my . . . romantic entanglements. That old story. The green-eyed monster. Or she would have, if that wire you wore had worked."

"If all Brenda wanted was to get back at you, why'd she take Billie Starr last night? I know it was Brenda who picked her up after the field trip. Billie Starr wouldn't get in the car with just anyone. She'd have to trust them. But I don't get why Brenda did it. She told me to ask you. So here I am, George, asking you. Why don't you try doing something different, something new, and tell the truth for a change?"

"Look, when I saw you, live, on air, tell Stephanie Shine that you slept with me in a hotel that rents rooms by the hour—"

"Which I hear is your go-to rendezvous spot, is it not? Your favorite place to take your lady friends."

George lay a hand over his left knee to stop it from jumping. "Who told you that?"

"It doesn't matter who told me. What matters is that I just lived through a night and most of a day when I thought my daughter might be dead."

"You tanked my campaign, Jenny. You've ruined me. Can we just call it even?"

"I don't think so. I didn't tank your campaign. You were behind before you even got started, before you even met me. And if you

were really listening to what I said to Stephanie Shine today, you might have noticed that besides talking about what we did at the Riverview, I also went on and on about how great you are, how generous and kind and selfless. What a joke."

"As much as I appreciated your kind words, I'm afraid no one will remember them. People tend to tune out everything after 'cheating womanizer.' And you're forgetting that all of this started with Lorne, with you in that slutty outfit saying you admired me from afar."

"So by dressing a certain way, I was just asking for my daughter to go missing."

"I didn't say that."

"What are you saying exactly?"

George stood up, limped around in a small circle, wiped a few drops of snot onto his sleeve. "I knew, when the faxes and calls and threatening emails started coming in, that Lorne was behind it all, pulling the strings—"

More things dawned. Jenny shivered. "Is that why you weren't worried about them?"

"Lorne's not exactly a criminal mastermind," George said. "Neither is Brenda. She's a weak woman, easily preyed upon. Lorne knows this. So, he convinced her to pay him and a couple petty crooks to see to it that my candidacy went up in flames. But, like everything else Lorne has done in his sad life, the scheme failed."

"That could have been the end of it all. Right there. You didn't have to bring Billie Starr into it. You didn't have to put me through hell."

"That first asinine fax, the one threatening to expose me for carrying on some secret tawdry affair, came in on the same day I happened upon a huge stack of cash in Brenda's jewelry box." George jingled the change in his pocket. "Brenda said she'd put it away for a rainy day, a trip to someplace quiet once the pressures of the campaign got to be too much, but I knew what it was for. She and Lorne hadn't

given up hope of framing me, of catching me red-handed, but with a different woman this time. Maybe a brunette. Or a blonde."

"Girls like me," Jenny mumbled.

"What's that?"

"Never mind."

"I confronted them, told Lorne I knew that he was the idiot behind the faxes and emails and phone calls, and I reminded them both that I'm a very good lawyer, told them that if they didn't want to end up on the wrong side of a very ugly court battle, they'd have to make it up to me."

"By kidnapping my daughter. Or pretending to."

"Would you believe me if I told you that that was Lorne's idea, too?"

"No."

"Jesus, Jenny, I wasn't let in on the details until this morning. I swear, I didn't know Billie Starr was even missing until Lorne told me the whole harebrained kidnapping plot over breakfast—"

"You're lying again. I know you're lying. And if it was so hare-brained, why'd you go along with it?"

George wasn't listening. He was pacing in front of the use-of-force poster, white cartoon drawings of guns pointed at the front of his head, the back, the side. "There I was, minding my own business, eating my cornflakes—I'm trying to be healthier—and suddenly I look up and my receptionist is on TV telling Stephanie Shine about me and some Black Suits and being stuck—"

"I don't care what you were eating, and I don't buy for a second that Lorne and Brenda left you in the dark. You were part of it, you knew. And you were willing to sacrifice a little girl for, what? Power, I guess? Ambition. Are you that empty? Were you that desperate?"

"It was a bit of theater, Jenny. A comedy of errors."

"A comedy of errors? My daughter was abducted. She spent the night with a person who might have done anything to her."

A silver-painted radiator creaked and banged in the corner. Jenny stopped, took a deep breath. The distressed, uneven thumping felt like it was coming from her own heart. "Brenda desperately wanted kids of her own. You said that yourself. What if she decided at some point last night to just take Billie Starr, to throw her in the car and drive away?"

"I would never let any harm come to your daughter. She's a special girl. I care about her. I care about you, too."

"Bullshit. You used her and you used me. There's no caring in any of that."

George raised his eyebrow. "Who are you and what have you done with Jenny Newberg?"

"I have a better question," Jenny said. "Who are you, George Shepherd? Do you really mean all that stuff you say about equal opportunity for all and being kind to your fellow man? Or is all that just an act? Do you even know who you are?"

"Let's not forget that you just spent the greater part of a week masquerading as a woman with a deep political résumé when I'd be willing to wager you've never actually voted in your life."

"You're right. I lied to you, too. I won't deny that. But I don't want a deep political résumé if it means saying all the right things and doing all the wrong ones. And, for your information, I do know who I am."

George sat back down, rested his chin on his folded fingers. "And who is that exactly?"

"I'm Pete Newberg's daughter. I'm Billie Starr's mother. I'm . . ." A work in progress, Jenny thought. On the right track. Not sorry anymore.

Jenny could tell that George had stopped listening again. She might as well be Brenda. Or an adoring face in a crowd.

"I thought, when I met you that morning in the grocery store, that it was my lucky day," George said. "Isn't that funny? For what it's worth, I really was in love with you. Who wouldn't be? Look

at you. You're a heroine." He gave her one more of his smiles. The sadness there. That's what hooked her from the very beginning. His vulnerability. Or what she'd taken for vulnerability and was probably in reality just an eagerness to be liked, the need to please. "How'd you figure it out? How'd you know where to find her?"

Jenny didn't answer right away. There'd been so much to consider and wade through, so many clues and missteps and wrong turns, the finger-pointing and backbiting and red herrings, the phone booth, the rabbit's foot, the ghost voices telling her to keep running. She opened the door, paused on the threshold. A pink scratch-and-sniff sticker curled up from the wood. Cotton candy on a stick, ripped down the middle.

Eventually, she said, "I did the math. I put two and two to-gether."

Jenny shut the door behind her. It made the same click Bil-lie Starr's did back at home. That sound. The end of something, the beginning of something else. Back in the reception area, Ruth Shields was telling Tony, Art, and the chief that emergency dispatch called, asking for a unit to be sent to Johnson Road, mile marker fifteen. "Near the Enyeart place."

"What for?" the chief asked.

"Caucasian male, deceased," Ruth said. "That transvestite Marcus Rye, frozen stiff on his way to see Trish Keck, apparently. Walked all the way."

"Until he didn't," Art said.

Tony chuckled. "Hey, Art, didn't you book him once on a public nuisance charge?"

"More like three times at least," Art said. "Maybe four. The man was always carrying loaded weaponry into crowded places, holler-ing about abject compliance and martial law."

Jenny glanced over at Billie Starr, hoping that somehow she hadn't heard. She had, though. She was trembling again, fists balled tight against her sides. Jenny thought of Marcus alone, lost, wan-

dering through whiteout conditions, a blizzard in his brain. Then she thought of him in his kimono, dancing in his kitchen, yelling at his cats, building birdhouses and solar systems and dolls for a little girl who didn't care that he sometimes forgot her name. Collecting women's clothes and weapons. Living his life, doing the best he could, just like everyone else. The station seemed suddenly smaller, the world, too. A colder, lonelier place without that weird, wonderful man.

"Who's gonna go?" Ruth asked the men. "Want to draw straws like last time?"

"I think it's my turn," Art said.

"Nah," the chief said. "Let's give this one to Chad. He could use the experience. You never forget your first dead tranny."

There was a roaring sound and Billie Starr ran at the chief, pummeling his big belly with her fists. Then she turned on Ruth, Art, and Tony, eyes blazing. "You're wrong, all of you. Wrong and mean and small and *you* should be the dead ones. Not Marcus. You."

"Now, young lady." The chief grabbed Billie Starr's hands, pushed her back. "Calm yourself."

"Don't tell me to be calm. I don't have to be calm. And don't talk about Marcus that way."

Ruth Shields looked affronted. "What way?"

"Like he's a joke. Like he doesn't matter," Billie Starr said. "He's my friend. He matters to me." Her teeth started to chatter.

Jenny went to her, folded her up. Then Lyd was there, too. She had emerged from one of the interrogation rooms, spotted Jenny and Billie Starr, walked slowly over, joined the hug. Arms steady and strong.

"You two," she said. "Thank God."

Jenny's face was smashed up against Lyd's chest. "Lyd, I'm so—"

"Don't say it."

"What?"

"You know."

Billie Starr sniffed. "She means sor—"

"I said don't say it."

So, Jenny didn't say it, and the police station was finally quiet, silent except for the tip-tap sound of Judd Pickens biting his nails. If only, instead of driving to Fort Wayne, Jenny had checked on Marcus that morning, everything might be different. He might still be alive instead of gone, erased, about to be identified by Patrol Officer Chad Leffert, who would almost certainly muse about getting to see a dead body on his second day on the job. *Can you believe my luck? Never a dull moment.*

Jenny swallowed her tears. Crying wouldn't bring Marcus back. Words wouldn't, either. The air in the station was thick somehow. Charged. With wishes. *If only if only if only.* With remembering.

Wings

Billie Starr had no trouble naming her favorite constellation. "Canis Major," she said. "No contest. It's Oliver's favorite, too."

Jenny gave the dog—full name, Oliver Boliver Butt—a few pats on the head. From the moment they'd brought him home from the pound, he followed Billie Starr everywhere: to school, the mailbox, the cemetery, where the previous morning they'd buried Carla and put flowers on Marcus's grave. And he slept with Billie Starr every night, shedding on the sheets and barking her awake. He was a medium-size red-furred mutt with a purple tongue, a long hound's face, and, in Jenny's opinion anyway, an old soul. Once in a while, when she looked into his eyes, she swore she could see all the way back to the beginning of time. Or time in reverse. Broken things fixed. Promises kept. The dead brought back to life.

There'd been a big party on the front lawn of the Cozy Cove Inn that afternoon to celebrate the first birthday of Randall and Eileen's son, Peter—named, it seemed, not for Jenny's father but for Eileen's brother, who'd died of a heroin overdose five years before. The party had long since broken up and Jenny and Billie Starr and Oliver were alone on the same public dock where, all those years ago, Pete had introduced Jenny to the wonders of the midsummer Milky Way. The night was quiet and dark and bats swung drunkenly over their heads.

"Which one do you like?" Billie Starr asked Jenny.

"Which constellation?"

"Yeah."

Jenny unfocused her eyes, let the stars swim, blend together into a spinning wheel of white. "I like all of them."

"That's boring, Mom."

"Okay, then. Pegasus."

"That's Dad's favorite, too."

Randall, who was still trying to be better—he had a job managing Johnson's Gas America and a paper route and covered for Buddy at Gill's Bar once a week—apologized to Jenny for the timing of the birthday party and for his and Eileen's absence from the funeral and the small wake Jenny held at her house immediately after. He'd wanted to pay his respects to Carla but had no choice but to spend the day mowing and cleaning and weeding to make the exterior of the inn as presentable as possible for the celebration. No one seemed to care about the motel's upkeep anymore. New management had given way to old hat.

"And I didn't really know when your mom was going to die," he'd said.

Jenny handed Randall the gift Billie Starr made for Peter—an unevenly stuffed blue bear—and watched while the little boy rabidly tore at the wrapping paper. "We didn't, either."

Holding the bear firmly by the neck, Peter promptly whacked Randall with it. Then, when Billie Starr ran over to ask Peter if he liked his present, he bit her on the hand. Billie Starr didn't seem to mind the boy's rough manner or the fact that Eileen went out of her way to make sure she understood she was only his half sister. She loved her new brother unconditionally. She'd even helped Eileen put him to bed, treating him to as many verses from "Hush, Little Baby" as she could remember.

"What do you think Peter will be like when he grows up?" Billie Starr asked now.

"We'll just have to wait and see," Jenny said.

"It's weird to think that someday he'll be a man like Dad and then an old man and then dead, like Carla and Marcus and Grandpa Pete. It almost doesn't seem real."

Billie Starr had delivered an impromptu eulogy at Carla's grave site and in her telling, her grandmother wasn't dead. She was living life over again as a butterfly, flitting around the cemetery and through the legs of the mourners, keeping the flowers and spiders and caterpillars on their toes.

"Terri Batchelder said that flowers don't have toes," Billie Starr complained. "Duh, Mom. Duh, I know that. I was trying to say something pretty, something different, but Terri said it was kind of crazy, not real, and she couldn't follow it at all. Then she made fun of Gertrude and Yo-Yo. She said they have fleas."

"They do have fleas."

"Still, it wasn't nice to say so. Why did she and her mom even come? They didn't really know Grandma."

Privately, Jenny wished they hadn't. The funeral was one thing. Fine. But then the wake, too? Terri stepped on a nail and made a scene. Ashley, clearly judging Jenny for having such a shabby yard, angrily ordered Mr. Richardson—they were married now and running the elementary school PTA together—to bring the car around. They needed to get Terri to the ER for a tetanus shot. Stat.

Poor Mr. Richardson. Whenever Jenny saw him—at school, the post office, the Brown Derby—he wore the slightly blinkered expression of a man who'd made a very big and permanent mistake.

"I thought your tribute to Grandma was sweet," Jenny told Billie Starr. "She would have loved it."

"But Grandma didn't really love anything. I mean, besides beer and cigarettes and Bob Butz. And the lottery money gown the funeral people buried her in."

Carla had died of lung cancer a year to the day after what many still considered to be one of the best weddings Benson ever saw. It

was Dr. Harme who'd diagnosed her. That was why she dropped him and went to Dr. Frank instead. Dr. Frank put her on a bunch of experimental drugs, but none of them worked and, after shrinking to nothing and losing all her hair, she was interred a little down from Doris, Bob Butz sobbing openly over the closed casket.

Apparently, Bob had genuinely loved Carla Newberg. Losing her left him brokenhearted. Good, Jenny thought. Now you know the feeling. Now you know what it's like. If Bob had had a hand in making Pete sick, she wanted him to suffer, to pay. At least for a little while.

Lyd had been right about her uncle. Bob wasn't evil, just predictably, pathetically selfish. Shortly after he and Carla moved into an airy, beige two-story in Juniper Ridge, the state opened up an investigation into his workplace practices—dust and people dying from it. The investigation wasn't enough to stop him being named to the board of directors of the Indiana Chamber of Commerce, though. That was the exciting business development he'd been referring to at the Brown Derby family bonding dinner. It was a lifelong dream, something he'd worked toward for years, but now that he'd achieved it, it was a lonely honor, he said, without Carla to share it with.

As for Carla's death, Jenny wasn't sad or shocked. Marcus's had hurt more. What she felt was mostly regret that they'd wasted so many years not understanding each other. What if they'd had more time? What if they'd given each other the benefit of the doubt? *What if what if what if.* That was the message the ugly mantel clock ticked off now, echoing what Jenny was almost positive were Carla's last words, but by then her mother's voice was so faint, Jenny supposed everyone in the room—Bob, Vi, the on-call nurse—heard whatever they wanted to hear.

Carla had gotten her fancy house in Juniper Ridge and died before she had the chance to decorate it. Her life seemed like nothing more than a missed opportunity. Too short, eaten up with pointless

work and petty cares and even pettier pleasures. It wasn't her fault and it wasn't her destiny, either. It was bad luck and a broken system. Jenny had learned that much working for George. The real loss, the real tragedy, was potential wasted. A chance at happiness and fulfillment squandered and erased. And how many Carlas were there in the world? Forgotten the moment they were gone because they left so little behind?

Billie Starr had turned her right hand into a telescope and was squinting through it. "Vi Gregor told me that Grandma's death was a blessing, that she was at peace and her suffering was finally over."

"She said the same thing about Grandpa Pete."

Vi had dumped her bail bondsman—or he'd dumped her—and came to the funeral on the arm of Troy from Pike's Pizza, whispering to Jenny when his back was turned that she was pretty sure he would become husband number five. If she played her cards right.

"Do you think Grandma's in heaven?" Billie Starr asked.

"I don't know. I'm not sure if heaven is real."

"The minister who gave the real funeral speech believes in it. He wouldn't stop talking about it, heaven this, the afterlife that, god god god and Grandma going up there to be with him. Being called, or something, to her celestial home. Do you have to be nice to go to heaven? Grandma wasn't always nice."

"I think you just have to be as good a human as you can be, and Grandma was as good a person as she could be, given the circumstances."

"Marcus is definitely in heaven if there is one."

"Definitely."

"And he gets to wear whatever he wants—dresses, skirts, feather boas, tiaras—and no one arrests him for it."

"I like that."

"What really happens sucks a lot. Have you noticed that?"

"I have."

"Hey, Mom?"

"Yeah, honey?"

"I'm not a honey. I'm a prodigy."

"Who told you that?"

"Sergeant Till. At the wake. I like him. Are you going to marry him? Or are you going to marry Buddy instead?"

"I have no plans to marry anyone right now."

"Yeah, me neither."

"That's good. You're a little young."

Buddy Winkler usually brought his toolbox when he came to see them. That and the newest dinosaur video from the library. So far, he'd fixed the birdhouse Marcus made for Billie Starr—"Look, Mom!" she said when she first saw it. "The birds can go in and out now!"—and repaired the faucet and the window above the kitchen sink. And he'd proposed to Jenny three times in the past four months. Every time, Jenny told him she'd have to think about it, and every time he said, fine, but don't think too long. Even he couldn't wait forever. He was so sweet, so easy to be around, and he loved Billie Starr and she loved him, but Jenny wasn't sure. She wasn't in a hurry. She wanted to wait, to see what happened next.

"Sergeant Till said I could shadow you guys next week on career day," Billie Starr said.

"Did he?"

"He said I could learn a lot from watching you take down the bad guys."

It was Zach Till's idea that Jenny join the police force in the first place. All her sleuthing skills, not to mention her plastic snowman ass-kicking moves, made her a natural, he said. He'd helped her study for the GED, talked her through getting used to the uniform, to carrying a gun, to the idea of arresting people. Jenny had graduated from the police academy a little over a year ago. The pay wasn't great but it wasn't terrible, either. Enough to cover the mortgage and buy Billie Starr a gently used computer from Heather's cousin who'd mostly used it to play *Oregon Trail*. Billie Starr did that, too.

Died over and over again of dysentery, but she also used the word processing program to write stories. About the adventures of Oscar the giant turtle and Oliver Boliver Butt the dog, about a girl named Billie Starr Newberg, who just might be president of the United States someday.

"You won't be shadowing me or Sergeant Till on career day," Jenny told her.

"I won't? Why not?"

"Because you don't want to be a cop. And because I talked to a friend of mine in the governor's office last week and he said he'll be more than happy to show you around."

"The governor's office?"

"Uh-huh."

Ted was surprised to hear from Jenny. Surprised, he said, and delighted. He'd been wondering how she was but thought that, by getting in touch, he might remind her of times she'd just as soon forget. They talked small at first—Billie Starr was doing great, thanks for asking, starting fourth grade soon; Ted had moved on from succulents, was keeping orchids now—and then rehashed the Shepherd scandal, Ted swearing he knew all along something weird was up with Brenda and George. They were like Bonnie and Clyde, he said, only dumpy. And now both were serving five years for kidnapping and aiding and abetting, while Roger and Wilfred languished in a no-kill shelter in Muncie, still waiting on their "furever home," one, ideally, without other dogs, young children, or carpet of any kind.

They talked, too, about the team. Max, who'd voluntarily put himself in anger management training after George's campaign fell apart, was working with Walter Mondale in a Democratic think tank in DC, and Hideo was in Chicago, training for an ultramarathon and studying for the bar.

At some point, Ted made the case for his new boss, the "milquetoast" incumbent who'd cruised to victory in a landslide. Ted said he was actually pretty wonderful once you got to know him. No

firebrand, but effective, smart, caring. A good leader. Jenny said she hoped Ted was right. She'd voted for him. And that's when she finally made her career-day pitch, said it was a school thing, no pressure, no obligation, but she and Billie Starr would be really grateful if he'd just consider letting her spend some time with him.

"I'd like her to see something of the world, other than the inside of a patrol car."

Ted laughed, then stopped suddenly. "Either Billie Starr has been working up one hell of a rap sheet for a third grader, or that's your way of telling me you're a cop now."

"Guilty as charged," Jenny said.

Ted didn't say anything for a while. Then he put her on hold. Another call, he said. When he came back, he told her he'd see what he could do. He wasn't sure about his schedule, things were crazy at the moment, etc. Jenny wasn't holding her breath. Then, just two days ago, Ted phoned with the good news.

"You'll even get a few minutes with the governor," Jenny told Billie Starr, who was giving Oliver a belly rub. "How does that sound?"

"The governor of *Indiana?*"

"My friend Ted works for him in Indianapolis. He's his press secretary. You remember Ted."

"He likes plants and bow ties."

"That's him."

"Lyd says politics is a crooked game played by egomaniacs and fragile jerkfaces in need of constant vaccination."

"I think you mean 'validation.'"

"I still want to do it."

"Good," Jenny said. "Lyd doesn't have to know."

Lyd, who'd moved in with Heather and was officially the head manager of Benson Bank and Trust—Larry had asked to go back to the teller line: he was tired of the pressure of being in charge—didn't just have a dim view of politics. Like Ted, she considered the

police force a pariah as well. The time she spent with Officer Chad was enough to convince her that all cops were cut from the same cloth. Bullies, she said. Bigots with axes to grind. So what if Jenny was determined to be a good one? What could one person really do to overturn a corrupt culture built on state-sanctioned violence? Did Jenny really think that by being a good apple she could magically fix the whole bunch?

"Give me a break," Lyd said. "You're in for a rude awakening. And just wait until you have to fire your gun. You don't have the temperament for the job, Jenny. You're going to flame out."

Maybe Lyd was right about that as well but it was too early to tell. In the fourteen months she'd worked as a Whitley County deputy, Jenny hadn't once been called on to discharge a weapon. She'd spent most of her time responding to petty theft and public nuisance charges. And she took a drunk and despondent Trish Keck home at least twice a month, home for Trish now being Marcus's trailer, which she'd bought with her first profits from Bulletproof Pies. On these trips, Trish never spoke of Lorne, serving four years in a medium security prison in Michigan City. She talked only of Marcus.

"Ironic, isn't it, that you only realize someone's the love of your life after they're so out of it with Alzheimer's they don't even know who you are half the time."

Jenny just nodded along, waiting outside long enough to watch Trish make it safely inside the trailer. Once in a while, Trish was so unsteady Jenny had to put her to bed herself, and on those nights, the older woman fixated not on late-in-life love but on Marcus's sad final moments.

"Do you know they found a bouquet of flowers next to him?" she would slur. "In the snow. He was bringing me a bunch of pink carnations. Life. It breaks your heart."

It did, Jenny thought. It broke your heart. Just ask Judd Pickens. It seemed like when Jenny wasn't with Trish, she was at the Pickens house, doing her best to get between Judd and his mother or Judd

and his mother and his little sister, Ruby, trying to keep them from tearing one another apart or burning their house down. At first, Jenny believed Tammy when she swore she would reform, be a better mother, but then she walked in on her smacking Judd in the head with a spatula for spilling syrup on the floor and scalding Ruby in her bath for pooping in it, and Jenny angrily informed Tammy she had no choice but to temporarily remove her children for their own safety. Then she took Judd and Ruby home with her for the night, a clear violation of her position, Sergeant said. She should have called child protective services. Stayed the hell out of the whole thing. That's what she should have done. Not gotten involved.

"We watched movies," Jenny told him. "Made cookies. We had a good time. What's the big deal?"

Zach was angry with her, worried she might lose her job, but then the sheriff, who had a soft spot for her and kids like Judd and Ruby Pickens, told her to never do anything like that ever again. Protocol and official channels exist for a reason, he said. Got it? Got it, Jenny said, and now that Judd and Ruby were in the Fort Wayne foster system—and Tammy in court-mandated rehab—Jenny reached out to the kids when she could, brought Ruby presents of dolls and candy and crayons and Judd baseball cards and comic books and notes from Billie Starr. The two of them had set *The Book of Sorries* aside, had turned their attention to a movie script instead. They were writing the script together in fits and starts and were very hush-hush about it, would only tell Jenny that it was sort of about life. And death. And everything in between.

Ruby, a flat-faced girl with curly black hair and a pigeon-toed walk, treated Jenny's visits like trials to get through. It was Judd who opened up, seemed to welcome her attempts at bonding. Jenny took him on ride-alongs on slow weekend shifts, chatted with him about his new school, his foster parents, a mouse he'd found in his closet and was now keeping as a pet. He told her he wanted to go back to Wetumpka, Alabama, which to him was still home and

always would be. He dreamed of making a life for himself along the Coosa River, fishing for his dinner and sleeping high up in a tall tree, not having to count on anyone ever again, excepting Billie Starr, whom he knew he could trust, or maybe his mom, if she could stay sober. Once, he'd cried in Jenny's arms, remembering Orville the cockroach and his grandfather, who'd been kind to him and whose cold eyelids his mother made him close before the ambulance came.

The boy's sharp-featured face was almost as familiar to Jenny now as her own daughter's. She could have drawn both with her eyes closed. Looking up, she saw them in the stars. Their own constellations.

"Mom," Billie Starr said. "Is the sky where Judd lives the same one we're looking at now?"

"Yeah, honey. It is. It's the same sky all over Indiana."

"Then I'm going to tell him that when he gets mad or sad, he should study the stars instead of crying or setting things on fire."

"That's a good idea."

"Yeah, and I'm going to tell him he should think about how millions of people are seeing exactly what he's seeing at that very moment. And then he'll know he's not alone."

Jenny put her arm around Billie Starr's shoulder. Buzzing low over the lake—mosquitoes. Clouds of them. But there were fireflies, too. Out in large numbers, their glowing bellies bright against the grass, appearing and disappearing, they were proof that dark would, from time to time, take over—no doubt about it, no arguing with it—but then light, just as stubborn, would show up again where you least expected it: in a girl's tangled hair, on the floppy ear of a bighearted mutt, atop a lily pad, bobbing. For the first time in a long time, Jenny had hope. She hoped the hope would last.

Acknowledgments

They say the second novel is the hardest, and they are not wrong. One thing that made this book possible was the generous support I got for my first. With that in mind, heartfelt thanks to Melissa Eden and Hanover College, the Mystery Writers of America, Indiana Humanities, and Glick Philanthropies for throwing some love *Tornado Weather*'s way. That love came at just the right time and made all the difference.

Speaking of love, big hugs to the following luminous humans: Liana Manukyan-Crosby, Jill Logan, Susannah Shive, Aaron Girard, Sinead Lykins, Evan Kuhlman, Shabnam Nadiya, Jonathan Davis, Alison Aldridge Raley, Jason Skipper, Michele Coppola, Gail Luciani, Tom Dorwaldt, John Krull, Sue Loechle, Jeff Chapman, Jean Hart, Bob Abbey, Jim Jatkevicius, the Literary Ladies of Forest Grove, and Michael Martone.

And, of course, I'm looking at you, Christine Kopprasch, editor without peer. Wisdom like yours is without parallel. You somehow take an amorphous blob of a rough draft and shape it into a story. And you do it with kindness and grace and humor. I'm in awe of your talent and am so glad we get to work and mom together at this surreal moment in time.

Abundant affection also to Yishai Seidman, exceptional agent, steadfast advocate, and heroically patient person. I will be forever

thankful we got to partner on two books—and for the countless others you selflessly read and took the time to comment on and make better. It's been a pleasure and honor that cannot be overstated. Man, I'm going to miss you.

Big thanks, too, to Megan Lynch, Marlena Bittner, Maxine Charles, Claire McLaughlin, Nikkia Rivera, Erin Kibby, Nancy Trypuc, Frances Sayers, and all the good people at Flatiron Books who make the world a better place by championing all kinds of words from all kinds of people.

And finally, a hat tip to Alec MacGillis, whom I do not know (but wish I did) and whose illuminating and essential *New Yorker* article, "The Case Against Boeing," gave me the idea for Jenny in the first place.

About the Author

Deborah E. Kennedy is a native of Fort Wayne, Indiana, and a recent graduate of the Iowa Writers' Workshop. Kennedy has worked as both a reporter and an editor, and also holds a master's in fiction writing and English literature from Miami University in Oxford, Ohio.